The Book
Stops Here

OTHER BIBLIOPHILE MYSTERIES

KATE CARLISLE

The Book Stops Here

A Bibliophile Mystery

AN OBSIDIAN MYSTERY

OBSIDIAN
Published by the Penguin Group
Penguin Group (USA) LLC, 375 Hudson Street,
New York, New York 10014

USA | Canada | UK | Ireland | Australia | New Zealand | India | South Africa | China
penguin.com
A Penguin Random House Company

First published by Obsidian, an imprint of New American Library,
a division of Penguin Group (USA) LLC

First Printing, June 2014

LIBRARY OF CONGRESS CATALOGING-IN-PUBLICATION DATA:
    Carlisle, Kate, 1951–
    The book stops here: a bibliophile mystery/Kate Carlisle.
    p. cm.
    ISBN 978-0-451-41598-1 (hardback)
    1. Women bookbinders—Fiction. 2. Books—Conservation and restoration—Fiction. 3. Rare
books—Fiction. 4. Murder—Investigation—Fiction. I. Title.
    PS3603.A7527B88 2014
    813'.6—dc23   2013045897

Printed in the United States of America
10 9 8 7 6 5 4 3 2 1

Set in Bembo

This book is dedicated to Mary Lou and Michael Debergalis, for the good times, good food, laughs, and love.

The Book
Stops Here

Chapter One

My mother always warned me to be careful what I wished for, but did I listen to her? Of course not. I love my mom, but this was the same woman who swore by espresso enemas to perk up your spirits. The same woman who performed magic spells and exorcisms on a regular basis and astral traveled around the universe with her trusted spirit guide, Ramlar X.

Believe me, I'm very careful about taking advice from my mother.

Besides, the thing I was wishing for was *more work*. Why would that be a problem?

I'd been in between bookbinding jobs last month and was telling my friend Ian McCullough, chief curator of the Covington Library, that I *wished* I could find some new and interesting bookbinding work. That's when Ian revealed that he had submitted my name to the television show *This Old Attic* to be their expert book appraiser. I was beside myself with excitement and immediately contacted the show's producer for an interview. And I got it! I got what I wished for. A job. A great job. With books.

That was a good thing, right?

Of course, I didn't dare tell my mother that I considered her advice a bunch of malarkey. After all, some of those magic spells she'd spun had turned out to be alarmingly effective. I would hate to incur her wrath and wake up wearing a donkey's head—or worse.

"Yo, Brooklyn," Angie, the show's stage manager said. "You look right into this camera and start talking. Got it?"

"Got it," I lied, pressing my hands against my knees to keep them from shaking uncontrollably. "Absolutely."

"Good," the stage manager said. "No dead air. Got it?"

"Dead air. Right. Got it."

She nodded once, then shouted to the studio in general, "Five minutes, everyone!"

I felt my stomach drop, but it didn't matter. I was in show business!

This Old Attic traveled around the country and featured regular people who wanted their precious family treasures and heirlooms appraised by various local experts. The production was taping in San Francisco for three whole weeks, and I was giggly with pleasure to be a part of it.

And terrified, too. But the nerves were sure to pass as soon as I started talking about my favorite topic: books. I hoped so, anyway.

Today was the initial day of taping and my segment was up first. My little staging area was decorated to look like a cozy antiques-strewn hideaway in the corner of a charming, dust-free attic. There were Oriental carpets on the floor. A Tiffany lamp hung from the light grid, which was suspended high above the set. Old-fashioned wooden dressers, curio cabinets, and armoires stood side by side, creating the three walls of my area. I sat in the middle of it all in a comfy blue tufted chair at a round table covered with a cloth of rich burgundy velvet.

Seated across from me was the owner of the book we would be discussing. She was a pretty, middle-aged woman with an impressive bosom and thick black hair styled in the biggest bouffant hairdo I'd ever seen. She wore a clingy zebra-print dress with a shiny black belt that cinched in her waist and emphasized her shapely hourglass figure.

She had excellent posture, though. I'd give her that much. My mother would be impressed.

Between us on the table was a wooden bookstand with her book in place, ready to be appraised.

"Are you Vera?" I whispered. I'd already seen her name on the segment rundown but wanted to be friendly.

She smiled weakly. "Yes. I'm Vera Stoddard."

I smiled at the sound of her high-pitched little-girl voice. "I'm Brooklyn. It's good to—"

"Settle down, people!" Angie shouted, and everyone in the television studio instantly stopped talking. Angie listened to something being said over her headset and then added loudly, "First on camera today is the book expert. It's segment eight-six-nineteen on the rundown, people! Stand by!"

"I'm so nervous," Vera whispered.

"Don't worry. We'll have a good time." I could hear my voice shaking but I smiled cheerfully, hoping she wouldn't notice. It wasn't like me to be this anxious. All I had to do was talk about books, something I was born to do. It was a piece of cake. Unless I thought about the millions of people who would be watching. It didn't help that several zillion watts of lighting were aimed down at me, and the stage makeup I wore, while it made me look glamorous, was beginning to feel like an iron mask.

"So stop thinking about it," I muttered, and plastered a determined smile on my face.

Angie caught my eye and pointed again at the television camera to her right. "Don't forget, this camera here is your friend. This is camera one. When you see the red light go on, it means you're on the screen." She turned and pointed to another camera a few feet behind her on the left. "Camera two will get close-ups of the book and the owner's reactions."

"Got it," I said, nodding firmly. "I'm ready."

"Good." Angie glanced around, then bellowed, "Here we go! Quiet, please! We're live in . . . Five! Four! Three! Two!" She mouthed the word *One* and waved her finger emphatically at me.

I took a deep breath and tried to smile at the friendly camera. "Hello. I'm Brooklyn Wainwright, a bookbinder specializing in rare-book restoration and conservation. Today I'm talking with Vera, who's brought us a charming first edition of the beloved children's classic *The Secret Garden*, written by Frances Hodgson Burnett."

I smiled at the older woman and noticed her lips were trembling badly and her eyes were two big circles of fear. Not a good sign. So instead of engaging her in conversation, I gestured toward the colorful book on the bookstand.

"This version of *The Secret Garden* was printed as a special limited edition in nineteen eleven."

I touched the book's cover. "The first thing you'll notice about the book is this stunning illustration on the front cover. The iconic picture of a blond girl in her red coat and beret, leaning over to insert a key into the moss-covered door that leads to the secret garden, is famous in its own right. There are some wonderful details, such as this whimsical frame around the picture, painted in various shades of green with thick vines of pink roses."

"I didn't even notice that," Vera muttered in her oddly charming sexy-baby voice.

"It's subtle," I said. "The artist was Maria Kirk, known professionally as M. L. Kirk. She was never as famous as her illustrations were, but she did beautiful work. Isn't this lovely?"

"I think so," Vera said softly.

I picked up the book and stood it near me on the table, keeping the cover turned toward the camera. "What makes this even more outstanding is that this illustration is actually an original painting on canvas."

"It is?"

"Yes," I said. "You can see that it's been signed by the artist here in the lower-left corner."

Vera blinked in surprise and leaned closer. "Oh. And look, there's a robin in the tree."

I grinned at her, happy that she was getting into the spirit of things. The show's director had urged us to keep the owner in the conversation, so I hoped Vera would play along. "Yes, that robin has a role in the story."

"I like birds," she said with a sigh.

Uh-oh. I shot a quick look at her. Was Vera going spacey on me? My smile stayed firmly in place as I spoke to the camera. "Another unusual feature is that the painting has actually been inlaid into the leather cover. You can see how the edges of the leather have been beveled so nicely." For the camera, I ran my fingers along the edge of the beveling and gave silent thanks to my friend Robin, who had insisted that I get a manicure before the show.

"I've never seen anything like that before," Vera said, her spacey moment apparently past.

"It's really quite rare," I agreed. "The bookbinder was clearly an artist, too, in the way he chose a rich forest green leather to blend with the painter's softer green frame. And the intricate floral gilding on the leather is patterned after the vines and roses on the painting." I glanced at Vera. "Do you have any idea what the book might be worth?"

"I don't have a clue," she said, shaking her head. "It cost three dollars at a garage sale last Saturday."

I choked out a laugh. "Wow. I don't think I'm giving too much away if I tell you it's worth a little more than that."

"Oh, good." She pressed her hands to her remarkable chest, obviously relieved by the news. Maybe now she would be able to carry on a normal conversation. Her voice was high yet sultry, but it seemed to suit her personality. I wasn't sure why I thought that. I'd never met her before this moment.

I opened the book and showed the frontispiece illustration to the camera. "There are eight color plates throughout the book, all in excellent condition and each with tissue guards intact."

I angled the book toward Vera. "They're charming illustrations, aren't they?"

She nodded politely. "They're very nice."

Nice? I thought. Was she kidding? They were *spectacular.* The entire book was fantastic. I couldn't believe it had been allowed to molder away in someone's garage. But I wasn't about to criticize Vera's lackluster response aloud.

I should've been used to that sort of attitude by now. Nobody gushed about books as much as bookbinders did. I would've loved to have mentioned how rare it was that a children's book printed in 1911 was this beautifully preserved. Children were not generally known for their ability to treat books gently.

I sighed inwardly and changed the subject. "Now, obviously not every copy of this book could be printed with original artwork attached to its cover. So let me explain briefly about this particular edition. Back in nineteen eleven, when this book was printed, a publisher would occasionally release two versions of the same book. A regular edition and a limited, more expensive edition. This version is obviously one of the limited-edition copies."

"How limited?" Vera asked, her gaze focusing in on the book.

"Very." I turned to the next page. It was almost blank except for two lines of print in the middle. "This is called the limitation page. It states here that only fifty copies of this numbered edition were printed. And the number six is handwritten on the next line. So this particular book is number six out of fifty copies made. It's beyond rare."

Vera gulped. "And . . . and that's good, right?"

"Yes, that's very good. And, of course, you will have noticed that on the same page we see that it's been authenticated with the date and original signature of the author, Frances Hodgson Burnett."

"I did notice that." She bit her lip, still nervous, though this time I figured it was from excitement, not fear.

Now that she was finally showing some emotion, it was time to bum her out. Earlier at rehearsal, Jane Dorsey, the show's director, had advised us to balance things out by mentioning a few negatives. So I flipped to a page in the middle. "I should point out a few flaws."

Vera's expression darkened. "No, you shouldn't."

I chuckled. "I'm sorry, but the book isn't without its imperfections." I faced the page toward the camera and pointed at some little brown spots. "There's foxing on a number of pages. These patches of brownish discoloration are fairly common in old books."

"Eww." She drew the word out as she leaned in to get a good look. "Are those bugs?"

"No. They're clumps of microscopic spores, but that's not important. Sometimes foxing can be lightened or bleached, but you should always hire a professional bookbinder to do the work."

Turning to the inside front cover, I said, "There's also an additional signature on the endpaper, right here." I made sure the camera could see what I was referring to, and then I took a closer look at it myself. "It doesn't look like a child's handwriting. It was probably a parent signing for the child. I can't quite make out the name, but I assume it's the signature of one of the book's first owners. They used a fountain pen, and it's faded a bit."

"And that's a bad thing?"

"Writing one's name in a book can diminish its value, but that's another topic altogether."

"But—"

"Let's not dwell on the negatives," I hurried to add, "because other than those items and a few faded spots on the leather, it's in excellent condition and—"

"And what?" Vera demanded, interrupting what was about to be my rapturous summary of the book's qualities.

I pursed my lips, thinking quickly. I had been given six minutes to talk about the book, but the director had warned me that as soon as I revealed my appraisal amount, my segment would be over, even if I had minutes to spare.

I wasn't ready to stop talking about the book—big surprise. But Vera was finished listening and it was time to put her out of her misery. More important, I noticed Angie hovering. And Randolph Rayburn, the handsome host of the show, stood next to her, looking ready to pounce into the camera shot and cut me off.

"And for a book of this rarity," I continued hastily, "in such fine condition and with the author's original signature included, it's my expert opinion that an antiquarian book dealer would pay anywhere from twenty to twenty-five thousand dollars for this book."

"Wha—?" Vera's eyes bugged out of their sockets. "Twenty . . . Say that again?"

"Twenty to twenty-five thousand dollars," I repeated, happy I'd finally gotten a reaction out of her. The producers were going to love that look on her face.

I turned the book over again to examine the rubbed spots on the back cover. "Frankly, Vera, it would take only a few hundred dollars to have the book fully restored to its original luster. Once you did that, you could probably add another three to five thousand dollars onto the value."

"Another five thou— Holy mother-of-pearl!" Vera slapped her bountiful chest a few times as if to jump-start her heart. "Oh, my God. Are you serious?"

"Yes."

"But that's freaking—"

Angie must have thought Vera was about to scream out some expletive because she shoved Randolph forward, and he rushed to stand in front of our table.

"Indeed, it is!" he said nonsensically to camera, grinning as he blathered cheerfully about some of the items coming up later in the show. He finished with, "We'll be right back."

"And . . . we're clear!" Angie shouted.

Vera looked shell-shocked. Everyone in the studio started talking again, moving here and there between the sets, carrying on normal conversations.

I had watched the program a bunch of times, so I knew that when they went in to edit the shows, they would plaster across the TV screen a green graphic banner announcing the amount of money I had quoted, accompanied by the sound of a cash register making a sale. *Cha-ching!*

Angie approached me, but suddenly stopped and cupped her hand over her ear to hear what was being said over the headset. Her arm shot up in the air. "Quiet, people!"

Everyone in the vicinity froze. *What awesome power she has,* I thought. It was all in the headset. I wanted one.

"Randolph, don't move," she warned, as though she suspected he would disappear if given half a chance. Then she announced to the group in general, "Okay, we're gonna need camera one to remain here. Jane wants to tape a short chat between Randolph and the book expert. For everyone else, we're moving on to the Civil War segment."

Most of the crew stirred themselves into action at the mention of Jane, the director. They pushed the cameras and the heavy microphone boom to the opposite side of the large studio where another cozy antiques-furnished set similar to mine had been designated the war room.

I had met Jane Dorsey earlier that day, during my orientation with the two executive producers, Tom Darby and Walter Williams. Jane was almost six feet tall and very attractive, but stick thin, with white blond hair pulled back in a severe ponytail. Today she wore knee-high black boots over her jeans and a black sweater. A long white scarf was tied around her neck and fluttered in her wake as she walked.

Apparently the long scarf was something she wore every day. Tom explained that they kept the air really cold in the director's booth so the equipment wouldn't overheat, but I figured she also enjoyed the dramatic effect. Not that she needed it. People paid instant attention to her when she walked into a room.

Camera one remained in place, still pointed in my direction, along with its operator and a couple of crew members who assisted with microphones and cables.

Angie looked around anxiously. "Where did Randolph wander off to?"

"I'm here," he said from halfway across the stage floor. "I'm here. I'm here. Don't pay the ransom."

A few of the crew guys chuckled and Angie's lips twisted sarcastically. "Can we get this show on the road?"

I wondered how he had escaped all the way across the room in mere seconds. The guy was speedy, for sure.

"Okay, let's do this," Randolph said, and flashed me a rakish grin. "Hello, beautiful."

"You are so full of it," Angie muttered.

"But you love me, anyway," he said, bumping his shoulder into her arm.

"Yeah, in the worst way," Angie said. She paused to listen to a voice in her ear, then said to us, "They're not quite ready upstairs, but don't anyone go anywhere."

Randolph snorted. "Famous last words. I'll be right over here." And with that, he wandered a few feet away to kibitz with one of the crew.

"You move and I'll kill you," she said.

He grinned and winked at me behind Angie's back. He was the worst kind of flirt, completely adorable and charming. I could tell Angie liked him. What woman wouldn't? Maybe she didn't want to like him, but she couldn't help herself. All of that was probably clear to Randolph, as well. Angie seemed pretty transparent with her feelings.

She was beautiful, with pale skin and a halo of thick, dark curly hair. They would make an adorable couple if hard-as-nails Angie could ever learn to deal with Randolph, the charming jokester.

The stage manager ignored the star as she rested her elbows on my table. "You did a good job, Brooklyn. Once we're finished with the chitchat, you've got at least two hours to kick back before we tape another book segment." She turned to Vera. "You okay, hon?"

Vera blinked a few times. "Oh. I'm . . . I'm a little shaken up, but very happy."

Angie pulled two pieces of paper from the clipboard she carried. "Almost forgot. You both need to sign these releases."

"Another one?" I'd already signed my life away that morning, indemnifying everyone in the universe in case of any possible occurrence of anything, including acts of God. "What are these for?"

"One of our local news stations is here, taping some footage for their nightly segment. It's sort of a Look What's Going On in San Francisco kind of thing."

"So we could be on the news?" Vera said.

"They're taping a bunch of short segments, so it's not a guarantee," Angie said. "But either way, they need your approval, just in case."

"Okay," I said, taking the one-page document from her and scrawling my name on the bottom line. "No problem."

"This is so exciting," Vera gushed, and signed her copy with a flourish. She handed it back to Angie, who slid both pages back onto her clipboard.

A young production assistant jogged across the set and slowed down as she approached the host. With a nervous gulp, she said, "Randolph, you have a flower delivery. They put it in your dressing room."

"Thanks, kiddo," he said, flashing her a million-dollar grin. "Hey, Angie, be back in two minutes."

He strolled away before Angie could protest. Exasperated, she turned to me. "Stand by, will you, Brooklyn?"

"No problem," I said, not minding the wait. I was having too much fun to complain about anything.

Vera flashed me a wide-eyed look. "Can I ask you a few more questions about the book?"

Before I could answer, Angie shook her head. "Sorry to interrupt, kids, but the second Randy returns, I've got to get that damn chat done and then clear this area. They'll start taping the next segment right after that, so maybe you two can set up a meeting later."

"Oh, sure." Vera stood and I got a look at her shoes for the first time. Patent-leather leopard-skin stiletto heels. Wow. They had to be six inches tall and the pattern should've clashed with her zebra-print dress, but somehow it all worked for her.

"Hey, dig those shoes," Angie said.

"Don't you love them?" Vera said, beaming. "They're my Christian Louboutin knockoffs."

Angie nodded. "They're freaking awesome."

Vera turned and bent her knee, lifting her foot behind her. "They've even got the signature red sole. See?"

Angie and I stared at the shiny red bottom.

"They rock," Angie said.

Vera gazed down at her sexy stilettos. "They were the first thing I bought myself after I left my no-good boyfriend."

"Best revenge, sister," Angie said stoutly.

"You know it," Vera said, and giggled.

I handed Vera the business card I'd pulled out of my pocket. "I'll be happy to talk with you about the book anytime you want. Or you can call me whenever you decide what to do."

She looked at the card. "Okay, good. The sooner, the better."

"Anytime," I said.

Looking relieved, she said, "Thanks, Brooklyn."

"And don't forget your book, hon," Angie said, extending *The Secret Garden* to her.

Vera stared blankly at Angie until she saw the book in her hand. "Oh, wow. I guess I'm still a little discombobulated. Thank you."

Angie pointed out the exit to Vera, and we watched her walk away, a bit wobbly in her sky-high heels.

I sniffed, feeling sentimental. Vera was, after all, a first for me.

"She's adorable." Angie grinned. "And you made her day."

"I loved every minute of it," I said, happy that so far my day was going pretty well, too.

But the same couldn't be said for Randolph. The star of the show crossed the wide stage and headed straight for Angie and me, his face drained of color and his jaw taut. He looked as if he might have just witnessed his own death.

Chapter Two

Ten minutes later, the director was ready to shoot our segment. I'd been watching Randolph carefully as he slowly shook off his mood and returned to his peppy, perky self. He was deeply involved in a conversation with Tom and Walter when Angie grabbed him and dragged him over to my table.

"Sit. Stay," she said, pushing him into the chair across from me.

He looked in much better spirits now than he had a few minutes ago and he took Angie's wrangling with good humor. I wondered if maybe he had a soft spot for her, too. Who could blame him? She looked like a pre-Raphaelite angel with lustrous black curls instead of the usual red.

I was nosy enough to wonder what had caused Randolph's look of despair earlier, but it wasn't the right time to ask. Something about that flower delivery had caused him to turn a deathly shade of white. I'd been itching to eavesdrop on his discussion with the producers, but I wasn't brave or stupid enough to do it. Not with so many witnesses standing around, anyway.

Whatever had upset him, he seemed to have brushed it aside and was in a good mood for our short teaser segment. The camera rolled and the two of us chatted for all of one minute. And then it was over.

"That was easier than I thought it would be," I confessed.

"It's my cheery inquisitiveness," Randolph said blithely. "Admit it: I make you feel both desirable and comfortable."

I couldn't help but laugh. "You really are a rascal."

"Rascal." He wiggled his eyebrows. "I like that."

"You would," Angie muttered.

Poor Angie had my sympathy. Randolph was in his thirties, tall and classically handsome, with dark blond hair worn in a casual, wind-tossed style. His vivid blue eyes were mesmerizing. He had a great smile and perfect teeth, and it didn't hurt that his voice could melt butter. Best of all, he had a charming sense of humor.

Angie yelled, "Civil War's up in ten minutes, people!"

I turned down Randolph's generous offer to buy me a free cup of coffee and headed off to the tiny dressing room I'd been assigned earlier that day. The schedule gave me two hours to research the next book I'd be appraising and I would need every minute to do my job well.

On the way backstage, I wasted a few long seconds worrying about my *Secret Garden* segment. Had I blathered? Had I laughed too loud? Had I sounded smart? Silly? Had my shoulders slumped? Had I droned on with details nobody else in the world would care about unless they were a devout book lover? Probably yes to that last one, and maybe to all of the above.

I wondered if my on-camera self-consciousness would ever wear off. Did it matter? I would be here for only three weeks and the most important thing was to have fun and give accurate appraisals and make the book owners happy. I thought I had accomplished all of that with Vera.

And with that conclusion, I shoved my angst aside. I didn't expect it to stay where I'd shoved it, but for now, I gave myself permission to ignore it.

As I crossed the massive studio, I glanced around and marveled that despite the large space, it had an air of intimacy. This was probably because of the twenty-five-foot-high wall of curtains that was hung from a curved ceiling beam that ran all the way around the room. The curtains were weighted and anchored to the studio floor, creating a wall between the main staging area and the backstage. The stage manager referred to the curtains as the backdrop.

The main staging area was further divided into six small sets where the different experts sat and appraised their items. Like my cozy space, the others were filled with antique furniture and interesting set pieces that corresponded to their field of interest. For instance, on my set, the cabinets and shelves were filled with old books. Sitting on the dressers were framed illustrations and frayed botanical prints taken from old books.

Since I would be sharing my space with a map expert and a historian who specialized in vintage correspondence and documents, my book illustrations would be switched out with framed drawings of maps or old letters and tattered certificates.

In the Civil War expert's area, an old rifle was displayed in a large glass cabinet. On one of the dressers were two elegant portraits of soldiers from that era. Apparently, the rifle could be replaced by a musket or a bow and arrow or another weapon, depending on which particular war was being discussed.

Another area featured shelves of vintage kitchenware, old toys, and folk sculpture. A child's painted rocking horse filled one corner of the space, and on the top shelf was an intriguing display of covered woven baskets.

The largest staging area was located at one end of the studio and would be used to feature larger pieces of furniture, grandfather clocks, and other big items, such as the old canoe one visitor had brought in for appraisal.

Even the largest area had the same rich, warm feeling as my

smaller set. If I ignored the studio cameras and the technical contraptions and the burly crew members, it was almost like being inside a beautiful home.

"Watch your step, young lady," one of the crew guys said.

I stopped abruptly and glanced down. I was close to tripping over the two-inch-thick cable that snaked down from the boom microphone pedestal, slithered across the shiny floor, and disappeared under the backdrop.

"Thanks," I said, flashing him a grateful smile. I really didn't want to break an ankle on my first day. Around me was a tangle of equipment. There were four television cameras along with two boom microphones that looked like heavy-duty fishing poles attached to rolling pedestals. These could all be wheeled from set to set, depending on which segment was being taped.

Besides all the hardware, dozens of people bustled about in a state of organized chaos. The lighting crew stood on ladders or used long poles to adjust the studio lights hanging on the grid high above our heads. Camera operators discussed the shooting schedules with the director and her team. A woman touched up Randolph's makeup and hair with brushes and sponges she had stashed in a tool belt around her waist.

Thick lines of electric cables went everywhere. It looked like one crew member was assigned to each camera and each boom, simply to adjust the wires and cables as the machinery was moved from here to there.

I found a break in the curtain and slipped through to the backstage area. I passed the green room—the walls of which were actually painted a pleasant light taupe—and the makeup room, then turned the corner and stared down a hallway that ran the entire length of the studio building. There had to be twenty doors on either side of the long, wide corridor and I was happy I'd memorized my dressing room number.

As I approached the room, I felt that odd buzzing sensation I always got whenever I was about to start work on a new book. I didn't know what else to call it but sheer exhilaration. I was itching to explore the old edition of the *Rubáiyát of Omar Khayyám* I'd been given to study, especially since it featured a unique wooden cover with art deco–style illustrations carved into it.

How cool was that?

And how geeky was I for getting so excited? I chuckled at myself as I started to turn the key in the lock.

"Yoo-hoo, Brooklyn!"

I glanced down the hall and saw Vera Stoddard teetering toward me in her death-defying heels. I grimaced, knowing that if she slipped and fell off those stilettos, she could break her neck.

"I'm probably not supposed to be back here," she said, giggling in that high-pitched tone I'd grown used to so quickly.

Probably not, I thought, but didn't say it aloud. She looked nervous enough already as she clutched *The Secret Garden* to her pillowy chest. I had to resist grabbing the book right out of her hands. The tiniest bit of perspiration could ruin that beautiful leather cover within seconds. But I held back. It wasn't easy, but it also wasn't my book.

"I wanted to ask you," she said, then paused, out of breath from her exertion. "I . . . I wanted to ask you about all that book stuff you said when we were on camera."

"Let's go in here." I opened the door to the dressing room and ushered her inside.

She stopped just beyond the threshold. "I don't want to take up too much of your time, but I'm anxious to—"

"It's fine, Vera. I'm happy to talk for a few minutes. Have a seat." I gestured toward the hideously ugly orange cloth chair that was a perfect complement to the ugly turquoise Naugahyde sofa shoved up against the wall. An imitation wood coffee table completed the ensemble.

Once she was seated, I held out my hand. "May I see the book again?"

"Oh, you bet." She handed it to me.

"Thanks." I sat in the swivel chair at the counter in front of the wide makeup mirror. I had turned it into a desk and set up my computer and a few reference books here. I took a moment to admire *The Secret Garden* cover again before looking up at my guest. "What can I do for you?"

With a nervous laugh, she played with the loose threads of the armchair. "I want to sell the book and I want to make as much money as possible. And I want to do it right away. The sooner the better. So, I want to hire you to do . . . you know, whatever it is you can do to make it perfect."

"So you definitely plan to sell it?"

"You bet I do," she said eagerly, then pressed her lips together as if she'd said something rude. "That is, I would love to keep it, believe me. It's a work of art, like you said. A real beauty. But when you told me how much it was worth . . ." She shook her head, giving up any pretenses. "I mean, wow. I could really use the money."

"I understand." I leaned forward in my chair. "But, Vera, I should warn you. I had only a limited time to research your book, so I'm not exactly sure how much work I might have to do. My guess is that my time would only cost you a few hundred dollars, but it could go as high as five hundred. I won't know for sure until I get a better look at the book."

"I hear you." She nodded slowly. "Five hundred would be okay, as long as it's not much more than that."

"No, I can promise it won't be any more than that." I turned the book over in my hand and carefully stroked the back cover. "Probably less."

"And then I could get a few thousand dollars more for it, right?"

"Yes." I wasn't going to tell Vera, but I believed a real collector would pay many thousands more than I had quoted her on camera.

"And when you're ready to sell, I can help you. I'll give you a few names of people to call." If she was going to sell the book, anyway, why not point her toward someone who would appreciate the book for the treasure it was?

"That would be great," she said with a sigh of relief. "I have no idea who to talk to about this kind of stuff."

"I'll be happy to help."

"Okay, let's do it," she said.

"Are you certain?" I asked. She didn't appear to be a wealthy woman, so I decided I'd better make sure. "It's a lot of money. I don't want to empty your bank account."

"You won't," she insisted. "As long as you guarantee that I'll get an extra couple thousand on the book when I sell it. Can you do that?" Her eyes narrowed suddenly. "I can trust you, right?"

I almost laughed. She didn't know me from Adam, so why would she trust me to give her an honest answer? But I wasn't about to lie to her. "Yes, I promise you can trust me, but you don't have to. I can give you some references before I take your money. I can also give you a list of bookbinders who can offer a second opinion."

She closed her eyes and pressed her hands together as if she were praying. "Just tell me again that I can sell it for the price you quoted."

I smiled. "Unless the world turns upside down tomorrow, I can pretty much guarantee it. And as I mentioned before, I can also give you the names of some reputable buyers in town who would be interested in looking at it." *Like Ian,* I thought. He would kill to add this book to the Covington children's collection.

She patted her chest again and took a slow, deep breath. Then she clapped her hands and let out a little shriek of joy. "Thank you! This is like a dream come true."

As I watched her bounce with delight, I noticed something odd. Her bubbly black bouffant hairdo seemed to shift slightly.

Is she wearing a wig?

I looked away, but from the corner of my eye I caught her surreptitiously tugging at her bangs.

That was so weird. But maybe she'd been sick. Maybe she'd lost all her hair. Maybe that's why she needed the money. I hated to stare so I busied myself with straightening my short stack of reference books. After a few seconds, I tried to be nonchalant. "I still can't believe you found this amazing book at a garage sale."

She glanced at the ceiling and around the room. "Gosh, I can't either. The guy I got it from didn't seem to know much about it."

"He couldn't have," I said firmly. "He wouldn't have given away a treasure like this for so little money."

"No, I guess not," she murmured. "Lucky for me."

I checked my watch. We'd been talking for ten minutes and I needed to get back to work. "Why don't I take the book home and look it over, then call you with an estimate? You'll have some time to catch your breath and figure out whether you want to spend the money or not."

She nodded. "That sounds good."

"If you decide not to go through with it, we can meet somewhere and I can return the book to you, no problem."

"I'm not going to change my mind," she said, and, reaching into a pocket of her faux tiger-skin tote bag, she pulled out a shiny green business card.

We both stood and she handed the card to me. "I own a flower shop at Nineteenth and Balboa in the Richmond."

I read the card. VERA'S FLOWER GARDEN. VERA STODDARD, PROPRIETOR. I looked back at her. "That's a pretty name for a shop."

"Thank you. I love flowers."

I was familiar with the Richmond District so I knew I wouldn't have any trouble finding it. "I'll call you with my estimate in the next day or two. Then, depending on which way you decide to go, I can either drop off my invoice and pick up a check, or I can simply return the book to you."

"Sounds perfect."

"And, like I said, you're welcome to get a second opinion."

She giggled as she reached for the doorknob. "You sound like a doctor."

"I probably do, but bookbinding isn't cheap." I followed her out. "And I want you to be happy with the final product."

She looked over her shoulder at me. "They wouldn't have hired you for this show if you weren't the best in town."

"Thanks," I said, feeling my cheeks grow warm with the compliment. "I appreciate that."

Before I knew what was happening, she let out a little squeal and came click-clacking back to me. She threw her arms around me and whispered, "Thank you."

"You're welcome."

"You don't understand," she said in a breathless hush as she stepped back. "I've met some real meanies during my lifetime, but everyone here has been so nice, especially you. I'm just bowled over."

"Thank you, Vera. That's really sweet."

"Well, I just think I should let people know when they've been helpful and kind." She frowned and pressed her lips together. "I had a really awful man in my life for a while, so I know the difference between nice and not so nice."

"I hope you got rid of him," I said.

"You bet I did." She laughed self-consciously. "I'd better stop bending your ear and get out of here."

"It was great to meet you, Vera." I walked with her down the hall and across the studio to the stage door that led to the parking lot, just to make sure she didn't get lost.

By the time I stepped back inside the studio door, my mind was already back to my next book. *The Rubáiyát of Omar Khayyám* was one of the most widely published books in the world, but the edition I was about to research was unlike any version I'd ever seen before. Excited to get back to work, I crossed the studio quickly and entered the backstage area. But while approaching the makeup room, I slowed down as I caught a snippet of hushed conversation.

"I'm sick of you two brushing this off," a man whispered harshly, and I realized it was Randolph. "Either you call the police or I will."

"And tell them what?" another guy said caustically. "That you stumbled over a broom?"

"No, damn it," Randolph said. "Tell them someone's trying to kill me."

The old freight elevator in my converted loft building came to a shuddering halt, and I dragged myself down the hall toward my apartment. Working in television was invigorating, almost manically so, but now I felt all of my high energy and perkiness collapsing from within.

Earlier, I had forced myself to shut off all thoughts of that short, ugly conversation I'd overheard, in order to give my work the attention it deserved. Concentrating on my job, I'd found some fascinating facts about the publisher of the wood-carved *Rubáiyát* I was appraising. Later I had managed to appear intelligent and sparkling during the videotaping of the segment. The book's owner was thrilled to be in possession of such a fabulous piece of art and history. I got high fives from the crew members and gushing words of praise from the production staff and I left the studio feeling proud and confident.

But now those ugly words came back with full force. *Tell them someone's trying to kill me.*

When I'd first heard it, my heart had clenched in my chest and my feet had stuttered to a stop just short of the open doorway to the makeup room. I'd been tempted to spin around and dash right out of the studio, jump in my car, and race home. I didn't want to be anywhere near someone who might be the target of a killer.

Been there, done that.

But because my innate curiosity outweighed my fear, I hadn't moved a muscle. Instead, I was still standing in the hall like a statue when Tom and Walter walked out of the makeup room, exchanging a derisive look.

Tom noticed me first. "Hey, Brooklyn. Nice job on the book segment."

"Thanks, Tom."

Walter winked at me and the two producers walked away, chatting quietly. They stopped halfway down the hall and went into another dressing room. They'd been chuckling and talking as if they didn't care that I'd obviously overheard their troubling conversation with Randolph.

I glanced inside the makeup room and saw Randolph gripping the counter as he stared at himself in the wall-length mirror. He looked pale, frustrated, and unnerved, completely unlike the flirtatious, smooth-talking dude I'd chatted with only a few minutes ago.

I lifted my arm in a casual wave. "Hi, Randolph."

"What? Oh. Hi, Brooklyn." He rolled his shoulders and neck as if to work out some kinks.

"Everything okay?" I asked.

Gritting his teeth, he muttered, "Just great. Couldn't be better."

I hadn't expected him to confess his deepest, darkest fears right then and there. He barely knew me. But my curious mind was itching to find out and I figured I would hear the truth eventually. At that moment, though, I had simply nodded and hurried back to my little dressing room, where I'd closed myself off to study more books.

Now I slipped my key into my front door, relieved to be home.

"Hi there," said a voice behind me in the hall.

I whipped around. My place had been invaded a few times in the recent past and I didn't like people creeping up on me. But the woman standing there didn't look threatening—unless you counted the fact that she was drop-dead gorgeous with long dark hair, exotic eyes, and supermodel legs. And she was tall. Taller than me by an inch or two, and I was no slouch at five foot, eight inches in my socks.

She stood by the door of Sergio and Jeremy's loft, at least twenty feet away. Not exactly invading my personal space.

"Hi," I said cautiously. "You must be Sergio's friend."

"Yes, I'm Alexandra Monroe," she said, and walked over to shake my hand. "But please call me Alex."

I worked up a smile. "I'm Brooklyn Wainwright. Nice to meet you. Are you settling in okay?"

"Oh yeah." She gave a quick glance over her shoulder at the apartment, then back at me. "The space is fabulous. I love all the exposed brick and the hardwood floors and the freight elevator. And this location is perfect. I'm really lucky I was able to work out a deal with Sergio."

"That's great." I felt completely outclassed and tongue-tied, probably because I was so tired. Alex Monroe was bright-eyed and vivacious. Didn't she know it was ten o'clock at night?

She wore a gorgeous pale pink business suit with a silky black tank top and fabulous shiny black stiletto heels. How could she be so friendly so late at night? And why was she still wearing high heels? Why wasn't she wrapped in a ratty old bathrobe? The woman was downright intimidating.

But I had to let that go. This was the good friend of Sergio and Jeremy's, my darling neighbors who had sublet their loft for the next year while they cavorted in Saint-Tropez. Alex was my new neighbor and I was determined to be friendly, even though I was so tired, I felt punchy.

"Have you met any of the other neighbors yet?" I asked. For a nanosecond, I considered asking her to come in to talk for a few minutes. I felt a bit aloof, carrying on a conversation out in the hall, but I wasn't quite ready to invite someone I'd just met into my home. Another residual effect of having my space invaded more than once.

"I met Vinnie and Suzie first thing this morning," she said. "And their adorable Lily, too. And then I ran into Mrs. Chung a little while ago. Everyone's been so welcoming and helpful."

I wasn't about to break the streak, so I smiled gamely. "I'm glad. We all love Sergio and Jeremy, so any friend of theirs is a friend of ours."

"That's so sweet of you," she said earnestly. Damn it, she sounded really sincere. Was there nothing truly hateful about the woman?

"I would ask you in for a glass of wine," I said apologetically, "but I'm completely beat. I've been working all day and I confess I'm not used to it."

She took a step backward. "I'm so sorry. I won't keep you. I just wanted to introduce myself."

"No, no, I'm glad you did. We'll have you over for that glass of wine as soon as possible."

"I'll look forward to it." Her smile turned thoughtful. "Vinnie said you worked at home. You're a bookbinder, right?"

"That's right." I wasn't sure how I felt about being the topic of conversation between the neighbors, but I guessed it was unavoidable. "I usually work at home, but I'm doing an outside job right now." I paused. "That sounds really weird."

She laughed, and the sound was so natural and friendly that it made me smile. For some reason, it also made me feel okay that Vinnie had been talking about me.

"Where are you working?" she asked.

"I've been hired to be the book appraiser on *This Old Attic*."

"I love that show!"

"Me, too." I grinned, pleased by her reaction. "It's just for three weeks and it's really fun, but I didn't realize how drained I would feel by the end of the day."

"You poor thing. You probably want to crawl into bed. But if you're up for it tomorrow night, why don't you stop by my place after work? I'll make cupcakes."

"Cupcakes?" I said slowly. "I love cupcakes."

"Everybody does," she said, smiling. "I'm hopeless at cooking much else, but I make fantabulous cupcakes. The best you've ever tasted."

"How can I say no?"

"You really can't."

"Then I'll be there."

"Good. I'll open a bottle of wine, too."

I laughed. "Now you're just pandering."

She laughed, too, and we stood there grinning at each other for a few more seconds until I realized how goofy I must look.

I shook my head. "I'm obviously tired or I wouldn't be standing here like a knucklehead. It was great to meet you, Alex. I'll see you tomorrow night." I started to walk away, made an instant decision, and turned back. "We're having a little party Saturday afternoon, very casual, mostly neighbors and friends. If you're not busy, we'd love it if you'd join us."

For a brief second she looked bewildered, as if nobody had ever invited her to a party before. I knew that couldn't possibly be true. Then, just as quickly, the look disappeared and she beamed with pleasure. "I would love to come. Thank you so much."

"Great." I turned, then remembered one more thing. "Tomorrow night I'll be home around this same time. Is that too late?"

She brushed away the question. "No, anytime is fine."

"Cool." I waved, then walked into my place and closed the

door behind me. And was instantly attacked by a tiny ball of fur that pounced on my shoes.

"Hello, silly thing," I murmured, reaching down to pick up my adorable new kitten and cuddle her against my neck. I set down my computer case on the floor by my workshop desk and carried the kitten into the living room. On the kitchen bar was an open bottle of wine and two glasses.

"This is a very good sign," I said to the kitten, then called out, "Is anybody home?"

Derek emerged from his office, also known as our second bedroom. "Hello, darling. How was your day?"

I turned at the sound of that silky, rich British accent and wondered if there was anything sexier than Derek Stone's voice. Not in my world there wasn't. "My day was exciting and fun, but now I'm exhausted."

He touched my cheek and nudged my chin up so that I was looking at him. Then he kissed me. "You do look a wee bit weary. Do you want to skip the wine and go to bed?"

"I think I can manage half a glass. And I want to talk and maybe watch a little television with you. It's so odd to be working outside of the house."

"It'll take some getting used to," he said, reaching for the bottle. "You take Pugsley and go relax on the couch. I'll bring the wine."

"Pugsley," I said, frowning at the kitten. "Really?"

He shrugged. It was his latest name for the kitten. Derek had surprised me a few weeks before with this fuzzy little white-haired darling, with a hint of tiger stripes around her face and a sweet personality. I'd fallen instantly in love with her, but we hadn't yet decided what to call her.

At first I had suggested the name Syllabub, after the ridiculously sweet and alcoholic English dessert I'd recently learned to make. But I had ended up calling her Silly and Derek had been calling her Bub. Neither of us were happy with that and I figured the poor cat was just confused.

So now we were trying out different names whenever they occurred to us, convinced we would recognize the perfect name when we found it.

As I walked to the couch, I nuzzled the kitten and she patted my nose with her tiny paw. "You're much too cute to be a Pugsley, aren't you? Let's sit down and think of a better name for you. How about Skeeter?"

"Absolutely not," Derek said immediately.

I laughed in agreement. "You're right, she's definitely not a Skeeter."

Derek set our two wineglasses on the coffee table and joined me on the couch. The kitten immediately abandoned me for Derek, who was holding a tiny stuffed mouse to entice her. As Derek teased the kitten, he regaled me with the story of his latest client who'd had a fortune in artwork stolen from his beach house in the famous Long Island Hamptons.

As one of the world's leading experts on security for the incredibly rich, Derek always had interesting work stories to tell.

"I might have to travel back east for a few days and I'm hoping you'll come with me. We can spend some time in New York."

"That sounds wonderful." I sighed. "But I can't go anywhere for the next three weeks, not until the show is over."

"I'll try to hold off, then, until you're free."

"That would be nice." I squeezed his arm affectionately. "I've never been to the Hamptons."

"Good. We'll make it a mini break."

"We'll have to find a kitten sitter," I said.

"Vinnie and Suzie can help out. You've taken care of their Pookie and Splinters any number of times."

"But they have Lily now."

"They won't mind," Derek said, tucking me closer to him.

"Of course they won't," I said. "And speaking of neighbors, I met Alex tonight."

"Alex?"

"She's the one who's subletting Sergio's place."

"I've yet to see her," he said. "Do you like her?"

"I do. Even though she's tall, smart, and gorgeous. She wears fabulous shoes and pink suits and still manages to look powerful and perky at this hour of the night. I should hate her, but apparently she bakes wonderful cupcakes."

"Ah," he said, finally reacting. "Cupcakes."

I laughed. "Yes, that got my attention, too. So far, it's her most outstanding quality."

He laughed, too. "I look forward to meeting her." He reached to pick up his wineglass.

"I should tell you something," I said.

He swallowed a sip of wine and studied my expression. "Yes, you should."

I related the conversation I'd overheard between the two producers and Randolph, the host. "Randolph was really upset, but Tom and Walter seemed unfazed."

"He believes someone is out to kill him?"

"Yes."

"Have you any idea what occurred before you came down the corridor and overheard them?"

"Not really." I mentioned the producer's throwaway line about Randolph tripping over a broom. It seemed a little silly, but given Randolph's reaction, it might be an important detail. Had he really tripped over a broom? Or was the producer being sarcastic? "I get the feeling from their looks and comments that they consider Randolph a prima donna who whines about everything."

"Does he seem that way to you?"

"No." I thought again of that moment when the two producers saw me in the hall. "And until Tom and Walter walked out of the dressing room, they didn't come across as insensitive, either. So I'm not sure what to believe. But I'm concerned."

Derek's lips twisted. "So am I."

Because of my penchant for finding dead bodies and facing down their craven killers? I didn't have to say the words aloud. They hovered in the ether and spelled out the reason for Derek's alarm. Mine, too.

"Let's change the subject." I grabbed the remote and switched on the television. The evening news was just getting started and I was happy to be distracted. The kitten diverted me, as well, trekking fearlessly up Derek's arm and across his wide shoulders.

The major news headlines had been covered and I was ready to call it a night when the anchorman switched to a more jocular tone. "And now here's Teddy to show you what's happening around San Francisco today."

The next thing I saw was a full-screen shot of hundreds of people standing in lines, clutching antiques and odd collectibles. Some pushed dollies that held larger pieces of furniture.

"Oh, my gosh, this is my show," I said, sitting up straighter.

The camera zoomed in on the line of people as a voice-over announcer said, "The popular antiques show *This Old Attic* has come to San Francisco, and if you're lucky, you could be invited to have your hidden treasures and old family heirlooms appraised by experts on TV."

The camera focused on a small leather case in the man's hand. He opened it to reveal several human molars.

"Maybe like this fellow, your great-grandfather was a dentist who swore he owned two of George Washington's teeth."

The video switched to a dignified-looking woman carrying an old-fashioned portfolio, and the jovial announcer continued. "Or you might have inherited a faded map of Africa that your aunt believes once belonged to Dr. Livingstone. You know, as in *Dr. Livingstone, I presume?* Yeah, that guy."

The camera pulled back to include the hundreds of people waiting in lines to talk to the producers. "Whatever your family treasure happens to be, bring it in. You could wind up having it appraised on camera by an expert. Like this woman did."

And suddenly, I was watching myself on television.

Derek grinned. "What a lovely surprise."

It was a surprise, all right. I watched myself pick up *The Secret Garden* and say, "What makes this even more outstanding is that this illustration is actually an original painting on canvas."

This was followed by a quick montage of camera shots and audio blips, ending with Vera saying, "It cost three dollars at a garage sale last Saturday."

Finally the camera cut to a close-up of the book with my voice-over saying, "And with the author's original signature included, it's my expert opinion that an antiquarian book dealer would pay . . ."

My voice cut out, and they went to Vera's reaction of stunned disbelief.

Suddenly the anchorman was back, wearing a big smile. "We promised the show's producers that we wouldn't reveal what the book is actually worth, but let's just say it's enough to feed a family of four for at least two years. Maybe more."

The anchorman began to chat with the weatherman, so Derek muted the sound.

I was wearing a silly grin as I reached for my wine. "That was so weird."

"It appears that you made someone very happy today," Derek said. "And you didn't look nervous at all."

"I was shaking like crazy, but the nerves faded away as soon as I started talking about the book."

"Of course they did," he said easily, as the cat tugged on his shirtsleeve.

I took a last sip of wine. "So, that's what I'll be doing for the next three weeks. What do you think?"

"I think they're lucky to have you. You came across as the consummate professional."

I gave him a big, smoochy kiss. "Thank you."

"You're welcome." His expression turned speculative as he added, "I also think the television studio will be crawling with newly excited book owners by tomorrow morning."

I pictured the place crawling with book owners and chuckled in anticipation. "Sounds like a good time."

"Yes, it does," he said, his lips pursing in thought. "And I plan to be there, as well."

Chapter Three

The next morning I was toasting bagels when Derek joined me in the kitchen and poured himself a cup of coffee. I watched him and managed to keep breathing, even though the man could take my breath away without trying. He was dressed for work in a perfectly fitted gazillion-dollar black suit, crisp white hand-tailored shirt, and gorgeous dark gold and black paisley silk power tie. Not that Derek needed a power tie to feel powerful. That came naturally. He was six feet tall with the lean, athletic build of a boxer. His hair was dark and he wore it cut short. His deep blue eyes gleamed with intelligence and wry humor and he had a commanding presence when he walked into a room. And he was hot, too. I was a lucky girl.

But, then, he thought he was pretty lucky for having found me. So I guess that made me even luckier.

I smiled as I slathered cream cheese on the bagels.

"Are you making breakfast, then?" he said.

"Yes. I figured it was my turn since you've done it three times in a row."

"How lovely." He kissed my neck, causing me to fumble the

knife. With a chuckle, he stepped away from me. "I'll let you get on with it."

"That would be smart." I slid the bagels back into the toaster oven to keep them warm. "Do you still plan to come by the studio today?"

"Yes. Not sure when I'll get there, though."

"As long as I know you're coming, I'll leave your name at the front gate."

He nodded as he sipped his coffee. "I'll call or text you when I'm on the way."

"Sounds good." I melted butter in a small frying pan, then cracked three eggs into a bowl and whipped them up. "I might have my phone turned off, but I'll let the guard know you're coming."

"Good." He took his coffee over to the dining room table, where a few days ago we had rolled out several sheets of architects' blueprints to study.

Derek had recently purchased the smaller loft next door to mine and our plan was to open up walls to enlarge the living area. We would also turn the master bedroom in the second loft into an office for Derek and create a guest suite with its own kitchen for our visitors. It would be an ideal place for members of my family to stay when they came to the city and I was also hoping we might persuade Derek's family to visit from England more often. After all, the last time his brother was in town, things had gotten very interesting. I couldn't wait to meet the rest of his family.

The only thing we hadn't decided on was where we would live for a few months during the most destructive and noisy phases of construction. We had already debated several choices. We could rent another apartment nearby or stay in a hotel. Neither of those options appealed to us.

Derek's company owned several hotel-type suites on the top

floor of their building, for visiting clients and corporate officials. We could live there for as long as it was necessary. I could commute to my home workshop and simply put up with the construction noise all day. Or we could both stay with my mom and dad in Dharma up in Sonoma County, where I grew up.

My parents still lived in their big ranch-style home, where they'd raised six children. Obviously, there would be plenty of room for Derek and me. It would be nice to spend quality time up there, and I could work in my old mentor Abraham's bookbinding studio, right down the street from my parents' place. But Derek would have to commute into the city and might be able to visit only on the weekends, so I wasn't happy about that choice, either.

The kitten played with a squeaky toy as we munched on our scrambled eggs and bagels with cream cheese and strawberry jam. "I'm nervous about taking little Snowball to Dharma."

"She'll be fine," he said absently as he studied one section of the blueprints.

"I'm probably being overprotective."

"Yes. If you're truly worried, just keep her inside." He flashed me a look. "And there's no way in hell she'll be named Snowball."

I bit back a smile. "I didn't think you heard me."

"I heard you."

I thought for a moment, then said, "What about Snowflake?"

He grunted in disgust. "Allow the poor creature some dignity, will you?"

I picked up the kitten and snuggled her soft, furry neck. "But she's just a widdle kitty."

"I see," he said, as he cut his bagel into smaller bites. "You've lost all your own dignity, so how can you possibly be expected to pass any along to the cat?"

I laughed and nuzzled her tummy. "It's hard to maintain much dignity around such a little cutie."

"I disagree. Watch and learn." He set down his knife and held out his hand for the cat. "Come here, Marlborough. There's a good lass."

"Marlborough?" I snorted a laugh, but handed the tiny creature over. "Sounds like the name of your butler."

"Hmm." He studied the cat. "Charlemagne, then." The kitten began to lick Derek's finger with its tiny pink tongue and he softened instantly. "Would you look at that? I'd say she approves of Charlemagne."

"No, she doesn't," I said, as I stood and stacked our empty plates. "But she loves you, anyway."

He glanced at me, one eyebrow raised in inquiry. "We could call her Charlie."

I considered it as I carried the dishes into the kitchen. Charlie was a cute name, especially for a girl kitty. "I'll think about it."

After Derek left for the office, I poured myself another cup of coffee and headed for my workshop, anxious to get started. I'd left *The Secret Garden* on my worktable the night before and now I rummaged through drawers and cupboards, pulling out the tools I would need to do a more thorough examination of the book: a metal gauge for measuring, a small scale for weighing, a super-high-powered magnifying glass to take a close-up look at its flaws. I grabbed my camera and began snapping pictures of the book from every angle, including the interior pages.

In only a few hours I needed to get ready for my day at the studio, but that would be enough time to study the book and write up an invoice. The sooner I gave Vera an estimate of the work I wanted to do, the sooner she would pay me. And then I could get started on the job.

I had long ago perfected the art of eating chocolate without getting any on my hands, so after popping two chocolate mint kisses into my mouth, I got down to business. The preliminary details came first. The book measured ten inches tall by seven and a quarter inches wide by two inches thick, and it weighed just over nine hundred grams, or almost two pounds. That was heavy for a children's book, but, then, any parent who would buy an exquisite book like this for their kid to play with had no idea what was appropriate, anyway.

I weighed and measured in order to establish a base of information. Once the book was finished I would do it all again and compare the original with my final work. My goal was to end up with the exact same numbers I'd started with.

In my notes, I listed the book's qualities as a conservative book dealer might describe them, which meant keeping my enthusiasm to a minimum.

Full goatskin binding, except for cutout on front.

Front cover with original painting on canvas signed by the artist M. L. Kirk.

Spine divided into six panels with raised bands between, each panel decoratively tooled and title lettered in gilt.

Fine condition externally, with crushed dark green Levant morocco leather decoratively tooled and gilded in a vine-and-rose pattern.

Gilded vine pattern extends to inside board edges with turn-ins decoratively bordered.

Leaf-pattern watermark on endpapers with date and unknown signature on flyleaf.

Sporadic light foxing internally, but otherwise paper clean and bright.

Eight tissue-guarded color plates by M. L. Kirk.

Limitation page indicates limited edition of fifty copies, of which this book is number 6.

Original author signature on limitation page.

Shaking off the dry bookseller's tone, I gazed at the book from my own perspective.

"You are a pretty thing," I murmured as I reached for another chocolate mint kiss and tossed it into my mouth. After lobbing the thin foil wrap into the trash can, I checked my hands to make sure they were chocolate-free. Then I picked up my magnifying glass and proceeded to study every inch of the leather cover, making more notes as I went along.

As I'd mentioned to Vera on the show, there were several faded spots on the back cover and I noted their locations. I was certain they wouldn't take too much time to repair, just a cautious application of the leather cleaner I used.

The spine needed more attention than I'd noticed at first. The gilding had all but disappeared along four of the raised bands, so I decided it would be best if I regilded them all so the intensity of the gold would match exactly. The decorative designs in each panel were still quite vivid so I wouldn't have to touch them.

I mentally patted myself on the back, knowing that that little decision would save Vera a few hundred dollars. Gilding could be time-consuming work and occasionally had to be repeated once or twice before it was perfect.

Moving on to the front cover, I noted that the unique beveled edge around the painting was rough in one spot. It was almost undetectable, but a good dealer would take money off the price if I didn't fix it.

I had friends who weren't this obsessive about their work, but I'd been trained by a bookbinder's version of a boot-camp instructor. During my apprentice years, Abraham would have gleefully ripped the book apart and made me start over if I'd missed the smallest detail. Consequently, I rarely skipped a step.

Besides that, I was halfway in love with this book. I was excited to get started and determined to give it the best treatment possible.

Once I finished examining the cover, I held the book in my hands and stared at it for a long moment. My throat tightened as my excitement was replaced with a wistful yearning for my dear old mentor, Abraham Karastovsky.

It wasn't something I ever would have shared with Vera or the viewing audience of *This Old Attic*, but my own childhood copy of *The Secret Garden* had been the very catalyst that led me to seek a career in bookbinding and restoration. My own book hadn't been nearly as grand as Vera's, of course, but I had cherished it all the same.

I could still picture the sturdy, pale pink cloth binding with its green cloth spine. The front cover had featured an illustration drawn by Tasha Tudor, a sepia-toned version of the little girl standing by the garden wall. She wore a plaid coat and hat and carried a jump rope in her hand. She appeared to be emerging from the secret walled garden through a heavy wooden door.

My clever parents had bought the book for me the summer they moved our family from San Francisco to the new commune in Sonoma County. They knew us kids well, had known we weren't happy about the move. Their solution was to surprise us with goodies to keep our minds off this major disruption. My gift was *The Secret Garden*.

I had adored that book and read it over and over again that summer. Then one day, I went to find the book and it was gone. Puzzled, I searched all over the house but couldn't find it anywhere.

I walked outside and saw my big brothers, Austin and Jackson, and a couple of their friends tossing something back and forth. It was my book! I screamed at them and they dropped it in the dirt and ran away, laughing.

I gingerly picked up my beloved *Secret Garden*. The cover had been ripped from the text block and dangled precariously, held on by a mere thread or two. I began to cry and tore into the house to find my mother, hoping she would agree to help me beat the boys with clubs.

Though she wasn't happy with what they'd done, she refused to punish them in the manner I'd suggested. I was inconsolable and ran to my room, sobbing. A few minutes later, Mom walked in and sat on my bed. As she rubbed my back, she suggested that I take the book over to the commune's bookbinder. Perhaps he could fix it for me.

The bookbinder was Abraham, my teacher and friend, who died last year.

He had taken one look at the tattered book and had called my brothers into his studio to put the fear of God into them.

"I am not happy about this," he'd said in his soft baritone.

I'd watched my brothers' eyes widen in apprehension, because when Abraham wasn't happy, people tended to run for the hills. The man was tall and husky, with a big head of wiry hair and really large hands. His voice grew softer the madder he became. All the kids agreed he would make a great bad guy in a science-fiction movie like *The Thing*.

He wasn't a monster at all, of course, but a big softy and a darling man. I loved him for counseling my brothers—after he had first frightened them thoroughly—that part of their job on this earth was to respect and treasure their family and to take care of the little ones, like me.

He'd added gruffly that anyone who didn't take care of books was downright stupid.

"You don't want to be thought of as stupid, do you?" Abraham

murmured. "Wouldn't you rather have us believe that you're intelligent young men?"

Jackson and Austin looked like bobblehead dolls as they nodded in agreement.

After listening to Abraham, I felt a little sheepish about having
asked my mother to beat up my brothers and their friends. But I
kept that to myself.

Abraham fixed my book and returned it to me in better-than-
original condition. After countless readings by my little eight-
year-old self, it had been admittedly a bit shabby, but Abraham had
made it look beautiful again.

As he'd worked on my book, I had hounded him, showing up
at his workshop hourly to check on his progress. His bookbinding
skills fascinated me, and once my book was restored I continued
to visit him almost daily to beg him to teach me how to do what
he did.

Finally, he reluctantly agreed, and I began the journey that
eventually made me the bibliophile expert I was today.

I sat back in my chair and checked the time. I still had another
hour before I had to stop, so I opened the book and found the
pages that contained the minor foxing I'd pointed out to Vera. I
wrote down each page number that contained even the slightest
discoloration. There was foxing on only twelve pages. That wasn't
so awful.

I still wasn't sure if I would bother eliminating the spots or
not, because the procedure could be destructive to the book. But
the sad fact was that while some buyers accepted that foxing was
inevitable, others were likely to downgrade the book's worth with
each instance.

Happily, the paper was a thick, creamy vellum, so if I decided
to go ahead with the bleaching procedure, the pages would be able
to withstand my gentle attempts to clean them.

Foxing was caused by various types of mold spores or mildew

that reacted to elements, mainly iron, within the paper itself. The problem with trying to clean or bleach the brown spots was that an individual spore could react completely differently, depending on the paper. You never knew exactly what you were dealing with until you saw the results.

It was frustrating. Spores, fibers, paper thickness, age of the paper, amount of iron—each of these factors could cause a completely unique reaction. So a bookbinder was taking a chance with every book. I never knew which formula of bleach or cleaner to use when trying to get rid of foxing. I could make an educated guess because I'd done it thousands of times, but I still couldn't say for sure what would happen in any given situation.

And even when the results looked good, the fact was that I would have broken down the microscopic cellulose fibers and this would eventually lead to the disintegration of the paper. And if there was one thing I didn't care to do, it was destroy the paper itself.

I'd had moderate success with a weak mixture of water and hydrogen peroxide, but I didn't dare use a chemical bleaching agent on a book as valuable as this one. I went ahead and added two hours of time to Vera's estimate, just in case I decided to try some of the nontoxic plant extracts I'd used in the past. The good news was that they wouldn't destroy the paper, but the bad news was that they also wouldn't entirely eliminate the spots.

I thought about the time I'd experimented by using a loaf of white bread as a bleaching tool. It hadn't been very effective, but it also hadn't damaged the paper. And it was fun to squish the pieces of bread into a ball, rub it against the brown spots, and watch the ball turn darker as it pulled bits of the stain away from the page.

I had a few minutes left so I picked up my magnifying glass again and studied the extra signature inside the front cover. I assumed the book's owner had written her own name in the book, because it was clearly not the author's signature. It also didn't look like a child's scrawl, although it did appear a bit immature and shaky, almost as if some young person had been practicing a more grown-up or flamboyant way to sign his or her name.

The first name began with a big, sweeping loop, followed by letters crammed up against one another. I started with the loops, determined to unravel the mystery of the bad handwriting.

The first name began with what looked like an *M*.

"Mary?" I whispered. "Martha? Marilyn?" I moved on to the second name and realized it wasn't a middle name so much as an adjunct to the first name. So . . . Mary Jo? Mary Sue? Martha Lou? Mary Tom?

Mary *Tom*? Probably not.

After a few minutes, I had to blink and look away to ease the tension in my eyes. It wasn't easy, staring at the crammed letters through the magnifying glass.

I stood and stretched. I didn't want to get a headache before I had to go off to work, so I gave up for the day. And, frankly, it didn't really matter if I couldn't figure out the name since I wasn't going to delete it or rebind the book because of it.

Leaving my tools where they were, I covered the book with a clean cloth.

I finished Vera's estimate and printed it. Before I jumped into the shower, I called the number on her business card. She answered on the first ring and we exchanged brief pleasantries. I quoted her my price and she was agreeable, thank goodness.

"Would you mind terribly bringing the invoice to me at the flower shop?" she asked. "I work every day except Sunday, from early morning until six each evening."

"I'll be happy to." We agreed to meet at her shop Thursday morning on my way to the studio. Her shop was far away from my usual route, but she was so excited that I didn't mind. She promised to have the check ready so I could get started on the work.

I grabbed my computer and shoved a few more reference books into my bag, then left my apartment, checking that the locks were secure before heading for the elevator. Even though I could do most of my research on the computer, I still liked to refer to the books written by the experts I most admired. Their unique views and experience couldn't always be found online.

The Peapod Studio complex was located at the base of Potrero Hill, just a few miles from my place. It was almost one o'clock and the sun was high as I drove into the studio parking lot. I stopped at the small booth and greeted Benny the security guard. He was a sweet, older man, and calling him a guard was probably a stretch since he was portly and a bit timid. But he took pride in his work and was friendly and attentive. And he already knew my name after only one day.

"Good morning, Miss Wainwright," Benny said, checking my name off his clipboard list.

"Hi, Benny. I have a guest coming to see me today." I watched him reach for a pen and added, "I'm not sure when he'll be here, but can you put his name on your visitors list?"

"For you, absolutely," he said.

He wrote down Derek's name and waved me through the gate.

I drove in and parked in my designated spot. As I walked toward Studio 6, I thought about Derek's prediction the night before and wondered if more people would show up today with their rare books. I hoped so. I was always happy to talk about books. The more, the merrier.

I smiled inwardly at the possibility of Tom and Walter agreeing to devote the entire show to just books. *Why not?* I chuckled and figured I would have to be satisfied with my two measly book segments each day. *Ah, well.*

"Hey!"

The angry shout startled me out of my reverie. I whipped

around and saw a tall, burly man stalking across the parking lot toward me. I glanced to either side and over my shoulder, wondering who he was shouting at.

"Yeah, I'm talking to you!"

I looked behind me again, thinking he had to be yelling at someone else. But I was the only one in the area and he was looking right at me. And getting closer. He wore a baggy pair of blue jeans and a stretched-out, dirty white T-shirt that barely covered his big stomach. A torn and faded flannel shirt completed the look.

At first I thought he was bald, but as he approached I realized that his head was shaved and he was actually pretty young. In his twenties, maybe.

The closer he got, the meaner he looked, and I was growing more alarmed by the nanosecond. I headed quickly toward the stage door and relative safety.

I noticed Benny watching from the shelter of his little booth by the parking lot entrance. I waved my hand frantically until he finally stepped out, but he didn't come any closer.

"Hold it right there."

Again I looked around. "Are you talking to me?"

"Don't play dumb with me," he said, jabbing his finger toward me. "I saw you on TV. That book is mine and so's the money."

"I'm not playing dumb," I said, irritated now. Was I going to be harassed by any big jerk who happened to see me on television? "I don't know why you're yelling at me, but I think you'd better leave."

Benny approached slowly behind the man. *Too* slowly for my taste. "Uh, everything okay here, Ms. Wainwright?"

"No, Benny," I said immediately. "I think you'd better call the police."

The brute moved closer and glowered at me. "If I don't get what's mine, I'll open up a whole can of *rude* on you."

"You'll have to leave, sir," Benny said nervously. I couldn't blame him for being afraid. The guy towered over both of us.

"I'm not leaving until I get what I came for."

"What is it you want, sir?" Benny asked cautiously.

He ignored Benny and stuck his huge sweaty face inches away from mine. "I want that book. Hand it over now or I'll kill you."

Chapter Four

Uttering a tiny shriek, I inched backward. "Get away from me."

"Sir, I'm going to have to ask you to leave," Benny said with all the authority he could muster, and grabbed the man's arm.

The big guy yanked himself free. "Not until I get my property."

"Call the police, Benny," I said urgently.

"Good idea, miss." He spun around and jogged away, leaving me alone to face the guy. It wasn't exactly my plan to be left alone with the guy, but I couldn't blame old Benny. He'd probably never experienced one minute of real danger in all the years he'd worked here. But couldn't he carry a cell phone, at least?

The stranger watched Benny run back to his booth and I managed to slide past him and make it to the heavy stage door that led into the studio. I grabbed the door handle but it wouldn't budge. At that very instant, an earsplitting siren blasted once.

"Damn it," I muttered. The siren went silent, but the bright red light over the door began to twirl, signifying that they had started taping another segment of the show.

Which meant that they wouldn't unlock the door until they

were finished. So I was stuck out here for at least five minutes, maybe longer.

"Looks like you and me have time for a little talk," my attacker said.

"The police are on their way." I set my heavy computer case down and folded my arms tightly. I was two steps up from him and could look him in the eyes. "You're trespassing and threatening me and I don't even know who you are. But I do know that the book doesn't belong to you. It doesn't belong to me, either. And even if it did, do you really think I'd hand it over to you?"

"That woman, that bitch, I saw her on the show. She stole that book from me."

"She didn't steal it. She bought it at a garage sale."

For a brief moment, he looked puzzled and uncomfortable; then he sputtered, "She stole it!"

The light dawned. "You're the one who sold it to her."

He looked befuddled again. Then his face turned even redder. "I didn't sell it to her!"

He didn't seem too smart but he was definitely mean. *You're an idiot,* I thought, but wisely kept my mouth shut. His face was a blend of humiliation and a growing temper made up of fury and frustration.

"That bitch is gonna be sorry she ever went on that show."

"You've already threatened me," I said, leaning backward to put more space between us. "Don't think I won't tell the police."

"Hey, I'm happy to talk to the police." He was obviously bluffing, but he blustered along. "They'll know who's in the right. They'll get the book back for me, along with the money. That belongs to me, too."

I frowned as something occurred to me. "They never said what the book was worth on the news segment. How do you know it's worth anything?"

"I'm not stupid," he snarled. "The guy on TV said it was worth enough money to feed a family of four for at least two years."

I shook my head. "He was exaggerating."

He ignored me. "I did the Google. A family of four eats about a thousand dollars' worth of food every month. That's twelve thousand a year, twenty-four thousand for two years. Twenty-four thousand dollars? That money is mine!"

You did the Google?

"You sold the book for three dollars." I was pressed against the stage door and couldn't back away from him any farther, so I started to edge sideways. "It doesn't belong to you anymore."

He took a step toward me and I stuck my hand out like a traffic cop's. "Get back. Get away from me. Right now."

Instead, he grabbed my wrist and twisted it, squeezing hard.

"Let go of me!" I slapped at his beefy hand to no avail. I'd never been attacked so publicly and viciously before. I'd taken self-defense classes, but anything I'd ever learned was useless because my mind went blank.

A police siren wailed in the distance.

That was enough to snap me out of my stupor. I kicked him and my pointed toe smacked his shinbone hard enough to make him howl like a wild dog. He let me go and started hopping around while clutching one leg, swearing the whole time.

I dodged away, out of his range, but he recovered quickly and came after me, grabbing my hair with one hand and my arm with the other. He yanked me back against him and I arched forward to keep from touching him. I was screaming as I tried to reach around and kick him again.

Benny came running back. "Hey! Take your hands off her!" He tried to pry the bigger man away from me, but the oaf wasn't cowed. Instead, he elbowed Benny out of the way, whirled me around, and grabbed hold of my chin, angling it so that I was forced to stare at his red, sweating face.

I tried to twist away, tried to plant my nails in his fleshy skin, but he barely reacted to anything I did. I scratched and slapped him, but he just eyed me menacingly.

"Nobody screws with me," he said in a harsh whisper. He squeezed my upper arm until I cried out. "I'll track down that bitch and get that book. Then I'll come after you. I'm gonna kill you both."

I'd been in a lot of scary situations and faced down sociopaths and murderers, but I'd never been confronted with such visceral evil before. I could see it in his cold, dead eyes. I had no doubt that if there had been no witnesses, if he thought he could get away with it, he would have tried to kill me right then and there. As it was, he was ready to snap my arm right out of its socket. I was bent over backward, trying to keep that from happening.

He was right on top of me. His skin was clammy and his hatred was terrifying and real. I could sense it eating away at him.

"I said get your hands off of her!" Benny shouted, bravely pushing and pounding on my assailant's back. "The police are on their way to arrest you." He tried to pry the guy's hand away from my arm, but it was like a minnow trying to prod a shark.

The brute had had enough of Benny. He shoved me aside and turned and smacked Benny across the face, sending him spiraling backward until he lost his balance and fell.

As Benny lay groaning on the blacktop, the police siren sounded again.

The man bared his teeth at me one last time. "I'll be back." Then he took off running across the parking lot and through the gate and disappeared into the neighborhood.

I'll be back? Who did he think he was? The Terminator?

I wished I was in the mood to laugh at that, but I could feel a bruise forming on my sore jaw. I brushed aside the pain and rushed over to kneel down next to poor Benny. "Are you all right?"

"Uhhhhn," he groaned. I helped him up to a sitting position and he shook his head, still disoriented. "Who was that guy?"

"I have no idea." But I did. He had to be the garage-sale loser who'd sold *The Secret Garden* to Vera for three measly dollars. I knew he was a vicious, scary psychopath who had brutalized Benny. He had threatened and assaulted and frightened the hell out of me. He could've killed me. But I still had no clue who he actually was. I didn't know his name or where he lived.

But Vera would know.

A cop car pulled into the lot twenty seconds later, siren screaming, but it was too little, too late. The vicious creep was gone.

"*I* love a challenge," Chuck the makeup man said, as he dabbed a thick liquid foundation onto my chin and along my jaw. With a clean white sponge, he began to blend the liquid into my skin, hoping to cover up the darkening bruise that the attacker had given me.

"I'm glad I could make your day," I mumbled.

"Don't sweat it; you'll look gorgeous on camera. I just hope you'll be able to talk with the swelling."

Oh, great. Now I had something brand-new to worry about. "Thanks a lot, Chuck." My jaw was really starting to hurt and talking didn't help. But I wasn't about to complain or say anything that would get me sent home, so I relaxed in the chair and let him work his magic.

After I'd given the two policemen a description of my assailant, I'd written down the address of Vera's flower shop and told them that she would be able to give them the bad guy's address. With any luck, he would be in jail for assault and battery by the end of the day.

Poor Benny had refused to go to the hospital, insisting he was fine. He'd just been a little shaken up. I couldn't blame him for wanting to brush off the incident. He might be worried about losing his job as a studio security guard if his employers didn't think he could handle an altercation like the one we'd just been through.

I wanted to call Vera and warn her that the police would be coming by, but I was running out of time. I needed to study up on my next book. And I had to telephone Derek before he showed up and saw my bruises.

But as I'd passed the makeup room, I'd run into Chuck. He'd taken one look at my darkening jaw and insisted on doing something about it.

"That's it, just relax." Chuck grinned as he worked. The man looked like a tall, skinny elf with his twinkling eyes, curly gray mustache, and meticulously trimmed goatee. His strokes were so light, it was like getting a mini massage. My eyelids fluttered closed and I was pretty sure I could've dozed off in this chair with no difficulty at all.

"What the hell happened to you?"

I flinched and my eyes flew open. Randolph Rayburn was staring intently at me, as if I were a strange-looking bug on a slide. I really must have fallen asleep because I hadn't heard him come into the makeup room.

"Did somebody hurt you?" he persisted.

"Sort of," I said slowly.

His eyes widened. "Who was it? Did he smack you? Should I call the police?"

"They were already here."

"They were?" He shot Chuck a questioning look. "Why didn't I hear them?"

"It happened outside in the parking lot."

"Who was it? Did the police arrest him?"

"No, he got away."

"Damn it. So, what happened?"

I took a deep breath and let it out slowly. It was hard to concentrate. I needed to pop some ibuprofen or I'd be a mess by the time I got on camera. And even scarier, it was getting harder to talk without my jaw aching.

"Maybe you should go home," Randolph said, watching me struggle.

"No. I'm just a little dazed, that's all." There was no way I was going home. "Anyway, some guy came by claiming to be the rightful owner of the book I appraised yesterday. He grabbed me in the parking lot and threatened me."

"Was it someone you know?"

I didn't feel like explaining the entire situation to Randolph. "No."

"So you've never seen him before today?"

"No."

Chuck snickered behind me. "Hey, Randy, maybe your imaginary stalker finally showed up for real."

"He *is* real," Randolph muttered, frowning.

"Sure he is," Chuck mocked. "Is he also the type to attack a woman?"

Randolph ignored Chuck and carried on with his questioning. "So, this guy actually attacked you?"

I wasn't about to let him change the subject. "Do you have a stalker, Randolph?"

Chuck snorted. "He'd like us all to believe he does."

I watched Randolph's expression turn cloudy. *Tell them someone's trying to kill me.* The words I'd overheard him say yesterday came rushing back.

If Randolph thought someone was stalking him, he seemed to be having a hard time getting anyone else to believe him. So why was I inclined to believe him without question? Maybe because I'd seen more malevolence in the last year than an average person saw in a lifetime.

My gaze met Randolph's in the mirror. "Are you being stalked?"

Chuck shook his head. "Oh, please. Don't encourage him."

Randolph scowled but said nothing more. A minute later, Angie arrived to take him out to the stage.

Chuck used a soft brush to give my cheeks the slightest touch of color. Then he patted my shoulder. "I think I've done all I can do for you, Brooks."

I smiled, amused that Chuck had called me Brooks from the first time we were introduced yesterday. Some people were the type to be familiar from the start.

I gazed at my face in the mirror and was pleasantly surprised. After turning my head to catch a few different angles of myself, I said, "Wow, you can't see a thing. And you made me look good besides. Thanks, Chuck."

"You look good without my help, doll," he said. "I just enhanced what was already there. Along with a little creative covering up."

"I really appreciate it." I stood and moved closer to the mirror to get a better look. "I owe you."

"I'll send you the bill."

I tried to smile, but it made my jaw hurt. Glancing around the room, I saw a stack of white facecloths. "Can I borrow one of your little towels?"

"Sure."

"I'll bring it back later."

"No problem, kiddo."

I walked out to the studio and found the catering table. At one end, tubs of crushed ice held cans of soft drinks and bottles of water. Grabbing a handful of ice, I wrapped it up in the towel and hurried back to my dressing room. I would need to ice my jaw for the next hour while I researched the book for my upcoming segment. I just hoped the ice wouldn't ruin my makeup.

"And right there, that makes you an idiot," I muttered. The fact that I was more worried about my makeup than my swollen, bruised jaw? Yup, that was crazy.

But I refused to be too hard on myself. It was only my second day in show business. I wasn't about to quit now. Once in my dressing room, I dumped my computer bag onto the desk, then rifled through my purse to find some ibuprofen. I took three pills with a big gulp of water and sat on the couch, pressing the makeshift ice bag to my jaw. The initial chill was a shock but it wore off quickly and the ice began to numb my jaw, easing the pain.

I reached for my phone and pushed Derek's number, turning on the speaker so I wouldn't have to hold it next to my ear. He answered on the first ring.

"Darling Brooklyn, what a nice surprise."

"Hi, Derek. I just wanted to—"

"Something's wrong. What happened? Are you all right?"

I frowned at the phone. "How can you tell something's wrong?"

"Your voice is subdued," he explained, "and you're never subdued. Are you hurt? Is somebody dead? Where are you?"

"I'm at the studio. Nobody's dead. There was a man in the parking lot. He wanted the book. He was a jerk. I'm okay, but he hurt Benny. It was pretty bad."

"He hurt you, too." It was a statement, not a question.

"Yes," I admitted. "But I'll be fine."

"I'm on my way."

"Wait. You don't have to rush. I just wanted to let you know what happened."

"You're hurt," he said simply. "I'll be there in half an hour."

"I love you, Derek."

"Dear God, Brooklyn. I love you, too. I'll hurry."

He ended the call. Derek wasn't used to hearing me tell him I loved him over the phone in the middle of the day. His reaction was a little frantic, and Derek, the epitome of cool and calm, never sounded frantic.

"He must think I'm dying," I said aloud, and sighed. I'd finally gotten used to saying those three little words to him, but it had taken a while. I didn't always trust my feelings because in the past I'd had a tendency to fall in and out of love a lot. Usually with inappropriate men, like my adorable and very gay friend, Ian.

In the beginning, I'd figured Derek was inappropriate, too. To start, his home was in London, so he was geographically inappropriate, to say the least. And his life was so different from mine. Derek had served in the Royal Navy as a commander before going to work with Britain's Military Intelligence. After a number of years, he left the government to open his own private security company. He had been in dangerous, deadly situations all over the world, while I had been raised in a peaceful, artistic commune in Sonoma County in northern California.

We had met under difficult circumstances when Abraham was killed and I was considered the number-one suspect. Derek had stayed close by my side throughout the ordeal, which would have been terribly romantic except for one little detail: he thought I was a murderer.

I met up with him again in Scotland when I attended the Edinburgh International Book Festival. Unfortunately, other murders occurred during the festival, but this time Derek knew I was innocent. Nevertheless, when we said good-bye, I never expected to see him again.

Then, out of the blue, or so it seemed, he returned to San Francisco and ended up opening a branch office of his security company there. And then he moved in with me. And never moved out.

I was growing more and more used to the fact that he was indeed my one true love.

I looked up and realized I'd left my dressing room door wide open. I got up and crossed to close it, but first took a quick look down the hall.

"Brooklyn! There you are." Randolph came bounding down the hall and stopped in front of my doorway. "I wanted to make sure you're okay."

"I'll be fine," I said, touching my jaw with one careful finger. "It's still a little tender."

"Can I come in?"

"I guess so." *More questions,* I figured. Under normal circumstances, I would've jumped at the chance to chat with Randolph. Given my usual nosiness, I should've been itching to ask him about his stalker. But my curiosity had been tempered by the attack of the vicious stranger.

I sat back down on the turquoise sofa, but Randolph continued to stand.

"What's up, Randolph?"

"First, you should call me Randy," he said.

"Okay, Randy."

"But." He held his index finger up in warning. "Never on camera."

I nodded. "Got it."

"It's bad enough that my name sounds so fake." He began to pace nervously back and forth from the door to the dressing table against the far wall, a distance of about ten feet total. "I mean, who names their kid Randolph Rayburn? Can you picture me getting beaten up every day after school?"

"Oh, dear." I tried to bite back a laugh. "I'm sorry."

He chuckled. "It was touch-and-go for a while, but I'm okay now. The name Randolph has some gravity to it, so it works for someone who's hosting a hoity-toity antiques show, right? Makes me sound smart. That's what I like to believe anyway. But Randy? Makes me sound like a horny goat."

"I can call you Randolph if you think it'll help."

"No, no, I actually prefer to be called Randy by my friends. But I'm under no illusions. I know what image the name conjures up."

"Horny goats."

"Exactly."

"I think it's a fine name," I said, trying not to laugh. "I'll be happy to call you Randy from now on. But not on camera."

He stopped pacing and peered at me for a long moment. "Wow, you really got nailed."

"Thanks a lot," I said, touching my chin. It was still sore.

"I mean, you're beautiful and all, but, well." He didn't seem to know what to say, so he began to pace some more. His handsome face was marred by those severe worry lines across his forehead.

I was getting a little dizzy watching him. "Why don't you sit down and tell me about your stalker?"

He stopped in his tracks, stared at me for several seconds, then picked up the pace again. His hands were clutched behind his back and he was gazing at the carpeting as he walked. He looked nervous or guilt ridden—I couldn't tell which. Finally, he stopped moving. "I'm worried my stalker might be the man who attacked you."

Now I understood why he was so upset. "I don't think you have to worry about that. Stalkers tend to be more nuanced. They don't show their faces. They move in the shadows and strike when you least expect it. This guy out in the parking lot was a big, mean creep, over six feet tall and heavyset. He was sweaty and in-your-face, you know? I'm pretty sure he doesn't have a nuanced bone in his body."

I just hoped Randy wouldn't ask how I knew so much about stalkers.

"Oh." He nodded. "Okay, good point." He sat down in the orange chair and crossed his leg so his ankle rested on his opposite knee. "Nuanced. I like that. You're probably right. Whoever's after me has been working in the shadows. I've never seen him, but I know he's there."

"I'm not sure what's worse," I said, as I adjusted the slowly melting ice pack. "The devil you know or the one you never see. I just wish they'd all go to hell."

"I'll second that. So besides being big, what did your guy look like?"

"I'd rather not think of him as *my* guy," I said, glowering.

"But like I said, he was about six-foot-four, two hundred fifty pounds, sweaty red face, dirty white T-shirt. Crappy dresser."

"Don't think I could miss someone matching that description around here."

"No, he stands out in a crowd." I tried to scowl but it hurt too much so I winced instead. "And his eyes give his real nature away. Mean. Soulless. He's a psychopath. I would hate to meet him in a dark alley."

"Or in a parking lot in broad daylight, either."

"No." With a sigh, I rested my head against the back of the sofa and closed my eyes.

"You poor dear," Randy murmured. "I should leave you alone."

"No, don't go. I really do want to hear about your stalker."

He sighed and scrubbed one hand across the back of his neck. "Sure, why not? Everyone can use a little schadenfreude once in a while to perk themselves up."

I heard his contemptuous tone and my eyes flashed open. *Schadenfreude* was a popular German buzzword that had to do with finding enjoyment from another's troubles. A lot of reality shows seemed to be based on the concept.

"You don't know me," I said slowly, "but the last thing I want is for you to get hurt. I know the producers have brushed off your concerns, but you shouldn't. Have you considered hiring a private security person?"

"You mean, like a bodyguard?"

"Yes."

"No, but I like the idea. I just don't think Tom and Walter will spring for the expense."

"Then you should cover the cost yourself."

"I'll think about it."

"I can recommend someone very good and very discreet."

"Okay, I'll get back to you on that."

"It's not just you, Randy. If there's someone skulking around the studio trying to hurt you, all of us could be in danger."

"I never even thought of that." His shoulders drooped a little. "I guess I've been selfish."

"You've been under some stress."

"Maybe." He studied me for a long moment. "I don't know anyone else who would've thought about the fact that everyone else would be in danger. You're sort of a big-picture gal, aren't you?"

"I've had a few run-ins with some bad people, so I like to know ahead of time what I might be up against in any situation. It helps to be prepared." I spoke lightly, but I was afraid I'd already freaked him out.

He grunted. "Now you sound like a Girl Scout."

"That's me," I said with a smile. "It's not a bad thing to be."

"I guess not."

"So, tell me about this person who's stalking you."

Randy sat forward and rested his elbows on his knees. The man never sat still. "He's subtle, like you said."

"How subtle is he? What makes you think you're being stalked?"

He chuckled but there was no humor to it. "You mean, what makes me think I'm important enough to be stalked? Is that what you were going to ask? Am I just a diva?"

"I didn't say that. If you think you're being stalked, I believe you."

He looked confused. "You do?"

"Of course."

"Well, that's a first." He'd been fidgeting with the paper rim of his empty coffee cup and now there were shredded bits everywhere.

He didn't seem to know where to begin, so I started the conversation rolling. "What has he done to you? Is it something specific? Have you been physically attacked? Has something important been damaged or destroyed? Or do you just feel like you're being watched?"

Randolph sucked in a big breath and let it go slowly. "Wow, you really do believe me."

I lifted my shoulders philosophically. "Like I said before, I've met some bizarre people in my life so I know they're out there."

"I hate to admit I'm relieved by that comment, but I am."

"Good. So, tell me what this guy has done."

He thought for a moment, seemed to measure his words, then said, "About six months ago, dead animals started showing up on my porch at home."

I tried not to react, but that was horrible. "Were they your pets?"

"No, I don't have any animals of my own because I travel too much. But every time I'd come home from being on the road, I'd find something. First there was a dead squirrel and a month later, a snake. Right there on my doormat. Then a rat. But I figured one of the cats could've killed them. We've got feral cats all over the place. But recently I found a dead cat, too."

I shuddered at the thought of discovering a dead creature on my front porch. Anyone who did that to an animal in order to scare another person? It went beyond evil.

Randy was still talking. "At first I didn't think much about it, because I live in a wooded area and there are plenty of wild creatures running around. But after I found the dead cat, I started to wonder."

"Yeah, I would, too."

"And while traveling with the show, I've noticed other things happening. The wrong breakfast order shows up at my hotel room. Sometimes I'll hear knocking at my door in the middle of the night and when I go to check, nobody's there." He tore another piece off the coffee cup and let it fall to the floor. "Once, I came back to my room and it had been ransacked."

"Was anything taken?"

"No." He grimaced. "It was almost more chilling to realize that nothing was missing."

"I know what you mean." I watched Randy as he talked and recognized that he was a man on the edge. And who could blame him? If someone had been harassing me for six months, I would have been a complete mess by now. "Has anything happened here in San Francisco?"

"Yeah." He blew out a breath and needlessly smoothed his perfect hair. "Yesterday morning, a bouquet of dead flowers was delivered to my dressing room."

I shivered. Dead flowers were damned creepy. "Wait. Was that the delivery you received just before we taped our short teaser segment?"

"Yeah."

"The production assistant came out onstage to tell you about it."

"Right. You're awfully observant."

I shrugged. "I notice things." I made a mental note to talk to the assistant. I felt like a cop. A good cop, of course. "Was that the first time an incident ever happened at the studio?"

"No. Scripts have disappeared, and once in a while a weird page has been slipped into my script book. I made the mistake of memorizing one of them and recited it on camera. We had to stop taping. Everyone must've thought I was nuts. Anyway, things don't happen every day, so Tom and Walter always chalk it up to human error—mine, of course—or plain old happenstance." He scowled slightly. It had to sting, knowing that none of his coworkers believed him.

"The script mishaps have happened three times. Once in Raleigh last month, and twice in Chicago the month before that. And then there's all the dead-animal stuff that happens at home."

"Where's home?"

"Minneapolis. I've got a place outside of town."

"So, he's been moving along with the show," I surmised. Then I added, "And I'm only saying *he* because it's easier to pick out a gender and stick with it."

"I get it." He stood and began to pace again, clearly out of nervous habit. "And, yeah, he's showing up wherever we tape the show." He stopped walking and blinked a few times. "Holy hell, he's probably someone I know."

He sat down, looking like the wind had been knocked out of him. Apparently, that thought hadn't occurred to him until this moment.

"Is there any chance it could be a woman?" I asked, since I'd brought up the subject of gender. "There are plenty of twisted female stalkers out there."

He made a face. "It's possible. But these don't feel like the sorts of things a woman would do. That's probably sexist."

"No, your instincts could be right," I said, although inside I wasn't so sure. He was a good-looking guy and could have easily attracted the wrong sort of female attention. I glanced at my phone and realized Derek might arrive at any moment. "Why haven't Tom and Walter called the police?"

"I don't know," Randy said, exasperated. "They think I'm either hallucinating or I've turned into some kind of a diva. Or *divo*, I guess. I haven't been with the show for very long so maybe they think I'm trying to stir up excitement with the media or something."

"Have they said that to you?"

"Not in so many words. But lately if I complain about something, even if it has nothing to do with the stalker, they ridicule me." He frowned more deeply and shook his head. "I happened to mention that I thought I was coming down with a cold a few weeks ago. Walter said that maybe my stalker had put sneezing powder in my talcum. Tom thought that was hysterically funny."

That seemed kind of cruel. And shortsighted, too. They were demeaning the star of the show, which couldn't be helpful to the morale of the staff and the reputation of the program.

"Think about it," I said. "Do you have any idea who could be doing this to you?"

"I have my suspicions, but I'd rather not say because it doesn't make sense."

"Would you like me to talk to my friend who owns the security company I told you about? He could make some inquiries and see if your suspicions make sense."

Randy chewed on his lip. "Oh, hell. I don't know what to do. If I have the guy investigated, won't it just make him angrier and more destructive?"

Before I could answer, there was a knock on the door. I called out, "Come in."

Derek opened the door and walked in. He took one look at my bruised jaw and swore ripely. "I'm not leaving you alone in this place for one more minute."

"I'm not quitting," I said, instantly defensive.

"Of course you're not." He sat on the edge of the couch and scowled as he studied the bruise on my jaw. "But as long as you're working here, I'll be accompanying you every day."

I beamed at Derek, then looked at Randy. "This is Derek Stone, the security expert I told you about. Looks like he just made your decision a lot easier."

Chapter Five

After formally introducing the two men to each other, I announced that I had work to do on the next book. Mostly I wanted to talk to Derek alone and was hoping Randy would take the hint and leave. But he looked perfectly happy to hang around until Derek mentioned that he was about to sign on to a conference call. Randy got up to leave then, right after securing Derek's promise to meet him later to discuss the stalker situation.

Once Randy was gone, Derek explained that he didn't have a conference call. He simply wanted to see me alone. He took a good, long look at my injuries, not happy at all about the bruising. And I wasn't happy that he could see it through my makeup, since it meant I would need another visit with Chuck before I went on-stage again.

I had discovered bruises on my upper arm, as well, where my attacker had gripped me and squeezed, but my long sleeves covered those.

"I know you're in a time crunch," Derek said with reluctance, "so go ahead and get to work. But this conversation isn't over."

"I know."

"I'll want to hear every detail of the assault."

"I know."

"You're sure you don't know where this animal lives?"

"I have no idea. But Vera can tell us."

"Good. I want that information."

I didn't like the tone of his voice. Derek was the most civilized and sophisticated of men—unless his loved ones were threatened. Then he turned into one of those guys who thought he had a license to kill. In Derek's case, he actually *did* have a license—for a gun. And while I appreciated his need to protect the people he loved, the fact that he often carried a weapon and knew how to use it didn't exactly fill me with serenity.

Derek made himself comfortable on the turquoise couch, pulled some papers from his briefcase, and began to skim through them.

No way did I trust his calm facade, but I didn't have time to dwell on it, since I had to finish my own work. Sitting down at the dressing table, I picked up the next book the producers had chosen for me. It was a first edition of Truman Capote's *Breakfast at Tiffany's*. Within minutes I was in my own world.

I went online to check some of my favorite antiquarian-bookstore sites. I wanted to determine the going rate for a first edition of this quality. I found copies worth anywhere from two thousand to ten thousand dollars. The most highly prized versions still had the dust jacket intact and were in excellent condition, which meant that the colors were still vibrant, and there were no torn edges and barely any fading.

Now that I had some parameters, I examined the book that was in my hand. The text paper had been gathered and sewn together in groups of eight, so the book was officially referred to as an octavo.

The binding was tight; the boards were straight and showed very little wear and tear. The pages were bright white and free of any writing, marks, or bookplates.

The big difference between the book in my hand and the ones online was that instead of the usual pink cloth cover, my book had been bound in pink morocco leather by a specialty bindery in England.

In the center of the pink front cover was a slinky black leather silhouette of Holly Golightly holding her trademark cigarette holder. She wore a diamond necklace and tiara. Tiny gems embedded in the black leather sparkled like diamonds. The cutout silhouette was elegant and fun, and I was looking forward to discussing the book on camera.

I had always loved the movie version of *Breakfast at Tiffany's*. George Peppard and Audrey Hepburn were magical together. I could still picture that last scene in the rain, looking for the cat. That damned wonderful cat.

After falling in love with the movie, I had read my mother's copy of the book. The ending was nothing like the movie's and it was my first realization that books and movies were completely different species.

The fact that I preferred the happy-sappy ending of the movie to the more starkly ambivalent ending in the book should've given me some insight into my own happy-sappy psyche.

My mind wandered for a moment as I considered the name Holly Golightly for my kitten. Would Derek approve? I glanced over at him and almost sighed. Without even trying, the man looked ruggedly handsome and masculine sitting there on that shabby turquoise sofa.

At that moment, he looked up at me and smiled.

I wanted to melt. Instead I said, "Tiffany?"

He paused for only a second, then scowled as comprehension struck. "Absolutely not."

"Audrey?"

"No."

I shrugged and returned to my work. I was jotting down the

last of my appraisal notes when Angie, our intrepid stage manager, knocked on my dressing room door to walk me out to the stage. Derek followed close behind us.

It was so much fun to see the book owner tear up at my announcement that his beloved *Breakfast at Tiffany's* was worth eight thousand dollars. The book had belonged to his recently deceased father, who had purchased the specially bound version in England. He assured me that he wouldn't dream of selling it for any amount of money because of all the sentimental value the book held for his family.

It was nice to know that not everyone wanted to run out and resell their treasures, like Vera planned to do. Not that I was judging her—much. Vera needed the money more than the book, and that was fine. But I had to admit, I really loved it when people appreciated the book itself.

I stood and said good-bye to the guest, then glanced around the studio, looking for Derek. I'd seen him standing off to the side earlier, watching my segment, but now he had disappeared. Maybe he was back in the dressing room. He'd left his office earlier than originally planned so he probably had some work to finish.

On the way back to my room, I passed Randy at the catering table and stopped to grab a cup of coffee.

"You do a good job with those books," he said.

"Thank you," I said, surprised and pleased with the compliment. "You obviously see a lot of different appraisers in this job."

"I do, so I know what I'm talking about. All the experts know their subject well enough, but a lot of them are as dry as dirt. You make the books come alive."

"Wow, I love hearing that. I guess I'm pretty crazy about books."

He grinned. "Lucky for you it comes across as enthusiasm, not insanity."

"Good to know," I said with a laugh.

Randy picked out a creamy buttermilk doughnut. "That last guy looked pretty happy about your appraisal." He bit into the doughnut and closed his eyes to savor it.

Why were there always doughnuts? I stared at a row of chocolate-dipped crullers and almost moaned. If Randy was still talking, I couldn't hear him over the hubbub those doughnuts were making. They whispered my name, murmured endearments, did all they could to get my attention. Doughnuts loved me in the worst way.

Randy was still talking. "It's great to see them go away happy."

I tried to pick up the conversation. "It is, isn't it? I was so pleased with his reaction. He said he plans to give the book to his son as a wedding gift someday."

"That's great," Randy said, but I could tell he was already distracted. Changing the subject, he said, "I've got another half hour before I'm due on the set. Do you think your friend Derek would mind talking to me for a few minutes?"

"Let's go find out."

I turned to cross the stage, but Randy grabbed my arm. "Wait. I know a shortcut to the dressing rooms."

I followed willingly, since Randy was more familiar with the studio than I was. He ducked through a break in the curtains and we walked along the narrow space behind the cyclorama, the secured backdrop that marked the outer perimeter of the staging area. It was fun to be backstage, where you could hear what was happening on the other side of the curtain, but nobody knew you were back here—except for the occasional stagehand or prop guy who passed by.

The lighting was dim where old props and faded stage flats were stored along the walls.

"Watch your step through this area," Randy warned as he approached a door and led me into the studio adjoining ours. It was a massive space with a ceiling that had to be at least three stories high. It was cavernous, dark, and empty, except for all the props and staging equipment stored against the walls.

This route didn't seem shorter to me and I had no intention of going this way again. Still, I was fascinated by the dozens of rolls of carpet leaning against one wall.

"Carpets?" I asked.

"No, those are painted canvas backdrops. They roll them up to store them more easily."

Next to the rolls were a few hundred wooden stage flats painted with various backgrounds. One had a living room scene painted on it. Others showed a kitchen wall, a tropical forest, and a circus tent. Shoved against the far wall were hundreds of fake trees and large plastic shrubbery, all planted in big barrels and crates.

We passed piles of square black metal boxes and I stopped to check them out. "What are these things?"

"They're light boxes." Randy picked one up to explain. "You've seen them hanging on the lighting grid above the stage, right? You put a bulb inside here, and these flaps can be opened wide or closed slightly in order to light up some specific spot on the stage."

I took the light box from him and moved the flaps back and forth. "I get it."

"Those movable flaps are called barn doors."

"Interesting."

"Yeah, it's a wonderland," he said dryly, and waited until I'd set the light box down before he continued our trek.

We tiptoed around more piles of coiled cables and past rows and rows of thick ropes that were hanging down from the rafters three stories above us.

I stared at the ropes. "What are all these for?"

"They pull the various curtains up and down, or raise and lower different backdrops, depending on which show is being taped in the studio." He pointed up at the ceiling. "Can you see the pipes up there?"

There was a bit of ambient light coming in from outside, so I could just make out the rows of pipes and beams that ran across the ceiling. There weren't any curtains hanging because the studio wasn't being used, but I could imagine it.

"How do they get the backdrops onto those pipes?" I wondered aloud.

"The canvas drops have grommets or cloth ties sewn into the edges."

"Oh. Kind of like a shower curtain."

"Kind of," he said, amused.

"Do you have a theatrical background?"

"Yale School of Drama and seven years on Broadway."

"Wow," I said.

He chuckled ruefully. "I was going to be the next Richard Burton. Instead, I wound up as the pretty face on *This Old Attic*."

"This seems like an awfully good job," I said. "The show's so popular."

"It's fine for now."

"Well, look on the bright side. It could be worse, right?"

He smirked. "Yeah, I could be the *ugly* face on *This Old Attic*."

"Oh, come on. You like working here, don't you?"

"It has its moments," he allowed, "but my ambitions are a little bigger than this." He kept walking through the deserted studio, which was dark except for the small wall sconces that beamed weak patches of light every fifteen feet or so. The light was too dim to do much except toss odd shadows onto the walls.

My stomach growled and I realized I was getting hungry. I wished I'd brought some of my doughnut friends along with me on this journey.

"The doorway to the dressing rooms is coming up on the right."

"Okay. This is some shortcut."

He shrugged. "I guess it's more of a scenic route than an actual shortcut."

"It's interesting, anyway. Thanks."

"I like to change things up. And sometimes I just don't want to run into anyone. Everyone wants to talk."

I chuckled, but didn't comment. We passed a dozen more stage flats leaning against the wall and I stopped to look at them. "Boy, they store stuff everywhere, don't they?"

The flats were made of thick wood planks wrapped in painters' canvas. These were bigger than the ones I'd seen a few minutes ago, at least ten feet high and several yards wide.

Despite the dimness of the space, I could see that the two in front had been freshly painted. One showed a lush garden scene and the other a sandy shore leading into a sparkling blue lake.

I squinted at the verdant garden scene and tried to imagine how it would appear on camera. "This looks so real."

"The guys do a great job, don't they? These were painted just yesterday and they'll be used for some of the segments in the main staging area. Just to give a different look." Randy leaned in to more closely examine the stage flat, then straightened. "Anyway, the dressing rooms are right over here. Let's go find Derek and . . ."

But I'd stopped listening as one of the green leafy plants in the garden scene moved closer to me.

"Whoa." My stomach did a little dip. Was I hallucinating? The painting was moving. Then I heard a creaking sound and realized it wasn't my imagination. The flats were moving forward. Falling.

"Oh no," I muttered, then yelled, "Help!" The entire stack of heavy panels was about to fall on top of me.

"What the hell?" Randy spun around and grabbed the edges of the wood, but the angle of his approach was all wrong and the flats kept coming at me. He shifted position and tried to get a better hold.

"Help!" I screamed again, loud enough for the entire studio to hear.

Everything happened in slow motion. The wood slipped out of Randy's grip. My leg muscles began to quiver and I fell to my knees while still keeping my arms outstretched, trying to keep the heavy boards up.

"Hold them!" I cried.

"I'm trying!" he yelled.

The planks were too heavy and I couldn't stop them from pressing down on me. My arm muscles gave out and the wood hit the top of my head and pushed me down.

"Get help!" I yelled, but my voice didn't carry far.

"Hold on there! I've gotcha." A wiry old man ran over, slipped under the flats next to me, and used one shoulder to keep the wood from falling farther. I could see his spindly back muscles starting to shake.

"Whoa, boy," he said. "That's heavier than it looks."

"Be careful," I shouted, pushing out with my arms again to try to keep the wood from trapping him, too. "Don't hurt yourself!"

"I think I'm . . . oh, boy." All that weight was too much for his skinny body to hold and he tottered dangerously.

My arms were shaking as badly as the old man's. I shifted again to use my back to hold the flats at bay, but now I could feel my neck muscles screaming.

The old man curled himself into a ball next to me.

I wasn't ready to watch his life being squeezed out of him, so I pushed his shoulder. "Crawl out the other side!" I shouted. "Move."

"I can't," he muttered, sounding feeble and defeated.

"Hang on! Help!" I yelled it louder, over and over again.

"Try to hold them back while I get more help," Randy shouted, and ran to the door leading to the dressing rooms. He hollered for help. For heaven's sake, where was everyone?

I was certain I could survive the weight of the flats for a short time, but I wasn't so sure about the old guy. And he'd been trying to save me! The guilt—or something—gave me a shot of adrenaline and I was able to push back on the crush of wood for a few more seconds.

"Nobody's coming," I shouted. "You need to get help."

"I'm not leaving you," Randy said, running back to me and sounding insulted that I'd suggested it. He reached under and tried to lift the flats, but they didn't budge. "How about if I hold them while you run and get help?"

"I'm already wedged under here!"

Randy bellowed, "Help!"

Footsteps pounded in our direction.

"Brooklyn?"

"Derek!"

"Damn it," he cursed loudly, and followed it up with a string of expletives. "What happened?"

"I'm stuck," I moaned.

"Duh," Randy said.

I almost laughed, despite being a little too close to suffocating to death.

"I'll get you out of there," Derek said.

"Thank God." My voice sounded desperate. I could only see Derek's shoes, but then he got down on his knees, bent over, and shifted the planks onto his shoulders. I wasn't sure how he summoned the strength to do it, but he managed to stand up slowly, steadily, with the full weight on his shoulders and back. After a moment, I could feel the load being lifted off me.

"You have room to crawl out now, Brooklyn." He said it gently, as if I were an injured animal.

"Thank you," I whispered, and reached out for the old man. "Come on, let's get out from under here."

The old guy didn't respond and I wondered if he had passed out from sheer fright. That had been a lot of weight pressing down on us. Up on my hands and knees with inches to maneuver now, I shuffled out backward, dragging the man with me to safety. It was slow going, but we made it. Thank Buddha, because my arm muscles were beginning to cramp.

Once we were both out from under the wood, I collapsed on the linoleum floor.

Now that the danger was past, Derek and Randolph were able to let go of the flats. The heavy wood crashed to the concrete floor with a loud reverberation. Dust clouded up. Randy bent over and rested his elbows on his knees, gulping in air.

Derek was breathing almost normally after his amazing rescue mission. He knelt down and rubbed my back. "Are you all right?"

"I'll get there. Is that old man okay?"

"He's winded but he'll be fine," Derek said. Then he lowered his voice and asked, "How did they fall?"

I twisted to look up at him. "I have no idea. I must've nudged them, but I didn't think I was that close."

He helped me stand up, then pulled me into his arms and held on tightly. "Damn it," he muttered. "I want to know how that happened."

"I do, too," I said. One minute the heavy flats had been secure against the wall, and in the next heartbeat, they were toppling over. It took too much energy to relive the nightmare, so I squeezed my eyes shut and clung to Derek for another minute.

"I wasn't sure where you went," I said.

"I was answering a phone call in the dressing room," he explained, stroking my back. "I'm sorry. I never should've left you alone."

"It's okay," I whispered, but I knew I wouldn't have come so close to being crushed to death if Derek had been with me.

From over Derek's shoulder, I watched my would-be rescuer stir, then wheeze as he crawled a few feet over to the wall.

"Let me help you," Randy said, and lifted the old man by the arms until he could sit up and lean against the wall.

The old guy was still trying to catch his breath. His hair was pure gray and matched his thick, gray eyebrows and bushy mustache. He was gaunt and his cheeks were hollowed with age. He was probably in his seventies and wore thin, round eyeglasses and a dark green janitor's uniform with an old-fashioned name tag sewn onto the front pocket. It read GARTH.

He was still wheezing. I couldn't believe he'd been so brave.

"You must be Garth," I said, pointing to his name tag.

"Sure am," he said, and gave me a shaky grin.

"You were really brave to help me," I said. "I'm Brooklyn, by the way."

He waved off the introduction. "I know who you are, missy. I've seen you doing those book segments. You're a smart one."

"Thank you, Garth. Thank you so much for trying to save me. You could've been killed."

"Ah, that was nothing," he said, embarrassed by my gratitude.

"Do you work here?"

"I've been a janitor here for a while now." He had to stop talking to suck in more air. He was completely worn out. "Good thing these young fellas came along when they did or we woulda been squashed like two bugs."

"Yes, good thing," I murmured, still trying to figure out how I'd caused the flats to fall. Maybe we'd had a small earthquake. I hadn't felt one, but it wasn't outside the realm of possibility that the earth had trembled enough to jar the planks away from the wall.

Randy helped Garth to his feet. I suggested that we call an ambulance to have him checked out at the hospital, but he refused to let me fuss over him.

We watched him walk unsteadily toward the door leading to the dressing room hallway and disappear.

"I hope he's okay," I said.

"I wouldn't worry about Garth," Randy said. "He's pretty spry for an old guy."

The three of us walked back to my dressing room and closed the door. Derek insisted that I lie down on the sofa and rest for a few minutes.

Randy sat in the orange chair and Derek took the swivel chair.

"That was weird," Randy said, raking his hands through his perfect hair, clearly shaken by the episode.

I nodded. "I was thinking there must have been an earthquake. Did you feel anything?"

"No," Randy said. "But something must've caused those flats to fall."

"Yes, something," Derek murmured, staring hard at him. "Or some*one*. Could it have been caused by your stalker?"

Chapter Six

"Stalker?" Randy said, taken aback by Derek's suggestion. "But it was an accident."

It was useless trying to relax now that Derek had brought up the subject, so I sat up and joined the conversation. "I was thinking it could've been the guy who attacked me earlier today."

Derek considered that possibility. "You described him as a rather large man. Did you see anyone like that in the vicinity?"

"No," I grumbled. "It was too dark to see anyone, but I can't imagine a guy that big sneaking up on us. He's not exactly stealthy."

But there might have been someone else. I thought back to that moment in the hallway and tried to be realistic. All those flats leaning together were at least two feet thick, possibly thicker. The hall was dimly lit at that end. Randy and I had been staring at the painted flat farthest from the doorway leading into the hall. All of those factors made me realize that someone might have been able to sneak up quietly if they'd stayed close to the wall.

But it couldn't have been the scary, oafish loudmouth who attacked me earlier. As Derek had said, the man was large. I couldn't imagine him sneaking up on anybody.

"It wasn't the guy who grabbed me in the parking lot," I concluded. "He was too big and cloddish to get away with it."

"Which means it's the stalker," Randy said, sounding miserable.

"Tell me why you think someone is stalking you," Derek said.

Randy went through the whole litany of incidents he'd recited to me earlier.

When he was finished, Derek nodded slowly and was silent for a long moment. I could tell he was thinking carefully because he had a habit of twisting his lips as he pondered possibilities. Finally, he said, "For the sake of argument, let's assume that your stalker caused the mishap with the falling stage flats."

Randy gritted his teeth. "Okay. So now what?"

"So up until today," Derek said, "this person has only been trying to scare you or embarrass you."

I felt my eyes widen. "But today he tried to hurt you. Well, and me." *Especially me.*

"Exactly," Derek said.

"So, what the hell does that mean?" Randy asked.

Derek's gaze was on Randy. "It means he might be growing more desperate."

Randy's eyes narrowed. "Are you saying he's escalating? Isn't that what they call it on TV?"

Derek nodded. "Yes."

"But Derek," I said, "causing the stage flats to fall on top of us had to have been a spontaneous act. He couldn't have planned it. How did he know we were going to take that route through the other studio?"

"True," he said. "The opportunity presented itself and he took action."

"But the dead animals and even the script pages," I continued. "Those had to be planned out to some extent."

Derek smiled and nodded. "Absolutely right. Those would take careful timing. Premeditation."

"Oh, hell." I turned and stared at Randy. "He could've been following us the whole time, just waiting for his chance to do something vicious."

"Do you often take the long way around to the dressing rooms?" Derek asked Randy.

He shrugged. "I'm always wandering around the place. I never know where I'll end up. People have gotten used to me telling stories of some prop or backdrop I discovered in some far corner. I just found this back entrance to the dressing rooms yesterday, so I don't see how someone could've known I'd come this way."

"Did you mention the new route to anyone?"

His shoulders slumped. "Yeah. I was telling a couple of the prop guys that I'd been looking over those planter boxes in the studio next door. They mentioned that they were going to be using them for a new show they're taping next weekend."

I shivered at the thought that someone might have been following us along the dark halls and through the empty studio. Given the way my life had been going lately, I had trained myself to be more aware of my surroundings. So much for awareness. And especially after the assault I'd suffered earlier, it was disturbing to realize how easily distracted I'd been by all the fascinating nooks and crannies and oddities of the studio.

Derek observed me for a long moment and I knew he was trying to read my mind. I'd bet it wasn't too hard to figure out what I was thinking. His mouth twitched in a slight smile and then he glanced back at Randy. "Since it sounds like he—or she—has been following you around the country, is it safe to assume that this person has some connection to the show?"

Randy's lips twisted in frustration. "Yes, but I hate the idea. I get along with everyone. Who in the world did I piss off so badly that now he wants to try to kill me?"

And me, I thought, but didn't say it aloud. Instead I tried to help him focus on the people who worked with him. "Think about it," I said. "Is there a stagehand or a camera operator you somehow insulted or irritated? Maybe someone on the production staff? Do you recall anyone acting weird around you?"

Derek chimed in. "You mentioned that these things started occurring six months ago. Is there a woman you rejected or broke up with six to eight months ago?"

"Oh, there are legions." But Randy quickly shook his head. "No, absolutely not. I flirt a lot, but everyone around here knows I'm not serious."

"Some women are a little more desperate than others," I said, having known a few of them. "And some can be downright delusional when it comes to men. One of them might've gotten the wrong idea from your casual flirting."

"That's disturbing," he muttered.

"What about Angie?" I said, regretting that I had to bring up her name. I'd grown to like the feisty stage manager.

"Angie?" Randy was taken aback at first, but then started to laugh. "No way. Absolutely not. We pretend to have a contentious relationship, but it's all in fun. She's actually my . . . she's a very good friend."

I hoped he was right. Even though he'd insisted earlier that his stalker wasn't a woman, he could be mistaken. So many stalkers I'd read about in the news were of the opposite sex.

"Wait a minute. Maybe Garth can help us," I said brightly. "He came running through the studio, so he might've noticed someone sneaking away."

"Good thought, darling," Derek said. "I'll talk to him."

I had a feeling that over the next few days, Derek would be talking to every last person who worked at the studio. He wouldn't take it lightly that I had been attacked twice in one day. I couldn't help but love that about him.

. . .

"**B**rooklyn?"

I turned and saw Frannie, the production assistant, standing a few feet away. "Hi, what's up?"

"There are some people asking for you in the guests' hall."

Who knew I was here? I was tempted to hide. Yesterday I had been accosted in the parking lot, had been nearly squashed to death by stage flats, and had discovered that a stalker might be running loose in the studio. What new and exciting horrors would this day bring? "Do you know who they are?"

"No. Should I tell them you're not available?"

"No, I'll go see what they want."

I followed her outside and across the parking lot to another studio on the lot that was being used as a holding area for all of the guests who came every day with their antiques in tow.

I walked inside and glanced around at the crowd.

"There she is! Yoo-hoo, sweetie!"

"Mom?" I laughed and rushed over to the slim blond woman in the rainbow skirt and crocheted vest and grabbed her in a hug. Then I noticed who was standing next to her.

"Robin? I can't believe it." I hugged my oldest and best friend tightly. "I haven't seen you in forever."

"It's only been a month or so," she said, laughing, "but I've missed you, too."

I pulled them over to a group of empty chairs and we sat in a circle. "What are you doing here?"

"We were all so excited to see you on the news the other night," Mom said. "And when I ran into Robin the next day, we talked about coming to visit you."

Robin jumped in. "I had to drive into the city to take care of some business today, so we decided this would be the perfect opportunity to surprise you."

"I'm so glad you did." Could they hear the sheer relief in my voice? I was so surprised and happy to see them, I'd forgotten to mask my ragged emotions. "Can you stay for a while? Please?" I glanced at the heavy shopping bag Mom was carrying. "What's this?"

Mom leaned forward and said in hushed tones, "We figured we'd better bring something old so they'd let us in. So before we left Dharma, I ran over to Abraham's workshop and grabbed a few old books."

I looked inside the bag and felt my stomach drop. "Mom, that Hemingway is worth at least ten thousand dollars."

She smiled brightly at Robin. "I guess that's why they were so eager to let us stay."

Robin and I exchanged amused looks. I had known her since we were both eight years old and loved her more than my own sisters. We'd met in Dharma when my parents moved there to be with their guru, Robson Benedict. Or Guru Bob, as we kids called him.

Robin and Mom could only stay for a half hour or so, but we still managed to catch up on all the latest news. Robin and my brother Austin were making noises about a possible wedding, but hadn't set a date, much to my mother's distress. My sister Savannah was starting to teach classes in vegetarian cooking at her popular Dharma restaurant and there was already a long waiting list to get in. My mysterious friend Gabriel was away from Dharma at the moment and the rumor mill had him on some clandestine operation in Southeast Asia. And, in more upbeat news, according to my father, the grape harvest would begin within a few weeks.

I told them about our new kitten and about our new neighbor, Alex, and I shared a funny story about one of Derek's recent adventures. I mentioned a few of the fabulous books I'd appraised on the show, but I didn't say a word about the attacks on me. It didn't matter, though, because as they stood up to leave, my mother took my chin in her hand and gazed into my eyes. With a sigh, she closed her eyes and began to mutter,

"Goddess, lend your help again,
Protect our girl from evil's sin,
Give her strength to walk through fire,
Help her forge through muck and mire.
Many thanks and blessed be,
As I speak, so mote it be."

She repeated the chant three times. Then she touched the middle of my forehead. "Om shanti, shanti, shanti."

Peace, I thought. I could use some. And, seriously, no one but my mother would break into a sacred protection spell in the middle of a crowd of two hundred people.

Her eyes opened and she gazed darkly into mine. "Did you think I wouldn't be able to tell that something was troubling you?"

"No," I admitted, smiling ruefully.

She glanced at Robin, who nodded once. I had a feeling the two of them had been talking about me. Great. Was this the reason they had shown up today? Was my mom now able to read my thoughts from two counties away?

But when Mom looked back at me, her eyes were clear and she was smiling. "You'll visit us soon."

Once I arrived home, I jogged across the hall to Alex's and begged for yet another rain check. I hadn't been able to make it last night because of my swollen jaw and the trauma of the falling stage flats. Tonight, I was simply too tired from my long day at the studio to enjoy an evening of wine and cupcakes with my new neighbor. And that was just sad. Derek was shocked, too, and probably a little disappointed that I wouldn't be bringing a cupcake home for him.

Alex was gracious and willing to postpone our get-together to the following night. I ran back to my place and fell into bed.

The next morning, after a quick phone call to my parents to invite ourselves up to Sonoma in two weeks for the annual grape harvest, Derek went off to work. As he left the apartment, he assured me that he'd meet me at the studio around noon.

I spent the next hour cleaning and organizing my workshop. I would start working on *The Secret Garden* once I had Vera's payment, so for now I wrapped the book securely in a white cloth and placed it in my built-in safe in the hallway closet.

The small closet was steel lined so the contents were safe from the elements, and the locking mechanism was the strongest one on the market.

Long before my building was converted to loft apartments, it had been a corset factory in the early 1920s. Back then, this closet had operated like a dumbwaiter. It held movable metal shelves that ran on ropes and pulleys, transporting supplies up and down between the floors. The airtight space underneath the metal floor panel was large enough to hold my important papers and emergency cash. It was also where I hid the most precious and expensive books I was working on.

An hour later, I drove out of the parking garage underneath my building and headed for the Richmond District and Vera's shop. I was excited about picking up her check and getting started on the book.

I was also anxious to commiserate with her about the horrible man who had attacked me and threatened her. Maybe the police had picked up the guy and he was already in jail. I hoped so.

I zigzagged over to Van Ness and took the busy thoroughfare up to Turk Street. As I drove west, I made a mental list of the people I would suggest Vera call to obtain bids for the book. Ian McCullough was number one on the list, of course, and I thought *The Secret Garden* would be an ideal addition to the new Children's

Book Museum. I owed Ian the courtesy of first refusal because he had been responsible for getting me the appraiser job on *This Old Attic*.

As I turned left onto Turk Street, I thought of another possible buyer. Joseph Taylor's son, Hunter, had taken over his father's bookshop after Joe's untimely death a few months ago. The charming old shop on Clement Street catered to a number of wealthy book lovers, so Hunter might have a client who would be interested in *The Secret Garden*.

A mile later, I crossed Arguello Boulevard where Turk became Balboa Street. This marked the beginning of the part of town known as the Avenues, so named because starting near the east end of Golden Gate Park, the streets running north and south were named numerically. Strangely enough, they began with Second Avenue. The avenues went all the way west to Forty-eighth Avenue, a block from the ocean.

When I got to Nineteenth Avenue, I started looking for a parking place and found one a full block away on the opposite side of the street.

I waited for traffic to clear before jumping out of my car and locking it. I crossed at the crosswalk and headed to Vera's shop, wishing I had an excuse to buy flowers. It would be a waste, though, because I would be going to the studio after I met Vera and chances were good that the flowers would be wilted before I got home.

In front of Vera's shop, a narrow patch of sidewalk was lined with planters filled with blooming flowers in every color of the rainbow. Two small café tables with wrought-iron chairs had been placed in the center of the space for customers to sit and enjoy a momentary pause in their shopping day. The setup was charming.

A tinkling bell above the door announced that I had entered the small, colorful shop.

"Vera, it's Brooklyn," I called as I stepped inside. I glanced around at all the intriguing floral arrangements and goodies and added, "What a pretty shop."

I didn't see Vera at the front counter, where the cash register was located. Behind the counter on the left side of the room was a tall, drafting-style table set up for cutting and wrapping bouquets of flowers. Rows of different-colored ribbons were lined up on dowels for easy access, and a large box of cellophane wrap was placed opposite the ribbons. Two pairs of scissors lay on the table, both tied with thick string and secured to the table through an eye hook screwed into the corner.

On the shelf below was a bright green canvas carrying case used to store gardening tools. It was spread open for easy access and eight pockets held different types of shears, a trowel, a small shovel, and other tools Vera probably used for potting plants and cutting thick stems.

One of the pockets was empty. I took that as a sign that Vera was off working on something.

On the right wall an industrial shelving unit contained rows of pots and vases in all colors and styles. The two bottom shelves held dozens of flower-themed knickknacks, garden gnomes, and clay animals.

A family of six green pottery turtles caught my eye. They descended in size from the papa turtle down to the baby, and I knew I had to buy them for my mother. She would love them for her vegetable garden.

The back wall held more shelves on either side of the doorway that was halfway open and led into some sort of storage room. The light was on and I could see rows of plastic buckets containing long-stemmed flowers waiting for the florist to bundle them together in colorful bouquets. There were sunflowers, delphiniums, cheerful gerbera daisies, deep red roses, white roses, and blue irises, along with several buckets filled with various types of greenery.

It occurred to me that running a flower shop, surrounded by beautiful plants and flowers every day, had to be a cheerful occupation.

"Vera?" I said loudly. "Are you back there? I've brought your invoice."

There was no answer and I was starting to wonder if I'd miscalculated the time. I didn't think so. I'd probably arrived just as Vera had dashed off to use the bathroom. Was there one in the back of her shop, or had she been forced to run over to another store?

I had a few minutes to spare, so I took the time to admire the flowers. There was a glass-covered, walk-in refrigerator case against the wall nearest the front door and I stared at the already-made bouquets that were waiting to be bought or delivered.

I was impressed with Vera's flair for flower arranging. Some of the bouquets were Zen-like in their minimalism. One had a single bird of paradise emerging from a dish of smooth pebbles. Another massive display looked as if it might be a wedding arrangement: every flower was white or off-white, and the combination of pale shades was dazzling in its simplicity. I could identify many of the blooms because my mother, who had always had a garden, had drummed the names of the flowers into our brains. At least a dozen white roses mingled with pale baby's breath, lilies, sweet peas, narcissus, anemones, and plump white peonies. White ribbon tied in a soft bow around the large, femininely curved vase completed the bouquet.

I glanced around to see if Vera had returned, and checked my watch. I was starting to get anxious.

"Vera?" I called again. "Are you back there? I have your invoice and I'd also like to buy these turtles here."

There was no response. I stepped outside and looked both ways down the sidewalk, thinking she might have stopped to talk to another shop owner. I didn't see anyone so I went back into her store to check that back room. If she wasn't there, I would leave a note to let her know I would try again tomorrow.

I stepped around the front counter and almost tripped over a pair of fake leopard-skin stiletto heels with bright red soles.

I recognized those flashy shoes. They belonged to Vera. And she was still wearing them.

I shuddered in horror and disbelief.

Vera lay curled on the cold cement floor, her back pressed up against the counter. Her glamorous black bouffant hairdo was indeed a wig and it had been yanked halfway off her head, revealing thin, stringy gray hair scraped away from her forehead and pulled into a messy ponytail.

Vera would have hated to be found like this. I had to physically stop myself from adjusting the wig to fit her properly.

Her left arm extended awkwardly across the floor and her elbow was smeared with the blood that had pooled beneath her. Dark red blood stained her white blouse, too, where a pair of English cutting shears protruded from her stomach.

Vera was dead.

Chapter Seven

I had found another body.

I let that thought go, temporarily ignoring the ugly reality and its emotional effect on my psyche. Instead, all business, I briskly called the police to report the murder. Then I telephoned Derek.

"Vera?" he said. "The woman from the television show?"

"Yes. I came by her shop to pick up a check and found her on the floor." I sounded calm, even to myself. Was I actually getting *accustomed* to finding dead bodies? "She's been stabbed."

I refused to think of all the blood she'd lost because I didn't want to faint and end up on the floor beside her. Murder was one thing, but blood was something else entirely, and I doubted I'd ever get used to it.

"Where is her shop?" he wanted to know.

"Derek, you don't have to—"

"Give me the address."

So I did.

"I'm finishing something up here," he said, "so it'll take me at least a half hour, perhaps longer. But I'll be there."

I knew he wouldn't take no for an answer, no matter how

much I protested. Of course, I didn't protest much at all since things were always a little better when Derek was around.

It wasn't as if I needed him here to take care of me. I didn't. Really. But he and I were partners. We worked well together, especially when it came to deciphering the puzzle, fleshing out the motives, and getting to the truth of why someone had been killed. It wasn't like we were trying to play detectives, but it was a horrible thing to have one's life touched by violent crime and even worse to be considered a suspect by the police.

Unfortunately, I knew the feeling. I'd been a murder suspect more than once and so had several people I loved. It was always a devastating and confusing and frightening time. So it was especially nice to have Derek around to help figure out what had happened and where to go from there. It also helped that he had an extensive background in law enforcement and security.

And I wasn't ashamed to admit that I just wanted my boyfriend there with me.

After giving him the address, I hung up and called the studio to tell them what had happened. Tom came on the line and assured me they would adjust the schedule so I could tape my segments later that afternoon.

Two police officers arrived within minutes. After questioning me briefly, they ordered me to wait outside on the sidewalk until the homicide detectives arrived to interrogate me further. I knew the drill, so before leaving the shop, I took off my shoes and handed them to one of the officers. "You'll want to check these for evidence since I almost stumbled over her. But I'd like them back as soon as possible, please."

He blinked a few times.

"The detectives always want to take my shoes," I explained.

His eyebrow rose in suspicion. "Always?"

"I've been present at a few crime scenes," I said, trying for nonchalance. From the way he goggled at me, I was guessing I didn't pull it off. "Anyway, this time I came pretty close to tripping over the victim, so your investigators might find some blood or other evidence on my shoes. And they'll also need to use them to eliminate my footprints from the others on your list of suspects."

He took my shoes from me, holding both of them tentatively with his thumb and finger. Saying nothing, he jutted his chin in the direction of the front door. I got the message and left the shop.

In my thin socks, I walked gingerly over to the sweet little wrought-iron table and chairs and sat down. I tried to appreciate that I was surrounded by beautiful plants, but my thoughts mainly centered on how long I would be stuck here. I hated to feel callous. I was truly sorry Vera was dead. She had been sweet and funny, maybe a little bit of a dingbat, but determined to get what she wanted. I had liked her, but I hadn't known her well and there didn't seem to be much point to my hanging around.

On the other hand, I was intimately familiar with the horrible man who had threatened to kill her. So I pulled a book from my bag and tried to read while I waited. It was useless. My mind was filled with images and thoughts of death and pain. And shoes.

Before I left the crime scene, I needed to remind the detectives to return my shoes. I'd bought them specifically for my television appearances so I was hoping they wouldn't keep them too long. Not that the camera had ever panned all the way down to my feet, but it could happen, right? The home audience might be dying to admire my girlish size-eight Ferragamo flats. It wasn't beyond the realm of possibility.

I felt more and more conspicuous as passersby stared at me. I didn't make eye contact, but it was clear that some of them were dying to find out what had happened. The two police officers had split up to carry out the procedures that went along with the discovery of a dead body. One was wrapping crime-scene tape across the front of the shop. The other cop walked down the street and stopped at each store to question the owners, in the hope that they had witnessed something crucial.

I turned away from the scene and absently studied the aged brick front of Vera's store. Hearty ivy vines grew from planters at the base and clung to the wall, making the storefront look like a charming country garden wall. It reminded me of the front cover of *The Secret Garden* and made me wonder how much of a coincidence it had been that Vera had been drawn to buy the book.

A crowd had begun to gather a few yards away. The cop with the roll of yellow crime-scene tape turned and studied the group but didn't approach them.

After a few more minutes, I glanced down the street and saw Homicide Detective Inspector Janice Lee heading my way. As usual, she was dressed more stylishly than your average San Francisco homicide cop and her gorgeous, straight dark hair was wrapped up in some kind of French twist. She wore the trim, black Burberry trench coat I'd coveted for months. She was Asian American, a year or two older than me, tall, thin, and pretty, an ex-smoker with a husky voice and a snarky attitude.

When she got close enough to realize it was me sitting there, she stopped and shook her head in resignation. "Doesn't it just figure?"

"It does," I said lightly, "seeing as how I asked the dispatcher to call you directly."

"I'm touched."

"It wouldn't be the same without you."

Her lips twisted and I could tell she was holding back a chuckle as she fumbled in her pocket for her notepad and pen. "Seriously, Wainwright, we've got to stop meeting like this."

"I'm pretty sure you've used that line a time or two before."

"Probably so, since I always seem to run into you at crime scenes." Her tone was laced with suspicion. "Funny how often that happens."

"You should be used to it by now," I grumbled. She was taking a jab at my disturbing tendency to stumble across dead bodies on a regular basis. Didn't she realize it bothered me, too? I had been involved in so many murders, I probably could have been forgiven for losing track of the exact number. But I hadn't lost track.

How could I? You didn't forget the blood, the cruelty, the faces of the people whose lives had been snuffed out so viciously and irrevocably. And you never forgot the tear-stained faces of their loved ones, who would grieve and suffer for the rest of their lives.

"Are you working alone?" I asked, wondering where her partner was. Inspector Nathan Jaglom had a much sunnier disposition than his partner, along with a laid-back style that camouflaged his whip-smart instincts. With his frizzy gray hair and kind smile, he usually played the good cop to Lee's bad—or, at least, snarky—cop.

The two of them had worked together on almost all of the murder cases in which I'd been involved.

"Yeah," she said. "Nate got tapped to cover the mayor's detail for a few weeks."

"I heard there were some threats on his life." I frowned. "I hope the inspector will be safe."

"Me, too," she said, then flashed a quick grin. "If he gets killed, his wife and I'll both kill him." She jerked her head toward the door to Vera's shop. "You might as well come in with me."

I jumped up and followed her. It was a lot better than sitting outside alone, being stared at by the looky-loos who had gathered to find out what all the hubbub was about.

It was silent as Inspector Lee took a slow turn around the shop. She jotted down notes of everything she saw, but stopped writing when she reached Vera's body. She set the pen and notepad on the counter and stared at Vera for at least two minutes.

Watching her, I got a little emotional. I appreciated her taking the time to simply absorb that image of the poor woman.

Finally, she grabbed her pen and pad and began writing notes again.

Glancing out the window, I saw the two police officers approach the people in the crowd, probably trying to find anyone who might have seen something relevant to the murder.

When I turned back to Inspector Lee, she was gazing steadily at me. "What time did you get here and find the body?"

"I walked in around ten thirty," I said. "I waited for Vera to show up, but she never did. After a while, I decided to check the back room and that's when I saw the body."

"After a while?" she repeated. "How long a while?"

I knew exactly how long because I'd checked my watch repeatedly. "It was eight minutes before I stepped around the counter and found her."

She stared at me as if I were a space alien. "You're telling me you stood in this shop for almost ten flipping minutes before you ever saw the body?"

"Eight minutes, not ten," I said, wrapping my arms tightly around my stomach. "And even though it sounds strange to you, I didn't see the body at first."

"Why the hell not?"

"Because," I said, my voice rising, "I'm a courteous customer, that's why." Not that I was a customer of Vera's, exactly, although I had been planning to buy those turtles.

Lee stood at the end of the counter closest to Vera's head, careful to avoid stepping anywhere near the body and thus destroying possible evidence. She was scribbling rapidly in her notebook, probably noting what a dolt I was. I didn't care. Well, I did, but I would get over it.

I liked Detective Inspector Janice Lee. Sometimes I wished we could be friends and I'd even invited her over to my house for a glass of wine a few times, but true friendship would probably never happen between us. Not when I was always the one finding a dead body and she was always the one showing up, taking one look at me, and wondering what the hell kind of murder magnet she was dealing with. It wasn't a great basis for a long-lasting friendship.

"I don't generally trespass beyond the front counter when I'm in a store," I explained more calmly. "But after waiting a few minutes, I saw those turtles and wanted to take a closer look."

Inspector Lee glanced down at the bottom shelf to see what I was pointing at. "Hey, those are fun."

"I thought so," I muttered. "I was thinking my mom might like them."

A thought flashed through my mind: *Why in the world were we talking about the turtles?* But it wasn't that odd, really. In the midst of a tragedy, we humans were inclined to cling to the most simple and mundane aspects of life.

"Sorry to disappoint you and your mom," Lee said, "but those turtles are officially a part of my crime scene now."

"Yeah, that's what I figured."

Lee moved over and stood next to me at the counter, where Vera's customers would normally stand. She set her pad and pen down on the counter and stared straight ahead for a long, nerve-racking moment. She glanced to her left and took in the wrapping table, then turned right to gaze at the shelves of pots and knick-knacks. Finally, she nodded. "Yeah, I guess it's possible. I can't see her from here, either."

I tried not to let on how important it was that she had just validated my own actions.

But she wasn't quite ready to let up on me. "So, what were you doing here for eight minutes while you waited for her to show up?"

"I was looking at stuff," I explained. "The turtles. The pots. The gnomes. Did you see all those arrangements in the refrigerator case? They're beautiful. It's a nice shop, don't you think? Everything is so cheerful and pretty."

"Except for that pesky corpse, right?"

I sighed. "Right."

Once again she grabbed her notepad and pen and started in with more questions. "So, what were you doing here in the first place, Wainwright?"

I gave her a brief rundown of my new job on *This Old Attic* and how I'd appraised Vera's book and how she wanted me to restore it so she could make more money selling it.

"So, you're like a celebrity now," she kidded. "If I watch the show tonight, will I see you on there?"

"These San Francisco shows haven't started airing yet. But they did feature a portion of my segment with Vera on the news the other night. You should watch it."

"Yeah, I'll get right on that." She kept writing.

"No, you should watch it right away." I knew she was only half listening to what I was saying, so I repeated myself. "I'm not kidding. You need to get a copy of that segment and watch it as soon as possible."

She glanced up at me and sighed. "And why is that?"

"Because that little bit they showed on the news is what motivated Vera's killer to come after her."

She pursed her lips sardonically. "Now, why am I not surprised that you've already got a theory worked out?"

I had known what her reaction would be, but I bristled, anyway. "It's not a theory, Inspector," I said flatly. "Vera's killer attacked me in the studio parking lot two days ago. He specifically mentioned that he'd seen that news segment the night before and that's why he was threatening to kill me."

She stopped writing midsentence. "Wait. Somebody attacked you? Threatened to kill you? Were you hurt? Why am I just hearing about this?"

I held on to my dignity, but I was ridiculously pleased to hear real worry in her voice. It meant a lot.

It was odd and a little upsetting that with each crime scene, Inspector Lee and I would start out almost as adversaries. Then slowly, throughout the process of solving the crime, we would rebuild the trust we'd had before and she would see me more as a cohort than a suspect. And then the mystery was resolved, the guilty party was carted off to jail, and Lee and I would go our separate ways. I just wished that the next time we saw each other at a crime scene, she would remember that we weren't enemies.

I quickly knocked on wood that there *wouldn't* be a next time.

"I was attacked in the parking lot of Peapod Studios, where we tape *This Old Attic*," I explained. "The security guard was knocked to the ground. He was hurt worse than I was, but I came away with bruises on my chin and my arms."

"Criminy, Brooklyn," Inspector Lee said, her concern growing. "Who was this guy?"

"He's a horrible man," I said, scowling at the memory. "A big, ugly brute who threatened to kill me and Vera." I waved my hand in the direction of Vera's body lying on the floor. "Clearly, he acted on his threat."

"But who is he?" she asked again.

I let out an exasperated sigh. "I don't know his name. Vera knew, or at least she knew his address."

"How did she know him?"

"She told me she bought the book at his garage sale."

Inspector Lee nodded slowly as she wrote down that detail.

I continued. "After the attack, the police came to the studio. I told them to talk to Vera and get the guy's name and address. They assured me they were going to talk to her that afternoon or the next day. That all happened two days ago."

"Do you remember the names of the cops you talked to?"

"Yes. Stern and Wilkins. The studio is at the base of Potrero Hill, so I guess they work out of whatever police station is closest."

"Good." She wrote down the names, then looked up at me. "Now tell me why this guy was threatening Vera."

"She found the book at his garage sale for three dollars," I explained again. "I appraised it on the show for twenty to twenty-five thousand dollars."

"What the hell? What's with these damn books?"

"They're art," I said. "They're rare. Collectors are willing to pay a lot of money to own them."

"Yeah, yeah." She brushed back her hair with one hand and exhaled in exasperation. "It's always got to be about a book with you."

"Books are my job!" I cried in frustration. "I work with books every day."

She grinned suddenly and I could tell that her happiness stemmed from being able to get a rise out of me. In some circles, that would brand her a sociopath, but I let it go. I liked her. We usually got along just fine, despite the barbs. She simply enjoyed giving me grief, as my brothers did. If we were in second grade, she would probably chase me around the playground, throwing rocks at me. And in second-grade parlance, that meant she liked me.

"The point is," I began patiently, "the guy who attacked me admitted right out loud that he'd seen that news segment Monday night. He threatened to kill me and Vera if we didn't give him the book. And now Vera is dead."

"Right. I'm pretty clear on everything now." She glanced around the shop again. "Do you think he found the book?"

"I know for certain that he didn't because the book is at home in my safe."

That stopped her. "You have the missing book."

"It's never been missing."

"Wainwright, you never cease to amaze me." She shook her

head as she flipped to a new page in her notepad. "How about if you start at the beginning again?"

*T*en minutes later, I was finished going over my story for the third time.

She folded her arms across her chest. "But the news didn't announce how much you appraised the book for."

"Right. The producers wouldn't allow them to tell the actual price I'd given. But the anchorman made a smart-ass reference to a family of four being able to live for two years on the money the book was worth."

"Oh, great." She stopped writing. "So basically he spelled it out for everyone."

"Yeah. The creep who attacked me admitted that he 'used the Google' to figure out that whole amount."

"The Google, huh?" She gave me a half smile.

"Yeah." I could see that she got the joke.

After taking a deep breath, she let it out slowly. "Sounds like we've got a motive for murder."

I smiled grimly. "That's what I'm saying."

"So, tell me more about the book itself," she said.

"It's a really rare, limited edition of *The Secret Garden*."

Her eyes widened. "*The Secret Garden* is a kids' book. This guy was supposedly willing to kill for a kids' book?"

"Yes." I braced myself, afraid I was about to get more book grief.

Instead, she smiled as her gaze drifted. "I loved that book when I was a kid. Must've read it a hundred times."

"Me, too," I said, pleasantly surprised that we had something else in common.

She waved over one of the uniformed officers who had just entered the shop. After writing something down, she tore the page out of her notepad and handed it to him. "Do me a favor, will you?

Track these two uniforms down and find out when's the soonest I can talk to them. They probably work out of Bayview, but if not, try Mission or Ingleside. They interviewed Ms. Wainwright Tuesday at Peapod Studios near Potrero Hill, and I want to know if they made it over here to interview our victim."

He stared at the page, then said, "You got it, ma'am."

"Thanks, Trent."

The cop jogged out to the patrol car to make the call.

Inspector Lee turned back to me. "That's some good work, Wainwright." She smirked. "We might get you that junior-deputy badge one of these days after all."

I patted my heart. "A girl can dream."

Chapter Eight

After the medical examiner and his assistant arrived at the shop with their gurney and bags of equipment, it was too crowded to remain inside. And even if it wasn't, I had no interest in watching them perform their gruesome tasks, so I stepped outside for some fresh air. Inspector Lee had told me to hang around for a while. I wasn't sure why that was necessary, but I wasn't about to disobey a direct order. I reminded her that I would need my shoes back as soon as possible and she saluted smartly.

Outside, the cold, rough surface of the sidewalk was another reminder that I had only my stocking-thin socks for protection. I walked cautiously back to my car, where I kept a pair of sneakers in the trunk for emergencies. Sitting in the front seat, I slipped on my shoes. The simple action brought a graphic image to my mind of Vera's feet in her flashy knockoff Louboutins.

"They were the first thing I bought myself after I left my no-good boyfriend."

I could still hear Vera's voice in my head. She had told me and Angie about her shoes that first night at the television studio. She had been so excited about the book appraisal, so ready to sell the book, make some money, and turn the page on her old life.

Poor Vera. I squeezed my eyes closed, but I couldn't erase the image of her lying on the chilly cement floor of her shop, after bleeding to death.

So much blood.

I rubbed my arms where goose bumps had taken up permanent residency. From experience, I knew the images of Vera's blood-soaked blouse, her sightless eyes, and her brand-new fake Louboutins would stay with me for weeks.

Locking my car, I headed back to the shop to see what else Inspector Lee needed from me. I was still a little shell-shocked, still couldn't believe I had found another murder victim. It had become a habit with me, but I would never be able to accept it as normal. How could anyone get used to finding dead bodies? And not just dead, but violently killed. Murdered. No, unless you were an undertaker or a homicide cop, it wasn't something you ever wanted to get used to.

"Brooklyn."

I stopped at the sound of that deep voice. Turning, I saw Derek walking purposefully toward me and noticed his black Bentley was parked a few spaces down the street.

"Derek." I met him halfway.

"Come here, love," he said, and hugged me close. Rubbing my back, he whispered, "Are you all right?"

I shook my head, upset about Vera, but so grateful that he had insisted on joining me. "Can you believe it?"

"Frankly, no," he muttered.

"I can't, either."

"Are you okay?"

"I'm fine," I said. "I didn't know her very well, but I liked her."

"I'm sorry, love."

I lifted my head from his shoulder and we walked to the flower shop. "The one good thing is that I know who did it. It's that hulking creep who attacked me at the studio. He warned me that he would come after us both."

Derek said nothing at first but kept his arm around my shoulders as we walked.

"How can you be sure?" he asked quietly after we'd gone half a block. "Couldn't it have been a simple robbery gone bad?"

I thought about it for a moment. "I suppose it could have been. But don't you think it's a remarkable coincidence that one day after a madman threatens to kill both of us, Vera is found murdered?"

"You know how I feel about coincidences."

I glanced up at him. "There's no such thing."

"Exactly," he murmured.

I scowled. "In this case, I agree."

We walked the rest of the way in silence.

*L*ater that afternoon I was back at work in the television studio, taping another segment for *This Old Attic*. It was strange to sit in the same place where I'd first met Vera, talking about books as though nothing odd or awful had happened that day. But I had a job to do. A job I loved. So I mentally set aside Vera's murder to concentrate on the book in front of me.

In this case, it wasn't just one book, but a set of them by Michael Connelly, the mystery author. I was appraising the first ten books in his Harry Bosch mystery series for the owner, Mr. Stanley Frisch, a self-described rabid mystery fan and Connelly devotee. Stanley was short and thin, with eerily pale skin, scruffy gray hair, and a sparse white mustache. He wore small, round steel-framed glasses that I feared might've been the exact same style worn by Michael Connelly.

The books he'd brought were all first editions and they had all been signed by the author. The first book, *The Black Echo*, included a rare five-dollar rebate deal marked on a blue band on the book cover. For serious book collectors, that little blue band was golden.

In addition, each of the dust jackets was in almost pristine condition, thanks to the owner having kept them wrapped in archival plastic covers from the first day he bought them. Frankly, the books appeared to be unread.

"This is an exceptional set," I said. "I commend you for keeping them all in such wonderful condition."

"Thank you," he said crisply. "Michael's my favorite author so I didn't want them to get ruined."

"Do you know the author personally?"

"Oh, no, but I've met him whenever he's come through on tours." He smiled bashfully. "I'd like to think he remembers me."

I nodded politely. "I noticed that he signed all the books with his name only. Did you ever ask him to sign any of them to you personally?"

"Absolutely not," he said. "I don't want my name on the books. I just want *his* name."

I glanced at the camera. "That's actually a good thing, because the market value of the book can be diminished if it's been personalized."

"I didn't know that," he whispered.

I picked up the first book in the series and held it out for the camera to get a better shot. "Do you know much about books, Stanley?"

"No. I just love them a lot."

"That's so nice to hear. But I ask because some collectors enjoy finding little quirks such as this blue rebate band on this copy of *The Black Echo.*"

He frowned. "Does that make a difference?"

"Yes, it does," I said, smiling as I angled the book so the camera could see the spine. "I also noticed that the bindings of all the books are unusually tight and straight. Have you actually read any of these?"

"Oh, gosh, yes. I've read them all several times. I'm a huge fan. I'm just extremely careful."

"I can see that you are." I paused for a dramatic moment before making my big pronouncement. "And because of all the care you've shown these books, along with the fact that this first book is extremely rare and in such fine condition, I've appraised the entire ten-book set at . . . fifteen thousand dollars."

"Oh." He sucked in some air. "Oh, my." His breathing grew shallow and his pale face quickly lost any color it had ever had.

"Are you all right?" I asked. But he wasn't; I was pretty sure he was going to pass out. His head wobbled. I reached across the table and grabbed his arm to keep him from sliding out of his chair.

I shot Angie an anxious look. "Is there a doctor nearby?"

She shook her head frantically.

"Stanley!" I finally shouted.

Stanley jolted. "What? Oh." Drawing in another big breath, he blinked and stared up at me. "What? No, I'm fine. It's just . . . oh, my . . . it's too much."

"It's exciting, isn't it? But—"

"No, I mean the amount of money. It's too much."

"It really isn't. That's the price you could probably get if you sold the books to a reputable book dealer or auction house."

"But I would never do that."

"You don't have to, Stanley." I let out a breath and tried to compose myself for the camera. "You can simply enjoy them for the rest of your life and never sell them. But isn't it nice to know that your efforts to keep them in fine condition have paid off?"

"But how can I enjoy them?" he wailed. "They're worth too much money. What if somebody steals them? Oh, God. What am I going to do?"

Randy was standing behind the cameraman and I caught his eye. He grinned, pointed to his ear, and made a circular motion with his finger, the universal sign indicating I was dealing with a crazy person.

Angie moved into my line of sight and gestured that I should wrap up the segment.

I reached over and patted Stanley's hand. "I'm sure the books will be perfectly safe with you as their owner. Thank you so much for sharing them with me and our audience today."

There was a long beat and then Angie yelled, "We're clear!" In a more sedate tone, she added, "Good job, Brooklyn."

"Thanks, Angie," I said, but I was still worried about Stanley. He hadn't moved from his chair, just sat there holding his head in his hands.

"Stanley?"

"What am I going to do?" he moaned.

"Please don't be upset," I said more gently. "The books are worth that much because of all the wonderful care you've given them."

"Yes." He scowled darkly. "And it was a big mistake. From now on, I'm going to mess them up just like every other slob does. What's the use of having nice things when you have to worry about them all the time? So forget it. I'll bend the corners to save my place, lick the pages when I turn them, write notes in the margins, you name it."

I cringed. "Don't do that."

He stared bleakly at me. "I can't live with the burden of having something so valuable in my home."

He stood and piled his books onto the little carrying cart he'd brought with him. Then he trudged off the stage, accompanied by Kristi, one of the production assistants, and disappeared behind the scrim.

Angie frowned after him. "Maybe you should offer to buy those books from him."

"He won't sell them," I lamented. "He's too big a fan. But now he won't maintain their condition anymore and that annoys the heck out of me."

"He's a wackadoodle," Angie muttered.

I scowled. "So why did he come on the show in the first place?"

"Can't say for sure," she said, and shrugged. "I've seen others like him. They want to be praised and recognized for being a good little boy and keeping their things in nice condition. They're fine until they hear about the money. Then they go a little crazy."

"So you think he just needed a motherly pat on the head?"

"Yeah, maybe."

"He would've been happier if I'd appraised the set for a few hundred dollars."

"Probably. Like I said, a wackadoodle."

We commiserated for another minute and then I left the stage for my dressing room. I was relieved that the segment was over, because I'd been distracted by thoughts of Vera the whole time— until the very end, of course, when Stanley went nuts on me. Now I just prayed that he wouldn't go home and do something stupid or dangerous, because my reputation would start to shred if word got out that my appraisals had led to two deaths.

"Oh, great," I muttered, cringing as I realized what a terribly self-serving thought that was. Vera was dead; Stanley was traumatized. But, hey, it was all about me and my reputation!

I stared at myself in the dressing room mirror and realized I was exhausted. I slumped down onto the turquoise couch and put my feet up on the rickety coffee table. I needed time to think. I'd already given up on Stanley's problems and was back to dwelling on Vera. Derek's words circled around in my head and I wondered if maybe he was right, that Vera's death might have been the result of a simple robbery gone bad. Maybe it hadn't had anything to do with *The Secret Garden*.

I had naturally assumed that her killer was the garage-sale guy who had threatened us both only a day before. The book was the best motive I could come up with for murder. Or, more precisely, the book's *monetary value* was the best motive. People had killed for a lot less.

On the other hand, Vera could have been killed during a simple robbery. I supposed I could survey other shop owners around there to see if robbery was a common occurrence. Not that it was my job, but once in a while I got a little curious and anxious to find out the real story.

Even if robbery was a problem in that area, why would a robber show up at midmorning to rob a store in such a busy, clean, well-traveled neighborhood? It didn't seem very smart. How much money could he expect to get from her cash register?

And why would he kill her? Okay, he might have gotten pissed off because there wasn't enough money, but wouldn't he just grab whatever there was and get the hell out of there? Would he really freak out so much that he ended up killing her? And even if the answer was yes, wouldn't he be carrying a gun or at least a knife? Why reach for her prissy English garden shears?

And wouldn't there have been a struggle? Vera's shop had been in shipshape condition when I walked inside. Nothing seemed to be out of place. But if a robber had been struggling to get money from Vera, wouldn't some items have been knocked off the shelves?

A robber would want to get in and get out quickly. If Vera had balked or if she hadn't given him enough money, he would have shot her and taken off. He wouldn't have looked around for the perfect pair of garden shears with which to stab her.

Damn, I should've asked Inspector Lee how much money was in the cash register. If it was empty, it might give more credence to Derek's simple robbery-gone-bad hypothesis.

But even if it was empty, that didn't necessarily mean it was robbery. The burly garage-sale guy could've stolen the money to make it look like a robbery.

I kept trying to picture that big oaf in Vera's store. How could he have walked through her small, tidy shop without disrupting everything? He was so loud and boorish, he would have made a mess just crossing the threshold. And he seemed like the kind of rotten jerk who wouldn't give a hoot if he left everything in disarray.

But nothing had been out of place in Vera's shop. I couldn't see him killing her and then taking the time to tidy things up before he left.

"Yeah, that's ridiculous," I said aloud.

So if it wasn't the garage-sale guy and it wasn't a robber, then who had killed Vera?

I was arguing with myself for argument's sake, but I still believed in my gut that Vera's killer was the garage-sale guy.

At this point, I hated calling him the garage-sale guy. *He really needs a name,* I thought, and wondered why I hadn't asked him his name while he was attacking me. Because, you know, that would've been the polite thing to do.

Idiot.

I shook those thoughts away, and after another moment of contemplation the name Horatio popped into my head. I didn't know why, but it worked. From now until we found out his real name, I would refer to garage-sale guy as *Horatio.* The name was close enough to *horrible* to work for me.

Horrible Horatio might be Vera's killer, but I still couldn't figure out why he'd grabbed those garden shears instead of just strangling her. He definitely seemed like the type to prefer physical brutality, the type who would enjoy using his hands to hurt someone. But Vera hadn't been strangled and I hadn't noticed any bruises on her. None that I could see, anyway.

A third possibility occurred to me. The killer could have been someone Vera knew. She'd mentioned an ex-boyfriend. Maybe the two of them had had a terrible argument and in a fit of passion the boyfriend grabbed the conveniently located garden shears and shoved them into Vera's stomach.

I grimaced at the thought and rubbed my own stomach in sympathy.

It made sense that her death might have been personal and had had nothing to do with *The Secret Garden*. But I still believed that Vera was dead because of the book.

I was so tired that my head was beginning to spin, so I stretched out on the couch. With my eyes closed, I was physically ready and willing to zone out into sleep, but my mind wouldn't stop circling around Vera.

I was so sure the book was the killer's motivation. At the same time, I had to ask myself: *Was that really enough to kill for? Do people really kill for a book?*

I jerked my head up off the couch. "Are you crazy?" I asked out loud. Of course someone would kill for a book!

If I wasn't so exhausted, I never would've had that ridiculous thought. I stood up and stretched my arms and shoulders for a minute. Maybe it would help me think things through more carefully.

What was it about this book *in particular* that would cause someone to kill another human being? Was it all about the money? Did Horatio just want the cash? Had he killed Vera when she refused to give it to him?

Or was there something else about the book that made Horatio determined to get it back? Had somebody else offered him more money for it? Had it belonged to someone else and that person had threatened to harm him if they didn't return it? Maybe his mother owned the beloved book and threatened to starve him out if he didn't give it back immediately.

My mind was coming up with reason after reason for why Horatio wanted the book back. It would probably be a good idea to write them all down, so I zipped open my computer bag and fumbled for a notebook. And a pen. Where were all my pens?

"Ah." I found one at the very bottom of the case, naturally. I was just starting to write out a list when my cell phone rang, causing me to jump. I yanked it from my jacket pocket, surprised to see Inspector Lee's name flashing on the small screen. "Inspector."

"I've got good news and bad news."

I slid down onto the swivel chair. "That's never a good thing."

"In this case, you're right."

"What happened?"

She took a deep breath. "Stern and Wilkins never got around to interviewing Vera. They caught a gang shooting in Ingleside Tuesday afternoon and didn't make it over to the flower shop."

"Damn it."

"My thoughts exactly," she said, then added, "I'm sorry."

"Yeah. Me, too." Annoyed, upset, and antsy now, I stood and began to pace the small room while we talked.

So we still didn't know who the garage-sale guy really was. Horatio would remain Horatio until further notice. I wallowed in that bad news for a moment, then remembered there was more. "What's the good news?"

"It's not exactly *good*, but it's a move in the right direction. We want you to come in and meet with our sketch artist. Do you think you can give us an accurate description of the guy who attacked you?"

My spirits lifted slightly. "Absolutely."

"Okay, good."

We set up a time the following morning for me to meet the sketch artist at the Hall of Justice on Bryant Street, just a few blocks away from my place on Brannan. We ended the call shortly after that.

I sat down on the couch, excited at the prospect of contributing any information that might lead to the arrest of Vera's killer. I just wished with all my heart that those two police officers had reached her in time yesterday. If they'd been able to talk to her, she would have given them all the information they would need to arrest Horatio. And she would still be alive today.

My shoulders slumped a little as that sad realization smacked me upside the head. It was true that I had barely known Vera, but I hated that she was dead simply because of bad luck and timing on the part of Officers Stern and Wilkins. The injustice was maddening.

Aiding the police sketch artist to create a picture of Horatio was important, but there had to be something else I could do to help.

A kernel of an idea sprouted in my brain. I jumped up from the couch and stalked around the room, the better to let the idea unfurl and grow. I've always thought better when I was moving.

The fact was, Horatio still didn't have the book. And if he was desperate enough to kill Vera to try to get it, then he would have no choice but to come after me again.

I could be the bait to draw him into the open.

"Oh, sweet Mary." I stopped midstep, picturing the smoke coming out of Derek's ears if he ever found out what I was thinking of doing.

But this could work.

My hours at the television studio usually began around noon, so I had some time to kill every morning. Why not spend them trying to lure Horatio out of hiding?

What was wrong with taking the time to stroll around the studio parking lot in the morning? I could always use the exercise.

It might be a long shot to think that anyone would be dumb enough to skulk by the studio, looking for a chance to attack me again. But we were talking about Horatio, after all.

If he'd been desperate enough to kill once, wouldn't he be

willing to approach me again? Even if he knew that I could identify him as the man who had threatened Vera?

My plan could work, as long as Horatio was really, really
stupid.

*T*wo hours later I had finished my last segment and was back in
my dressing room with Derek. We were packing up our computers and files for the night when my cell phone rang. I checked
the screen; Inspector Lee was calling again.

"Inspector," I said.

"I've got more news. It's a little better this time."

I sat on the swivel chair and grabbed a pen. "What's up?"

"We're not going to need you to meet with our sketch artist."

"Why not?" I dropped the pen. "I can do it." Darn it, I'd been
looking forward to describing Horatio to the police artist, just like
I'd seen people do on television.

"I know you can do it, Wainwright, but now you don't need
to. Stern and Wilkins are really pissed off about Vera. We all are.
We're pretty sure her death could've been avoided if they'd had a
chance to talk to her and get the guy's address."

"Yeah, I was thinking that, too."

"So now they're working their asses off to find the guy. They
went back to the TV studio to retrace your attacker's movements
and had a long talk with the security guard who got beat up."

"They talked to Benny?"

"Yeah, Benny. So the day of the attack, Benny was too addled
to think of it, but today he told them that there are security cameras everywhere. They're on all the studio doors and at the entry
gate."

"Holy cow. That's great."

"Yeah," Inspector Lee said. "So we got hold of the tapes and
your guy is all over it. There's video of him walking through the

gate, grabbing you, punching Benny, running out. We're putting a group of photos together and sending them out to all the news outlets. With any luck, we should have him ID'd by the weekend."

"That's wonderful," I said, letting go of the breath I'd been holding. "I'm so relieved."

"Yeah, we got a break."

I rested my elbows on the desk surface and sighed in relief. "Thank you so much for calling to let me know."

"Figured you deserved to hear the news since you have a stake in all this."

In other words, I was still in danger as long as Horatio was free to walk around the city. I rubbed my arms to ward off a sudden chill. "Do me a favor and find him fast, please."

"Your wish is my command, princess," she said with a snicker. I shook my head as I ended the call.

Chapter Nine

Derek and I arrived home at ten o'clock that night, both of us dead tired. As we stepped out of the elevator, I noticed right away that our new neighbor's door was ajar. A sharp chill shot up my spine and my mind immediately leaped to the worst-case scenario. Had Alex been burgled? Was she lying in her apartment, hurt? Dead? I was halfway down the hall and ready to shout out her name when I recalled her invitation.

"Cupcakes," I said, as relief poured through me. "How could I forget?"

"Beg your pardon, love?" Derek said as he slid the key into our lock.

"Cupcakes. Alex invited me over for cupcakes tonight. That must be why her door is open."

"Ah," he said. "Well, go and enjoy. I have a conference call with the Tokyo office in ten minutes, so perhaps you'll ask her to take pity on me and send you home with an extra treat."

"I'm sure she will." I followed him into the house and un-loaded my computer and purse inside the door. Shoving my keys in my pocket, I reached up and gave Derek a kiss. "Back soon."

I was so tired that for a moment I thought I might have to beg for another rain check, but that moment of panic on seeing her open door had given me a quick blast of energy. I was wide awake and ready for conversation and cupcakes.

I nudged her door open farther, and breathed in the sugary, delectable aroma of freshly baked yummies. Oh, mercy. It smelled like my version of heaven.

I knocked lightly on the door and called out, "Hello? Alex? Something smells wonderful."

With a happy smile, I strolled into her apartment—and skidded to a halt. Sitting alone on the elegant living room sofa was a very handsome man. He looked tall, with blond hair, blue eyes, and broad shoulders.

And he was naked. Completely and utterly naked, except for a colorful wide strip of blue painter's tape across his mouth.

And from the way he was sitting, it looked like his hands were bound behind his back.

"Are you all right?" I whispered.

He nodded.

At least he can breathe, I thought. Painter's tape, like masking tape, was paper-based and porous, unlike duct tape. I knew this because I worked with paper and tape, but how ridiculous was it to have that thought at a time like this?

My heart rate zipped up and I swallowed nervously. I took a quick glance around, but didn't see Alex. Was my new neighbor in danger? I was about to race out and call the cops when the naked man winked at me.

I didn't imagine it. The guy winked at me.

"Are you sure you're all right?" I asked again.

He wiggled his eyebrows at me and I could plainly see that his eyes were twinkling with humor. I couldn't see his mouth because of the painter's tape, but I was pretty sure he was wearing a grin. And not much else, as I already mentioned.

He seemed friendly enough, despite the bizarre situation.

"So . . . you're all right," I said lamely.

He nodded slowly, then shifted slightly so I could see that he was wearing handcuffs. He gave me a little thumbs-up sign and winked again.

"And Alex is okay?" I asked, glancing around.

This time he nodded eagerly, his head bouncing up and down with enthusiasm.

Wow. Okay. Clearly, I was interrupting something. Cupcakes were a distant memory as I raised my hand and returned a weak little wave. Then I tiptoed out the door and closed it behind me.

Thirty minutes later, there was a knock at my front door. I was almost afraid to answer it, but Derek was still on the phone with his Tokyo partners, so I soldiered up and headed down the hall, back to my workshop where our front door was located. I checked the peephole and swung the door open.

It was Alex, wearing skinny jeans, a tunic-length black sweater, and orange sneakers. She was holding a pretty, three-tiered tray filled with the most amazing-looking cupcakes I'd ever seen. The frosting was piled high and looked so fluffy and moist, it almost sparkled. She must have used a pastry bag to heap on the frosting in such dramatic swirls and curls, just like a professional baker would. I did a quick calculation. There were twelve cupcakes in three different colors: pretty pink, lemony yellow, and chocolaty chocolate.

"Brooklyn," she began. "I'm so sorry."

"Come in," I said, opening the door even wider. She was, after all, bearing gifts.

As she walked in, she apologized again. "Can you forgive me? I left the door open for you, but I was in my bedroom, changing out of my work clothes, and I didn't hear you knock. Jason told me you walked in and saw him and . . . well. This is awkward."

She was right about that. "No need to explain." Then, pointing to the tiered tray, I added, "Can I help you carry that?"

"It's just that he was supposed to arrive later, after you were gone. But since he was already there, well. I guess I should explain." She laughed nervously. "It's a little role-playing game we like to indulge in. I'm the Black Ops interrogator and he's the—"

"Stop!" I laughed. "Alex, please. You don't have to explain." *Just give me the cupcakes and all will be forgiven.* I didn't say that to her, of course, but I was thinking it. Many of the world's problems would be solved if people would just shut up and pass the cupcakes.

I saved her the trouble of having to decide what to do next and took the tray from her. "Come on in." She followed me into the kitchen, where I set down the tray and grabbed a half-filled bottle of Cabernet to show her. "It's an awfully good wine. Would you like a glass?"

"Yes, please, and you're so sweet to brush off what happened." She wrung her hands together. "But I know it must've been a shock to walk in and see . . ."

"A naked man, bound and gagged?" I said, when her voice faded. "Sitting on your couch as if he'd come to tea? Yes, I admit it was a bit of a shock. But he looked pleasant enough. I was going to call the police, but then he winked at me. That's when I decided to leave. I figured if he was winking at me, he probably wasn't in any danger. And, more important, you weren't in danger, either. Were you?"

"Absolutely not," she insisted. "If anything, Jason's the one in danger. He showed up early and will have to be punished at some point."

"Eek!" I instantly held up my hands. "Stop. Please. You really don't need to explain."

"I'm sorry!" She buried her face in her hands and I was afraid she was going to burst into tears. Instead she started to giggle. She really didn't seem like the giggling type and neither was I, most of the time. But the sound of that giggle, and the fact that her cheeks were now bright pink with embarrassment, were enough to make me smile.

After a few long seconds, I gave up pretending that the situation was normal. "Okay, it was weird."

"Of course it was," she said, and gestured toward the cupcake tray. "I'm not going to apologize again, but, luckily, I have brought a peace offering."

"Accepted."

I checked to see if Derek was still on his conference call. He signaled that he would be a while longer, so Alex and I sat down at the kitchen bar with glasses of wine and the twelve cupcakes. I chose a pink one first because they were so pretty.

I took a bite and closed my eyes. "Oh."

She frowned. "Is it okay?"

"Oh." I nodded, but couldn't seem to form words, just kept repeating, "Oh. Oh."

With a satisfied smile, she said, "They're good, aren't they?"

"Oh yeah." I took another bite. The icing was just as fluffy and moist as it looked, and it tasted even better than that. It wasn't the usual buttercream frosting I was used to. It was incredibly soft and sweet without being cloying. "Better than good."

How did she do it? Was it something you could learn or did you have to be born with that ability? I was pretty sure that baking was harder than cooking. Although I could barely cook, I was still willing to learn how to bake if there was a chance that one day I might produce something this transcendentally scrumptious.

"This cupcake actually tastes pink," I whispered. "How do you do that?"

"I've been experimenting with reducing pink lemonade down to its essence. It seems to work."

"And how do you get the frosting so fluffy?"

"I make my own simple syrup instead of using commercial corn syrup. It makes everything lighter and fluffier."

"I have no idea what you're talking about, but you are a genius."

She smiled. "Thank you."

Alex chose a lemon cupcake while I continued to savor my pink one. She asked me how the television show was going and I told her about the books I'd appraised so far. I left out the part where I'd been attacked two days in a row. Instead I chatted on about the books and she seemed interested. At least her eyes didn't glaze over, so I considered that a real win.

"I love books," she said.

"I do, too."

"I mean, I love to read. I don't know anything about bookbinding, but it sounds fascinating. You actually take books apart and put them back together in better shape than they were before?"

"That's the goal."

"It sounds like such rewarding work."

"It is," I said. "I love it."

She told me briefly about the company she ran, a successful brokerage firm in the financial district.

"It's your own company?" I asked, as I stared at the tray of cupcakes. How could I possibly eat a second one?

I could have just a bite and save the rest for later. Happy with my decision, I reached for a chocolate one.

"Yes," she said, and took a sip of wine. "I started it with a guy I used to work with at another firm. We've done pretty well for ourselves."

Her statement was modest, but I had a feeling she was underplaying it. I'd seen the way she was dressed the other night and the way she carried herself in general. Anyone could tell that Alex was a successful, high-powered businesswoman and probably worth millions. She would be the alpha dog in any relationship.

Her submissive friend Jason would probably agree.

Meanwhile, I was having a hard time concentrating on the conversation after taking a bite of the cupcake. I considered myself a chocolate aficionado, but nothing I'd ever tasted could come close to this flavor.

"I work really hard," Alex was saying, and I had to focus to hear her words above the buzzing in my ears. When was the last time chocolate had caused me to temporarily lose my hearing? I swallowed the bite and the buzzing decreased.

"I don't have a lot of friends," she said, "except my work-related associates. All they ever want to do is talk shop, so when I come home at night, I want to shut out the world and relax, bake something, or just read. I feel the same way about dating. I don't like to go out with the domineering alpha types. I much prefer men like Jason, who's sweet and submissive and—"

I raised my eyebrows and she held up both hands in retreat. "That's all I'm saying on the subject. My point is, I don't have many girlfriends."

"My friends are mostly work-related, too," I said, and tried to ignore the image of Jason in handcuffs. He had looked happy. To each his own, I supposed. Where was I? Right. Girlfriends. I took a quick sip of wine and continued. "My best friend, Robin, used to live in the city, but she moved to Dharma last year and lives with my brother Austin. And my sisters are my friends."

"That's nice," Alex said wistfully. "I don't have any sisters."

"I have three, but they all live up in the wine country."

"I could be your friend," she said, then cringed. "That sounds so pathetic. But I'd like to be friends—unless what happened earlier has completely soured you to the possibility."

Rather than dive back into that odd little quagmire, I waved it aside with a smile. "I would love to be friends."

"Good."

I couldn't imagine Derek ever having this conversation with another man. It was definitely a girl thing. But having made our decision to be friends, Alex and I were able to relax a little. After a sip of wine, I asked, "How does someone so busy have time to bake such artistic cupcakes?"

"It's just something I'm good at," she admitted. "My job is so frenetic sometimes that I enjoy coming home and baking. Especially cupcakes, because they're so small and cheerful and fun. Plus, you make a dozen at a time, so if you make a mistake frosting one, you have eleven chances to fix it."

"Good point."

"And if you're fond of frosting, like I am, you've probably already noticed that the frosting-to-cake ratio on cupcakes is truly outstanding."

"No wonder I love them so much," I said. "And I'm impressed by your use of mathematical formulas when making desserts. You really are smart."

She laughed, then asked me about my family. I told her about Dharma and my parents and my brothers and sisters.

"I don't have much family," Alex said. "Just an aunt who lives back east."

She didn't say much more about her past, just talked about the brokerage firm and some of the charity work she enjoyed.

"Shall I open another bottle of wine?" I asked.

"No, I should be going." She glanced down at the floor. "And who's this little darling?"

I followed Alex's gaze and saw my kitten tugging at her orange shoelace. "Oh, that's our newest resident. We haven't named her yet."

"She's adorable." Alex tweaked the kitty's nose, then glanced at me. "Kittens should have happy names."

"I agree." I was pretty sure Alex could carve and slice up a business opponent with almost no effort, but I had a feeling that she was also cursed with a soft marshmallow middle. I could relate, and it made me like her even more.

With my friend Robin living so far away, it would be nice to have a new friend close by. Although I couldn't help but wonder how Alex would react when my mother got ahold of her and tried to read her aura or tickle her chakras.

I reached out to pet the kitten, who batted my hand with her tiny paw. "What do you think of the name Cupcake?"

"I like it." Alex laughed.

*A*lex insisted that I keep the entire tiered tray of cupcakes for Derek and me to enjoy. That was how awesome friendships were created and nurtured.

Still, I made a weak attempt to convince her that I couldn't possibly eat all the cupcakes. She simply gazed at me in silence and eventually I just sighed. Who was I kidding? Of course I could eat them. And Derek would help.

Alex was long gone and I was getting ready for bed when Derek finally finished up his conference call.

We talked as he hung up his suit jacket and undressed. He mentioned a new client his company was working with. I told him all about Alex, her cupcakes, her job.

I held back any mention of the naked man. Instead I said, "I forgot to tell you that I invited her to the party."

"That was neighborly of you." He glanced over at me. "Alex is short for what? Alexis? Alexandra?"

"Alexandra," I said. "Alexandra Monroe."

He nodded thoughtfully. "Monroe. That name sounds familiar."

"James Monroe was one of our Founding Fathers and an American president."

"Thank you for that history lesson," he said dryly.

"Marilyn Monroe was an iconic American actress of the nineteen fifties and sixties."

He shook his head.

"Monroe. It's both a doctrine and a shock absorber. And our new neighbor."

"You're a sassy wench."

I laughed as the words rolled off his tongue. Amazing how

that British accent could make a cheeky insult sound like a heart-
felt compliment.

"We have a lot in common," I said, trying to return to the
subject of the moment.

"You and James Monroe?"

"No, you nutball," I said, still laughing. "Me and Alex. Our
neighbor. I think you'll like her. She loves books and reading and
wine and good food. Wait till you try her cupcakes."

"I plan to have one for breakfast."

"Great idea."

"I have a million great ideas. Here's another one." He climbed
into bed, turned off the light, and pulled me close. It was late and
I was sleepy and content, but something he'd said a minute ago
was gnawing at a tiny corner of my brain. Finally, it hit me.

"You're going to investigate her," I said, affronted.

"Hmm?"

"That's why you asked about her last name. You're going to vet
her, whether I agree to it or not. I think I should be insulted."

Ever since someone I liked very much and invited into my
home had turned out to be a vicious killer, Derek had been overly
cautious about the people I allowed myself to befriend. I appreciated his concern but I believed I'd become a lot more discerning
since then.

"Go to sleep, love." He wrapped his arms around me and
kissed my neck and I didn't want to think too much after that. But
I was so going to give him grief in the morning.

Chapter Ten

Over coffee, eggs, and, yes, *cupcakes* the next morning, Derek and
I discussed the last-minute plans for Saturday's party. It promised
to be a beautiful day in the Bay Area. The food order had been
placed with Piccolo, our favorite local Italian deli, and the guest
list was finalized. And speaking of guests, I broached the sore subject of him insisting on investigating Alex. "You should trust my
judgment and leave her alone. I have a good feeling about her."

But Derek wasn't about to bend to my wishes. I could tell by
the cute way he furrowed his brow. He probably considered it
more of a stern look than a cute one, but what did he know?

"I do trust your judgment, darling, but this isn't about that at
all." He reached out and caressed my cheek. "Indulge me. I'm
merely concerned about keeping both you and our home safe from
harm."

I didn't know how to counter that. Naturally, I appreciated his
concern. I had suffered too many perilous moments over the past
year, and we'd had several actual break-ins by bad people who'd
damaged my stuff and scared me to death.

And in case my short-term memory was slipping, I had been

threatened twice just in the past few days. And the other person who'd been threatened along with me was dead!

Still, I was annoyed on general principle. I liked Alex a lot and I was sort of afraid that if Derek did investigate her, he might find something to prove me wrong about her. But it looked like I was going to have to live with the annoyance.

"All right, fine. But I hope she doesn't find out about it."

"She won't find out," he assured me. "It's a normal background check, the sort that's done when someone applies for a job or rents an apartment."

"If you say so," I muttered, knowing Derek's background check was probably going to be a lot more thorough than he would admit. By tonight, thanks to his friends in high places like Interpol, MI6, the FBI, and the NSA, he would know what size shoe Alex wore, who her third-grade teacher was, and whether or not she had cheated on any spelling tests. Derek took our security very seriously. And who could blame him? Not me.

"When you meet Alex," I said staunchly, "you'll realize that all of this intrigue is unnecessary. She's a good person."

His eyes warmed. "I'm already feeling kindly toward her after tasting this cupcake."

"Aren't they amazing?"

"Yes," he said, wiping away a few cake crumbs. "Truly amazing. Do you think she'll bring more to the party?"

His voice was so tentative and hopeful that I began to laugh. "I'll ask her."

"And that's why I love you."

As I walked with him to the door a few minutes later, I remembered a subject I'd completely forgotten to bring up the night before. I didn't quite know how to broach the subject, so I decided to take the direct route. "Derek, how do you feel about handcuffs?"

"They're necessary in certain circumstances," he said absently. He stopped at my desk, set down his briefcase, and opened it to shift around some files. "They're essential when apprehending a particular type of criminal. I try to leave it to the cops, but I do have a pair of my own in case of emergency."

"You do? Right, of course you do." I chewed on my lip, trying to figure out how to rephrase the question. "But I mean, have you ever worn them yourself?"

"Have I worn handcuffs?" He looked at me as if I had grown horns. "Of course not. And I hope I never do. The thought of being arrested and incarcerated sounds like the lowest circle of hell to me."

"Boy, you're right about that." Feeling stupid now, I decided it was best to drop the subject. "Well, have a fun day at work."

He snapped his briefcase shut and gazed at me. "What's this all about, Brooklyn? Why the sudden interest in handcuffs?"

Oh, rats. He wasn't going to let it go. "All I meant was, do you like them, you know, for fun?"

"Handcuffs? For fun?" He stared at me for a long, weighty moment. Then he nodded slowly. "Ah."

"What do you mean, *ah*? It's nothing. Never mind."

He took two pantherlike steps toward me, wearing a look that suggested he was still hungry and I was a yummy cupcake, and wrapped his hands around my upper arms. "Is there something you'd like to share with me, darling?"

"Share with you? No." I blinked. "Oh. No! No, it's not about me. Really, no. I was only asking because . . ." But I was suddenly reminded that he was intending to run a background check on Alex, so why should I give him any extra ammunition to use against her? "It's nothing. Never mind. Oh, look at the time. You're going to be late. Better go. Love you. Bye-bye."

He laughed and began to run his hands slowly up and down my arms. "Do you honestly think I'm going to leave you now, with that subject hanging there in the wind?"

"What subject? Nothing's hanging. There's no wind. Off you

go now. Ciao." I tried to push him toward the door. "*Hasta la vista,* baby. See you later. Go on. Am-scray."

He yanked me into his arms and kissed me like no other man had ever kissed me before. I was breathless by the time he lifted his lips from mine.

He kissed my earlobe, then moved on to that tender spot under my jaw. He whispered, "Are you going to tell me why you're so intrigued by the idea of wearing handcuffs?" The sensation of his breath against my neck was causing my knees to wobble.

"Okay, okay," I said, giving in. It was no surprise to hear how gravelly my voice was and I had to cough to clear my throat. "This isn't about you and me, I promise."

Although I was willing to give it a try if he was. But wait: he was on his way to work and I had things to do.

What were we talking about? Oh yes. I had to take another deep breath and let it go before I could speak.

"I didn't get a chance to tell you last night," I said, "but when I first went over to Alex's place, I didn't see her. Instead, I saw a man sitting all alone on her sofa."

"A man?" His eyes narrowed. "What does this have to do with handcuffs?"

"He was . . . wearing them."

"Wearing them. Handcuffs?"

"Yes, his hands were cuffed behind his back. And there was a piece of thick tape across his mouth."

"What the—? Did you call the police?"

I shook my head. "No. I just left and came home."

"You left him there?"

"I should, um, probably mention that he was naked."

Derek stared at me, nonplussed. I believed this might have been the first time I'd ever seen him at a loss for words. It made me smile.

"Okay, I admit I was worried at first, but then he winked at me. That's all," I said briskly. "End of story. Bye-bye. Enjoy your day."

"Yes, I really should get going," he said slowly. "But first I want to make sure I have a clear picture of what happened."

"Okay." He still had a grip on my arms and wasn't going anywhere. And neither was I.

His gaze was trained on me. "You walked into Alex Monroe's apartment last night and saw a naked man wearing handcuffs with a piece of tape over his mouth. And you didn't tell me?"

"I meant to, but you were on that conference call and I didn't want to disturb you. Besides, the guy looked perfectly happy. Like I said, he winked at me."

"He winked at you."

"Yes. It turns out he wasn't in any danger."

"How do you know that?"

"Well, there was the winking, plus he gave me the thumbs-up sign. And later, Alex told me all about it. She said she likes submissive men. So I guess that's where the handcuffs question came from. Because, you know, inquiring minds want to know."

He frowned. "You wanted to know if I was submissive?"

"Oh, God, no," I said with a laugh. "You're the last person in the world I'd call submissive. But still, I wasn't sure about the whole naked, handcuff-wearing question."

He tilted his head and pierced me with a questioning look. "So you're asking whether I would be interested in getting naked, being bound and gagged, and then agreeing to sit passively on a couch as though I didn't have a care in the world? While you did . . . what?"

I tried not to smile. "I hereby withdraw the question."

"Not fair."

"Alex says they do a role-playing game. She's the Black Ops interrogator and he's . . . well, I made her stop talking, so I'm not sure what role he gets to play."

"Probably just as well," he murmured. "But let's be clear. I'm not submissive."

I laughed. "That was clear from the first minute we met."

Derek Stone was indeed the last person in the world I would ever call submissive. He was—how had Alex put it last night? He was a domineering alpha type and proud of it. Derek was the Big Dog. Leader of the Pack. He ruled not only the porch but the entire yard and all the fields beyond.

"Good," he said. "I'm glad we've straightened that out." He shot me a look. "We have straightened it out, haven't we?"

"Yes, we have." I nodded smartly.

"Excellent. But now this begs the question."

I didn't like that gleam in his eye. "What question would that be?"

He leaned closer and pressed his forehead against mine in an intimate gesture I had always found endearing. "How would *you* like to be naked on a couch, wearing handcuffs, darling Brooklyn?"

A shiver zigzagged up my spine and across my shoulders. "The handcuffs don't appeal to me," I said carefully. "But we could talk about the rest."

He grinned wolfishly and kissed me once more. "That visual will stay with me all day."

Saturday was one of those exquisitely warm October days in San Francisco that made all the dreary cold and rainy days of winter worth it. The sky was a deep blue with barely a cloud to be seen from here to the horizon. A slight breeze blew in from the East Bay with just enough oomph to remind us that we did indeed live in cool San Francisco and not in some insipidly warm place down south.

It was so pretty outside that Derek and I decided to start the party upstairs on the rooftop patio. I dressed in a pale crocheted top; a long, crinkly skirt; and strappy sandals. Derek seemed to approve.

I held open the door that led to the patio as Derek carried a tray of glasses and utensils up the stairs. He had worked too late the night before, so I'd forgotten to ask him a question I'd had on my mind. Now as he reached the top step, I said, "Did Alex survive your background check?"

He stopped. "Are you looking for a yes-or-no answer, or do you want to know the details?"

I glared at him. "I want to know that you're not going to arrest her and ruin our party."

He gave me a lopsided grin and carried the tray over to a side table. "As long as she behaves herself, I shouldn't have to arrest her."

I barely kept myself from pouting. "That's not the most encouraging response you could've come up with."

"Darling Brooklyn." Derek came up close and squeezed my shoulders affectionately. "Nothing will ruin the party. The background check was clean and I'm looking forward to meeting our new neighbor."

I was still stressed out about the party but I felt my muscles relax by a degree or two. "You're just looking forward to getting more cupcakes."

"That, too," he conceded with a quick laugh.

"Me, too," I confessed. "The woman is a genius with frosting." I returned downstairs with the empty tray and loaded it up again with cocktail napkins and plastic cups for the kids' drinks.

Our plan was to serve appetizers and drinks upstairs on the patio while the sun was out and the air was still warm, then move downstairs for a casual dinner around the dining room table. We had expanded the table as far as it could go and had added a sturdy card table at one end to make room for twelve adults and the three Chung children. Their mom, Lisa, had assured me that her kids wouldn't feel excluded if we wanted to set the smaller table off to the side and have them sit by themselves, but I thought it would be more fun to include them at the big table.

Six-year-old Tyler had developed a strong crush on me when we first met. And when I'd seen him the other night in the hall, he'd told me he wanted to come home with me. He was a smart little boy with so much charm, I was pretty sure he could hold his own with the grown-ups.

His five-year-old twin sisters, Jessica and Jennifer, were adorable, as well, but much more shy. The girls were actually Tyler's cousins, but Lisa and Henry had adopted them when their parents were killed in a boating accident a few years ago.

Derek grabbed the tray loaded with napkins and cups to take back upstairs. He had decided to grill vegetables, so he remained on the roof to prepare the grill and arrange the patio furniture while I stayed downstairs to set the dining room table.

The grilled vegetables reminded me of a little-known fact I rarely shared with the world. Namely, Derek had turned out to be a much better cook than I could ever hope to be. This, despite his having been raised in a large home with a mother who employed both a housekeeper and a cook.

I understood that men in general were endowed with some kind of weird gene that allowed them to grill meat without any prior knowledge or experience. But it didn't seem fair that Derek was also capable of throwing a complete meal together despite never having ventured into the kitchen while growing up.

I, on the other hand, had been helping my mother in the kitchen since I could walk. But in all that time I hadn't soaked up one lousy thimbleful of cooking ability. Nope, my sister Savannah got it all and became a Cordon Bleu chef just to rub my nose in it.

Lately, however, I'd been trying to improve my cooking skills. I could now make a passable pasta sauce and a yummy coleslaw. I had a signature dessert, too! Maybe I wasn't the greatest cook yet, but to give myself some credit, I had been blessed with a truly awesome talent for *eating* food. And if you could be good at only one part, I much preferred it to be the eating one.

It helped that I wasn't a picky eater; I loved food of all kinds. The thought of Derek's grilled vegetables was almost as thrilling as the thought of Alex's cupcakes. I would be mocked for saying so out loud, but grilled vegetables could be very exciting. To me, at least.

Derek had already slathered olive oil and a dash of pepper and sea salt on zucchini, red peppers, skinny Japanese eggplants, fat red onions, and curly radicchio. The rest of the meal—all sorts of fabulous treats we'd ordered from Piccolo—had arrived: three different pasta salads, plus a Caesar salad; thick slices of cold, rare tri-tip roast; a big antipasto platter; and lots of chunky, crusty bread and butter.

I had transferred everything to pretty serving bowls and platters, and now it was all in the refrigerator, waiting for our friends to arrive. Not that I expected to fool anyone by using my own bowls and plates. Even my newer neighbors had somehow learned that I couldn't cook, so every single person I'd invited had promised to bring a side dish. It was demoralizing, but I would live with it.

The doorbell rang and I jogged out to answer the door.

"Hello, neighbor," Alex said. She looked smashing in black jeans, a silky green tunic, and gold-flecked flip-flops.

"Hi. You look great."

"We both look fabulous," she said with a quick grin.

I stepped aside as she pushed a three-tiered serving cart into my house. "Good grief, how many cupcakes did you bake? And thank you, thank you, thank you!"

"Four dozen," she said, grinning. "We had a new-client meeting yesterday at work and it got testy, so I came home and went a little crazy in the kitchen."

"I'm sorry about your meeting, but . . ." I homed in on the top

tray. I could see its contents through the clear plastic top. "Oh,
God. Are those red velvet?"

She laughed. "Yes. Aren't they pretty?"

"They're . . ." I stared, mesmerized, unable to speak for a long
moment. I itched to try one right away but managed to control
myself. "They're beautiful."

"They taste good, too."

"I believe you." I led the way back to the kitchen. "Still, I'm
sorry you had such a bad day yesterday."

She shrugged. "It's a small thing about the meeting. I was just
hoping to promote one of my newer brokers to deal with this client, but he's not going to be able to manage the guy."

"So you'll have to handle him?" I realized what I'd said and
slapped my hand over my mouth. "Oh, dear. I didn't mean . . ."

She burst out laughing and grabbed me close in a friendly,
one-armed hug. "I love you, Brooklyn."

"As do I."

I whirled around at the sound of Derek's deeply distinctive
voice. He stood a few feet away with one eyebrow raised in spec-
ulation.

I smiled and held out my hand to draw him near. "Derek,
come meet our new neighbor."

I introduced them formally and they shook hands. For the
briefest moment, they stared as though sizing each other up. After
an awkward second or two, they both seemed to relax. Was I
imagining things? Was I the only one who felt awkward? What
was that confrontation all about?

Derek's smile was smooth. "Your cupcakes are fantastic."

"I'm so glad you're enjoying them." Alex smiled, too, and
glanced around, looking completely relaxed. "Brooklyn, I love
how you turned your front room into a workshop."

"Thanks." I supposed they were both being perfectly cordial,
but I felt a coolness. I wasn't sure why. Did they already know each

other from somewhere in the past? Or did Derek not like Alex? What was there not to like? The woman was gorgeous and smart, ran her own business, and made great cupcakes. Still, I supposed it was a matter of taste.

More important, why wouldn't Alex like Derek? He was one of the most intelligent, caring, funny, awesome men I'd ever met, as well as being the absolute best-looking manly male on the planet.

Another thought occurred instantly. Maybe Derek liked her more than he thought he would. Was the coolness I sensed actually a strong attraction he was trying to tamp down?

Did Alex feel the same way?

Oh, hell. I hated the sharp sting of doubt that streaked through me at lightning speed. I had no reason to mistrust either of them, especially Derek. Nuts. I was seriously being nuts. Derek loved me and I knew it. I was just grasping at mental straws, trying to find an answer to why Derek and Alex weren't hitting it off.

I must have been staring into space because I didn't see Derek move closer until I felt his arm around my shoulders. "Darling, everything's ready upstairs, so why don't I pour you both a glass of champagne?"

"Thank you." With a vague smile, I returned to my task of carefully wrapping the utensils in colorful cloth napkins and placing them on the dining room table.

"Will you have champagne?" Derek asked Alex.

"Sounds wonderful."

I watched as Alex maneuvered the cupcake cart against the wall nearest the kitchen bar. "Can I leave this here until we're ready for dessert?"

"That's a perfect spot for it," Derek said. "Can they be served right from the cart?"

"Oh, sure," she said. "It'll be more fun that way."

Derek hovered a few inches away, staring at the treats as

though he hadn't eaten in a week. He glanced up. "Does everyone react to them with such . . . fervor?"

She laughed. "Yes, and I love it."

"What are the flavors?"

"I made chocolate mint, pineapple coconut, red velvet, and marshmallow cocoa. Twelve of each flavor. And they all have a special treat baked into the middle."

"Dear Lord," Derek muttered. "You are a witch."

"A *good* witch," I added quickly.

She beamed with delight. "Thank you."

And just like that, the tension between them seemed to dissipate. It was just as I'd noticed before: all the world's problems could be solved by sharing a few dozen cupcakes.

Derek's eyes became dark with purpose. "I definitely choose the marshmallow cocoa."

"Excellent," I said. "I'm red velvet."

He nodded. "Good to know we won't have to fight for the same flavor."

A few minutes later, he jogged up the stairs to check the grill. Alex joined me in the kitchen while I washed and dried a few dishes. "Derek seems like a great guy."

"He's the best."

"How did you meet him?"

I sighed. "We were involved in a murder together."

"Ah, romantic." She took a sip of her champagne and then leaned in closer. "So, tell me. Was he with Scotland Yard? Interpol?"

I backed up. "What?"

She smiled knowingly. "I recognize that International Man of Mystery type."

"What do you mean?"

Ignoring my words, she reconsidered her choices. "Oh, wait. He's got to be with MI6."

Moving deliberately, I reached for the dish towel and dried my hands. "If you know enough to recognize the type, then you must know that if I told you what you wanted to know, you wouldn't live long enough to enjoy the party."

Her eyes widened and she began to laugh. She finally had to set down her champagne glass, she was laughing so hard.

"Did I miss something funny?" I asked.

She took a deep breath as her laughter subsided. "I really do like you, Brooklyn."

"Lucky me." I hung up the dish towel before facing her directly. "Let me ask you something. What do you really think of Derek?"

Alex seemed to seriously consider the question as she pursed her lips in thought. "He's gorgeous, obviously. Wonderfully tall. I imagine he has good taste in everything. He's smart, especially for choosing to be with you. Sharp sense of humor. Dangerous. Calculating. A risk taker. Ridiculously alpha. Not my type at all."

"Why not?"

"Way too dominant."

I frowned. "He likes kittens."

"Everybody likes kittens," she said with another quick laugh.

I took a moment to pull a cheese platter from the refrigerator and set it on the counter to allow the cheeses to soften. "So, how did you know he . . . I mean, why do you think he worked in intelligence?"

She took another sip of champagne before answering. "I've had some experience in the field."

"Oh? What did you do?"

She grinned. "If I told you, I'd have to kill you."

*T*he party was a huge success, if I did say so myself. It was lovely to see my friends and neighbors enjoying one another's company. The Chung children managed to behave well while having a blast at the same time. And none of them got hurt or cried too loudly.

Six-month-old Lily, the baby that Suzie and Vinnie had become guardians for, was a naturally happy child. She giggled and smiled for everyone and we all took turns holding and cuddling her.

Each of the guests came up with names for the kitten. Frisky and Dusty were suggested, and Bookie, because of my job, of course. A few of us argued over Snowflake and Mrs. Bigglesworth. Mrs. Chung liked Sweetie Pie, Tyler preferred Killer, and Jessica voted for Poofy. Jennifer, who was naturally more introspective than her twin, gave it a lot more thought and finally whispered her choice in my ear. "Tickles."

"That's a good one," I assured her. I wrote all the names down and Derek and I promised to consider each one. But I didn't think we'd arrived at the perfect name for our kitten yet.

After my odd moment with Alex earlier in the kitchen, I wasn't sure what to think. But an hour into the party, she found me at the kitchen sink again while everyone else was laughing and talking upstairs. Taking a deep breath, she leaned against the counter and faced me. "I was a covert operative for many years."

That was the last thing I had expected her to say. "Did you work for the CIA?"

She smiled. "I'm not giving you any details except to say that I had a talent for languages. I was recruited right out of college, a fresh, young thing determined to make a difference in the world. I found myself working for men whose only interests were in gaining power and control." She shrugged. "So what else is new, right?"

"Sad, but true," I said.

"I was a slow learner," she said with a rueful twist of her lips. "After a year of hitting my head against a wall, I started playing their game, fighting for every crumb I could get—while still upholding the highest standards of conduct, of course." Alex's smile dissolved as she dipped into memories that were clearly not pleasant. "I managed to rise up the ranks fairly quickly after that. I refused to let anything stand in my way."

She paused for too long.

"What happened?" I asked finally.

"My team was sent to the Balkans. Kosovo."

I frowned at her. "You're too young to have been involved in that war."

"It was long after the war was over, but the country was still a mess. Criminals were in charge. The economy was running on drug and human trafficking. We were on a covert mission to supply the opposition with the means to take over the government. I figured we'd be cleaning up corruption and replacing the criminals with patriots."

"Let me guess. You were wrong."

"I was a fool."

"You survived," I said quietly.

"Not exactly."

"What's that supposed to mean?"

She stared at the bubbles in her glass. "I died."

I squinted at her. "Say what?"

"I died." She added quickly, "Just for a minute or so. They were able to revive me and I was sent home to recuperate."

"You're omitting a few details."

She nodded. "Yeah."

My curiosity was killing me. "Well? How did you die?"

"I was ambushed," she said darkly. "I trusted the wrong people. Let's just leave it at that."

"I'm sorry."

"I was, too, at the time." She took a fast sip of champagne, maybe to wash down the memories. "And once I recovered, I was just plain angry. I hated everyone. One of my superiors suggested, in the nicest way possible, that I go and find a quiet place to be alone for a while. So I rented a cabin up in the San Juan Islands

near Seattle. It was so damn cold, but beautiful. It took a long time
to sink in but I finally concluded that I wanted to go on living."
She groaned. "And isn't that the worst cliché imaginable?"

"Yes."

She laughed. "But it was true. For years before that, I'd been
in pure survival mode. Now I wanted more. I wanted to live and
work and laugh and have boyfriends and be normal. So I quit the
job. And here I am."

She was still leaving out a lot of details, but I figured she
would fill in the blanks as we got to know each other better.
Something occurred to me. "Have you ever met Derek before?"

"No."

"So what were you thinking when I introduced you? It looked
like you were sizing each other up."

"We were," she admitted.

"Why?"

"It's simple," she said. "We're both determined to be your champion."

"My champion?"

She leaned her back against the refrigerator. "Look, I got an
instant good vibe from you the first minute we met in the hall the
other night. That doesn't happen often. I told you I don't have any
girlfriends. The women I've met in the business world tend to be
paranoid and too desperate to be good friends with anyone."

"That's sad."

She waved away my concern. "Hell, they probably think the
same of me. Anyway, yes, when Derek and I met, we tried to read
each other. It's what you learn to do in an instant in the field. Your
first instincts can save your life. So I knew he was looking at me
and thinking, Does she really want to be Brooklyn's friend or is
she going to use her? Hurt her? Betray her?"

I shook my head. "You can't honestly believe he was thinking
all that."

"Yes, I can, because I was thinking the same thing of him. Is he good enough for you? Does he treat you right?"

"Of course he does."

"I know," she said, smiling. "I got that from him almost instantly."

I was taken aback. "You figured all that out in two seconds?"

"Yes. We both did." She smiled. "He's madly in love with you, Brooklyn. It's lovely to see. You have no reason to ever doubt him."

"I-I don't." And I really didn't. Still, it was nice to hear.

"Good." She gave me a fierce hug. "Now I need more champagne."

I pointed toward the stairs to the roof, where the ice chest was. She wandered off to replenish her drink and chat with the other guests.

Over dinner, I had tried to pace myself so I would have room for a cupcake. It wasn't easy because everything was so delicious. But I'd had my eye on one of those red velvet delicacies from the moment Alex had showed up and I had no intention of missing my chance at it.

Neither did anyone else. As we all bit into our chosen treats, the oohs and aahs and orgasmic moans made us all laugh.

"This was so worth the wait," Suzie said. She used her napkin to whisk away bits of coconut clinging to her lips and cheeks.

Vinnie sighed. "I have reached nirvana."

The cream cheese frosting on top of my red velvet cupcake had been whipped until it glistened. Its gravity-defying peaks curled and twisted every which way and I almost hated to take a bite and destroy its dramatic beauty, but I managed to get over my hesitation and was not disappointed.

"Oh, dear God," I whispered. The cupcake was sweet, creamy, and substantial but not heavy, with a melt-in-your-mouth lusciousness that sent waves of delight to every single one of my taste buds.

It might have been the best thing I'd ever tasted, but I couldn't be sure. So I took another bite. And another. I looked around at all the smiling, frosting-smeared faces and had to laugh.

Derek met my gaze and nodded. "Best party ever."

Lisa and Henry Chung had left to put their sleepy children to bed. Suzie had taken Lily home, too, while Vinnie insisted on staying to help me clean up. Alex stayed, too, after having packaged up cupcakes for everyone to take home.

"I would love a tour of your bookbinding workshop one of these days," she said.

"Anytime you want," I said as I filled the dishwasher. "There's not much to it."

"You're used to it, but I've never seen anything like it before. It's fascinating."

"Oh, it is," Vinnie agreed, as she stacked several clean serving dishes in one of the wide bottom drawers. "And when you think of all the nefarious creatures who have broken in and tossed the place, it makes it even more exciting."

Alex gaped at me. "Vinnie told me you'd cornered a killer or two, but she never mentioned that some of them had actually broken into your home."

I flashed Vinnie a sardonic smile. "I'm surprised you left out that part."

Vinnie blinked and her cheeks turned pink. "Please do not despise me, Brooklyn. I let my tongue get away from my brain."

"I was teasing you," I said hastily. "It's fine to let Alex know about the break-ins so she'll be more careful."

Alex jumped in. "Vinnie's covering for me. It's all my fault for being so nosy. Sergio told me about some of your exploits before I moved in. He considered it an extra perk of living here."

"A perk, huh?" I shook my head. "I love Sergio, but they're hardly my exploits. It's not like I go out looking for trouble. More like me having a gift for being in the wrong place at the wrong time."

"Brooklyn, you are much too modest," Vinnie insisted. "Everyone knows how heroic you are." She twisted her fingers nervously. "And since Alex explained that Sergio had already given her a hint of your audacious spirit, I felt it best not to mention the break-ins but instead assure her that she would never be in danger living with you nearby."

I wanted to argue, but Vinnie was so earnest and goodhearted, I didn't want to hurt her feelings. Instead I reached for her hands and gave them an affectionate squeeze. "I appreciate that."

"Thank you, Brooklyn," Vinnie said. "I'm glad you can see how my conversation with Alex would naturally proceed to the subject of you saving so many people from the jaws of imminent death."

I laughed and gave Alex an imploring look. "Please. She's greatly exaggerating my abilities."

"I don't know either of you that well, but I believe Vinnie." Alex enclosed several chunks of cheese in plastic wrap and tucked them inside the refrigerator.

As my friends bustled around my kitchen, I suddenly remembered Horrible Horatio and his threats. I'd had such a good time all evening that I'd somehow managed to forget all about him. I fervently hoped he was safely locked up by now.

But what if he wasn't? What if he was still on the run? What if he found out where I lived? I spun around to Vinnie. "I want you and Suzie to be very careful. Don't let any strangers into the building. Keep your doors locked." I glanced from Vinnie to Alex. "You too, Alex. You probably know some good self-defense moves, right?"

"My goodness." Vinnie touched my arm. "You look so unhappy all of a sudden. Why are you talking like this, Brooklyn?"

"What's going on?" Alex asked quietly.

"Has there been another killing?" Vinnie asked.

My teeth clamped together in anger and frustration. I didn't want to worry my friends, but I couldn't lie to them, either. "Yes. Somebody I know was murdered a few days ago and I'm concerned because the police haven't found the killer yet."

Vinnie gasped.

"You've got to be kidding," Alex whispered, but somehow she didn't look surprised.

Oh, boy. My words hadn't come out quite as calmly as I'd hoped they would. I tried again. "I mean, they expect to arrest him this weekend, so please don't worry. Really. He's probably already in jail by now. I shouldn't have said anything."

"Yes, you should've," Alex said firmly. "I want to hear more."

I exchanged wary glances with Derek, who had been standing on the other side of the kitchen bar, listening in on the conversation for the last minute or two. He came into the kitchen, reached for the half-full wine bottle, and poured a small amount in each of our glasses. "Why don't you all go relax in the living room? I'll finish cleaning up in here."

Vinnie stood on her tiptoes and kissed him on the cheek. "You are the best of men, Derek."

He shot me a grin and grabbed my dish towel.

Once we were ensconced in the living room, I told Vinnie and Alex all about *The Secret Garden* murder.

"Good heavens, you could still be in danger," Vinnie said. "Should not Inspector Lee assign you a bodyguard? Or perhaps she feels that having Derek here is more than enough protection for you?"

"He is. And he's been coming to the studio with me every day."

Alex sat forward on the couch. "That's reassuring, but Vinnie's right, Brooklyn. Even Derek can't be with you twenty-four/seven. You need to take responsibility for your own protection."

"Derek taught me a few self-defense moves."

"I'm sure that was helpful," Vinnie said. "You know that Susie and I—and our chainsaws—are always here for you in times of danger, but Alex has a point. Perhaps there is more you could do for yourself." Vinnie glanced at Alex. "Have you taken many self-defense classes?"

She hesitated. "Yeah, a few."

"A few?" I studied her for a long moment. Knowing a little bit about her background, I figured she'd taken more than a few classes. "What level are you?"

She met my gaze and shrugged. "Fifth-degree black belt in tae kwon do and Kenpo."

"Only fifth degree?" I muttered.

She smiled. "My dojo awards a sixth degree only after twenty years of study."

"Ah." I shut up and drank my wine.

"My goodness," Vinnie whispered, eyes shining with complete awe. "You are a killing machine."

"When I have to be," Alex said with a grin. "Come to my class sometime. I'll teach you some moves."

"*Your* class, Alex?" Vinnie said.

She stared at her wineglass. "I teach Krav Maga and Brazilian jujitsu, along with tae kwon do and kickboxing."

"When?" I demanded, wondering why the heck I'd never thought of doing something like this before.

"Saturday mornings. I'll e-mail you the info."

"I'll be there."

"And Suzie and I wouldn't miss it for the world," Vinnie chimed in. "This will be fun, will it not?"

Alex bowed her head slightly, acknowledging our enthusiasm. "Meanwhile, you need to continue to practice the few moves you're familiar with."

I didn't have a lot of confidence in my kicks and hand chops. "Any quickie suggestions in case that guy comes around again?"

"Yes." Alex set her wineglass on the coffee table and stood up. "I can teach you every martial arts technique known to man, but in the moment when you're fighting for your life, my advice is to fight dirty. Bite him, gouge his eyes out, pull his hair, kick him in the groin, stomp on his feet. Scream. Do whatever you have to do to get away. Then run your ass off. You got it?"

"Got it." I stood up and faced her in the middle of the living room. "Now show me."

Chapter Eleven

As soon as our last party guests left, I pounced on Derek. I told him everything Alex had said earlier in the kitchen and demanded to know if he had been sizing her up, too.

"That's one way to put it," he hedged, as he filled two water glasses for us.

"How else would you put it?"

"I'd put it this way." He bided his time, pulled a clean dish towel out of the drawer to dry the last of the coffee cups, and put them away. "I had never met her before, and yet you were determined to be friends with her. Given your recent history, I resolved to proceed cautiously. As you know, I ran the background check on her and it came up clean. Interesting, but clean."

I pulled the barstool out and sat down. "Did you find out that she worked for the CIA?"

"Yes," he said slowly, giving me the impression that there were other interesting details to be found in Alex's background check.

But first things first, I thought. "So what was with the Vulcan mind meld happening between you two when I introduced you?"

"There was no mind melding involved," he said easily. "I simply wanted to take some time and gauge my own first impression of her."

"And what was your conclusion?"

He turned away from me to hang up the dish towel. "She'll be a good friend to you."

"That's it?"

He looked back at me. "But that's everything. That's all I wanted to know. I needed her to answer a critical question and she did."

"Silently? In one brief instant?"

"Sometimes that's all it takes."

I frowned. At times, his sense of British resolve was hard to appreciate. "It shouldn't be that simple."

"It is precisely that simple, my love." He pulled me into his arms and held on to me for a long moment before speaking again. "You weren't the only one devastated by the betrayal of a person you thought might be a good friend. I watched you suffer and it tore me apart. You've an open, generous heart, Brooklyn, and mine broke to see you in so much pain."

"I'm sorry." I had my arms wrapped around his waist and I hugged him a little tighter. British stoicism or not, he was wonderful. "Mary Grace fooled us all, but especially me."

"I've had a hard time forgiving myself for that."

"So have I," I admitted, "but she turned out to be a psychopath. She was hardwired to lie. It's like her life depended on it."

"It did."

Unwilling to dwell on the bad memory any longer, I said, "Let's come back to the current situation."

"All right, love." He kissed the top of my head. "I like Alex."

I leaned back to look him in the eye. "You do? Just like that?"

He chuckled. "Yes, just like that. She won't take advantage of your good nature. She'll return your friendship in equal measure. And she'll make us awesome cupcakes."

I choked on a laugh. "All true."

"And I've elicited her solemn promise," he said, frowning reflectively, "to kick anyone's ass who comes around making trouble when I'm not here."

"We got him," Inspector Lee announced when I answered the phone early Monday morning.

My heart jumped once, then settled down in my chest. I took in a big, slow breath and let it out. I hadn't realized how flipped out I'd been, waiting to hear her say those words about Horatio. "Thank you."

"Don't thank me yet," she said. "I'd like to swing by in a few minutes and have you look at a few six-packs."

I was pretty sure she didn't mean beers. Or, sadly, half-dressed male models with good stomach muscles. "What do you mean by six-packs?"

"Photos of suspects. They're on cards, six photos on each."

"Got it. Do you want to come right now?"

"Yeah. I'll be there in fifteen minutes."

It took her only ten minutes to drive over from the Hall of Justice, where she worked in the Personal Crimes Division, which included Homicide. I poured her a cup of coffee and we sat at the dining room table. She handed me the cards one by one. Each five-by-eight-inch card showed mug shots of six different men. It was odd to see the faces of so many men who'd gone through the prison system. Most of them looked either wasted or angry or dazed, and I realized that getting a picture taken for a mug shot was not anyone's best moment.

A shiver scuttled up my spine the moment I saw the mug shot of Horatio. He looked half-asleep, but his eyes still managed to convey malice and his lip was curled in a mean snarl. I tapped his picture, then dropped the card on the table. "That's him."

"You sure?" Inspector Lee held up all the cards I hadn't seen yet.

"I'm absolutely positive, but if it helps strengthen the case against him, I'll look at a few more cards before pointing to the same guy."

"Not necessary. You've already looked at a couple dozen, at least. But I want you to be sure. Look at him again. Is that the man who attacked you in the Peapod Studio parking lot?"

"Yes."

"Would you say you're one hundred percent sure that's him? Or eight percent? Sixty percent?"

"One hundred percent sure that's the guy."

She wrote out a short statement on a printed sheet that included the time and date of the attack, checked a few boxes, and had me sign it.

"Is that it?" I asked. "Are we finished?"

"For now." Pushing her chair away from the dining room table, she stood and gathered her cards and papers. "The district attorney might want you to come in for an in-person lineup. It depends on the lawyers."

I stood, too. "I'll do whatever you need me to do—just let me know. I want this guy behind bars."

"You and me both. Problem is, he won't stay in jail for long on a mere assault charge. And except for your statement that he threatened to kill you and Vera, we don't have anything substantial tying him to Vera's murder. It's all circumstantial at this point."

"What about fingerprints? Or witnesses."

"There were no prints on the murder weapon." She seemed to realize what she'd said and scowled. "If I hear that repeated on the evening news, I'll come after you with a pipe wrench."

"Ouch." I pretended to clutch my chest in pain. "After all this time, I should think you would trust me a little more."

"I do, actually." She huffed out a breath. "Sorry. Just, you know, keep it to yourself."

"I will." I walked with her down the short hall, into my

workshop, and over to the front door. "I wouldn't dream of doing anything that could jeopardize this case. I want him to go to prison forever."

"If he killed Vera Stoddard, we'll make sure he gets what he deserves."

"Good." I opened the door for her. "Let me know if you need me to identify him in a lineup. That would be so cool."

"You're a twisted woman, Wainwright."

"I know," I said, smiling. "It's part of my charm."

"Yeah, charm. Or something."

*T*wo hours later, Inspector Lee called. "The district attorney met with our suspect's lawyer. They're demanding a police lineup and they'd like to do it tomorrow morning."

"That was fast."

"Can you make it?"

"Absolutely."

She gave me the time and place and we ended the call. I wanted to jump up and do a happy dance, but I restrained myself. After all, there was nothing happy about Vera being dead. And I was the one who would be fingering her killer.

"Fingering," I muttered. When had I started to talk like a Mob boss?

I stared at the one-way glass window. "Can they see me?"

"No, they can't see you," Inspector Lee muttered.

I was pretty sure every last person who had ever gone through this procedure had asked the very same question.

Besides Inspector Lee and me, there were two men in a small viewing room. Both wore suits and I guessed they were attorneys. I wasn't introduced to either of them. I figured nobody wanted to get too chummy with me, seeing as how I was there to finger the perp, as they said. Good grief, more fingering.

Lee spoke into a small intercom speaker. "Send in number one, please."

I watched through the glass as a uniformed officer opened the side door of the room. A large man walked slowly halfway across the space. He was told to stop there and look straight ahead. He stared right at me, although Inspector Lee insisted again that he couldn't see me.

Nobody else walked in with him.

I frowned. "Where are the others?"

"We don't do it with a group anymore," Lee explained. "We do what's called a sequential lineup. It's supposed to be better for you, the witness, so you're not comparing the suspects to one another. Instead, you're judging them each individually against your own memory of the person you saw. It lowers the chance of a false positive."

"I'm not sure I understand."

She thought about it for a few seconds. "Okay, you've described your attacker as a large man. So if we lined up four skinny guys and one great big guy, you might identify that one larger man as the perpetrator, even though he's innocent. All you're seeing is one large man out of five or six, so you're assuming he's the guy."

"But I would never do that."

"Maybe you wouldn't, Wainwright, but plenty of people would. Especially if they didn't get a good look at his face up close."

"I see," I said, still a little thrown off, because this wasn't the way they did it on television. But I could definitely see the benefit of a sequential lineup. And I was learning a sad truth, that cop shows didn't always portray these procedures exactly as they were done in real life.

"Let's do this," she said. "I want you to take a good long look at this guy."

I stared at the first guy for another minute.

"Seen enough?" Lee asked.

I nodded.

The first man was instructed to leave by the same door he came in, and a few seconds later, the next guy walked into the same space and stared straight ahead at me.

It was Horatio.

I flinched at the sight of him. He was as huge and frightening and menacing as he'd been a week ago and I had to remind myself that he couldn't see me.

I sucked in a breath, exhaled slowly, and then whispered, "That's him."

"So noted," she said, and shot a glance at the taller man in the suit standing next to her.

A moment later, she said, "Send in the next person, please."

I didn't say another word as the same routine was repeated for the rest of the suspects. There were a total of five and all of them were tall and heavyset.

I looked at every one of their faces, their clothing, their height, their shoes, their hair, and the shape of their heads. Horatio was the second man in. Number two. He was the tallest and heaviest of the five, and he looked the meanest. I had recognized him the instant he walked into the room. The memory of seeing him so close made me shiver again. I still wasn't 100 percent confident the guy couldn't see me through that glass wall.

He had to know that I would be one of the people who would identify him. But that didn't mean I wanted to have a face-to-face confrontation with him. I'd done that already.

"Did you recognize any of these men as the one who attacked you?" Inspector Lee asked, her voice a bit stilted and formal.

"Yes."

"Can you give me his number, please?"

"He was number two."

"Are you certain?"

"Yes, absolutely one hundred percent certain that's the man who attacked me and Benny the guard at the studio last week. He's the one who threatened to kill me and Vera Stoddard."

"Number two," Lee repeated.

I nodded. "Yes."

She turned to the two men standing next to her. "You got that?"

"I got it," the shorter one grumbled.

"Let's go," the other man said. He looked at me and said, "Thank you for your time."

They walked out and I looked at Inspector Lee. "Who were those guys?"

"The unhappy one is number two's lawyer. The other one is the ADA."

Assistant district attorney, I thought. The prosecutor. "Cool. Just like on TV."

"Get out of here, Wainwright. I've gotta go take care of number two."

She snorted and I swallowed a laugh as we left the viewing room.

*B*efore heading to the studio, I found out from Inspector Lee that Horatio's real name was Larry Jones. But he was better known by his street name, Lug Nut.

Lug Nut. Good grief. Had his parents called him that as a baby?

I walked out of the Hall of Justice building and turned east on Bryant. My apartment was only five blocks away, so I could've walked here from there. But they were five long city blocks and since I knew I would have to drive directly from here to the studio, I'd come by car.

It was getting chilly and I pulled my short navy jacket closer around my waist. I'd heard the weather report predicting rain tonight, so I'd brought my new raincoat and an umbrella with me, but I'd left them both in the car. Too bad, because it looked like it would start pouring any minute.

I had parked in a lot on Boardman Street, a block south of Bryant, but I had my sights set on checking out a food truck I'd seen at the corner of Bryant and Harriet, one block past Boardman.

I had developed a dangerous affection for food-truck dining and was currently on the lookout for the perfect *pupusa de queso*, a yummy little fried treat made of thick cornmeal and stuffed with cheese.

I walked faster and checked over my shoulder to see if it was safe to cross the street. That's when I noticed a man on the opposite side of the street, staring at me.

My breath hitched and I stopped in my tracks. The guy was huge and mean-looking and his mouth was set in a permanent sneer.

Horatio?

How? He was in jail. Did he have a twin? Whoever the hell this guy was, he noticed that I had seen him and he was jabbing his finger toward me in a menacing way.

"You!" he shouted. "I'm gonna make you sorry you ever went to the police."

Damn, it couldn't be Horatio—or, rather, Lug Nut. But he looked exactly like him. And he sounded like him, too, with that deep, harsh voice. But that was impossible. Lug Nut was in jail.

Had he escaped already? They couldn't have let him go. But who was this guy? Lug Nut had to have a brother. In fact, this guy could be his twin. But why was he gesturing and yelling so angrily at me? He didn't know me! Did he? Had he seen me coming out of the viewing room after identifying his brother?

Had he and his brother been spying on me? The thought made my head spin. But how else would he know who I was?

I stared dumbly for a few more seconds until I realized he was checking the traffic, too. Was he waiting for a break so he could cross the street and— What? Threaten me? Kill me?

Damn it! I turned and ran up the sidewalk, back to the crosswalk directly in front of the steps leading up to the Hall of Justice. But Lug Nut—or whoever he was—kept pace with me on the other side of the busy street. I couldn't believe it. He was standing right in front of police headquarters, threatening me, blocking my access. So how was I supposed to get from here back into the building without running right into him?

I looked around for a cop. We were directly in front of police headquarters, for God's sake. Where was a cop when you needed one?

At that very moment, a cop car approached the intersection and stopped to allow me to cross in front of him. I rushed around to the driver's side of the car and the cop rolled down his window.

"Can you help me?" I asked, pointing toward my tormentor. "That man over there in the black T-shirt is following me."

"The big one?" he said.

"Yes. I've been trying to get into the building to talk to the police but I'm afraid to go near him."

The two cops in the car stared directly at Lug Nut's twin. He stared back for a long moment, and if looks could kill, I would have dropped dead. After another few seconds, he shook his head in disgust, uttered some rude words I couldn't hear, and stomped off in the opposite direction.

The police officer driving the car gazed up at me. "Do you want us to go after him?"

Yes, please! I thought, but I couldn't ask them to do it. "He hasn't actually done anything yet," I admitted, glancing back at the hulk retreating from sight. "He was just trying to frighten me."

"If you want to file a restraining order, you can get the forms online and file them at the McAllister Street courthouse over at the Civic Center."

"Okay, thanks," I said, smiling tightly. I knew I could probably file some kind of protective order against him, but he looked too vicious to care. To him, it would just be a piece of paper, no matter how legal it was. Besides, I didn't even know his name! So how was I supposed to keep this guy from coming near me?

With the path cleared, I scurried across the street and raced up the stairs. A woman was exiting the building as I approached, so I grabbed the door and slipped inside.

I stared out at the street and was shocked to see that the Lug Nut twin had already reappeared. The police stare-down hadn't frightened him away. He was on the other side of the street now, just standing there as plain as day, studying the trio of massive glass doors leading to the Hall of Justice. As he stood there, he lit up a cigarette and lazily blew out a lungful of smoke. His calmness unnerved me.

Watching him carefully, I could detect subtle differences between him and his brother—or twin, or whatever his relationship was with Lug Nut. This guy's head was bullet-shaped instead of round. He looked slightly older, more hardened, and more in control of his emotions, if barely.

The hazy sky cast enough light to reflect off the glazed windows of the glass doors, blocking any outsider's view inside. I knew he couldn't see me, but it still freaked me out to see him staring my way.

He was waiting for me. There had to be a back exit somewhere. I wasn't about to give him a chance to hurt me like his brother had.

My whole body shook with fear. I needed to find Inspector Lee and tell her about this new threat. But first I pulled out my phone and snapped a few photos through the glass. I zoomed in for a close-up but the shot came out a little blurry because the big jerk kept moving back and forth along the sidewalk, watching and waiting. So instead of a photograph, I switched the camera to video and recorded his moves for about fifteen seconds. This was something I could show Inspector Lee.

My phone buzzed in my hand, causing me to jolt before I came to my senses and answered the call.

"Derek," I said. "Thank goodness it's you."

"What's wrong?" he said. "Where are you?"

"I'm still at the Hall of Justice. I identified the attacker from the lineup and he's in jail now, so that's done. But . . ." How could I explain this? "Derek, the guy who attacked me must have a twin brother." I briefly explained how I had been followed to my car by yet another big, mean-looking guy and how I had managed to evade him—for the moment.

"You're inside the Hall of Justice right now?"

"Yes."

"Then you're safe."

"Are you kidding?" I whispered. "I'm surrounded by criminals and scoundrels, and those are just the lawyers."

"I'm pleased to see the experience hasn't affected your sense of humor."

"Trust me, it's a defense mechanism," I said. "I'm scared to death. I was on my way to find Inspector Lee when you called."

"I want you to ask her for a police escort to walk you back to your car. Or, better yet, have someone drive you home. I'll meet you there. We can come back for your car later."

"I can't," I murmured. "I've got to go to work."

He swore under his breath. "Then get a cop to walk with you to your car. Drive straight to the studio and I'll be there as soon as I can."

"Okay." I hated dragging him away from his own work to babysit me, but I wasn't about to turn down his offer.

"Until the police investigate this brother or whoever he is," he continued, "I don't want you going anywhere alone."

"Did I mention I'm scared?" I hated to sound so helpless.

"So am I, love," he said softly.

"I'm sorry it's all happening again."

"Just stay safe. Don't go anywhere without a police escort. I'll see you at the studio in less than two hours. Call me if there's anything you need."

"I'll be fine," I said, then whispered it again to convince myself. "I'll be fine."

"Of course you will," he said calmly, for my benefit, no doubt. "Because once I get there, I'm not letting you out of my sight again."

"Thank you. I love you."

"I adore you."

I ended the call before realizing that my eyes were damp with tears. "Idiot," I muttered, and brushed them away. I hated crying as much as I hated feeling powerless and afraid.

I glanced outside and my heart literally jumped in my chest. The big guy stood leaning against the stair railing, less than twenty feet away.

I managed to make it through the long security line without screaming and ran to the elevator, pounding on the button until the door opened.

Inspector Lee was standing there, holding a bag in one hand and waving her cell phone in the other. "I can't let you out of my sight for one minute without you causing more trouble."

"Lug Nut has a brother," I said. "They could be twins."

"I know. Derek already called me. Come on," she said, leading the way to another elevator that had just arrived. "I'll drive you to your car. Oh, here. These are your shoes."

"Thanks." I took the bag from her. "I've got some video of the guy if you need it. He's standing outside on the front steps."

"Yeah, e-mail it to me. It might come in handy."

We rode the elevator to the basement garage and Lee climbed into the driver's seat of a black-and-white police car. I jumped into the passenger's seat, and she drove up the narrow driveway, then out to the street and once around the block to see if the brother was still waiting for me.

He was no longer standing out front, but we saw him farther down the block, jogging toward a parking lot.

"Jeez, they really could be twins," Lee said.

"If I hadn't seen him with my own eyes, I wouldn't believe it," I muttered. I didn't bother to add that if Derek hadn't called Inspector Lee, I wasn't sure she would've believed me, either.

As I turned in my seat to get one last look at the man, I silently calculated the length of time it would take me to earn a black belt in some kick-ass martial arts discipline. Too many years, unfortunately. But, anxious to get back some of my old self-confidence, I couldn't wait to start Alex's self-defense class next Saturday. I was tired of feeling like a weakling.

Inspector Lee dropped me at my car and then followed me to the studio. I hated to inconvenience her, but I was pitifully grateful for her presence. Once she saw that I was inside the studio gate and parked safely, she waved and drove off.

It was starting to rain, so I was glad once again that I had my new red raincoat with me. It was a gift from Derek, who had brought it back from the Burberry store in London a month earlier. I was a little hesitant to wear it in the rain, even though it was made for the rain. Duh.

I jumped out of my car, quickly draped the coat over my shoulders and pulled up the hood, then locked the door and ran across the lot to the studio door.

I was still nervous at the thought of Lug Nut's brother watching and waiting for me outside police headquarters. I knew he hadn't seen me in Inspector Lee's car, but if Lug Nut had told him about me, he probably knew that I worked here at the studio every day. He could've jumped in his car and driven over here. He might've been watching me at that very moment.

Shivering, I yanked open the stage door and took one last look behind me before rushing inside to safety.

*A*lmost two hours later, I had taped my first segment and was back in my dressing room, studying up on my second book, a small, charming, slightly shabby leather-bound copy entitled *The Thoughts of Marcus Aurelius*. He was an early Roman emperor who was said to be wise and relatively kind—for an early Roman emperor.

A sudden knock on the door caused me to jump again.

"Stop it," I said to myself. I was still so agitated, I was driving myself nuts. Standing up, I shook my hands and shoulders loose as I crossed the room to get the door. I whipped it open and almost leaped into Derek's arms.

"The door was locked."

"Sorry," I whispered. "Thank you for coming. I really appreciate it."

"You'd better get used to seeing me around here," he murmured, his breath ruffling the strands of hair near my ear. "Because I'm not leaving your side until the danger is over."

"I'm so glad." I didn't care how wimpy that sounded. After a few minutes of catching up with Derek and retelling my story of being followed and taunted by Lug Nut's doppelganger, I went back to my research. Derek sat down on the couch and opened his briefcase to finish up some work before starting in on two conference calls. In between the business calls, he telephoned Inspector Lee for a quick update on Lug Nut's brother.

Clearly, Inspector Lee had plenty of information for him, because Derek began to jot down notes. I was glad Derek was the one who'd called her, because I knew she would be willing to give him much more scoop than she would ever give me.

"What did she say?" I asked as soon as he hung up the phone.

He scanned the notes he'd taken. "The man who followed you this morning is Larry Jones's brother, Gary."

"Gary," I repeated in disbelief. "That's so . . . normal."

He glanced at his notes. "Better known by his street name, Grizzly."

"You've got to be kidding." I almost laughed, but nothing about this situation was funny. "It suits him, though. Lug Nut and his brother, Grizzly. What a charming family." I couldn't believe their real names were Larry and Gary Jones. Such ordinary, down-to-earth names for two extraordinarily vicious creeps.

"The brothers grew up in the Tenderloin, and according to the authorities in that area, Grizzly is reputed to be even more dangerous than his little brother."

"He looked it." I rubbed my arms to calm down the goose bumps that sprang to life at the memory of my brief confrontation with Grizzly.

Inspector Lee had told Derek that the two men weren't twins, but looked enough alike to have caused plenty of grief for their parents, teachers, and local law enforcement throughout their teenage years. They had both landed in the prison system and had been in and out of jail for years. They were known to be major screwups and mean sons of bitches.

"Do they still live in the Tenderloin?" I asked, wondering how in the world Lug Nut could've held a garage sale. The Tenderloin was mostly filled with seedy hotels and disreputable apartment buildings. There were plenty of bars and pawnshops, but I couldn't picture any houses in the area suitable for a garage sale.

The neighborhood was located a few blocks west of upscale Union Square and had long been known as one of the most seamy, dangerous parts of town. That reputation was changing slowly, though, as the area became marginally safer, thanks to an influx of immigrant families. But it was still said to have the highest concentration of parolees in the city.

It was also home to some of the best Indian restaurants in town, but that was beside the point.

The point *was*: how in the world had a no-good lowlife loser like Larry "Lug Nut" Jones gotten his hands on an exquisite and rare copy of *The Secret Garden*? Had he stolen it? But if he'd stolen it and knew its value, why would he ever sell it in a garage sale? Of course, he had denied selling it to Vera, but he would've said anything to get his hands on the book. It was clear from the short conversation I'd had with him the day he attacked me that he'd discovered the book's value only on the night he saw our short segment on the evening news.

Maybe his brother, Grizzly, had stolen it. Maybe Lug Nut had discovered it among his brother's belongings and sold it at the garage sale for a few bucks, not realizing how much it was worth.

If that scenario was true and Grizzly had found out that Lug Nut sold the book, he might have threatened his little brother with severe bodily harm unless he got it back. Under those circumstances, Lug Nut might have been willing to do whatever it took to retrieve the book—even commit murder.

My mind was spinning off in ten different directions.

"They moved out of the Tenderloin last year," Derek explained, "after they came into some money. Found a small house in the Sunset District, close to the beach."

"*Came into some money?* Is that code for robbing a bank?"

Derek shot me a half smile. "Perhaps."

Regardless of where their money had come from, their move to the small house answered my question about where the garage sale had been held.

Derek continued. "Inspector Lee drove out to their place a little while ago to talk to Grizzly, but he wasn't home. She'll check back tonight and again tomorrow."

"I hope she's taking someone with her," I said with some concern. "Inspector Jaglom is on another assignment, so she's been working this case alone."

Derek frowned at the news and was about to say something

when Angie knocked and yelled through the door. "You're wanted on the set, Brooklyn. Five minutes to taping."

I grabbed the door and swung it open. "Thanks, Angie. Be right there."

As she hustled back down the hall, I turned to Derek. "I'll be back in a few minutes, if you want to stay here and work."

He shut his briefcase and flashed me a purposeful grin. "What part of *I'm not letting you out of my sight* do you not understand?"

Chapter Twelve

"Two thousand dollars?" Mitchell whispered reverently.

"Yes," I said, holding the Marcus Aurelius book up for the camera. "Your thrift-shop bargain was a little more valuable than you thought."

"That's fantastic."

I was so relieved by his reaction. While it was probably interesting for the audience to see the owners burst into tears or hyperventilate or nearly faint, I was really starting to appreciate the more sedate responses, like Mitchell's.

"My wife is going to be tickled pink."

"I'm so glad."

He just grinned and after a short, silent pause, Angie announced, "And we're clear. Next is segment three-forty on your rundown. We're doing World War Two posters on the war stage. In thirty minutes, people."

"Thank you so much," Mitchell said, shaking my hand with enthusiasm as the crew and camera operators began the slow move of equipment and cables to the other end of the studio.

"You're welcome, Mitchell," I said. "It was fun. Enjoy the book."

"Oh, you betcha. Gotta go tell the wife."

Frannie, the production assistant, smiled as she led Mitchell off the stage and back to the production room, where his wife was waiting.

I was getting to know more of the staff and crew in my second week of working at the studio. It was nice to be able to greet them by name.

Derek was talking to Tom on the other side of the studio, so I stepped down off my little stage and headed their way.

"Hey, Brooklyn."

I turned and saw Tish, one of the gaffer's assistants, approaching me. She was in her twenties, a tall, pretty redhead engaged to the assistant prop guy. She was tapping the screen of an electronic notepad.

"Hi, Tish. What's up?"

"I'm taking orders for pizza and salad. Do you want anything?"

"No, thanks." I had never known them to order food for the evening.

Angie joined us. "I'll have two slices of veggie pizza and I'll split a green salad with someone."

Tish tapped out the order on her tablet. "I'll split the salad with you."

"Excellent. You want money now or later?"

"Now would be good. I'm asking for ten dollars from everyone. That should cover it. We're getting eight pizzas, so I'll make sure one of them's a veggie."

Angie pulled out a coin purse from her fanny pack, zipped it open and handed her a bill. "Thanks, kiddo."

"No problemo."

Tish walked away and I turned to Angie. "I didn't know you all were working late tonight."

"Not late," she said dryly. "We're working all night long."

"Ooh." I cringed. "Why?"

"We're loading a new show into Studio Two." She jutted her thumb toward the studio next door. "The entire crew will be pulling an all-nighter."

"But you're going to be wiped out tomorrow."

"That's why the schedule was moved back. Did you notice we don't start taping until three o'clock?"

"I saw that, but I didn't know why." I hadn't stayed up all night since college and didn't miss the experience one bit. "I guess you'll all have a good time."

"Yeah, right." She laughed and glanced around the stage. "Some of these kids will actually think it's fun. But I expect to work my butt off, go home and crash for a few hours, come back tomorrow, and do it all over again."

"That's rough."

She shrugged. "That's showbiz. And, hey, I'm just glad to have a job."

"I don't blame you. It must be such a relief whenever a new show comes in." I knew most of the crew members and some of the production staff had been hired locally, so they would all be scrambling for work once *This Old Attic* left town.

"A huge relief," Angie said, pulling off her headset to shake back her hair. "I don't mind working the long hours because it means there's a paycheck waiting at the end of the week."

"Okay, guys, I'm out of here," Tish said, slipping the strap of her purse across her chest for security's sake. "Be back in an hour with the food."

"Can't you call and have it delivered?" I asked.

She shrugged. "Some of the guys want beer and cigarettes, so I offered to go to the pizza place and the liquor store, and the guys will pay for my dinner."

"Sounds like a deal," Angie said.

She waved. "See you in a while."

"I hope you brought a raincoat," I said. "It's pouring outside."

"It is?" She glanced down at the white linen blouse and thin gray vest she had on. Her shoes were dainty black flats worn without socks.

"Did you bring a coat?" Angie asked.

"No. It was sunny when I left my house this morning."

"Yeah, me, too," Angie muttered. "I didn't bring my coat. Otherwise, I'd let you borrow it."

"That's okay," Tish said.

"Brooklyn," Angie said. "You brought a raincoat, right?"

"Um, yeah," I said, and regretted it immediately. Regret was followed quickly by guilt and I winced. It was just a raincoat, for goodness' sake.

But no, it was a *Burberry* raincoat. A gift from Derek. From *London*. Did I mention that it wasn't just red—it was *claret*?

Oh, shut up, I thought, and sighed, knowing poor Tish would get drenched without a coat. I couldn't have that on my conscience.

"I've got a key to your room," Angie said. "Wait here. I'll go get it."

"Are you sure, Brooklyn?" Tish said, as Angie took off running.

"Absolutely." I flashed her what I hoped was an upbeat smile and we traded small talk for another minute until Angie jogged back with my coat.

"Here you go," she said.

"Oh, it's beautiful," Tish said, pulling it on. She grinned at me. "And it fits great. Thank you."

"You're welcome," I said, biting my tongue. "Be careful. It's wet out there."

She gave a thumbs-up as she walked quickly to the door leading to the parking lot.

Angie started to speak, but then held up her hand. Her eyes glazed over and I knew that someone was speaking to her over her headset. With a wave, she went off toward the kitchen stage area.

I turned and saw Derek watching me from just a few feet away.

"That was very kind of you," he said.

"If you knew what was going through my mind, you wouldn't think so."

He laughed as he swung his arm around my shoulders. "I knew exactly what was going through your mind."

I buried my head on his chest. "Oh, God, I'm transparent."

"Only to me, love," he said, still chuckling. "Only to me. And no worries. We'll just take a trip to London and get you a spare Burberry. How's that sound?"

"Wonderful," I said, delighted by the very idea of traveling to London, one of my favorite cities, accompanied by my favorite man. *And who couldn't use a spare Burberry coat?* I thought with a smile.

"What were you talking to Tom about?" I asked, changing the subject.

"I suggested he hire some extra security," Derek said.

"That's a great idea. Did he nix it?"

"Pretty much," Derek said affably. "But I'll still be hanging around as long as you're working here."

"My hero."

We were almost to the hallway leading to my dressing room when a woman screamed from somewhere out on the stage.

"What the hell?" Derek took off running and I followed.

We found Randy Rayburn sprawled on the floor near the craft-services table, struggling for air. A cup of coffee had spilled all over the floor.

"He can't breathe!" Sherry, one of the assistants, yelled, clutching her hands helplessly over her chest. She must have been the one who'd just screamed.

Derek knelt down and loosened Randy's shirt and tie. He looked up at me. "Call nine-one-one."

I didn't have my phone so I shouted, "Somebody call nine-one-one"

"I've got his pen! I've got it!" Todd, another production assistant, came dashing around the corner from the direction of the dressing rooms. He ran over and handed something to Derek. "He's allergic."

Derek didn't hesitate to slide the injector out of its tube. He ripped off the cap, gripped the injector, and shoved the needle into Randy's thigh.

I had to look away, and noticed a few others making faces.

Derek held the injector tube against Randy's leg for at least ten seconds, then pulled it away. He'd obviously had experience dealing with anaphylactic shock and EpiPens. A good thing, because I wouldn't have known what to do.

A few seconds later, Randy jerked his head up off the floor and sucked in a huge breath of air. He did that a few times, wheezing like an asthma patient.

"Can you sit up?" Derek asked after a minute.

"Yeah," Randy muttered, then coughed a little. When he stopped coughing, Derek lifted him by the arms to a sitting position.

I was standing near Todd and my curiosity was killing me, so I leaned close and whispered, "What's he allergic to?"

Todd looked at me in surprise. "Peanuts. Everybody knows that."

"I didn't," I confessed.

"But everybody else knows," he insisted, despite my words. "On our first day, he took all of us in to show us exactly where he keeps his EpiPen. And we were all warned that nobody's allowed to bring anything with peanuts onto the set."

I didn't argue with him. The fact was that I'd had no idea Randy had a peanut allergy, so it was a good bet there were others who were as much in the dark as me.

But it didn't matter who didn't know about the allergy. What mattered more was who *did* know. Because it was possible that someone right here in the studio had meant to kill him.

I scanned the room. Could a killer actually be roaming the studio? Had someone nearby slipped peanuts into Randy's food?

Hell. I stared at the cardboard coffee cup that had rolled under the table. Just moments ago, it had been filled with coffee. Randy had taken a sip or two before spilling the entire contents on the floor. On a hunch, I bent over, picked it up, and folded it in half.

I knew the basics of anaphylactic shock, knew that Randy's tongue and throat must have become swollen enough to cut off air to his lungs. No wonder he couldn't talk. He was lucky to be alive.

"I'm okay," he finally whispered. "But I might need some help getting back to my room."

"Stay where you are," Derek said, and signaled to Tom, who stooped down to talk.

"He's got to go to the hospital," Derek said.

"No, no," Randy mumbled.

"What the hell were you thinking, eating peanuts?" Tom demanded. "You know better than that."

"I didn't eat anything," Randy muttered. "Just had a cup of coffee."

"The EMTs should be here any minute," Derek said.

Randy waved his hand weakly. "I'll be fine."

"You damn well better be," Tom grumbled.

Derek shook his head. "The amount of epinephrine in the EpiPen is only intended to keep you alive long enough to get you to the hospital."

Tom sighed and pulled out his cell phone. He spoke quietly for a minute, then disconnected the call. "Jane says we'll tape your segments tomorrow or the next day."

Randy nodded and closed his eyes.

I nudged Derek and held out the cardboard coffee cup. In a low voice, I said, "Smell this, please."

He gave me an odd look but took the cup and held it to his nose for a quick whiff. He glanced at me, scowling, but didn't say anything right then.

I couldn't be certain, but I thought there was the faintest odor of peanut butter under the coffee smell.

As Tom continued to pace restlessly, Derek knelt back down next to Randy. "What exactly did you eat tonight?"

"Nothing," he repeated, his voice still weak. "I never eat while we're taping."

"Did you drink anything?"

"Well, yeah. I always have a couple cups of coffee."

I hunched down to join in. "Everybody knows your routine, right?"

"Well, sure. I usually announce that I'm going to get coffee, so the whole crew knows where I am." He flashed a feeble smile. "Angie tends to get riled up when she can't find me."

Derek and I exchanged glances and I asked, "Was anyone standing near you at the coffee table?"

He struggled to sit up straighter. "No one in particular. Plenty of people were milling around, though, since we were on a break."

"Think about it carefully," I persisted. "Did you see anyone hovering nearby, watching you?"

He took in our somber expressions and began to shake his head vigorously. "No, no. Come on, you can't be serious. Nobody here tried to poison me. This was an accident, pure and simple."

"Was it?"

"Absolutely," he said, waving away our concerns.

"Absolutely," Tom said through gritted teeth.

"But what about your stalker?" I said quietly.

Tom frowned. Was he finally starting to realize that Randy wasn't joking about the stalker? That there might be a real problem here? I hoped so, because Randy's stalker was obviously getting bolder.

"Okay, okay," Randy said. "I get what you're saying. But he's never done anything to actually hurt me. He just seems to get off on scaring me."

"You could've died tonight," I said.

His cheeks ballooned as he blew out a heavy breath. "Everyone knows where I keep my EpiPen. And someone ran and got it. If the stalker wanted to kill me, they would've done it when I was all alone with nobody else around, right?"

It was such a lame argument, I thought, but didn't push it. Instead I said, "Todd ran to get it."

Randy blinked. "Get what?"

"Your EpiPen," I said.

"Try to keep up," Tom muttered.

I wanted to scowl at him, but I managed to compose myself. Randy frowned. "Which one is Todd?"

"The tall, skinny guy with the spiky blond hair," I said.

"He's a good kid," Tom said defensively.

I glanced from Tom to Randy. "How well do you know him?"

Tom stopped pacing. "You're not actually accusing someone on my staff of doing this, are you?"

Derek jumped in to defuse his anger. "We're just looking for answers."

"I know, I know. Sorry." Tom raked both hands through his hair in frustration. "But maybe Randy's right. Maybe it was just an accident."

"Maybe," I said, but I doubted it. Looking at Derek, I could tell he was thinking the same thing I was. Namely, that there was no maybe about it. Someone had tried to kill off the star of the show.

The EMTs arrived a few minutes later and Randy was taken to the hospital for observation. One of Tom's assistants followed the ambulance in his car in order to take him home later.

Tom's sarcastic treatment of Randy had bothered me from the start, but it seemed to roll right off Randy's back. I supposed they'd known each other for a while, so maybe Randy was used to the snarky comments.

I had one more book segment to tape that night, so Derek and I headed for my dressing room, where I planned to do some quick research on the next book.

"Will you have that analyzed?" I asked when I noticed he was still carrying the coffee cup.

"Yes," he said. "I smelled something other than coffee, as you did."

"I smelled peanuts or peanut butter."

"The most minute smear could've killed him."

I frowned at the thought that Randy could've died tonight. "Someone must have dabbed some peanut butter in his cup. Or maybe they tossed some ground-up peanuts into the coffee itself."

"Good point. I'll check the coffee urn while you're doing your appraisal."

"The first time he told us about the stalker, he was so nervous about it," I mused as I unlocked my dressing room door. "Now he's pretending it's nothing. An accident."

"He's afraid," Derek suggested, following me into the room.

"He should be. This time was different."

"Yes," Derek said, adding ominously, "His stalker's threats are escalating."

"I agree." I sat on the swivel chair. "Those other occurrences were creepy and scary, but this is life-and-death. It's terribly real and he's got to be more afraid than he's letting on."

I held up the lovingly restored, leather-bound copy of *Leaves of Grass* by Walt Whitman so the camera could get a closer shot of it. I explained how the book had been made at a bindery in England that had mass-produced thousands of well-made copies of the classics during the fifties and sixties. There were countless numbers of similar volumes available online, although this copy, owned by a woman named Ruth, was in stellar condition. In the end, though, I was only able to quote her a value of two hundred dollars.

Ruth took the news with good grace.

I wrapped up the segment with a word of encouragement to both Ruth and the audience at home. "Not all the books on the show can be appraised for thousands of dollars. I consider myself lucky when I get to work with a simple, nicely bound book that has been well taken care of and will give someone years of quiet pleasure."

Ruth admitted she'd been given the book by a friend who had inherited it from her mother. The friend couldn't care less about it so she'd passed it on to Ruth.

"I didn't pay a dime for it and I've enjoyed it immensely," she said. "To be honest, knowing that it's only worth two hundred dollars fills me with relief. Two hundred dollars is plenty for a little book like this. If it had been worth thousands of dollars, I wouldn't feel comfortable having it in my house. Now I can continue to enjoy it and have peace of mind in the bargain."

Her words reminded me of Stanley Frisch, the book owner who had been so shattered by the news that his Michael Connelly first editions were worth so much money.

When I'd first taken this job, the thought had never occurred to me that someone wouldn't want to own a rare, valuable book. Now I was finding it was a common sentiment. Which made me wonder again why the people who felt that way would come on a show like this in the first place. If they didn't want their treasures to be worth too much money, why find out either way?

Were they just looking for a fun new way to spend the day? Probably. I guessed I was taking it all too seriously.

Once Angie cleared us to go, Derek walked me back to the

dressing room, where he pulled a half-filled plastic ziplock bag from his pocket and placed it in his briefcase.

"What is that?"

"Coffee grounds from the caterer's coffee urn," he said.

"I'm glad you remembered."

We packed up the rest of our things and headed out.

They were still taping the last segment and there were more crew members working than usual. Most of them were waiting to clean things up on our stage before starting in on their all-nighter next door.

Halfway to the stage door I stopped. "I forgot my raincoat. I have to get it back from Tish."

Derek shrugged in resignation. "Let's go find her."

I glanced around but didn't see her onstage, so I grabbed Angie as she walked by. "Have you seen Tish?"

"She went to the store, remember?"

"That was almost two hours ago."

"Oh yeah." She glanced around. "I haven't seen her in a while and I'm getting hungry, now that you mention it. She probably snuck off to the prop room to visit Kenny."

"I'll go check." I led Derek back around the scrim and we crossed to the adjoining studio where the prop room was located.

I knocked on the half-open door and saw Bruce, the head prop guy, look up. "Hey, girlie. What do you need?"

Bruce was a tall, good-looking, whip-thin black man. His speech was a colorful combination of fifties cool cat and eighties cool dude. He called most women girlie while all the men were bro.

I walked inside to ask about Tish and stopped suddenly. "Oh, my God."

Huge papier-mâché puppets were hanging from the ceiling and stacked together along the back wall of the two-story-high prop room. There were at least twenty of them and they were

gigantic, nearly fifteen feet tall. Grotesque and misshapen creatures with human bodies and oversized animal heads, all grinning
madly.

"Cat got your tongue, girlie?" Bruce asked, shaking me out of
my transfixed state.

I pointed at the puppets. "What are those?"

"My in-laws," he said, and cackled. "Nah, they're puppets.
You like? We used them for a Mardi Gras special a few years back
and I couldn't let them go. They're cool, aren't they?"

"Yes. Can I touch them?"

"Sure, sweet cheeks. They're a little fragile, so be careful, but
help yourself."

"Brooklyn?"

I whipped around and saw Derek standing in the doorway. I'd
completely forgotten what I was doing there.

"Puppets," I said, pointing, before I realized how idiotic that
sounded. I smiled at Bruce. "Sorry. I'll come back another time to
check out the puppets. Right now, we're looking for Tish."

He sat back in his big chair and crossed one leg over the other.
"Tishy girl's in here all the time, flirting with Kenny, but I haven't
seen her for a few hours. Did you check the control booth? She
might be up there with the lighting director."

Since Tish was the gaffer's assistant, she worked closely with
the lighting director and often took notes during the tapings.

"I'll check. Thanks." We ran upstairs to the control booth. It
was a large room with a massive plate-glass window that looked
out over the stage. Jane, the director, sat at a long console, surrounded by the tech crew that worked with her. She and the script
supervisor, associate director, technical director, and lighting director all stared at a wall of monitors that showed every camera's
view, along with whatever graphic was about to come up.

Jane was on headset to the camera operators, the stage manager, and everyone in the booth. She told the cameras which shots

to take and she cued the technical director to cut between the shots, blending it all together with lighting and sound.

The audio man had his own soundproof booth behind them. There were a few tall stools along the back wall for the producers and guests to sit and watch the action.

Tish wasn't up there.

I turned to Derek. "I guess we could leave, but I really don't want to go without making sure she got back safely."

"Let's check downstairs again," Derek said. "We'll take one last turn around the stage. Maybe she's back by now." We walked down the stairs and took the shortcut behind the scrim until we got to the curtain break. The cameras and crew were gathered down at the opposite end of the studio, still taping the last segment on the kitchen set.

I glanced around and easily spied tall, good-looking Kenny, Tish's boyfriend, standing back behind the kitchen set. Not wanting to disrupt the taping, Derek and I stood where we were for another three minutes until Angie called out, "We're clear, people. That's a wrap for this shoot, but anyone working on the Studio Two load-in, take a fifteen-minute break and then meet on the stage next door."

"Let's go talk to Kenny," Derek said, and reached for my hand. We started across the stage when all of a sudden, a thunderous boom rang out.

The stage door had been flung open and had crashed against the wall, causing the loud noise.

Garth, the nice old janitor who had tried to help me lift the stage flats, stumbled through the open doorway in a daze, dripping wet. He flailed his arms and cried out at the top of his lungs, "She's dead! She's dead! Call the police!"

His voice cracked and he began to cough and hack miserably. One of the stagehands grabbed him and slapped him lightly on the back a few times.

"Call nine-one-one!" Derek shouted for the second time that night as he went racing across the stage and out the door. I grabbed my cell phone from my purse and made the call as I ran after him. I told the dispatcher that someone had been attacked outside the studio. I gave her the location and she paused briefly, then informed me that an ambulance would arrive in five minutes while the police would be there in two.

I tucked away my phone and dashed out to find Derek. The parking-lot lights were dimmed by the pouring rain, but I spotted Derek right away. He had just found Tish. She lay curled on the tarmac halfway across the lot, between a black SUV and the wall of the next building. Derek knelt next to her and gently pulled back the red raincoat hood. I leaned over him and could clearly see the blood that had trickled down her temple.

"Is she alive?" I asked, unwilling to accept that she might be dead. A siren began to wail in the distance.

"She's breathing," Derek said, looking up at me. "She's unconscious, but she's alive."

Chapter Thirteen

I watched the ambulance drive away, red lights and siren blazing. Kenny raced to his truck to follow it to the hospital. "I'll be with her until they let me take her home."

"Let us know how she's doing," Tom yelled, shielding his eyes from the rain.

"I'll call you," Kenny shouted, then slammed the truck door shut and drove out after the ambulance.

It was still pouring and I was soaked to the skin. I wrapped my trembling arms around my waist as cold and dread sent shivers throughout my system.

The police officers insisted that we all go inside. They had some questions to ask.

Despite the urge to jump in my car and escape, I walked with Derek as calmly as we could back into the studio.

Once we were wrangled onto the stage, Chuck and Florence, who worked in the Wardrobe Department, walked through the crowd, handing small white makeup towels to everyone to help blot some of the rain.

The officers took a cursory survey, asking for a show of hands from anyone who had seen something suspicious outside. Nobody admitted seeing anything. We had all been working. Besides, it was raining. Who wanted to be out in that?

It occurred to me that it was too late to determine if someone had followed Tish outside—because they would have gotten wet. *Duh!* We could have checked everyone's shoes and hair and coats and maybe discovered Tish's attacker. But once Garth came in and broadcast the fact that Tish was hurt (or *dead*, as he had first reported), we'd all gone racing outside to see what had happened and ended up getting equally drenched.

So much for preserving evidence, if getting wet could be considered evidentiary. It was all beside the point, though, because Derek and I already *knew* who had assaulted Tish. We weren't about to announce it to the gathered staff and crew, though.

The cops took down everyone's names and phone numbers, and passed out their business cards, on the off chance that any of us recalled something significant.

"Was she robbed?" Todd asked. "She had a bunch of cash on her."

"We can't comment on that," one cop said.

Derek whispered in my ear, "I didn't find any money on her."

I grimaced. Had Tish's attacker stolen the money?

"So you're saying she was robbed?" one of the women said, her voice high and shaky. "Shouldn't we get more security for the parking lot?"

"She wasn't robbed," the officer said bluntly, in an obvious attempt to keep things calm. "But hiring more security wouldn't be a bad idea."

With that equivocal advice, the cop changed the subject and asked for a room to conduct interviews with a few of the witnesses. Namely, Derek and Garth.

"You can use one of the empty dressing rooms," Bruce said, taking charge. "But first, can you just tell us if you found a bunch of cash on Tish? She went out to buy pizzas for the crew."

"Ah," the taller cop said. "Guess that's why there's a stack of pizza boxes in her car."

There were a few muted sighs. It was hard to cheer for pizza when Tish was on her way to the hospital. The tall cop left with Bruce and two of his prop men to retrieve the food from Tish's car.

The other cop tracked down Garth, who had first announced the bad news about Tish. He looked scared to death as he was led away.

So Tish hadn't been robbed and that led some of the crew members to try to figure out why she'd been attacked. As if I didn't know! It was because she was wearing my new red raincoat. She was attacked because someone thought she was me. And there could be only one person who would do that: Grizzly Jones.

And that was bad news.

I'd had a premonition earlier that day when I arrived at the studio. Now I knew my gut check had been right on. Grizzly must have given up waiting for me at the Hall of Justice and decided to drive over to the studio to watch for me until I arrived. I had to assume his brother had told him where I worked. He must've arrived at about the same time I had and seen me in my red raincoat.

Had Grizzly been lying in wait out there until he saw me leave the studio for the night? Had he mistaken Tish for me and attacked her with deadly force? I knew the answers to all of the above were yes.

Luckily, Tish had survived, but that just meant that Grizzly would try again.

Earlier, as we'd waited for the ambulance to arrive, Tish had regained consciousness briefly. Her eyelids had fluttered and she'd mumbled something incomprehensible.

"Thank God," I'd murmured.

Derek had lifted her head up slightly. "Did you see who hurt you?"

"No," she'd said in a weak whisper. "Hit me from behind. Couldn't hear. The rain. I couldn't see."

She'd closed her eyes.

"Don't push her," I'd said, although I'd wanted to. I'd been so relieved that she was alive and I hoped that once she was feeling stronger, she might give us more details. It didn't matter, though, because I knew who'd done it to her.

A half hour later, Derek was finished with his police interview. "Let's go," he said, reaching for my hand. We got as far as the studio door before Tom hurried over and blocked our escape route.

"Okay, I admit it," he said in a rush. "You were right: we need more security. That stalker has gone too far this time. He's not targeting just Randy now. He's creating havoc with my people and I can't pretend to ignore it any longer." He rubbed both hands over his face, obviously upset. "I guess I figured Randy was just being a whiner, but this attack on Tish is too much. Can you get me the people I need?"

Derek and I exchanged glances. We'd agreed that Randy's stalker, whoever it was, had not been the one who'd attacked Tish, but we kept silent. If Tom was willing to hire Derek's security team to protect his staff and crew, I didn't care what justification he used. All that mattered was that everyone in the studio would be safer.

"I'll have two men and two women in place tomorrow," Derek said, all business now. "They'll be in plain clothing and you'll introduce them as new production assistants. They'll blend in—don't worry. I'll be here every day, too."

"Okay." Tom took a deep, shaky breath and let it out. "Okay. Sounds good."

"A brief word of warning," Derek added. "The fewer people who know why we're here, the better it'll be for everyone. Do I have your assurance that you'll keep the reason for our presence under wraps?"

"Absolutely," he said, nodding briskly. "Nobody will know except me and Walter."

Derek suggested that he introduce Tom and Walter to the new security agents and they agreed on a time to meet the following day in my dressing room. Then the two men shook hands. "See you tomorrow."

We left the studio and drove home together in Derek's Bentley. I didn't want to leave my car all night, but I was too tired to drive alone. Derek would come back to the studio tomorrow and stay with me all day, just as he'd promised. At some point, I would drive my own car home.

I couldn't imagine anything more boring for Derek than sitting in my dressing room all day, so I was extra grateful that he meant to keep his word. He really was a hero.

*T*he next morning we woke up to sunshine pouring through the windows. I was so glad the rain had passed—and not just because I didn't have my red raincoat anymore. The memory of Tish lying on the wet tarmac with blood trailing down her face was so awful, I had to jump out of bed and start moving, just to distract myself.

A while later, over bacon, eggs, and scones, we chatted about today's meeting with Derek's security team. I was excited at the prospect of getting to know some of his people, though I hated the circumstances under which we were meeting.

I must have had some kind of telling look on my face, because Derek reached over and squeezed my hand. "You're going to need a new coat, darling."

"Are you reading my mind again?" I asked lightly.

"I just know you. I had a feeling it might be bothering you."

"It is. I admit it." I set down my coffee cup. "I hate to be such an idiot, but I know I won't be able to wear it again. And it was so beautiful and you were so thoughtful to bring it home for me and

I really love it. But after seeing Tish lying there in the parking lot, with her head bleeding from that vicious attack, I can't . . ." I shook my head. "I know I could take the coat to the dry cleaners and it would probably be as good as new, but I'm not sure I can wear it again."

I shut my eyes tightly, so tired of listening to myself whine. "Oh, just ignore me, please. This isn't about the coat. I'm just so worried about Tish."

Derek squeezed my hand a bit tighter. "The coat was damaged in the commission of a violent crime. Tish was attacked precisely because she was wearing your coat. It makes me ill to think it could have been you out there in the rain. I refuse to let you wear it again."

"Well, when you put it like that."

He smiled with resolve. "That's exactly how I'd put it. Now, we can ask Tish if she wants to keep the coat. I can't imagine she will, but you never know. If she doesn't want it, we'll give it to the homeless shelter."

"All right," I said, somewhat mollified.

His smile widened. "Someone who needs it will have a warm coat. And I will have the pleasure of taking you to London and we'll make new memories together—while also getting you a new coat."

A little lump of emotion got caught in my throat. I jumped up from my chair and wrapped my arms around him. "You are the best thing in my world."

He rubbed my back. "And you're the best thing in my world."

"What a happy coincidence," I whispered.

"Come here, thing," he said, and pulled me onto his lap. We both smiled contentedly and sat snuggled up to each other for a few more minutes. It was a good start to the day.

As Derek drove the car out of our garage, he brought up the subject of *The Secret Garden*. "I keep circling back to that children's book. I know it's worth a lot of money, but I can't see those two brothers killing to get it back."

"We've both seen people kill for less," I reasoned.

"But this time the players are two extremely violent criminals. Psychopathic thugs. They're not your typical book lovers, to say the least. So why do they want this book? Why are they so willing to kill to get it?"

"I don't know. And it's not like they'll get away with it," I added. "The cops already know who they are. So even if they do manage to steal the book, they'll spend the rest of their lives in prison."

Derek glanced in his rearview mirror before changing lanes. "Let's play with the theory that they're not just after any old valuable book, but they're determined to track down this specific one. So there must be something about this book, in particular, that makes it beyond valuable to them."

"Yes, exactly. And I've been trying to come up with some possible motivations." I glanced over at him. "If you'll indulge me?"

He flashed a lopsided smile at me. "Please proceed."

"Okay." I readjusted myself in the seat so I was sitting facing him. "One scenario I came up with is that Grizzly was the one who originally stole the book. And don't ask me where he found it. I haven't worked that out yet. Anyway, let's say Lug Nut inadvertently threw the book in with a bunch of stuff for a garage sale. When Grizzly found out, he threatened to kill Lug Nut if he didn't get it back."

"Not bad," Derek said, nodding in accord. "That gives him a very strong motive. Namely, fear. He recognizes that his older brother wouldn't hesitate to kill him, so he's willing to kill someone else."

"I wouldn't be surprised to find out they've been beating each other up since they were kids."

"Or worse," Derek said. "Perhaps their father was abusive."

"Ugh." I shuddered at the thought, though even if it was true, it didn't give them the right to continue the cycle of violence. "Okay, another theory is that maybe they have a mother or a sister who always loved the book. Maybe Lug Nut wasn't paying attention the day he sold the book to Vera, and now he needs it back because his sister is dying of, I don't know, consumption. Or something." I wrinkled my nose. "That scenario's a little weak."

Derek chuckled. "It's a bit less plausible. But it makes sense in that they need *this* specific book as opposed to any old rare, expensive book."

I took another shot at it. "What if someone hired them to get the book back?"

"Who would hire them?"

"Someone mean who doesn't care if anyone gets hurt. I'm just offering possibilities."

"All right." Derek considered it. "But whoever it is, why would that person condone their killing someone?"

"Because it's a valuable book?" I said lamely, out of answers. "I don't know why anyone in their right mind would give the brothers permission to kill in order to get the book."

He nodded thoughtfully as he turned right on Sixteenth Street. "I assume the book is still in the safe."

"Yes. I was keeping it there until I got paid by Vera. Now I'm not sure what to do with it."

"Perhaps she has relatives who would inherit it."

"Maybe." Although I couldn't imagine Vera's relatives having any more interest in the book than Vera had had, other than the money they could make by selling it.

I pictured the beautiful book with its dazzling original cover painting and stunning craftsmanship. Then I pictured the hideous Jones brothers. Grizzly, standing on the street, threatening me. His equally disgusting brother, Lug Nut, grabbing me, bruising my arm, and smacking down Benny the guard.

On one hand, the precious book. On the other, the repugnant thugs. The two images were so incongruous, they made me dizzy. But I needed to figure out the connection between them before I became a target again.

Derek pulled to a stop at the red light at Sixteenth and De-Haro Street. "Love, perhaps it's time you did a little more research into the book itself."

"I was just coming to that same conclusion."

Everyone I met in the studio wanted to talk about Tish. Most of the women were still worried about security in the parking lot.

In an effort to quell nerves and get people back to work, Tom gathered the entire staff and crew together on the stage to make an announcement. "I just heard from Kenny. Tish is doing great. She's sitting up in bed and demanding that he get her the hell out of there." Everyone laughed and some began to applaud.

"But the doctors want to keep her there for one more day," he continued. "Just to make sure her concussion isn't more serious than they think."

Low murmurs of concern escalated quickly through the crowd.

"Hey, hey, it's just a precaution," Tom added quickly. "She's feeling great and expects to be back here working by Thursday."

This seemed to satisfy everyone enough to drop their security issues for the moment and they ambled back to work. I was thrilled to know that Tish would recover completely, but the knowledge did nothing to ease the guilt that was causing my stomach to twist and dip. Because, let's face it, she was in the hospital because of me.

"No," I muttered aloud. She was in the hospital because of those jackass Jones brothers.

That thought intensified my desire to seek a solid connection between the Thug Brothers and *The Secret Garden*. I headed for my dressing room to spend some time doing research on my computer, but when I got there, I found it packed with people.

"Oh, hello," I said. I'd forgotten Derek had chosen my room to meet with his small security force and introduce them to Tom.

"Brooklyn," Derek said, grabbing hold of the knob to keep the door open. "Let me introduce you to everyone."

I walked in and was soon shaking hands with George, Barbara, Steve, and Mindy. They were all in their late twenties or early thirties and looked smart and capable. Each wore casual street clothes except for George, who was wearing the same style guard's uniform that Benny wore.

"George isn't quite as undercover as the others," Derek explained. "I thought it would calm some of the frayed nerves to have an outward show of increased security on the set."

"I'm sure it will," I said. "Tom and Walter should be here any minute. I just saw them out onstage."

"Good," Derek said. "Before they get here, I want to reiterate that we've two security objectives. First and foremost, Brooklyn."

I waved weakly. "That's me."

Derek shot me a wry smile and then sobered. "We believe the man who attacked Tish last night is the brother of the man who assaulted Brooklyn last week. Brooklyn's assailant is currently in jail, but his brother is still on the loose. He's a dangerous thug who goes by the street name of Grizzly. I e-mailed descriptions of him and a short video to all of you last night."

"Grizzly." Mindy frowned. "His name suits him."

"It does," I assured her, glad that Derek had shown them the video from my phone.

"So he'll be hard to miss," Barbara added.

"He's a big, ugly sucker," I said. "There's no disguising his height and weight. Be careful if you run into him."

It was probably an unnecessary tip. These women—and men—worked security for Derek so they had to know every form of self-defense move known to man. *Unlike me,* I thought. But that would change soon. I couldn't wait for Alex to show me some moves that would make me feel a little more kick-ass and less wimplike.

Derek switched subjects. "Tom Darby and Walter Williams are the show's producers and you'll meet them in a moment. They're the only ones who know your true reason for being here. You three will be introduced to the other staff and crew members as new production assistants and you'll be expected to do whatever the job entails. George, you're the new security guard Tom hired. You'll act accordingly, patrolling the stage areas, keeping your eyes and ears open for any trouble. If any of the women want to be escorted to their cars, go ahead and do that."

"It'll be my pleasure," George said smartly.

Mindy batted her eyelashes. "Who doesn't love a man in uniform?"

The others snorted with laughter and I joined them, pleased to know that Derek had hired such likable people.

"We've got a few wrinkles," Derek said, interrupting the merriment. "First of all, Tom believes he's hired us to protect his people from a stalker who's been tormenting the star of the show, Randolph Rayburn. Randy has been stalked for the past six months by an unknown person, so we have no physical description."

Derek gave them all a brief rundown of the things the stalker had done in the past, the last of which may have been the peanut-allergy scare. "He—or she—has never threatened Randolph physically before, so his behavior appears to be escalating."

"The stalker could be anyone in this building," I added. "Randy's a good-looking guy, so I thought we might be dealing with a woman, but he's not convinced."

"So, to be clear," George said, "our assignment is to protect Randolph and Brooklyn, not the general population."

"Brooklyn and Randolph," Derek corrected, spearing each of

his employees with a meaningful stare, just so there would be no mistaking the fact that I was their primary job. I wished us all luck with that.

"Yes," Derek continued, "they're the primary assignments. However, there's an adjunct problem. While the stalker seems obsessed only with Randolph, the assailant who attacked Brooklyn is capable of hurting anyone who gets in his way."

"So everyone here is at risk," Barbara said.

"Yes," Derek said. "Hypervigilance is called for at all times."

George gave a brisk nod. "Got it, boss."

After the producers and Derek's security force went off to work the studio, I spent the rest of the day—whenever I wasn't working onstage—holed up in my dressing room, doing more research on *The Secret Garden*.

I went back to all the rare-book sites I had visited during my original research of Vera's book. The books I'd used for comparison were still available at each site, so I pored over their history and origin again, soaking up whatever skimpy background information they could provide on Frances Hodgson Burnett, the author.

Because I worked on books for a living, I often studied the writers and other book industry professionals, as well. If I was hired to track the provenance of a particular book, it was important to check out the publisher and even the original bookbinder and his bindery. That's where I often found some interesting connections.

So in the hope of finding a connection, *any* connection, between Lug Nut and Grizzly Jones and this particular copy of *The Secret Garden*, I was willing to dig deeply into the background of Frances Hodgson Burnett. If that entailed going out on a limb or sliding down a rabbit hole to discover some helpful snippet of information, I would do it.

Not that I seriously believed the author of *The Secret Garden* would turn out to be Grizzly's long-lost grandmother. Or great aunt. Or their mother's third cousin's beloved fifth-grade teacher. Or whoever. On the other hand, anything was possible. It didn't pay to ignore the tiniest clue.

Reading about Frances Hodgson Burnett reminded me that authors were truly an odd bunch. I always enjoyed discovering little ironies in their lives, and in Frances's case there were some fascinating ones. She had begun writing *The Secret Garden* while plotting out her own garden at the home she was building on Long Island. The young characters in her book began to thrive once they were able to draw from the redemptive power of nature, as one reviewer called it, referring to the plants and flowers within the walled garden of the book.

Frances evidently had thrived in the garden, as well. By every account, she loved gardening, right down to the dirty job of weeding. In one passage, her description of pulling weeds sounded more like a fierce warrior describing a battle than a gardener noting a small infestation of plants.

On another Web site, I found one measly tidbit of a story about Mrs. Burnett visiting New York City and taking in a Broadway play. It didn't connect to any other aspect of her life in New York, though. Did she have an interest in playwriting? The theater? Big-city nightlife? It seemed to be a throwaway line, but I wanted to know more.

According to friends, Frances had a strong temper, but I couldn't find out who or what it had been aimed at. She was said to have suffered mentally and physically, but nothing explained why or to what extent.

I smiled when I read that her close friends called her Fluffy. It didn't jibe with the claim that she had a strong temper, and other than the theory that she occasionally wore wigs and frilly clothing, I could find no satisfactory explanation for the nickname.

On a hunch, I Googled *Frances Hodgson Burnett heirs*, but all that produced was a brief outline of *Little Lord Fauntleroy*. The main character, poor young Cedric, receives a message from his grandfather, the earl, that with the death of his brothers, Cedric is now a lord and *heir* to the earldom and a vast estate.

A horrifying image sprang to mind, of Grizzly and Lug Nut wearing blue velveteen jackets and knee pants with ruffled collars and curls in their hair.

I shuddered in revulsion and shut down the computer. There had to be more information, but I'd reached too many dead ends on the Internet. All of these short biographical bits and sketches were leading me nowhere.

If I wanted to know more about Frances Hodgson Burnett, I was going to have to access a more extensive database than was available on my own computer through Google or Wikipedia or even her book publisher's Web site with its page devoted specifically to the author and her books.

But would anything I found relate back to Lug Nut and Grizzly Jones's relentless pursuit of *The Secret Garden*? Was I wasting my time? I wouldn't know until I did the work. I just knew I wasn't willing to give up yet. There had to be a connection somewhere.

My mood brightened as I realized exactly where I could do my research. The Covington Library, one of my favorite places in the world. I would run over there as soon as it opened tomorrow morning and work for a few hours before going to the studio. Maybe I could mix a little business with pleasure and convince Ian to have lunch with me. After all, my showbiz career would soon be coming to an end and Ian was good at coming up with new bookbinding gigs. I was even willing to pay for lunch.

Chapter Fourteen

The following morning, Derek drove me across town to the Covington Library. He brought the Bentley to a stop directly in front of the imposing building at the top of Pacific Heights, but kept the engine running. "I'm still not sure this is a good idea," he said.

"Then park the car and come inside with me," I said gently, resting my hand on his thigh. "You can take a look around and make sure things are copacetic."

He scowled for a moment, but quickly shook off the gloom. "All right." It was early still, so he found a parking spot within a few feet of the front of the main building.

Derek was rarely unsure of himself, but this week had been a strange one for both of us. We had decided over breakfast that he would drop me off at the library, knowing I would be safe inside the building while Derek spent a few necessary hours at his office over on California Street, near the top of Nob Hill.

But when he was faced with actually leaving me and driving away, he was having a difficult time. His protectiveness tugged at a tender little spot near my heart. I knew what a dilemma it was for him, so I slid my arm through his and held on as we walked.

"I'll be fine," I assured him. "This place is crawling with security guards."

"And I'm certain they're all nice people," he muttered. "I'm just not sure they've run a hundred-yard dash in the past ten years, or jogged down a flight of stairs in pursuit of a vicious thug."

"I'm not in any danger here," I insisted. "I plan to hide away in a quiet cubbyhole on the third floor. Nobody will even know I'm there."

He stopped and stroked my hair. "So beautiful, yet so naive."

I laughed and smacked his chest. "Oh, shut up."

We entered through the main doorway of the dignified Italianate-style mansion and I took a moment to breathe in the magic. I'd been coming to the Covington since I was a little girl and had never grown tired of it.

We lowered our voices as we walked through the main library. Not because it was a church or some other holy place, but because the dignity of the room itself and the magnificence of the ancient and rare books displayed behind glass walls conveyed a silent message: *Take time to look, listen, learn, revere.* There were universal secrets within these walls, within these books.

One of my teachers used to say that a civilization that didn't respect its books was destined to die off.

The guy had probably stolen that quote from someone else, but I believed it completely and felt it anew every time I walked into the Covington.

Derek and I trekked through the east gallery and down the arched hall that led to the new Children's Book Museum. A door to the left led to the administrative offices.

At the end of another hall, we came to a closed door. Unintimidated, I pushed it open and we entered a big, bustling office that fanned out as wide as the length of the building. Eight large cubicles were spread across the expanse, each one occupied by an assistant who played gatekeeper to whomever was working inside the executive offices behind those eight doors.

The impressive double doors in the center led into Ian's office. I'd started calling him the Grand Poobah since he had recently been promoted to president of the museum and still acted as their chief curator. A very notable achievement, although he still had to answer to a distinguished board of trustees as well as to old Mrs. Covington herself, whose bazillionaire father had first established the elegant museum, library, and gardens back in the twenties.

"There's Wylie," I said, waving at Ian's longtime assistant. "How are you?"

"I'm living the dream, Ms. Wainwright," Wylie said, flashing me an angelic smile that hid a keen wit. Picking up his phone, he whispered something. After a few seconds, he hung up. "You can go right in. He can't wait to see you."

"Thanks, Wylie."

Derek knocked, then cracked open the door.

Ian stood and met us halfway across the office. "Hey, you two."

"Hello, mate," Derek said. The two men shook hands, then gave each other one of those manly hugs with lots of back slaps.

"Hi, Ian," I said, and hugged him, too. "Can you join me for an early lunch today? My treat. We can go to the Rose Room."

The Rose Room was the Covington's charming tea shop situated outside the main building near the terraced rose garden on the northwest side of the library. The quaint Victorian-style restaurant was a big draw on sunny days because you could sit and stare out at the Golden Gate Bridge and the rugged Marin County coastline.

"I can't," Ian groused. "I've got a damn lunch meeting scheduled. Can we do it tomorrow?"

"Yes, but I have to leave for the studio by one o'clock."

"Shouldn't be a problem."

Derek checked his watch and I took the cue. "I'm in good hands."

"Yes, I see. So I'll be going. Great to see you, Ian."

"You, too. And don't worry. I'll make sure she stays out of trouble."

Derek shot me a stern look, then nodded at Ian. "I trust you've ordered in extra security."

I laughed lightly and kissed him good-bye. The fact that he was willing to leave meant that he trusted I would be safe here.

A few minutes later, after settling on a time for our lunch the next day, I left Ian and headed back to the large foyer at the entrance to get the elevator for the third floor.

Passing through the main room of the library again, I gazed up at the elegant coffered ceiling three stories above me. I loved this upward-facing view, with its stunning art deco light fixtures and intricate wrought-iron balconies that wrapped around the outer perimeter of the second and third floors.

Glass-fronted dark oak bookshelves lined the narrow walkways. Every few yards, an open door led off to an even narrower hall that ended up in a cozy reading room or in a tiny nook big enough for an individual study carrel, one chair, and a lamp. This was where my computer and I were headed and I was excited to get to work, plug into the Covington's international database, and do some deep Internet surfing.

As I pushed the elevator button, I had a flashing thought that the only thing I was in danger of here was running into Minka LaBoeuf, my archrival, worst enemy, and the world's most disastrous bookbinder. Ian had a kindhearted but misguided tendency to hire her for contract book jobs when he couldn't get anyone else to do the work.

I shuddered from the instant chill I got whenever Minka's visage passed through my consciousness. I shook my head vigorously to dislodge all thoughts of her before stepping inside the elevator.

The only good that came from being reminded of Minka was that I wasn't focused on Grizzly and Lug Nut for the moment. It was the lesser of two evils, I supposed, but not by much.

Once on the third floor, I turned right and found the long, narrow hallway. This place was a rabbit warren of passageways and alcoves and dead ends. It was all part of its charm, and yet I was often tempted to bring bread crumbs with me to find my way out.

I finally found a comfortably isolated carrel and arranged my computer and notes and got to work.

Two hours later, my cell phone buzzed. Knowing my tendency to get drawn into my work, I had cleverly set the alarm to alert me when it was time to go.

Derek would be swinging by to pick me up in thirty minutes. That would give me just enough time to finish up and find my way back to Ian's office.

Based on what I'd read, I wanted to ask him a few questions.

"We have a number of collectors of her children's books," Ian said when I asked him about Frances Hodgson Burnett. I had caught him getting ready to leave for his lunch meeting so I walked out of the building with him.

"But no experts on the author herself?"

"No. That is, no one who's expert enough to give you the kind of intimate background knowledge you're looking for."

I had expected as much, but I was still disappointed. "In that case, I'll just download her biography onto my phone reader."

"You can read off that little screen?"

"I can skim," I hedged, hating to admit that I didn't like to read books on a screen. As a bookbinder, I was partial to holding the book in my hand. I liked the feel of paper and leather and cloth. But I wasn't about to judge anyone else's choices when it came to reading. Any contraption that got people to read was a good thing.

We reached the sidewalk and I spied Derek's black Bentley a few parking spots down the hill. I gave Ian a quick hug. "I'll be back tomorrow. Don't forget lunch."

"I've already made reservations for eleven thirty."

I turned. "Oh, but I'm buying."

He chuckled. "I'm happy to let you buy. I just called ahead to make sure we get the best table in the house."

"Wonderful." It was good to have friends in high places.

"*A*nd we're clear!" Angie pressed her fingers to her earpiece to listen for a moment, then announced loudly, "We'll shoot the next segment on the kitchen stage in fifteen minutes, people. Fifteen minutes!"

I had finished the research for my next book segment earlier, so Derek and I could remain onstage to watch some of the other experts on camera. It was a nice change from being cooped up in my dressing room.

A flurry of excited voices rose behind us. Tish was walking into the studio, and even though she looked wiped out and had a bandage taped across her temple, I felt a flood of relief at seeing her.

She leaned heavily on Kenny's arm as she greeted her close friends, but then left them all and approached me.

"I'm so sorry," she said, her voice a whisper. "I had to give your coat to the police. They thought they might be able to retrieve a fingerprint from the leather strap around the neck or one of the buttons."

"I hope they can," I said, and gave her a light hug. "But please don't worry about the coat. I'm just glad you're okay."

"I'm getting there."

I glanced around, then leaned closer. "Did you get a look at the person who attacked you?"

"I didn't. The police asked me all kinds of questions, but I was no help at all."

"Did you hear anything? Footsteps or breathing or a car taking off or . . . anything?"

She pursed her lips in thought. "I thought I heard someone coughing, but that could've been the guard."

"I know I'm being a nudge, but did you smell anything unusual? Perfume or garlic or something?"

Her eyes widened. "Oh. I did. I smelled cigarette smoke. I remember thinking it was weird because I don't know anyone who smokes anymore."

"See? You know more than you thought you did."

"Wow, you're good, Brooklyn. You should be a cop."

I almost laughed out loud, imagining what Inspector Lee would say to that.

Tish and Kenny wandered over to the gaffer's podium and I turned to Derek. "It was Grizzly—I know it was. I saw him smoking a cigarette out on the steps of the Hall of Justice."

"A lot of people smoke, darling," Derek said, playing devil's advocate, no doubt.

"Yes, but not a lot of smokers go looking for someone in a red raincoat so they can knock her unconscious." Angry all over again at the picture of that big creep attacking Tish, I bared my teeth. "I can't wait to see that slug behind bars with his creepy brother."

"Nor can I."

"I'm sick of just waiting around for him to attack again." Saying the words aloud jogged my memory, reminding me of my idea of luring Lug Nut out into the open using myself as bait. I could still carry out the plan with Grizzly.

Derek was studying my expression and his own turned icy. "Don't even think about it."

"Think about what?"

"Using yourself as bait."

I blinked, astonished and annoyed that he could guess my thoughts so accurately. "Why would you think I would ever do that?"

"Because I know you too well." He wrapped his arm around my shoulders and pulled me close. "And sometimes you scare me to death."

An hour later, I left my dressing room, carrying the next book I would be appraising. It was a Geneva Bible from 1583, and it was huge. Over fifteen inches tall and ten inches wide, it was five inches thick and the heaviest book I'd ever appraised. I was hoping the book's owner and the show's producers would enjoy this segment as much as I planned to.

I'd been told by the producers that the show didn't usually appraise family Bibles because they didn't have much commercial value. In the late eighteen hundreds they were being mass-produced and many families had been able to buy one. In general, they were well made with good-quality paper and leather and often remained in the family for generations. But other than their sentimental value, they weren't worth a lot.

This Geneva Bible was different. I knew there were books similar to this one out there, but I'd personally never seen anything like it before. It gave me a thrill just to hold it in my hands.

I stopped in the hall when I realized I hadn't checked the condition of the interior back hinges. I'd spent time examining only the front hinges because the front of the book was so striking, with its decorative gilding and ancient brass workings.

I couldn't go out onstage without completing the work, so I glanced around for a place to set down the book and check it out. It had to weigh at least ten pounds and was growing heavier by the second, so when I noticed Randy's dressing room door was ajar, I quickly knocked and walked in. He wasn't there, so I placed the book on the dressing table, where the light was strongest.

The door slammed shut.

It must've been a gust of wind in the hallway, I thought, and ignored it. I turned the book over. The back cover was in need of a decent polishing but the hinge and brass works were in fine condition. This entire book was beyond fabulous. I was pretty sure it would win the prize for the highest book appraisal of any of the San Francisco shows.

But after dealing with a few people who couldn't quite handle the fact that they had an expensive book on their hands, I was a little concerned that the owner . . .

I heard an odd rattling sound and glanced around. I didn't see anything, so I went back to the book. The back endpapers were in better condition than the front ones, which was typical, since people tended to expose the front papers more often than the back.

I picked up the heavy Bible and adjusted it in my arms, then reached for the doorknob. It wouldn't budge. "What the heck?"

The rattling sound echoed through the room. I turned again but didn't see anything.

Suddenly a deadly-looking snake slithered out from under the sofa and headed straight toward me.

I froze in complete horror and screamed louder than I'd ever screamed in my life. I pressed up closer to the door, but there was nowhere to go.

The thing had to be five feet long!

Scared to death, I shook the doorknob but couldn't open it to save my life. Literally.

"Help!" I screamed over and over as I banged my hand against the door. "Somebody help me!"

The snake moved closer. It was only a few feet away now. If I stood very still, would it ignore me and go away? I kind of doubted it.

Its head wafted up off the floor and I screamed. "Get away from me!"

That's when its tail began to shake again, making the dreadful rattling sound I'd just heard.

Desperate, I realized I had only one weapon: the Bible. With both hands, I slammed it down on the head of the snake and heard a squishing sound. I knew I'd crushed it or at least made serious contact.

Tremors overtook my body, rushing up and down my spine and arms and legs. I was still screaming and collapsed back against the door. At that moment, someone yanked it open and I fell backward into the hall.

"What were you doing in there?" Randy demanded.

I scrambled and grabbed hold of him and held on for dear life.

"What's wrong with you?" But he wrapped his arms around me and patted my back. "You're shivering. What happened?"

"Oh, God." I gasped for breath. "Oh, God. Thank you."

"Brooklyn, are you all right?"

"Derek. Oh, Derek." I spun around and threw myself into his arms. He clutched me tightly.

"What is it, love? What happened?"

"Snake." The word came out like a breath of air.

"What?"

"Snake."

"A snake?" Randy said loudly. "What the hell are you talking about?"

"Snake." I pointed at the doorway. "Dressing room. Dead."

"Christ almighty," Derek said, and turned on Randy. "What the hell were you thinking, bringing a snake in here?"

"Me?" he shouted. "No! I didn't do anything!"

"How did a snake get into your room?"

"How the hell should I know? I was out onstage when I got a text from Walter telling me to meet him here. I get here and find Brooklyn in there with the door closed."

"I couldn't get the door open." I could hear myself whimpering, but I didn't care. I clutched Derek's arms for dear life.

He continued to hold me close with one arm and pushed the door open wider with the other.

"Looks like a rattler," Randy said, and whistled. "Holy mother."

The Bible lay splayed on the floor on top of the creature. The back cover was hanging loosely off its hinges. I felt a twinge of guilt, but not enough to keep me awake at night. The value of the book might have been momentarily diminished, but at least the snake was dead.

*T*he snake survived.

Bloodied and bruised, it nonetheless began to wiggle while we were standing there staring at it. I screamed and Randy jumped three feet backward, then ran out to the stage. Derek pulled me out of the room and slammed the door shut.

Seconds later, Bruce came racing down the hall and took over. He managed to wrangle the injured reptile using a lighting pole and one of the pretty covered baskets they used as set decoration on the kitchen stage.

It turned out that Bruce was a certified exotic animal trainer, a prerequisite to working on an Animal Network show a few years back.

Obviously, Randolph had been the intended victim of the snake. It was just my luck to wander into his room. Derek cornered Walter and asked him if he'd sent the text to Randy. He denied it and then couldn't find his phone. Someone—Randy's stalker, no doubt—had taken it. One of the prop guys found it a while later, tucked behind one of the boxes of doughnuts on the catering table.

I was shaken and still breathing heavily, but I needed to tape my segment. Derek suggested that I ask to postpone it, but I wanted to get it over with. And I was pretty sure it would take my mind off killer snakes and broken Bibles.

Derek picked up the heavy Bible and took care of wiping the bits of snake blood and guts off the book. I couldn't watch. I was too busy wondering what excuse I would give the book's owner for breaking and bloodying a holy book that had managed to survive in this world for almost five hundred years—until the moment I got hold of it.

"How did you come to own this Bible, Jack?" I asked casually. Nobody would ever know I'd just been threatened by a rattlesnake.

"I recently inherited it from my grandfather, who was a biblical scholar. It's my understanding that he never had it appraised because he thought that would be blasphemous."

"Rendering unto Caesar?" I said, trying for a bit of levity.

He grinned. "Exactly. Grandfather was not known for breaking the rules."

I slipped into appraiser mode to describe the woodcuts on the title page and in the text throughout the book, many of which were printed in red ink. It was a quarto edition, which meant that the pages were sewn together four at a time. Without moving the book too much and giving away the fact that the back cover was hanging by one hinge, I pointed out that the dark brown leather cover was framed and paneled in heavy gilt with raised bands on the spine and gilded lettering.

"The most unusual aspect of the cover, and typical of Bibles of that age," I said, "are these brass corner protectors. The hinges of the book are brass, too. The engravings on this brass clasp and closure are spectacular. And they still work."

"I've tried to keep my kids from playing with the clasp," Jack said. "I'd like it to last another five hundred years, if possible."

"That would be nice." I smiled and added, "There are very few cracks in the leather. He really kept it in great condition."

"He loved that book," Jack said with a sad smile. "I'm not very religious myself, but I could tell it was worth a little something."

"Oh, it is," I said enigmatically. "The paper is thick and bright, with hardly any tearing. There's a bit of foxing, but that's to be expected. It's still easy to read."

"I can't believe something that old is printed in English," he said. "I figured it would be old German or something."

"It was the first English Bible printed after the Reformation," I explained. "The reason it's called a Geneva Bible is because it was first printed in Geneva, Switzerland. It was meant to be affordable so that a family could purchase it and study it together." I lifted the book carefully and opened it to a representative page. "As you can see, there are margin notes, which were meant to aid in the study of the Scriptures."

"Wow."

"So all of that means that it's a very important book historically. And visually, as well. You can see that it's exceptional."

"I can see that it's huge," Jack said with a grin.

"And very heavy." *Thank goodness,* I added silently. Otherwise, I wouldn't have been able to almost kill a freaking five-foot-long rattlesnake with it. "By the way, I don't know if you've noticed, Jack, but the back cover has come loose from its hinges. It's a simple fix and I'll be happy to take care of it for you after the program."

"Really? That's great. I didn't know you did that here."

"This is a special case, and there's no charge," I added with a bright smile. *Because I'm the one who smashed it against the head of the snake and damaged it all to hell.* No guilt there.

"Well, thank you very much."

"You're welcome," I said. "Thanks for bringing it in today. It's an exceptional book and easily worth my appraisal price of forty-eight thousand dollars."

His mouth opened and closed a few times. "W-what?"

"Forty-eight thousand—"

"D-dollars? Holy moly." He tried to swallow a few times but couldn't, and he looked like he was struggling for air. A stagehand rushed over with his own cup of water and handed it to Jack, who gulped it down. He wheezed a few times and coughed.

This was getting to be a regular occurrence.

"Are you going to be all right?" I asked finally.

"Holy moly." He buried his face in his hands for a moment, then lifted his head. "Damn, Grandpa, what were you thinking?"

"Why do you say that, Jack?"

He pressed his lips together, swallowed once more, and whispered, "He said he didn't have enough money to go through with an operation, so he stayed home and died."

"I'm so sorry," I said, reaching over to squeeze Jack's arm lightly. "Perhaps the book was more important to him than his health."

"Yeah." He shook his head, still a little bewildered. "Like I said, he was pretty religious."

"It's obvious that he revered the book, so my hope is that you'll be able to enjoy it as much as he did. It really is a work of art."

"Oh, I will. The whole family will. It was a part of him and his father before him, so I'll keep it as a centerpiece of our home."

"That sounds wonderful."

"But wow," he said. "Forty-eight thousand dollars coulda put a lot of meat on the table, I'll tell you that for nothing."

"It was definitely a rattlesnake," Derek confirmed, and handed me a glass of red wine.

I couldn't say anything to that, just clutched my wineglass and tried to keep from trembling again.

It took two glasses to calm me down. Derek shot back two fingers of scotch. We sat sprawled on opposite ends of the couch with our feet touching.

"Bruce informed me that snakes can be quite resilient," Derek continued. "He'll take the creature to a rescue facility he's familiar with and it'll be nursed back to health."

"I'm glad," I said, though my tone didn't fit the words. It wasn't that I wished the snake were dead. I just wished I'd never seen it before.

"The door lock had been switched out," Derek explained. "So someone could lock it on the outside as usual, but anyone inside the room couldn't open it."

"Jeez." I took another long sip of wine. "That took some time and planning. They would've had to do it overnight, because they'd have been seen during the day."

Derek scowled. "I'm sorry I didn't foresee this, but from now on I'll have a team on duty at night. George and Barbara are staying there tonight, and Mindy and Steve will take tomorrow night. They'll switch off as long as necessary."

"Good," I said. "I mean, too late for me and the snake, but good going forward."

Derek moved to my end of the couch and wrapped his arms around me. He felt comforting and warm and I leaned into him.

"The peanuts were a dangerous threat," he said, "but at least Randy had his EpiPen."

"Yes, but now a rattlesnake?" I said, starting to shiver again. "What kind of lunatic brings a rattlesnake to work?"

Chapter Fifteen

A little while later, we were heading for bed when I realized I couldn't sleep before reading some of Frances Hodgson Burnett's biography. I took my phone to bed with me and vowed to stay up for fifteen minutes only.

Skimming through the pages, I read that Frances was born in England but lived for a long time outside of New York City. She was married, then divorced, then married again but for only two years. She had two children but one died at age sixteen. Did the child who lived go on to spawn the parents of Lug Nut and Grizzly? That was a long shot.

I shook my head. No, it wasn't just *long*. This was the *longest* shot I'd ever taken. But I couldn't afford to pass up a possible clue.

I found more references to Broadway shows and now the reason was obvious. *Little Lord Fauntleroy*, Frances's best-known book at the time, had been turned into a Broadway play.

Tucked into the anecdotal comments made by her contemporaries was one reference to another show she attended that starred a young Mae West. Frances had been amused by the bawdy young actress and had invited her and the other cast members to her Long Island home for tea. Frances's friends also mentioned how they all

enjoyed seeing George M. Cohan and an up-and-coming inge-
nue, Helen Hayes, on Broadway.

I thought it was charming that the creator of *Little Lord
Fauntleroy* could also enjoy a risqué revue like the one that had
featured Mae West. But I still couldn't quite picture Mae West
sitting down for tea with an English gentlewoman. They must
have made quite a pair.

But so what?

"Have you found what you were looking for?" Derek murmured.

I flinched. "I'm sorry. Did I wake you up?"

"No, darling." He sat up and drank some water.

Glancing at the clock, I saw that it was almost two o'clock in
the morning. My eyes were raw from reading off the little screen.
"I'm probably wasting my time with this."

"Nothing is a waste of time when you're following leads," he
assured me. "Everything you're looking into will either confirm
or eliminate the book as the prime motive for killing Vera. You're
checking every possible scenario, weighing all the odds. All of it
will add to the big picture. And, love, no one else is capable of
connecting the book to her death but you."

"I know you're right, even though it feels like I'm grasping at
straws." Seriously, how could Frances's random run-in with a fu-
ture movie star like Mae West or Helen Hayes have even the
slightest connection to Grizzly or Lug Nut Jones?

With a sigh, I plugged in my phone to charge it and turned off
the light.

And in the dark, I wondered how Derek had managed to
sound so articulate at this hour of the morning.

Early the next day, Derek was dressed and hard at work in our
second bedroom office. He would be tied up on a conference
call with his London office for the next hour, so I pulled Vera's

copy of *The Secret Garden* from its hiding place in my hall closet. Could it hold the answers I was looking for? Perhaps it had a secret pocket in the back cover that was stuffed with money or the deed to a ranchero somewhere.

Fine, I probably wouldn't discover a deed. But maybe something about the author's signature or the original painting on the cover would give me a clue to a connection to the Jones brothers.

Perhaps they were related to the illustrator. I made a mental note to check later at the Covington.

Or maybe there was something to do with the binding itself. I'd disregarded the bookbinder's connection before but now I wondered if the original bindery was an important one.

I yawned as I headed for the kitchen. I'd been up way too late the night before. Now I was desperate for coffee. Thank goodness Derek had turned on the coffeemaker.

I took my coffee to my workroom and gathered my supplies— mainly, my most powerful magnifying glass. Once I'd scanned the book up close, I would figure out what needed to be done next.

I took a few big gulps of coffee and then left the mug on my desk. I never allowed myself to keep liquids on my worktable. That was a disaster waiting to happen.

I unwrapped the soft cloth around the book and gazed at it for the first time in more than a week. It was like seeing a museum masterpiece after a long while. I noticed new details, new colors. A piece of chalk on the ground by the little girl's booted feet. The swirls of vibrant blue ribbon at the end of the title banner above the artwork. The depth and luminescence of the gilding on the edges of the front cover.

With a contented sigh, I picked up the magnifying glass to examine the painting of the little girl in the red coat again. The swath of red was so joyful, so—

I dropped the magnifying glass and sat back in my chair, staggered. The girl in the red coat. That was me! Or it was supposed to have been me, anyway, until Tish had taken my place and suffered the hurtful consequences.

How weird was that? There were those shivers again. What were the chances? Was there possibly a connection between . . . ?

I almost groaned out loud. "It's not always all about you, miss."

Maybe not, but wasn't it interesting that I had a red coat and the little girl on the cover had a red coat, too?

It's just a silly coincidence, I insisted silently, and mentally smacked myself. *Now get back to work.*

I picked up the magnifying glass again. And prayed I wasn't the only weirdo in the world who carried on these little arguments with herself.

Soon I was lost in the book again. After serious examination, I came to the sad realization that there were no secret pockets anywhere in the book. But as I studied the book, I decided to go ahead and do the work I'd planned to do for Vera, for free. The book deserved to be spruced up, and it was my way of honoring poor Vera, as well.

If Vera had any family, they would be able to obtain the highest price possible for the book. And if none of Vera's relations came forward to claim it, then the Covington Library might want it. In that case, I could recoup my time from them.

After checking the outer covers and the end pages, I opened the book to study the limitation page again. Frances's signature was original and seemed to be in order. To be certain, I compared it to several ephemera Web sites that sold cards and books autographed by her. It wasn't the most comprehensive way to ensure authenticity, but it was close enough for my purposes.

I turned to the flyleaf page inside the front cover to study the second signature and date. This time I used the powerful magnifying glass to take a good, close look. I hadn't examined it in much detail the first time because it wasn't something I was willing to erase or repair. But now, if I could figure out whose signature it was, it might provide a clue. It was a long shot but I didn't have much more to go on.

I was able to decipher the date more quickly than the signature itself. It read *Sept. 7, 12.* I'd seen dates jotted down this way in the early days, with only the last two numbers of the year represented. So the person whom I assumed was the original owner had signed the book on September 7, 1912.

The signature itself was trickier. Through the magnifying glass I could see the concentric swirls and dips typical of a young woman's signature of this era.

I'd already established that the first name began with *M*. The second name began with either a *J* or a *T*.

Mary Jo. Mary Jane. Mary June? Mary Theresa. Mary Todd?

"Hey, Mary Todd Lincoln," I muttered. "Not likely."

I moved to the last name. The last three letters looked like *est*. So it was a matter of figuring out the first letter. I went down the alphabet. *Best. Jest. Nest. West.*

West was the most likely guess, given the dramatic swirl of the first letter. Mary Jane West? Mary Jo West?

I had a lightbulb moment and decided I could Google all of these possible names together with the year 1912.

A minute later, I stared in stunned silence at the computer screen.

Mary Jane West, known as Mae West, was an American actress, singer, playwright, screenwriter, and sex symbol whose . . .

Mae West.

"Oh, my God." I almost laughed. I'd read about the two women having had tea together. Still, how was it possible that this rare edition of *The Secret Garden* was once owned by Mae West, one of the most famous sex symbols in the world?

My father had loved W. C. Fields, so I had seen Mae West in *My Little Chickadee* at least six or eight times while growing up.

She was coarse and earthy and in-your-face funny. I remembered all of us laughing at the double entendres flying back and forth. Even as kids, we understood many of the naughty jokes, except for the most provocative ones.

Mae West hardly seemed the type to own a copy of a beloved children's book, but the connection was there. Vague, but it was there. So now that I had established a tenuous relationship between Frances and Mae West, how was I supposed to figure out how those two women were linked to Lug Nut and Grizzly?

I felt a wave of guilt for ever ridiculing the possible bond between Mae West and the two thugs.

"Because you just never know," I mumbled, still not over the shock of finding an actual connection.

I wrapped the white cloth around the book and slipped it into my computer bag. I needed more information and I knew exactly where to get it.

"You must meet Edward Strathmore," Ian said enthusiastically. "You'll love him. He's charming and a bit eccentric but extremely generous. He's given so much to the library."

"He sounds like a dream come true for you," I said, and took a small bite of my chicken salad.

"He is," Ian said with a smile, before adding, "And for you, too, because he's quite possibly the world's foremost expert in all things related to Mae West."

I blinked. "Are you kidding?"

"Nope."

"Well, why didn't you say so?" I said. "When can I meet him?"

"I'm not sure." He bit into his curried chicken sandwich. "I'll try to reach him after lunch."

We were seated at the best table in the lovely Rose Room, right by the bay window that overlooked the colorful rose garden, the wooded Presidio, and the sparkling Bay with the Golden Gate Bridge in the distance.

I could barely concentrate on the view because I was dying to know more about Edward Strathmore. On the other hand, I had no problem concentrating on my delightful lunch of tea and a variety of crustless mini sandwiches, followed by scones, jam, and tea.

"Does he live in San Francisco?" I asked, as I slathered homemade jam onto my scone, topped by a blob of clotted cream. "It doesn't matter. I'll travel to wherever he is."

As soon as I said the words, I knew I had a problem. I wouldn't be able to travel anywhere with my television schedule. "Or maybe we can talk on the phone."

Ian took a quick sip of his tea. "He lives in Belvedere and works out of his home, so he's probably available almost any day you are."

Belvedere was a small, upscale community in Marin County. *Upscale* as in "multimillion-dollar Bay-front homes with incomparable views of the city and the Bay."

"I'm available tomorrow," I said promptly, "or anytime he's willing to meet me."

He grinned. "I'll call him and set it up as soon as I get back to my office."

I secretly feared I would be struck with some sort of posttraumatic snake stress when I returned to the studio, but it didn't happen. Randy, on the other hand, looked horrible. I met up with him at the coffee and doughnut table and his face was pale, almost chalky.

"Are you all right?"

He groaned and rubbed his stomach. "No."

"Why don't you go home?" I asked.

"Because I've got post-segment interviews with the owners

and eight intros, plus a bunch of teasers to tape." He grimaced and grabbed a can of cola. After popping it open, he took a long swig.

"You seriously look like hell."

"I appreciate that," he drawled, but couldn't quite pull off the sarcasm.

"I'm worried about you. Do you think you have the flu?"

"I never get sick."

I peered closely at him. "Is this about the snake?"

He shook his head. "No, every trace of it is gone. Derek and George, that new guard, searched my dressing room to make sure there weren't any more surprises. And then Garth went in and cleaned and disinfected the place from top to bottom. It's just psychological, I guess."

"Psychological stress is as real as any other kind."

"Thank you, Doctor Freud."

I chuckled as I poured a dollop of cream into my coffee. "You've still got your crappy sense of humor, so I guess you'll be okay."

"I'll be fine." We took our drinks and walked backstage toward the dressing room hallway. "I'm going to have Chuck add a little bronzer to my makeup so I look healthier."

"Good. We wouldn't want to have to shut down the show just because you were too ugly to go on."

"They could always call Gerald," he muttered. He leaned against the wall of the hall and closed his eyes.

Now I was really worried. He looked exhausted, first of all. And second, Randy always laughed when I teased him about his looks. And I had to tease him regularly. The man was gorgeous, much prettier than any woman on the set.

"Who's Gerald?" I asked.

"Gerald Kingsley, the former host of the show?" He glanced at me. "Don't you remember him?"

"Oh yeah, the old guy."

"He wasn't that old, but he was with the show from the very beginning. Then last year he had an appendicitis attack while on the road and landed in the hospital. His recovery was going to interfere with the schedule, so they called me in to do a few shows. I guess they liked me because they decided to keep me, and Gerald retired."

"Do you really think they'd call him?"

He shrugged listlessly. "I think he's still active. I heard he was working at a local station back in Minneapolis or Cleveland." He frowned. "Indianapolis? Somewhere in the Midwest."

"I vaguely remember him. Tall, good-looking older man with glasses?"

"Right." He shot me a sideways look. "Except for the tall, good-looking part."

"He wasn't nearly as good-looking as you."

"That's better." He managed a weak grin. "And he's not quite as tall as me, either. But I have to admit, Gerald knew this show backward and forward. And he was much more knowledgeable about antiques than I'll ever be. He got along great with all the owners, whereas I'm just a pretty face with a charming personality. I don't know squat about the junk these people bring to the show, but I look good on camera."

"And you're humble, too."

He bowed graciously. "That, too."

*L*ater, alone with Derek in my dressing room, I repeated Randy's story about the former host of the show being replaced by a newer, younger version. "Apparently he's still working somewhere in the Midwest so he can't be our stalker, but I wonder if he really did retire gracefully."

"Use the Google," Derek said.

I smirked at him. "I'll get right on it."

Neither of us said aloud what we were both thinking: that

Gerald had been pushed aside and replaced by Randolph, a newer, shinier model. If Gerald could eliminate his rival, he might get his old job back. What better motives could a stalker have than jealousy, rivalry, and revenge?

I Googled the former host, and a minute later I recited to Derek everything I'd learned about the original host of the show. "Gerald Kingsley not only hosted *This Old Attic* for eight years; he was also the show's creator."

Derek leaned back on the couch. "It would be hard to accept that you were no longer wanted by the very thing you had created."

"Yes, it would be," I murmured. After skimming another few paragraphs of Gerald's bio, I paraphrased for Derek. "It says he studied acting in college but then inherited his parents' small chain of high-end antiques stores around Ohio. That's where he first came up with the idea of having regular people bring their family treasures in to be appraised on television. Because of his acting background, he gave himself the job of host and interviewer, and at first he even did the appraisals himself. The original season was aired on a local PBS station. The studio they used was on the campus of Kenyon College." I looked at Derek. "That's in Ohio."

"Where's he working now?" Derek wondered.

"I'll check." I ran a few more searches and even looked at Wikipedia, which was notoriously unreliable.

"The most recent mention of Gerald Kingsley is in an ad on the Mount Vernon news Web site." I glanced up at Derek. "Again in Ohio."

"So he's back in his own neighborhood," Derek surmised.

"Close enough."

"Where everyone would know him. And they would know that he was no longer hosting the show he'd originated." Derek returned to the couch and leaned forward, elbows on knees. "Could he put a positive spin on why he was no longer working on the

show that made him famous? Tell everyone it was he who'd grown
tired of them instead of the other way around? Could he hold his
head up high? Or would he be awash in humiliation? Unable to
cope with the shame?"

"You're creeping me out." I scanned the advertisement.
"Okay, this is basically an announcement for a new local talk show.
I guess that's what Randy was talking about." I clicked on the link
and read what came up. "But according to the TV listing, they've
got someone else hosting the show."

Derek gazed at me. "So where, oh where has Gerald gone?"

"He seems to have disappeared," I said. "At least, according to
the Google."

"Can you pull up a picture of him?"

I clicked over to Google Images and typed Gerald's name, and
several dozen photographs flashed across the screen. "Come see."

Derek crossed the room and leaned over my shoulder. "Do
you recognize him?"

I nodded. "I've been watching *This Old Attic* for a few years, so
he looks familiar. But I've never seen him in person. Have you?"

"No." Derek frowned and stared more carefully at the pictures
on the screen. "Do we know how tall he is?"

"I would guess he's at least five foot ten." I repeated what
Randy had said about Gerald being slightly shorter than him.

"And I'd estimate that Randy is six feet tall, so five foot ten
sounds right." Derek stood. "Let's go talk to him."

"They were doing three weeks of shows in Madison," Randy
explained, "and Gerald got an appendicitis attack halfway
through. Tom had seen my reel and liked my work, so I was called
in to substitute. The producers decided Gerald was getting too old
for the gig and he was fired."

"While he was still recuperating?" Derek said "That must
have been devastating for him."

"Yeah, maybe." Randy frowned. "He continued coming to the tapings because I guess he felt it was his show, you know? Some people probably thought it was weird, but I didn't really mind. He's such a nice guy, and he never took it out on me."

"So Gerald stayed around."

"Yeah, he'd go hang out in the guest hall with the antiques owners. They got a kick out of it. Probably thought he was still associated with the show. And nobody ever said anything to the home audience. There was no fanfare. One day, Gerald was hosting the show. The next day, he was out and I was in. He kept coming around for a while, like I said, but eventually he just stopped showing up."

Derek nodded thoughtfully. "How long has it been since you've seen him?"

Randy thought about it. "Probably about six months."

Derek and I both stared at him.

Randy blinked as he put it together. "Wait. You think Gerald could be my stalker?"

"It makes sense."

"But he was so nice to me. And he was really helpful during the whole transition."

Derek wasn't buying his nice-guy story. "Can't you see he has every reason to try to get rid of you?"

Randy looked stricken. "You think he wants me dead? Just so they'll hire him back? That's sick."

"Stalking is sick," I said. "You mentioned that he took a job back in Cleveland, but I can't find him listed as working anywhere."

"I can't imagine he took the enforced retirement well at all," Derek mused.

I jumped in. "Put yourself in his shoes. Even if we ignore the fact that the producers coldly fired him while he was recuperating from surgery, the fact remains that he created this show. It was his baby all these years. And then some young whippersnapper comes along and takes it away? It might not make him too happy."

Derek leaned forward. "Have you seen him in the studio or on the set?"

Randy paced restlessly. "No. I haven't seen him in months. It's got to be someone else."

Derek and I exchanged glances and I sighed. "Okay. Let's make a list."

"Fine." Randy frowned. "You start."

I was happy to begin. "It could be a woman. Someone who works here."

"But who? Everybody likes me."

"You drive Angie crazy."

He looked hurt. "What are you talking about? Angie loves me."

There was a fine line between love and hate, especially when love was unrequited. But that was a little heavy-handed so I kept it to myself. "One of the stagehands, then. Or maybe you pissed off the caterer."

"No." He looked doubtful for a second, but then repeated himself. "No. Absolutely not. I haven't pissed anyone off. It's a good group. We all have a great time. Don't you think so?"

"Sure, except for snakes and stage flats and Tish being attacked and . . ."

"Yeah." He grimaced. "Sorry. No wonder you want to find this guy. You're the one suffering the brunt of his anger."

Derek glared at him. "You noticed that, did you?"

"It's been six months since he last saw Gerald," I whispered on our way back to the dressing room. "And it's been six months since his stalker started dropping dead animals on his front porch. Coincidence? I think not."

"But nobody's seen Gerald around here," Derek reasoned. His features were a study in frustration, but I could see the gleam in his eyes, which told me his always razor-sharp mind was working through dozens of scenarios.

"True." I glanced up at him. "I still think it's a woman. Have you seen the way Angie looks at him sometimes?"

"You've brought her name up before," Derek murmured. "I thought she was your mate."

"I like her a lot. But you and I both know I haven't always been the best judge of character."

He wrapped his arm around my shoulders. "You're getting better."

"Aw, thanks."

We both chuckled as I unlocked the door.

"So, now what?" I wondered aloud.

"We can ask the crew if anyone has seen Gerald around. But I'd rather not open it up for general discussion. George has been chatting with some of the crew members, so I'll have him broach the subject in a subtle fashion."

"Maybe he comes in disguised as a guest and brings a new antique with him each time."

"It's possible," Derek said. "But I doubt he'd waste time sitting around all day in the guest hall. He's already tried to kill Randy twice. He's deadly serious. Look at the time he put into changing out the dressing room lock."

I thought about it. "Maybe he's working for the caterer. He could get into the studio several times a day if he brought boxes of doughnuts and fresh coffee."

"Possibly."

"I'm still dealing with the fact that in all this time, Randy has never considered Gerald a threat."

"He doesn't honestly grasp that he's in danger."

"Because he isn't. I am."

"True," Derek said, scowling. "It was you who confronted the snake. And you who got trapped under the stage flats."

"The only close call he's suffered was the peanuts."

"And he's had allergic reactions before, so, if you'll recall, he didn't even connect that event to his stalker."

"And Tish's attack?" I asked.

"Tom believed it was the stalker, but we know it wasn't. Randy never said much about it."

"Maybe because it happened outside the studio. That's not his realm."

There was a brisk knock at the door. "Ten minutes, Brooklyn!"

"Thanks, Angie," I yelled back.

Derek opened his briefcase. "While you're out onstage, I'm going to text my people to meet me here for a briefing. I want them to be on the lookout for someone matching Gerald's description."

"Sounds good."

As I was closing the door, I heard him mutter, "We just have to figure out what that description is."

Chapter Sixteen

Early Saturday morning, Alex stopped by my place to pick me up for her Krav Maga class. Derek offered her a cup of coffee and the two of them began to discuss the short drive to her Hayes Valley gym as if they were conducting a Black Ops incursion into a hostile foreign land.

Alex poured a dollop of cream into her coffee and took a sip. "I'll work with her from oh-eight-hundred to oh-nine-twenty. That's when you'll arrive, correct?"

"Oh-eight-hundred?" I said. "You mean, eight o'clock?"

"Roger that," Derek said, ignoring me. "I won't park and take the chance of being blocked in. At oh-nine-twenty you'll see me pull directly in front of the doorway. I'll keep the motor running."

"Not for long," Alex assured him. "We'll walk out at precisely oh-nine-twenty."

"I'll leave the motor running regardless."

"Ten-four, Tango Bravo," I muttered. I'd heard the guys on *NCIS* say something like that once or twice.

Derek paid no attention, just gave Alex a brief nod.

"You realize we're just going to a mini mall," I said.

Relaxed at the dining table with his coffee and a scone, Derek continued to tap out messages on his smartphone. No doubt he was plotting the takeover of a minor planet.

"Great coffee—thanks." Alex set her cup in the sink and smiled at me. "All ready to go?"

I looked at the two of them. "You people are sick."

"Is that a yes?"

Derek smirked. I grabbed his shirtfront and kissed him hard on the lips. He smacked my butt. "Have fun."

"I'll try to survive."

We drove to a small gym in the Hayes Valley neighborhood where Alex taught her Krav Maga and kickboxing classes. Walking into the large space, I saw a row of punching bags hanging from the ceiling. Mirrors lined the opposite wall. The entire floor space was covered by one-inch-thick gray matting.

Alex introduced me to her three fellow instructors, and that's when I found out that she had arranged for me to be their only student for the next hour or so.

"So you're all Krav Maga teachers," I said, and looked at Alex. "I thought you were mostly into jujitsu and black-belt-type stuff."

"I'm into a lot of things," she said. "I would usually recommend that you balance your self-defense fighting with some sort of Eastern discipline, but right now, we want to teach you how to kick someone's ass and leave him crying in pain."

"Sounds good to me."

For the next hour, the four experts taught me some great moves. Even if Grizzly came at me with a gun, I knew in theory what to do to change the balance of power.

Unless he decided to shoot me at point-blank range.

I shook off the little chill that skittered across my shoulders at that thought.

We talked about how large Grizzly was, and two of the men showed me how to use Grizzly's own weight against him. I hoped it wouldn't come to that. The brief training session gave me a little boost of self-confidence, but I knew I would need a lot more before I would be ready and willing to tackle Grizzly.

At precisely oh-nine-twenty, I walked out of the gym with Alex and ran to Derek's car. As I slid into the passenger's seat and slammed the door shut, I glanced across the street. Leaning against the wall of a seedy check-cashing center, smoking a cigarette, was Grizzly Jones.

His look was one of pure arrogance, as though I was helpless to stop him from harassing me.

I screamed and pointed. "That's him, that's him! Right there! Do you have your gun? Shoot him!"

Derek jumped out of the car. "Go inside and stay with Alex. Call the police."

"He's getting away!"

Grizzly flicked the cigarette into the gutter and took off running. As soon as there was a break in traffic, Derek raced across Hayes and down the block. Instead of going back inside, I ran right after him, afraid to leave him alone with that horrible creep.

For a man as stout as Grizzly, he could run pretty fast. It figured with the kind of life he'd led, he had to be used to being chased down by cops or other violent criminal types all the time.

Sadly, Grizzly jumped into a car and screeched away before Derek could grab him.

Derek turned and saw me. "I told you to call the cops."

"I was going to, but . . ." I had no reason not to call the cops, except that my first instinct had been to join Derek in the chase.

"You could've been hurt."

"You, too."

"I can defend myself," he said, his voice a low growl.

"So can I," I said, my fists bunching up in frustration. "I just learned some moves. Want to see?"

He muttered some expletive and grabbed me by the arm.

I pulled away, anger and adrenaline still coursing through me. "Don't do that."

He yanked me into his arms and held me, rubbing my back like a recalcitrant toddler until I calmed down. "I will kill that man if he comes this close to you again."

I was still annoyed, but his words and touch helped dispel it. I breathed in his masculine scent, an intoxicating blend of expensive leather, exotic spices, a touch of the rain forest. I relaxed against him. Damn it, I loved the way he smelled.

I was bordering on delirious. Probably from too much exercise or endorphins or something.

After another minute, we walked silently, arm in arm, back to the car.

Alex was standing outside her studio, watching us. She nodded once at Derek, then went back inside.

We didn't speak on the drive home, but once we were inside our apartment, I turned on him. "You might think you're James Bond or some superhero, but you're not. I was scared to death that you'd be hurt. That guy is huge and mean and completely evil. I couldn't let you face him alone."

"And just how could you have helped me take him down?" Derek demanded. "I'd have been so distracted by you possibly being hurt that he would've ended up clocking me royally."

I fumed. He was right, but that didn't mean I was going to admit it out loud.

He cupped my face with his hands. "And let's get one more thing straight right here and now. I *am* James Bond."

He sounded exactly like Sean Connery, and he spoke so seriously that I laughed out loud. "Now that you mention it, I might've noticed a slight resemblance."

After a long moment during which he studied my face intently, he leaned in and kissed my neck. "And you bear a rather striking resemblance to a former associate. Miss Moneypenny. Perhaps you'd be interested in a bit of role-playing?"

"Perhaps," I said, smiling as his lips moved up to my earlobe. "As long as it doesn't involve handcuffs."

Way too early the next morning, Ian called. "Edward Strathmore can meet with you for one hour if you can get there by noon."

It took me a few seconds to shake off my sleepiness and realize it was Sunday. Derek and I had nothing planned that day, so I figured I'd better jump at the opportunity Ian presented.

"That's perfect," I said. "Where and when? And thank you." I wrote down the details.

"Have a good time," Ian said. "It'll be an experience you won't forget."

"That sounds ominous."

"I swear it's not," he said with a soft chuckle. "He's an interesting fellow, an old-fashioned gentleman, and a bachelor, to boot. And his house is, hmm. Let's just call it unusual."

Edward Strathmore's home in Belvedere was almost twenty miles from my place south of Market, across the Golden Gate Bridge in Marin County on a strip of land that jutted out into the San Francisco Bay.

Derek was adamant about driving me there and although I tried halfheartedly to talk him out of it, I was just as glad he insisted. We had just run into Grizzly Jones yesterday, so I had a feeling he was hovering nearby. As if there was a disturbance in the Force, I could *feel* him out there. He knew I worked at the studio. I had to believe he knew where I lived, too, and was waiting in the shadows to attack again.

That was too horrible a thought to dwell on, so I chose to ignore it. It helped to have my hunky boyfriend bodyguard along for the ride.

Once across the bridge, we wound our way through Marin and took the Tiburon turnoff. It was a roundabout journey to reach Mr. Strathmore's opulent mansion on Belvedere's westernmost promontory overlooking the Bay. We drove a hundred yards down the driveway until Derek pulled off to the side and came to a stop.

"It looks pink," I said, staring at the huge stucco home clinging to the steep hillside.

"I think it's a warm shade of beige," Derek countered. "But the sunlight on this side of the house gives it a pinkish glow."

The Strathmore home sat on a large piece of property that sloped all the way down to the Bay. It was a glorious example of the Mission Revival style that had been popular in the Bay Area since the 1920s. The style took its influence from the early California missions that had been built by the Spanish as they attempted to colonize and civilize the territory. It was epitomized by red tile roofs, arched windows, a bell tower, and often, as in this case, several balconies.

"Are you sure you don't mind waiting?" I asked as Derek turned off the engine.

"Not at all." He checked the dashboard clock. "I have a conference call starting in six minutes. It should last an hour, perhaps longer."

"I shouldn't be longer than that."

"If the call ends early, I've got a briefcase full of work to do. I'm not going to drive off and leave you. I'll be here waiting when you're ready to go."

"Thank you." I leaned over and kissed him. "I love you."

He pulled me back for a longer kiss. "I know."

I was smiling as I shut the car door. For the longest time, I hadn't been able to say those three little words without stumbling over them. It wasn't him; it was me. I couldn't trust my feelings after getting myself tangled up in a number of disastrous relationships in the past. But times had changed. Now the words rolled off my tongue with ease. Because they were true. I loved Derek so much. And I knew he loved me, too.

A little scattered by my thoughts, I strolled dreamily down the drive to a paved stone walkway that led to the oversized front door. From here, the house appeared to be only one story. It was still lovely, but not nearly as intimidating as the side view of the entire three-story mansion.

Before knocking on the front door, I took in the picturesque fountain and terraced garden that made up the front yard. Indigenous shrubs and flowers meandered up the hill, and old oaks and palm trees lined the top of the ridge. I stopped and breathed in the subtle scents of lavender, rosemary, and ocean breezes.

Pulling myself together, I rang the doorbell, and was immediately greeted by a jovial housekeeper. "Oh, Miss Wainwright, we're so happy you found your way. Come in."

"Thank you." I glanced around the large, sunny foyer. "It was no problem finding the house."

"Isn't that nice?" She was a woman in her sixties and she wore a classic white uniform with a black apron and sturdy white shoes. She was almost the same height as me, but stockier, with wide shoulders and an impressive chest. Her blond hair was braided and wrapped around her head, and she was almost bursting with cheeriness. "Such fun to have you visit Mr. Edward."

"Thank you. It's lovely to be here." She was so happy and welcoming, I felt instantly as ease.

"He's waiting for you in the living room." She held out her arm to indicate the direction. "Please go right in. May I bring you a refreshment? Coffee? Tea? Aperitif?"

"No, I'm fine, thank you."

"If you want anything, anything at all, you just ring for me. I'm Mrs. Sweet."

"Thank you, Mrs. Sweet."

She smiled brightly and bustled away.

I walked through the wide arched opening into the large, open living room and came to an abrupt stop.

Holy guacamole, as my mother would say.

The walls were covered with dozens of photographs of Mae West. Some showed her with other people, costars, friends, politicians, studio heads, partygoers. There were also framed playbills, probably featuring the shows in which Mae West had starred. Along one wall were six life-sized mannequins that displayed flashy, glittering floor-length gowns that must have been the ones she wore in her movies and plays. Around the mannequins' necks were jeweled necklaces of all sizes. Were the stones real?

On the mantel was a row of mannequin heads that held platinum blond wigs, each coiffed in a convoluted hairstyle that was similar to the styles I'd seen her wear in her movies. Several featured diamond tiaras.

The room was a museum completely dedicated to Mae West.

In the middle of it all, a thin, older gentleman sat on the couch, quietly fiddling with a computer tablet. Probably checking his stocks and bonds. He was dressed comfortably in an old oxford-cloth blue shirt with the collar buttoned down and a gray cashmere vest. His trousers were a dark plaid. He looked eccentric and very wealthy. And frail, but that might've been because he was so thin.

A Siamese cat sat next to him, purring loudly as the man petted his sleek coat.

Despite the outlandish displays around the room, the furniture itself was comfortably contemporary. Two pale yellow couches faced each other, separated by a wide coffee table. Matching toile chairs were placed nearby and faced the fireplace. Another seating area was arranged at the opposite end of the spacious room.

The man noticed me after a few seconds and gave me a wide smile. He nudged the cat. "We have a guest, Prinny." The cat jumped off the couch and skedaddled out of the room.

Mr. Strathmore walked toward me with both arms extended. "Miss Wainwright, what a treat." He took my hands in his and shook them gently. "It's delightful to meet you."

"Please call me Brooklyn, Mr. Strathmore. Thank you so much for agreeing to see me."

"It's my pleasure. And you must call me Edward." As he walked me toward the glass door leading to the outside balcony, he whispered conspiratorially, "We don't get many visitors. Unless we throw a party, that is. So we try to throw them quite often."

Was that the royal we? I wondered. Ian had mentioned that Edward was a bachelor, so was he including his housekeeper in the equation?

"Your house is magnificent," I said, gazing at the high, beamed ceiling and stone fireplace. In the ceiling above the stone wall was a recessed panel that would open to release a screen. Did Edward watch old Mae West movies in this room? It would be the perfect setting.

"We like it," he said pleasantly.

At the sliding glass door, I stared out at the expansive sight of city skyline, Bay, and Golden Gate Bridge. "What a stunning view."

But I had to be honest. Who could concentrate on the view when the room itself was so bizarre and compelling?

His eyes twinkled. "Would you like the five-cent tour?"

"I'm willing to pay more."

"Aren't you delightful?" He chuckled and slipped his arm through mine. "I like you."

I liked him, too. He was an old-fashioned gentleman, as Ian had said, with a twinkle in his eye and a lively sense of humor. The tour was mind-blowing. Mae West memorabilia filled every room. He was a true collector and had to have spent millions of dollars on his favorite hobby. Except for the fact that the rooms were pristine and orderly, I would've been tempted to call him a hoarder. Instead, he was merely obsessive. He owned thousands of items from Mae West's life, including furniture. And he appeared to know the minutest details of every piece.

He opened the door to a bedroom off the main hall that was used as a sitting room. "Everything in this room is from the set of *She Done Him Wrong*, right down to the wallpaper and wainscoting."

"It's amazing," I whispered. Although spotlessly clean, the room smelled a little musty, probably because everything in it was decades old. A red velvet chair. An old-fashioned lampshade with crystal fringe. A gold rococo mirror. A spinet piano that displayed sheet music from 1933. A vase filled with colorful feathers on the ledge of the piano. A brocade fainting couch filled one corner, covered in a mass of colorful pillows. In another was a curved love seat in a shiny gold satin fabric. Some of the pieces were of good quality; others looked a bit shabby.

The room was a wild mishmash of colors, textures, and styles. But it was all great fun. I didn't know what to look at first.

When Edward closed the door, I noticed a small brass plaque screwed into the wood. It read, SHE DONE HIM WRONG, 1933. He showed me a few more rooms furnished in items collected from Mae's other films, including a Western-style saloon from *My Little Chickadee*. But none of the others were as riotously garish as the *She Done Him Wrong* room. I wondered if he spent much time in these rooms and what determined which room he would choose. Did it depend on his mood? The day of the week? The phase of the moon?

Edward led me back to the living room and offered me a chair while he sat at the end of the sofa nearest me. "Now, Ian tells me that you've come across something that might be of interest to me."

I opened my satchel and pulled out my copy of *The Secret Garden* and handed it to him.

"Ah," he whispered. "Excellent."

Prinny, the Siamese cat, strolled into the room and stopped at my feet. Could he sense my little kitten's scent on my shoes? After a few seconds of sniffing, he returned to his master's side and Edward rewarded him with long strokes along his back. The cat purred with happiness.

At that moment, Mrs. Sweet bustled in with a tray of tea and cookies. She set the tray on the table and poured the tea into fine china cups. She was about to walk away when she noticed the book her employer was holding and blinked a few times. "Oh, my. That is a lovely one."

Edward looked up and smiled. "Isn't it, Mrs. Sweet? It's a duplicate of the one I have in the library."

"You have the very same book?" I asked. I wasn't exactly surprised. The man had everything that Mae West had ever touched. But had his copy of *The Secret Garden* been signed by her, as well?

"Yes, the very same," he said, smiling as he stroked the spine gently. "This limited edition is exquisite, isn't it?"

"I love it," I admitted.

"Enjoy," Mrs. Sweet said, and toddled off.

Reaching for my teacup, I said, "There's a signature on the inside front cover. Would you be able to verify that it's Mae West's?"

"Certainly." He laughed lightly. "That is what you're here for, after all." He opened the book carefully and raised his eyebrows. "Oh, my. Yes. It's definitely Mae's signature. From the early years of her career. It changed as she grew in fame. Became grander, more flamboyant." His smile softened. "This was the signature of her youth."

He set down the book, got up, and walked slowly over to a small escritoire in the corner. He returned with a magnifying glass and sat and stared at the writing for another long moment. Then he gazed at me. "Tell me how you came to possess this book."

"I'm working as a book expert on *This Old Attic* while they're taping in San Francisco. Do you know the show?"

"Absolutely. I never miss it." He chuckled. "In fact, this will confirm that it's a small world, because the producers called to ask if I would come and be interviewed on their 'Collector's Corner' segment next week."

"That's wonderful. I'll see you there."

"I'm delighted. But go on with your story."

I told him how Vera had found the book by chance and brought it to the show. I mentioned that she had died a few days later, but left out the gorier details of her death. I didn't want to shock him.

"My goodness, that is tragic." His head tilted as something else occurred to him. "But what will happen to the book?"

"If the owner has no living relatives, it might be put up for auction. The Covington would probably be interested in bidding. I suppose any money made from the sale could go to charity."

"Oh yes." He nodded briskly. "The Covington would be a wonderful place to display it. But, dear me, I'm stunned that the young lady found it at a garage sale."

"Yes, it was one of those crazy things," I said lamely. I wasn't about to mention the bad luck that had followed me, not to mention Vera, ever since.

"I used to enjoy poking around garage sales," Edward admitted. "These days, I prefer to use the services of the established auction houses." He added with a wink, "And usually by telephone from the comfort of my humble abode."

He spent a few more minutes studying the book, turning the pages slowly, touching only the outer edges so any oils in his skin didn't mar the leather surface. He was clearly experienced in handling rare books.

When he handed the book back to me, I said, "Thank you for treating it so respectfully. I can tell you're a true book lover."

"Yes, I am, and I appreciate your saying so." He took a cookie and bit into it. "I'm very careful with my own books and would be highly agitated if someone were to mistreat one of them."

"I would, too," I said firmly. "I'm sorry to say it, but many people don't treat these rare books with the reverence they deserve."

He scooted forward on the couch. "I don't share my library with most people, Brooklyn dear, but I know you would appreciate it. Do you have time for me to show you some of my special treasures?"

"I would love to see your library," I said eagerly, elated by the offer.

On the way down the long hallway, he entertained me with the story of how Mae West met Frances Hodgson Burnett. It was the same basic story I'd read in her biography, but Edward peppered it with interesting details and humorous asides.

Both women had been living and working in New York in 1912. Mae came to see Frances's *Little Lord Fauntleroy* on Broadway and Frances was thrilled. She'd seen Mae onstage in a little-known revue the previous year, and then again more recently in the opening performance of *A Winsome Widow*.

"Frances told Mae that she was destined for stardom."

"She was right about that," I said. "But how did you discover all these stories? I've been looking everywhere for information like this."

At the end of the wide hall was a closed door. Edward pulled a key from his pocket and unlocked the room before glancing at me. "Mae told me the stories herself." He walked into the room, leaving me aghast.

"You met her?" I followed him into the room. "Really?"

"Yes. She had long been an idol of mine and I made it my goal to meet her one day. And to become friends. And perhaps more."

"Wow."

He smiled at my expression. "It's good to have goals, don't you think?"

I laughed. "Definitely. But . . . I'm not sure how to say this, but weren't you quite a few years younger than she was?"

"Oh, my, yes," he said, chuckling. "But I still loved her as a man loves a woman."

I blinked at his words, but they faded from my mind as I turned and gazed around the big, elegantly wood-paneled room. "This is a beautiful space."

"Thank you. Have a look around."

The ceiling was at least twelve feet high, with solid wood beams running its length. The walls were paneled in a rich mahogany. Two arched windows faced south and west, allowing for stunning views in both directions. Bookshelves and glass display cabinets lined the walls. In the center of the room were six pedestals holding one book each, displayed under glass domes.

"The surface of the windows is coated so the sunlight won't damage the books." He strolled past glass-fronted cabinets filled with rare collections of beautifully bound works. "I couldn't bear to block the view."

"I don't blame you," I said, following him slowly, taking it all in. It was as though a treasure chest had been opened and I was trying to keep my greedy fingers from grabbing the jewels.

In one oblong, glass-fronted case were six finely bound books by Jane Austen. Each had a miniature portrait of the author or the subject matter encased in glass and inset into the leather binding.

"I can't believe what I'm seeing," I murmured. "Are they all by Cosway?"

"Yes." Edward stared at the display with his hands clasped together. "I do love his miniatures. The detail is exceptional. I have other artists' works on the shelves, but Cosway's are so special to me."

Richard Cosway was a Regency-era artist famous for his miniature portraits. Book lovers knew his name because so many of the portraits had been set into the covers of the finest leatherbound books of his time. They had come to be known as Cosway bindings and were beyond rare.

On a nearby shelf was a collection of six delicate, colorful, gem-encrusted eggs, each set on a matching three-legged stand. One was studded with diamonds. Another was fashioned to look like a flower basket. Yet another was opened to reveal the tiniest royal coach. I was pretty sure it was made from solid gold.

"Are these Fabergé?" I asked in a whisper.

"Yes. Aren't they fun? I couldn't resist."

It must have been nice to buy priceless artwork just for fun.

Several paintings on the walls were familiar to me and I wondered if they were original. There was a large Titian that I thought I'd seen at the Palace of the Legion of Honor. Or was it in Los Angeles at the Getty Museum? How had it ever ended up in Edward Strathmore's library?

I stopped to admire a lavishly jeweled binding of Chaucer's *Canterbury Tales*. "This is fabulous."

His eyes lit up. "It is, isn't it?"

I frowned at him. "Don't tell me Mae West was a rare-book collector."

He tossed his head back and laughed out loud. "Oh no, no. These are my own little obsessions. But Mae did enjoy spending time with Frances and collected her books."

"Did they have much in common?"

"You wouldn't think so, would you? But both had strong feminist sensibilities, even before the term was coined. They were outstanding in their chosen fields. They both enjoyed the company of younger men."

I smiled as he chuckled and went on. "They were both successful writers on Broadway as well as in other genres. Both were destined to suffer through at least one unhappy marriage."

"Do you think Frances gave her this book?" I asked, holding up my copy of *The Secret Garden*.

"Probably. Frances gave Mae several autographed copies of her books. I have three of her most famous works on display here." He stopped at a glass display case mounted on a pedestal at eye level. It held three books: *The Secret Garden, Little Lord Fauntleroy,* and *A Little Princess.* They were all standing and held open to the title page. A viewer could circle the cubicle and see the front-cover illustrations and gilding designs as well as the signature of the author on all three books.

"And these all belonged to Mae?"

"Yes."

The Secret Garden in the case looked like the exact same limited-edition version that Vera had bought at the garage sale. The other two books on display were similar in style, but not quite as elaborate.

I turned and looked at him. "I just realized I never asked. Would you be interested in acquiring the copy I have?"

He chuckled again. "As you can see, I'm fascinated by anything connected with Mae. But I already have two copies of the same book, both signed." He pointed to the three books within the glass case. "These were in her home when she died, and they mean so much more to me, knowing they were with her throughout her life."

"I understand," I murmured.

He sniffled once and collected himself. "It simply wouldn't be right to bring in another book and disturb the balance I've achieved in this room." He wiped away a tear and shook his head. "Forgive me for unloading my personal feelings on you."

"I don't mind at all. I appreciate your honesty."

"Good," he said, with a stiff exhalation of breath. "Good. Then I would rather see your book go to the Covington Library or another worthy organization that would display it for all the world to see."

"That's very generous."

"Mr. Edward."

We looked over and saw Mrs. Sweet standing in the doorway, beaming at us. "You have a phone call, sir."

"Oh, I think I know what this is about." He patted my arm. "Would you excuse me for just a moment, my dear?"

"Of course."

Edward strode out and Mrs. Sweet toddled along after him. I probably should've taken the opportunity to say my good-byes, but I wanted to wander and explore more of the library. I might not ever have the chance again.

I took a quick look out at the view before reaching the display case I'd noticed before. It contained the complete works of Shakespeare, in folio.

In between the Shakespeare cabinet and the next one was a burgundy velvet curtain hanging on the wall. Without thinking too much, I pushed it aside to take a peek at what was hiding behind it.

It was a single oil painting. I pulled the curtain back farther to catch the light and saw a startlingly lifelike depiction of Mae West and Edward Strathmore in a romantic embrace.

"Whoa." It was obviously somebody's idea of a fantasy, since the two appeared to be contemporaries and both looked young enough to be in their late twenties. Her platinum blond hair was curled around her in sexy disarray. He wore a tuxedo and was as wildly handsome as a movie star.

Definitely a fantasy, I thought. Especially since Mae West had died years ago and Edward, despite his Old World manners and frailty, was probably only in his late sixties.

I stared at the painting and realized something else was odd about it, beyond the creepy fantasy factor. What was I missing?

I heard Edward's footsteps on the hardwood floor of the hall and quickly returned to my study of the Shakespeare folios.

"I should probably be going," I said, as soon as he walked back into the room. "I've enjoyed myself so much, but I think I've taken up enough of your time today."

"It was a pleasure," he said, with a slight bow. He slipped his arm through mine again and led me out of the room. "You're a delightful girl."

"Thank you. I'm so grateful you allowed me to see your library."

"I don't let every Tom, Dick, and Harry come in there."

"I don't blame you," I said. "You have so many treasures and not everyone would appreciate them."

"Exactly so."

"And thank you again for all of your insight into Mae West. It was so helpful."

"Oh, my dear," he said, "anytime I can talk about Mae is a special day for me. Never a chore."

"I'm glad."

As we headed back down the hall toward the front door, he said, "We're having a party next Saturday. I know it's late notice, but I would be so honored if you could come."

That took me by surprise. "I would love to."

"Be sure to bring your husband or your beau."

I smiled. "He's my beau."

"Wonderful," he said with enthusiasm. "It's going to be quite a get-together. Lots of movers and shakers, as they say."

"It sounds like fun."

He squeezed my arm in a friendly gesture. "It will be, as long as you're here."

Chapter Seventeen

Early Sunday evening, Derek stayed home with the kitten, the latest James Bond film, and a briefcase filled with work, while I walked across the hall to Vinnie and Suzie's place for an impromptu ladies' night. It was the three of us and our new neighbor, Alex.

In the good old days, Vinnie and Suzie used to go out for dinner every night of the week. I loved those old days because they usually brought me their leftovers.

Now that they had baby Lily, though, the two women had turned into homebodies. Vinnie had become addicted to the Food Channel and was always experimenting with new and strange meals, much like my own experimentation with food. The difference was, Vinnie had talent. Everything she tried turned out to taste really good.

The same couldn't be said for me and my experiments. I couldn't count the number of times I'd tossed a pot of mushy pasta into the trash or poured a watery pudding disaster down the drain. It was so unfair.

Vinnie opened the door seconds after I knocked. "Brooklyn is here," she cried. "Come in." She led the way into their two-story living room and I was stopped in my tracks by the sight of the most

amazing wood sculpture I'd ever seen. And that was saying something, because Vinnie and Suzie were talented chainsaw artists
whose unique works were on display all over the country.

The piece stood in the middle of their high-ceilinged living
room and looked like it had been carved from a ten-foot-tall, two-
foot-thick square slab of redwood. The top half of the thick wood
piece had been sliced and split into hundreds of thinner pieces.
These had been painstakingly bent and curved and extended out
from the center. The thinner pieces were split even farther, and
farther still, and so on, until the entire piece ultimately resembled
a tree, with a thick tree trunk and branches spreading out in all
sorts of wild directions. The branches sprouted smaller and thinner
boughs and limbs that grew and spread out every which way. The
ends of some of those limbs were as thin as a splinter.

"It's fantastic," I said. "So you started with a tree and you
ended up with a tree."

"Exactly so. We call it *Endings and Beginnings*." Pleased, she
took hold of my arm. "Come have a margarita."

Alex was sitting at the bar, and the first thing I spotted was a
tray of cupcakes on the counter. So this party was already a big
success.

"Brooklyn!" Suzie cried. "The party is now official. I'm rev-
ving up the blender."

"I wish you had let me bring something besides chips and
salsa," I said, setting my shopping bag on the kitchen bar.

"But that was the only thing we were missing," Vinnie insisted.

"I brought homemade guacamole, too." I pulled everything
out of the bag and set it on the counter. I'd brought matching
bowls from home so they wouldn't have to clean more dishes than
necessary.

"You made this?" Vinnie's eyes were wide and I sensed a
touch of fear in her voice.

"Yes. And it's good," I said defiantly.

She pursed her lips and stared at the green substance.

"My sister Savannah loves my guacamole," I said, bringing all the umbrage I could muster to the statement. Savannah was a world-class chef, so, in theory, if she liked something, it had to be good.

"Hmm." Vinnie exchanged a glance with Suzie.

"Sounds great," Suzie said doubtfully.

"You'll love it and you'll be sorry you mocked me," I promised.

Vinnie grabbed me from behind in a quick hug. "You know we love you, Brooklyn."

"Yeah, yeah. Just taste the damn guacamole." I went and sat down on one of the barstools. "I'll be waiting over here for your apologies."

Alex had been watching the scene with a hesitant look on her face.

"We kid," I explained.

"Brooklyn is a lovely person," Vinnie said, her lyrical Indian accent strong as she explained herself. "But she cannot cook, poor thing, though she does try."

"I'm sitting right here," I said, laughing. "I can hear you."

"Here," Suzie said, thrusting an icy margarita into my hand. "I think you deserve the first drink."

"Thanks, Suz."

She passed the glasses around and we all clinked, then sipped.

"Oh," Alex moaned. "So good."

"Delicious," I agreed.

Suzie dunked a chip into the guacamole, took a bite, and her eyes widened. "Wow, Brooklyn. That really is delicious."

"Really?" Vinnie bent over and stared into Suzie's face so she could gauge her sincerity. "Are you serious? Tell me the truth."

By now I could tell that she was teasing me, so I sat and enjoyed my cocktail and chips, while they sampled my special dip.

We took turns telling everyone how our day had gone. When

it got around to me, I retold the story of my visit to Edward Strath-more's odd home.

"I've met Edward a few times at various fund-raising events," Alex said. "He's charming and old-fashioned. I never would've guessed he lives in a shrine dedicated to Mae West."

"Oh, it's way more than a shrine," I said, sipping my drink.

"Who's Mae West?" Suzie asked as she poured more mixer into the blender.

There was silence as we all turned and stared at her.

"Are you kidding?" I asked.

Vinnie looked both horrified and worried. "Suzie, you can't be serious."

"I am serious," Suzie said with a shrug, and squeezed limes into the mixture. "I've never heard of her."

"Oh, my gosh," Vinnie said. "I can't believe it." She raised her hands in surrender. "But, then, I cannot talk. You thought it was sad that I'd never heard of Ella Fitzgerald."

"That *was* sad," Suzie agreed.

"Vinnie, how did you hear of Mae West in India?" Alex asked.

Vinnie giggled. "It is a good question because we are such a puritanical country. And Mae West was a wicked woman with many lecherous moves and suggestive phrases. Her dresses were much too tight and her sense of humor was blatantly lewd. Naturally, my father was a huge fan."

I laughed. "My father was, too."

"I enjoyed her very much, as well." Vinnie thrust her shoulders back slowly, let her head sway a bit, and before our very eyes, she switched personalities. She splayed her hands on her hips and began to sashay sensuously in Suzie's direction.

"What are you doing?" Suzie asked, giving her a suspicious look.

Vinnie nudged her playfully with her shoulder. "Why don't you come up sometime and see me?"

I let out a surprised giggle. Vinnie's Indian accent, always so cheerful and chirpy, was gone. Instead, she sounded low and sultry with a slight nasal quality. It was a surprisingly good imitation of Mae West.

"I've heard that line before," Suzie said.

Vinnie nudged her again. "When I'm good, I'm very good. But when I'm bad, I'm better."

Suzie laughed. "You're very good, babe."

She batted her eyelashes. "I've been in more laps than a napkin."

I snorted a laugh. "I've never heard that one before."

"Me, either," Alex said.

Vinnie turned and winked at us. "I used to be Snow White, but I drifted."

Alex actually giggled.

"Marriage is a great institution," Vinnie drawled, swaggering around the kitchen. "But I'm not ready for an institution."

Suzie laughed. "How do you know all these lines?"

"They're from Mae West movies," Vinnie said, dropping the character. "She's famous for them. But if you did not grow up watching her movies, you probably missed them."

"I missed the movies," Suzie said, "but somehow I've heard a few of those lines."

Vinnie strutted again. "I generally avoid temptation unless I can't resist it."

We all laughed, and I said, "Vinnie, you do a great impression of her."

Suzie shook her head. "You never cease to amaze me, babe."

Vinnie slipped her arm around Suzie's waist. "That was fun. We will rent some of those old movies so you can see the real Mae West in action."

"Good idea." Suzie looked at me. "So, this guy you met today is an expert on Mae West?"

"Yes. It was really interesting."

"And a little freaky?" Suzie said.

"Yeah," I admitted. "He's sweet and gentlemanly, but there was definitely a touch of the weird."

"I can imagine," Alex said. "With mannequins and wigs all over the place? You do meet the most interesting people in your job."

"I do. Just wait till I tell you about the snake."

They stared at me. Alex held out her glass. "I'm going to need a refill first."

*M*onday at noon Derek and I showed up at the television studio and met up with Randy in the parking lot.

"You look so much better today," I said.

"I feel a hundred percent better," he said. "I don't know what hit me—maybe a little food poisoning or some twenty-four-hour bug—but it's gone."

"I'm so glad," I said. "Make sure it stays gone, because none of us wants it."

"I hear you," he said with a smile, and strolled away to talk to the director. Derek and I took off toward the dressing rooms.

"Hey, Brooklyn," Tom said, stopping us near the makeup room. "I'm glad you're here. Let's talk."

Derek gave me a curious look and I shook my head. I had no idea what he wanted to discuss.

"The first show aired over the weekend," he said as he led me back toward the studio door.

"I know." Yikes, I had completely forgotten. "I taped it but I haven't watched it yet."

"Thanks to you and that first book you appraised, we've had a tremendous increase in requests from people who want to bring in rare books, so we're going to add one more book segment to your day."

"That's great," I said cheerily. "I just hope I'll be able to do justice to the appraisals. The research is what takes most of my time."

"That's what I wanted to talk to you about," he said. "We've hired two more prescreeners. One of them starts today and the other one will be here tomorrow. So now you'll have more people getting the books from the owners and checking them out. They'll write up their usual short reports and all you'll have to do is a little fact-checking."

I didn't tell him that I would still be compelled to conduct my own research. I couldn't make an appraisal based on someone else's notes. It wouldn't be ethical.

But he probably didn't care, and why should he? The show was basically entertainment. He wasn't worried about my ethical issues.

Still, I was happy. It was so good to hear that the show would feature more books. "That's wonderful, Tom. I can't wait to meet the new appraisers."

"Yeah, let me introduce you to one of them right now." He led the way outside and I saw the throngs of people lined up to enter the guest hall. Tom looked around and pointed. "There she is. You wait here. I'll bring her over."

He jogged off into the crowd. There were so many people standing around, I couldn't catch a glimpse of who he was talking to.

Without warning, the sun slipped behind a dark cloud and I trembled involuntarily. I wasn't cold, exactly, but I felt a darkness enveloping me.

A sharp spasm of pain stabbed at my stomach. What the hell was that?

As I rubbed at the pain, the woman talking to Tom turned to look at me. And I knew the dark forces had collected to try to destroy me.

"No, no, no," I groaned under my breath.

Minka!

Like in the movie *Beetlejuice*, I usually hesitated to say her name aloud, just in case the devil was summoned forth. But despite my precaution, here was Minka LaBoeuf in person. My worst enemy.

She took one look at me and her upper lip curled in a snarl that only a mama dingo could love. She was wearing too much lipstick, as usual, in a shade of orange that could not be found in nature. From ten yards away I could see the oil slick it left on her front teeth.

She wore a plaid skirt seven inches too short, with black pleather boots that stretched up and over her knees. Her sweater was so tight that anyone in the immediate vicinity could be in danger of losing an eye if it unraveled and her boobs sprang loose.

Seeing her here brought to mind all the hateful things she had ever said or done to me. There were too many and they were too vile to mention.

Otherwise, it was just dandy to see her.

I rarely had such unpleasant thoughts about anyone, but she brought out the meanie in me.

Who could've possibly recommended her for this job? If it was Ian, he'd only done it to keep her from begging for work at the Covington Library. Still, that was no excuse to ruin my life.

I was going to kill him.

"Minka tells me you two know each other," Tom said jovially. "I guess it's a small world."

I nodded and she grunted.

Tom glanced back and forth, still smiling. "I've got to get back inside, so I'll leave you two to chat with each other. Glad to have you with us, Minka." He ran off, deserting me.

I mentally girded my loins and waited for the insults to roll off her tongue.

"I can't believe they hired you for this job," she said in a hiss. "I would look so much better on television than you."

"Because orange teeth are so photogenic," I drawled. As an insult, it was weak, but when she was around I always felt winded. The air grew thick and oppressive and it was hard to breathe.

Rather than listen to more of her slurs, I turned and walked away with only one thought in mind.

Ian was a dead man.

*T*wenty minutes later, I was still fuming in my dressing room. I couldn't believe I was being forced to work with Minka. She was useless! She didn't know a thing about appraising books. She barely knew anything about bookbinding. She couldn't tell a kettle stitch from a slipknot. And I was still certain she'd tried to stab me back in college when the knife she'd handed me had "slipped" and almost sliced the tendon in my hand. She'd physically attacked me more than once and blamed me for every bad thing that had ever happened to her. Not to put too fine a point on it, but she hated me with the heat of a thousand suns and I felt the same way about her.

I knew that if she could find a way to sabotage my job, she would do it. I didn't have the time or energy to worry about what she might do, but now I would have to anyway.

Derek knew Minka, too, and he was almost as annoyed as I was. She had caused way too much trouble for both of us over the last year.

I finally decided to telephone Ian. I couldn't be too angry with him because he had set up my meeting with the fabulous Edward Strathmore. Still, it wasn't right for him to sic Minka on me.

"Hello, Brooklyn," Ian said cheerfully.

"I can't believe you recommended Minka!" So much for not being angry with him.

"What are you talking about?"

"She's working here." All of the fury drained away when I realized Ian had no idea what I meant. "I take it you didn't suggest her to the producers."

"Absolutely not," he insisted. "I wouldn't do that to you."

"I appreciate that. But somebody did. I don't think I can take it."

"I remember what she did to you the last time she came to see you in Dharma."

I scowled at the memory. Minka had interfered with a murder investigation and almost gotten us both killed. I had been forced to save her life, but had she thanked me? Of course not. She'd blamed me for causing the problem in the first place. Horrible woman.

I sank onto the couch. "I'm glad it wasn't you. But who do you think recommended her?"

"Maybe someone at BABA?" he suggested.

"Oh, maybe so," I said slowly. BABA was the Bay Area Book Arts Center, where I occasionally taught bookbinding classes. The director might have recommended Minka for the job in order to get rid of her. I couldn't blame her.

Nobody liked having Minka around. Maybe we could send her an anonymous letter suggesting that she move far, far away and never bother us again. But I doubted she would take the advice. Meanwhile, I was stuck with her for the next five days.

*A*n hour later, I had finished my first segment and was back in the dressing room, studying my next book. My cell phone vibrated, so I grabbed it and checked the screen. "Alex, hi. Everything okay?"

"Hi, Brooklyn. Um, no." She sounded distracted and ill at ease, which wasn't like her at all.

"What's wrong? What is it, Alex?"

"I hate to tell you this, but somebody tried to break into your apartment."

*T*he producers tweaked the schedule to allow Derek and me enough time to rush back home to see what had happened.

The studio was barely a mile away so it didn't take us long, but I was on pins and needles the whole trip.

As soon as the elevator door opened, I saw Inspector Lee standing outside in the hall, talking to Alex. I had called the Inspector as we left the studio and she had rushed to our place in minutes.

"Thank you for coming," I said to her.

"What happened?" Derek asked.

"You go ahead and tell them," Inspector Lee said, waving to Alex.

"I happened to be home in the middle of the day because of an appointment I had." She was avoiding meeting my gaze and I realized she must have been meeting up with one of her hand-cuffed men.

"I heard a noise out in the hall," Alex continued, "so I peeked out and saw a big guy wearing a ski mask, trying to jimmy your lock."

"With what?" Derek said caustically. "It's impossible to jimmy that lock."

"He had a tire iron," Alex said. "I called the cops right away. I thought he was going to rip the door off its hinges."

"What an idiot," I muttered. "He should be arrested for stupidity."

"I went out into the hall to get in his face."

"Oh no. Alex, you could've been—"

"I happened to be carrying a whip." Alex glanced at Inspector Lee. "Don't ask."

"I don't want to know," Inspector Lee said, holding up her hands in mock surrender.

"I yelled at him," Alex continued. "I told him I'd already called the cops. He hesitated a second and I figured he would at-tack. I was ready to fight him, but instead, he took off in the opposite direction and ran down the stairs. I didn't want him to get away, so I raced after him. I managed to crack the whip at his feet a few times. It caused him to trip and fall down the stairs."

"All right!" I said, clapping my hands.

"Smart move," Inspector Lee, sounding impressed.

Derek flashed her a grim smile. "That was fast thinking, Alex."

"He still got away," she said, scowling. "But the good news is, he was limping. So I was just telling Inspector Lee that they should be on the lookout for a big, ugly guy with a limp."

"One minute to air!" Angie shouted.

I took my seat on the stage. We had rushed back to make it in time, so I was a little out of breath. But I still managed a smile for the book owner sitting across from me. "Hi. You must be Joanne. I really enjoyed your book."

"You must be the blonde the screener told me about," she said, her tone a little haughty. "I hope you plan on giving me a fair appraisal."

"Of course I do," I said, my smile faltering. "I've done quite a bit of research on your book and I'm looking forward to talking to you about it."

She folded her arms tightly across her chest. "That makes one of us."

"Am I missing something?"

"Somebody is," she said, her tone still snide. "What I don't understand is why the show hired you. Based on what I've heard, they made a big mistake."

I did a slow burn. I so didn't need this aggravation. "What exactly did you hear and from whom?"

"The book expert."

"Which one?" I asked, as if I didn't know.

"The chubby one with the black hair. She may be a little sloppy, but at least she's honest."

"No, she isn't honest," I said through gritted teeth. "She doesn't know the meaning of the word. You'll get a fair appraisal from me, but you were wrong to believe a word she said."

Angie leaned close and whispered, "Everything okay here? You look pissed."

"Yeah," I said. "Everything's just great."

"Okey dokey, then." She stepped back and shouted, "Ten seconds!"

Joanne left in a happy mood. I was still annoyed with her for believing one word of Minka's nonsense. *Stupid woman.* I had given her book a fair appraisal and, in fact, it was worth substantially more than she'd thought it would be.

My last words to Joanne off camera were not the most pleasant, but I didn't care. It had taken a lot of nerve for her to sit there and accuse me of being unethical. And anyone who would believe one word coming out of Minka's snarly, orange-stained mouth deserved the short, succinct rant I delivered.

I knew it wasn't right, but I also wanted to run after Joanne and smack her upside the head. Just once. I was pretty sure it would've made me feel better, though it probably wouldn't be too good for the show.

Instead, I hiked back to the dressing room, anxious to tell Derek what that jackass Minka had done this time. As I passed Randy's half-opened door, I heard moaning and my brain went on automatic red alert. I hesitated to knock, wondering what fresh hell might await me inside, but concern for Randy made me push the door open wider.

Randy lay on the couch, writhing in pain.

"What in the world?" I rushed over to him. "What happened? You look awful."

"I'm so sick," he cried.

"I thought you got over whatever was making you feel bad."

"I thought so, too. But it came back."

He kept groaning and I was tempted to back away a few feet, like all the way out into the hall. I didn't want to catch whatever he had. But he was so miserable, I couldn't leave him. I grabbed a bottle of cold water from his mini fridge and opened it for him. "Here, drink this."

He moaned again. "I can't."

"It'll help. God, you're sweating." I pressed the cold bottle against his forehead. "You need to go to the hospital."

"No," he croaked. "I have to tape the intros."

"Not tonight, you don't."

"I just need a little extra makeup. Call Chuck, would you?"

"Yeah, sure." I jogged down the hall to find Tom, but ran into Derek instead. He followed me back to Randy's room.

"What did you eat for lunch?" Derek asked.

"Nothing bad," he whispered. "A tuna sandwich."

I exchanged a glance with Derek. *Bad tuna?*

Randy grunted in pain.

"I can bring you some soda water," I said.

He grunted in response.

"He looks like he's lost weight," Derek said. "His skin is clammy and pale. I'll go find Tom, but I think he'll agree that Randy belongs in the hospital."

The following day, Randy remained in the hospital. His condition was improving slowly but he was still dehydrated and the doctors weren't ready to release him.

Tom and Walter were borderline frantic when I ran into them at the coffee table.

"Tomorrow we're taping our three 'Collector's Corner' segments," Tom explained. "I'm concerned that we still won't have a host."

"What are you going to do?" I asked.

Walter sighed. "We're tempted to call Gerald to do the interviews with the collectors."

"Gerald, the former host?" Trying to look innocent, I asked, "Is he in town?"

"No, he lives in Cleveland," Walter explained. "So we'll need to decide soon if we want to get him onto a plane and out here in time for tomorrow's taping." He turned to Tom. "I'd like to check on Randolph in the morning to see if—"

"Forget it," Tom said brusquely, signaling his assistant to join them. "We need to get Gerald Kingsley on the phone right now."

Chapter Eighteen

The next afternoon, I had just finished taping my book segment when Edward Strathmore strolled onto the stage. He looked positively jaunty in tan trousers, a navy sports jacket, a crisp white shirt, and an ascot. *Not enough men wear ascots anymore,* I thought. I waved and walked his way.

"Brooklyn," he said, smiling brightly.

"Hello, Edward."

He took my hands in his and squeezed, then gave me a light kiss on the cheek.

"Thank you again for meeting with me Sunday," I said. "I had the best time."

"It was good fun for me, too."

Tom and Walter approached and I asked, "Have you met Edward Strathmore?"

"Not officially," Tom said. "It's an honor."

Edward shook hands with both men. "What a delight. I've been watching *This Old Attic* for years. Thank you so much for inviting me on the show."

"We're the grateful ones," Walter insisted. "I've heard rumors that we're going to be treated to many wise and witty stories."

"I hope I don't disappoint," he said, bowing his head ever so slightly.

"You won't," I said loyally, and earned myself a wink in return.

In every town the show visited, they always featured several of the local antiques collectors. The experts would come on to talk about their personal collections and the different antiques favored by the show's audience. Sometimes they brought odd or interesting items and would share stories of their adventures in the antiques world.

"Ten minutes, people," Angie shouted. She listened on her headset, as usual, but this time she grimaced in disgust. She seemed edgier today than usual, so I caught her as she was walking over to the side of the stage.

"Are you okay?"

"I'm pissed off."

"Why?"

"Where the hell is Randy?"

"I thought you knew. He's in the hospital."

"Really? Because I just tried to call and they said he wasn't there."

I frowned. "Maybe the switchboard was told not to disturb him. He's sort of a celebrity, right?"

"A celebrity?"

"Well, he is the host of a popular TV show."

"Great, Brooklyn. Glad to see you've turned into yet another groupie. Well, I'm sick of all you bitches." She turned and walked away.

"Hold it." I went after her. "I'm not a groupie, damn it. And I'm not a bitch. What's wrong with you?"

"Nothing." But then I noticed that her eyes were damp with tears. I'd never seen Angie cry, not once. She was tough. All-powerful. She practically ran this place. Her superhero motto should've been, "Have headset; will kick ass."

I pulled her off to the side—or tried to. She balked and refused to pick up her feet and walk with me, but I pulled her by the shirt and her shoes slid easily across the polished studio floor with me. "Tell me what's going on, Angie. Maybe I can help."

"Just leave it alone, Brooklyn."

"Nope." I shook my head stubbornly. "We might not ever see each other again after this week, but right now I consider you a friend and I'm not going to let you suffer alone."

"I'm in love with him," she wailed.

"I'm sorry." I rubbed my ears. "What did you say?"

"Don't make me repeat it. It's too humiliating."

"Okay, you don't have to. I heard you." I shook her arm lightly. "But that's not humiliating—it's wonderful. Oh, wait. Does Randy know? Is he interested?" I gasped. "Wait. Did he hurt you? That bastard."

"Shush," she said, giggling like a schoolgirl now. "He knows. He loves me, too. He wants to live together."

"That's so cool. Aww."

"Oh, God. You're as bad as Tish."

"Why? I'm happy for you."

She buried her face in her hands. "But I'm stuck in San Francisco and he travels with the show." She looked up and her eyes widened. "Or else he's dead in the hospital. Who knows? I can't talk to him!"

"He's not dead," I said with a certainty I had no right to feel.

"Okay, we'll go with that theory for now." She gnawed on a fingernail. "So he's alive, but he's leaving town next week and I'll never see him again."

"So leave with him. Join the show. You've got to be the best stage manager they've ever had."

"I'm damn good, and it would be nice to have a permanent job." She let out a wistful sigh. "Usually a show moves in here for a few months, you meet people, become friends, and then they're gone and you never see them again. I hate that."

"If you stayed with the show, you'd be able to see Randolph and all the other people you've become friends with."

"But I live here. You don't understand—I was born and raised here. My mom is here. My friends."

"So in between shows, you come back here and live."

"But he lives in Minneapolis."

I gave her a look. "If he turns down San Francisco in favor of Minneapolis, you might want to rethink your opinion of him."

She groaned. "I don't know if you've noticed, but he's got this real Midwestern sensibility. It's charming and all, but a little weird."

"You're just making up excuses. I've been to Minneapolis and it's filled with smart people. They like to read."

"Because it's always snowing," she muttered.

I laughed. "You could live there half the time and here the rest of the time. Or what the hell? Move to Minneapolis. It's really pretty."

"Hello? It snows," she reminded me.

"Snow is exciting," I said. "What do you care? You want to be with him, right?"

She stared at the floor. "What if he's dead?"

"Oh, God, she's hopeless," I muttered. "We're finished talking."

"No! I thought we were friends."

I walked away, chuckling.

Gerald Kingsley sauntered onto the set and all conversation faded.

He smiled at everyone he passed and waved to the few people he recognized. He shook hands and introduced himself to others. He was friendly and warm and acted like a politician returning to his hometown. Not in a bad way, really. I just wasn't overly thrilled to see him under the circumstances. I was on Team Randy.

Tom came out to the center of the stage and introduced the crew and staff to Gerald. "I want you all to make him feel welcome, because he's doing us a big favor, helping us out while Randolph recovers in the hospital."

I waited until some of the crowd dispersed before walking over to introduce myself.

"Hello, Brooklyn," he said, his voice clear and pleasant. "I've heard you're doing great work."

"Thanks. You know, you look so familiar to me," I said, studying his face.

"I'm hearing that a lot today," he said, chuckling. "Did you ever watch the show before?"

"All the time," I said, and laughed. "That's why you look familiar. You must get people telling you that a lot."

He chuckled again. "Happens all the time."

I could feel my cheeks heating up. That was how I knew I was acting like an idiot. "I'm sorry. Anyway, welcome back."

A few minutes later, Angie called for quiet on the set, and they began to tape the expert collector segments. Gerald had done his homework and the questions were thoughtful and entertaining.

Edward was the third one to speak and he was so charming, he won everyone's hearts. Even the toughened crew members were laughing at his recollections.

He had brought a few items from his vast array of vintage Mae West memorabilia, including one of her fashionable hats. He told stories about the movie stars he'd met and which of them had contributed their own personal items to his collection.

"I must tell you one last thing about the most fascinating book I saw yesterday," Edward said. "It was *The Secret Garden*, a children's book that was recently featured on this very show. Your book appraiser wanted to verify that Mae West's signature was indeed on the book. And I was able to confirm that yes, the book once belonged to Mae. It was a sweet moment, and very special for me. I won't be surprised if your appraisal price goes up a few more dollars after this."

Edward winked at me again and I smiled. Feeling both gratified and self-conscious, I glanced around the set to see if anyone had noticed. And saw Minka snarling at me from twenty feet away. My smile grew even brighter.

"We're clear," Angie yelled.

"Simply wonderful," Tom said as he rushed forward to shake Edward's hand and congratulate him for an excellent segment.

"Thank you. Thank you so much. It was awfully fun. I hope I didn't jibber and jabber too much."

"You were fabulous," Gerald said, standing and shifting into a more relaxed stance.

"So were you," Edward said in a loud whisper. "Thank you for your insightful questions."

"It was my pleasure."

Edward looked around and laughed. "I don't want to leave. I've had such a jolly time. Perhaps we can extend the good feelings." He raised his voice to get the attention of the crowd. "I'd like to invite you all to a party at my home this Saturday night."

Excited murmurs rose and spread and the crew moved closer to the stage.

"Let me explain," Edward continued, his voice growing thready from shouting to be heard throughout the studio. "There will be many important people attending. You know the type. Movers and shakers, power brokers looking to make connections and raise money for their various causes. It can be such a bore!"

When the laughter died down, he continued. "I want to make sure I have a good time at my own party, so I'd like lots of fun people there. I hope you'll all come."

The entire group burst into cheers and applause.

"I'll put a stack of invitations on the table near the coffeepot, so make sure you all get one. The directions are a bit tricky, but you all look smart enough to find your way."

That garnered more chuckles and applause, and when Edward stepped off the stage, he was surrounded by grateful staff and crew members.

"A generous man," Derek murmured in my ear. I hadn't noticed him approach.

"He really is," I said, smiling fondly at Edward before turning to Derek. "I know he's eccentric, but I can't resist his charm."

"It should be an interesting party."

"Yes," I said. We wandered over to the side, away from the crowd. "I didn't see you in the studio. Were you able to watch his segment?"

Derek nodded. "Very entertaining."

"I thought so. And Gerald did a good job." I glanced around to see if Gerald was still in sight. "And why not, since he . . . oh, crap."

"What is it?" He turned and saw what I was seeing. "Oh no. That's hard to watch."

And yet, we couldn't stop.

Minka had made her way through the crowd to shake Edward's hand. For some unfathomable reason, Edward seemed taken by her, and instead of shaking her hand, he kissed it. The crowd thinned out, but the two of them remained together. It seemed that they had eyes only for each other.

Edward was inches away from her now, speaking intimately into her ear and studying her expression as he continued to hold her hand. Minka was giggling. That couldn't be easy on poor Edward's ears. She sounded like a hyena.

Edward didn't seem to mind. Maybe when one reached his age, a hyena was better than nothing.

That was rude and I was sorry I'd let myself think it. I liked Edward and I didn't want to judge his behavior, but . . . Minka? Really? Why?

"I have to walk away," I muttered. Derek grabbed my hand and we escaped back to the dressing room. It was a long while before we were able to speak again. We were too traumatized by what we'd just witnessed.

When I returned to the stage to tape my next segment, I heard through the grapevine, otherwise known as Angie, that Edward had taken Minka out to dinner. They'd been seen running out of the studio, giggling and holding hands like two kids being let out of school for the summer.

My stomach did a little dip at the thought of the two of them together. I hoped I wouldn't have to witness their lovey-dovey act again, but when it came to Minka, my wishes were rarely granted.

Angie shouted something and it reminded me that I needed to talk to her right away. I was worried there might be a little misunderstanding.

Now that I knew her true feelings for Randy, and apparently his for her, I wanted to know why he had allowed me to suspect Angie of being a potential stalker. Why hadn't he explained that they were dating?

Maybe they had promised to keep their relationship a secret, but that was no excuse for him to put up with my accusations.

And besides that, Angie had been hired in San Francisco only a few weeks earlier than me. There was no way she could've put dead animals on his front porch six months before she ever met him. That had only occurred to me recently.

I would've liked to have discussed everything with Randy first, but he wasn't around. So I decided to talk to Angie right after my segment was finished.

. . .

"Thank you so much," Betsy said when Angie had given us the all-clear sign. "My husband is going to be so thrilled when I tell him what that book is worth."

"It's a wonderful book," I said, gazing at her first-edition collection of Hans Christian Andersen fairy tales.

"But eleven thousand dollars for an old book of fairy tales? He's going to *plotz*!"

I chuckled. "The fairy tales are wonderful, but it's the bindings and paper and engravings that brought the price up. I hope you continue to keep it in great condition. You might try rubbing a little tea-tree oil into your bookshelves. That should help keep the silverfish away. Don't get the oil near the book; just rub it along the edges of the shelves."

"Thank you, Brooklyn," she said. "You're so much nicer than I thought you would be."

My smile faded. "That's good, I guess."

"And you appraised the book for a lot more than I was told it was worth."

Now that my last nerve was hanging by a thread, I had to hear the rest. "Whom did you talk to about the appraisal?"

"Oh, that first girl I talked to in the hall." She leaned closer and whispered loudly, "She said it wasn't worth much because it was so old."

Oh, for God's sake. My head was spinning. "Betsy, you do realize that around here, an old book is usually a good thing, right?"

"Yeah," Betsy said, chuckling uncomfortably. "It didn't make a lot of sense to me, but she was so sincere and really seemed to know what she was talking about."

"She doesn't," I muttered.

"I almost took her up on her offer, but now I'm glad I didn't because you appraised it for so much more than she was going to give me."

I almost swallowed my tongue but I tried to appear calm. "She offered to buy it from you? What was she going to offer?"

She quoted me Minka's amount, almost five thousand dollars less than what the beautiful book was worth. Why was Minka offering anything? She didn't have the money to buy these books outright. I knew she wasn't working at the Covington, so who was backing her offers? Not that the Covington would ever consign Minka to buy books for them, but I was at a loss as to whom she was in business with these days.

The production assistant arrived to escort Betsy back to the guest hall. I wished her good luck as she strolled away.

I spotted Derek talking to Bruce at the far end of the stage. I was tempted to storm across the space like an army general so people would sense my fury and clear the path. But I couldn't do that. Instead, I walked casually, professional and composed as I passed the friends I'd made over the past few weeks. But as I approached the two men, Bruce must've seen something scary in my eyes because he made a quick getaway. I figured my true feelings had sprung loose.

"You won't believe this one," I said to Derek. My jaw was clenched so tightly, I wondered if my skull would crack. In a low voice but with many hand gestures, I repeated everything Betsy had said. It wasn't easy to rant quietly, but I tried.

"I'm wondering why you're so surprised."

"Good point." I shook my head in dismay. "Nothing about Minka's behavior should surprise me."

Minka had devised a scam to rip off the guests. Betsy hadn't realized what was happening or what she was saying, but it had been clear to me instantly.

"She'll pay them some lowball amount and then turn around and sell the book to a legitimate buyer for twice as much money."

"Yes," Derek added quietly. "And there's the not insignificant fact that she has defamed you on several occasions now." He took my arm and led me away from the main stage to a deserted area backstage.

"I want to catch her in the lie," I said, thumping my fist into my palm.

"I do, too," Derek said. "I think this calls for a covert sting operation."

"I really like the sound of that." I was still angry, but now I could smile. "What do you have in mind?"

*M*inka was fired the next day.

Derek's security operatives each played their roles to perfection. He'd brought in another female agent from his company to play the role of book owner. I supplied the book from my own library and made up some background information for her. Minka fell right into the trap, offering a lowball figure for the book on the condition that the owner would sell it to her instead of going on the show. Minka told her it was probably her best option because I wasn't capable of assessing it properly. And then she made up a bunch of lies about my own experience and how shoddy my appraisals had been.

If I were the violent type, I would've been tempted to go after her with a baseball bat. But I was all about peace and love. Still, I was thrilled that our little sting was successful and that Minka had been dumb enough to play right into our hands. She had insisted that it was all her cousin's idea. She never would've taken the money. Liar.

Earlier, Tom had called the four guests who had worked with Minka. After a few discussions, it became clear to Tom that Minka had been lowballing the worth of the owners' books and then offering to buy them for more money than she'd quoted. One man claimed that she'd followed him all the way out to the parking lot, trying to get him to deal with her.

Now, as the police dragged her out of the hall, she pointed at me. "I know this is all your fault! You set me up!"

"You tried to defraud these people," I said, not mentioning the fact that minutes ago, she'd tried to blame her cousin. "Maybe it's time you took responsibility for the fact that you're just a lousy grifter."

"I'll get you for that!"

"Oh, shut up," I muttered, but still refused to be too angry when the moment was so sweet.

One of the cops pushed her head down and shoved her into the squad car. She howled in protest and twisted and squirmed as the two officers jumped into the front seat and drove away.

As they left the parking lot, the sun came out from behind a cloud and birds began to sing. It was a beautiful day.

Soon after Minka was gone, I ran into Angie inside at the catering table.

"I heard you were the one who recommended Minka for the job," Angie said as she stirred sugar into her cup. "Did you know she was like that?"

I looked at Angie in horror. "You heard wrong. I would never recommend her for anything. She's my worst nightmare."

"I'm glad to hear that. I thought she was kind of mean."

"She's criminally insane," I said, pouring myself a cup of decaf. "There's no other way to spin it."

Angie held up her hand to stop talking as she listened to her headset.

That's when I remembered that I owed her an apology.

"I'd better get back to the stage," she said.

"Wait. Do you have one quick minute to talk? I have a confession to make."

"Ooh, boy. That doesn't sound good."

I laughed, then lowered my voice. "You know that someone has been stalking Randy, but what you don't know is—"

"Stop." She squinted at me. "What did you say?"

Whoops. "I'm sorry. I didn't realize you didn't know."

"Of course I know," she whispered tightly. "But nobody else is supposed to know." Her eyes were filled with suspicion. "How did you find out?"

"Randy told me." Judging by the expression on Angie's face, she wasn't thrilled to hear that. "Look at the time!" I exclaimed. "I've gotta get back to the set."

She grabbed my arm and pulled me off to the side. "Not so fast there, missy."

"All right, all right." I scanned the area to make sure we were alone. "I happened to overhear him talking to Tom and Walter. And when Tish was attacked, they hired Derek's company to provide security for everyone here, but mostly for Randy." I didn't mention that security-wise, Derek's priority was *me*.

Angie nodded. "So what's the confession?"

It was my duty as a girlfriend to spill my guts, even if it made her angry. "When we were making a list of possible stalker suspects, I mentioned your name."

"Me?"

I grimaced. "I'm sorry! But I've seen you get so annoyed with Randy. With some people, that would be enough to set them off."

"Oh, he gives me grief, for sure."

She was silent for a moment, just long enough for me to wonder if she'd been telling the truth. Was she really dating Randy? Maybe she was delusional. Maybe she really *was* stalking him. This could get ugly.

On the other hand, if it was true and she was dating Randy, she could be in danger. What if Randy's stalker found out about their involvement? Would he—or she—go after Angie? The thought made my stomach lurch in fear.

Her bottom lip began to quiver. "I thought you liked me."

"What? No. Don't do that!" She was going to cry! I grabbed her arm. "I do like you. But love can make even the smartest people go a little crazy. And how was I supposed to know you guys were seeing each other? Randy never said a word. Oh, God, please don't cry."

Angie slowly grinned. "Gotcha."

I gaped at her. "You are a sick puppy."

"Maybe," she said, laughing. "But you're so gullible."

Staring at my hands, I said, "I deserved that."

"A little," she said, chuckling. "You can make up for it by telling me who else is on your list."

"No way."

"Oh, come on."

"Nope. I refuse to embarrass myself further. It's all guesswork at this point, anyway." Besides, I'd already said too much. I trusted her, but I should've kept my mouth shut.

She checked her watch and stood. "Damn it, I've gotta get onstage. Otherwise, I'd stay here and torment you until you told me everything."

"Gosh," I said brightly, "you'd better go, then."

She walked away laughing.

My laugh faded fast as I worried about the possibility of her being in danger. I rushed off to find Derek. He would have to add Angie to the growing list of people needing protection from a stalker who was getting more dangerous every day.

*L*ater that afternoon, Derek and I were both working in the dressing room. I was munching on a chocolate peanut butter granola bar when Inspector Lee called.

"I won't say it's good news or bad news," she began.

"That means it's bad news," I said, glancing at Derek.

"Not necessarily. Gary Jones, better known as Grizzly, was arrested near Daly City last night."

"Really?" My neck and shoulder muscles relaxed instantly. "That's great news."

"No, it's not," she said sharply. "They let him go."

"What? Why?" My poor neck ached all over again.

"A technicality," she muttered. "They didn't have the latest updates on their computers or some such crap. Something fell through the cracks."

I slumped down, resting my elbows on the dressing table. If my mother were here, she'd have given me the look. No elbows on the table. "Damn, I hate cracks."

"You and me both, Wainwright."

I stood and stomped my feet on the carpet, too antsy to just sit there. "Can't you assign someone to follow him around so we'll know if he's coming near me?"

"That would be nice, wouldn't it?" she said pleasantly.

Derek crossed the room and spoke clearly into the speaker. "Nice, but not necessary, Inspector. Brooklyn will have my protection twenty-four hours a day until the bugger's behind bars for good."

I kissed him soundly on the cheek. "Thank you. My hero."

"Aw, that's adorable," Lee said. "I'm going to go lose my lunch now."

Derek laughed. "Keep us posted, Inspector."

Inspector Lee called again on Derek's phone four hours later. We were in the car, driving home from the studio. He was wearing his Bluetooth and answered, listened, and began to swear a blue streak. When he hung up, he looked grim.

"What in the world happened?" I asked.

"Larry Jones is out on bail."

I gasped. It was the last thing I'd expected to hear. Grizzly was freed last night. Now Lug Nut was free. And I was terrified. "How? Why?"

Derek's jaw was so tightly clenched, I thought it might shatter. "His lawyer petitioned the court. Claimed there was nothing linking him to Vera's murder. No fingerprints, no evidence, nothing. So the judge told the police to let him go."

I had to sit back in the passenger's seat and catch my breath. "B-but he attacked me. He hurt Benny. He threatened to kill Vera. He *did* kill Vera. He's a vicious criminal."

Tears welled up and I had to blink them away. I hated this damn case and those two horrible brothers. I felt so helpless and stupid and . . . scared.

"The police have found nothing to tie him to the flower-shop killing," Derek reiterated with deadly calm. "And his attack on you is a separate case. A lesser crime. He was eligible for bail on that one, and he got it."

"I'm scared," I admitted. "And I hate the feeling."

Derek reached for my hand and gripped it during the rest of the drive. The expression on his face was lethal. I'm glad it wasn't directed at me. But if I were Grizzly and Lug Nut Jones, I would be packing up and heading out of town in a hurry.

*E*arly the next morning, the phone rang.

"Who in the world could that be?" I said in mock surprise as I sipped my coffee.

The phone was closest to Derek, so he answered and put it on speaker. "Inspector, what a pleasant surprise."

"Yeah, yeah. Look, I've got good news and—"

"Wait," I said. "I can't handle any more bad news." We had been enjoying toasted bagels and cream cheese with our eggs and onions, but I was afraid I was about to lose my appetite.

And *that* would be bad news, in my book.

"Nope, no bad news—promise," she assured me. "I was going to say, I've got good news and you're going to want to hear it."

"Let's hear it, then."

"Hope you're sitting down."

I gave Derek a quizzical look. "We're sitting."

"Lawrence Jones," she began, "also known as Larry Jones, also known as Lug Nut Jones, was shot and killed early this morning during the commission of a crime."

I shook my head slowly. "What?"

"Is this true, Inspector?" Derek asked, to be sure. I was glad to know I wasn't the only one shocked by the news.

I sagged in my chair, truly stunned. I couldn't call it good news that someone was dead, but I knew I wasn't sorry about it. Lug Nut Jones had made my life a living hell. Still, karma was a bitch. He got parole when he shouldn't have and ended up dead for his trouble.

Unfortunately, his meaner, uglier brother, Grizzly, was still around to carry on the family business. And somehow I knew that he would be more determined than ever to terrorize anyone he might blame for his brother's death.

"It's true," Inspector Lee said. "I thought you'd be throwing confetti."

"We're a bit gobsmacked at the moment," Derek admitted. "How did it happen, Inspector?"

"He was caught burglarizing a home over in Belvedere. The owner heard a noise, got out of bed, and found Jones crawling out a window, and shot and killed him."

Derek and I stared at each other in disbelief. Finally, he said, "Pardon me, but did you say Belvedere?"

"Yeah," she said. "Not my jurisdiction, but I was contacted when the cops on the scene discovered Jones's connection to my murder investigation."

I sighed. "Did it happen to be the home of Edward Strathmore?"

"Ah jeez, Wainwright," she said. "You know I don't like it when you're privy to little details like that."

"I know," I said with a rueful smile. "And I'm sorry. But I know Edward Strathmore. I was at his house a few days ago. He owns a book very similar to the one Vera had."

"*The Secret Garden,*" she said.

"Yes," I said, pleased that she remembered the book. "He's a big book collector. I needed him to authenticate a signature in the book, so I drove out to his place last Sunday."

"I'd call that a remarkable coincidence."

"Which means it's no coincidence at all, right?"

"Right," she said. "Looks like I'll be paying a call on Mr. Edward Strathmore."

Chapter Nineteen

After breakfast, Derek closed himself off in the second bedroom office to get a few hours of work done.

I jogged down the hall to return a plate to Alex. She had surprised us the other morning when she appeared at our door with breakfast cupcakes.

Bacon-and-pancake cupcakes.

I had raised a cynical eyebrow when she told us, and Derek was even more skeptical. But once we tasted them, we were sold. The cake portion had been made with pancake batter mixed with maple flavoring and chunky bits of savory bacon. Extra bacon and maple syrup had been added to the frosting and thick chunks of bacon were crumbled on top. Besides being tasty, they were pretty, too. The woman was a genius.

Alex answered the door, dressed for work in another fabulous suit with skyscraper heels.

"You look sensational," I said.

"Thanks. Come in."

I pointed at her shoes. "How can you wear those all day?"

"They're part of my Intimidating and Powerful Boss Lady

uniform," she said with a smile. "It used to be shoulder pads, remember? Now it's stilettos."

"I remember those awful jackets. I looked ridiculous in them."

"Everyone did." She led the way into her kitchen, where she slipped the plate into her dishwasher. "I take off my shoes as soon as I get to my office. With any luck, I can go a few hours without having to put them back on."

"Good. I hope today's one of those days."

"We'll see." We walked to her front door. "Hey, I meant to tell you, my firm received an invitation to Edward Strathmore's party Saturday night, so I'll see you there. I can't wait to check out his house."

"Oh, that makes me happy. And Derek will be glad to hear it, too. Would you like to ride with us? Unless you've got plans for afterward."

And if she did, I so didn't want to know what they were.

"I'd love to," she said. "I have no other plans that night."

"Great." But in an instant my smile turned to a frown. "Oh, ugh. I have to go shopping for something to wear. I always wear the same thing to any dressy event we go to and it's so boring."

"Why?"

"Because shopping is my least favorite job in the world."

"It's one of my favorites," she said, grinning. "In fact . . ." She gave me a quick once-over from head to toe. "We're pretty close to the same size. You can borrow something of mine. Why don't you stop by tonight after work and try on a few things? I'd do it right now but I have a staff meeting this morning."

"I wouldn't feel comfortable borrowing from you. What if I spilled something all over it?"

She waved her hand at me. "Oh, please. You won't spill. And I have a thousand different outfits you can choose from." Seeing my doubtful expression, she added, "I'm serious. My third bedroom is my closet. You'll see."

"The whole room?"

"Yeah. I go out a lot."

My shoulders slumped. "I can't believe I said I might spill something. Now I absolutely will."

She laughed. "That's why God created dry cleaning. Come on, it'll be fun. More fun than shopping, right?"

That was all she needed to say to get me to agree. "Okay, I'll stop by after work tonight."

"See you then." She started to close the door but stopped. "Wait, Brooklyn. I almost forgot! I made something for you." She ran to her kitchen and picked up a large pink box tied securely with pink string. "Today's your last day at work, right?"

"Yes. What is this?"

She smiled at my suspicious tone. "I made cupcakes for you and your work friends."

"You did not."

"Well, they're actually mini cakes, so they're small, but they're still yummy. This box holds thirty-six. I hope that's enough. Some people might have to share."

I gazed at the box, then at Alex. "You are so good."

"I like having you for a friend." She handed the box to me.

I stared at the box again, almost embarrassed in the face of her warm generosity. "Thank you. This is so sweet. I wish there was some way I could pay you back."

"Just come over tonight and try on dresses. We'll have a totally girly-fun time."

"Okay." I gave her a kiss on the cheek. "I like having you for a friend, too."

"Why would Lug Nut break into Edward's home?" Derek wondered aloud as we drove to the studio.

"Now that he's dead, I refuse to call him Lug Nut anymore," I said. "The name just bugs me."

"I'm not calling him *Lawrence*," Derek drawled.

I chuckled at his tone. "*Larry* will be sufficient. So, back to your question. Why would he try to break into such an obviously well-secured home?"

"Perhaps he's done it before."

I glanced at him. "You think he stole *The Secret Garden* from Edward and sold it for three dollars in a garage sale?"

"Possibly."

"I like my old scenario better. *Grizzly* stole the book from Edward, and Larry found it and stupidly sold it in the garage sale to make a little money. When Grizzly found out, he threatened to kill Larry if he didn't get the book back."

"So, now what? He went to steal another book from Edward?" Derek scowled. "Seems a ridiculous plan."

"It is," I said. "It's like painting the white roses red instead of planting new red roses."

"That's a simplistic analogy," Derek said, shaking his head. "And yet I understood it completely."

"That's why you're my guy." As Derek flashed a smile, something more sinister occurred to me. "Do you think Grizzly followed us to Edward's house the other day? He saw how expensive the house was and convinced Lug Nut to try to steal something. How else would he have considered breaking in to Edward's house?"

"It's possible." At the stoplight, Derek added, "So, he might not have been going after a book. He might've been targeting something more valuable."

"I can't figure it out," I said. "It doesn't make sense. But, then, Lug Nut wasn't too bright, was he?"

"No. Seems Grizzly got the one brain cell in that family."

I laughed but then sobered. "I feel terrible for Edward. He's such a gentle soul. It can't be easy for him, knowing he killed someone in cold blood."

"He was protecting himself and his property," Derek reasoned. "And he has a housekeeper living there. She was in danger, too."

"I know it was a protective instinct. But what an awful experience for the poor man, having to face down that big creep and pull the trigger."

I shivered and he patted my thigh. Then something else occurred to me and I moaned. "Oh no. He'll probably cancel the party. What a bummer."

*I*t was a minor miracle but I managed to hustle the big pink box of cupcakes to my dressing room without being stopped. My plan was to present the cupcakes to my fellow workers at just the right moment, but first I wanted to set a few aside for me and Derek. During those long research breaks, it was nice to have a little treat. Especially homemade cupcakes from Alex.

After the first few segments had been taped, Tom asked everyone who worked on the show to join him in the studio for what turned out to be a pep rally.

"I want to thank you all for helping put together the best group of shows we've ever produced."

We all cheered and congratulated ourselves.

"I'm sorry Gerald had to take off this morning, because it was nice to have him on set yesterday." He waited for the polite applause to finish. "He was a real trouper to fly out and help us. But I'm really glad to have Randy back with us."

That brought more enthusiastic cheers. Randy was right about everybody liking him. Almost *everybody,* I added to myself. He stood and waved from where he'd been sitting on the war set. He still looked weak but happy to be acknowledged.

"Thanks to all our local staff and crew," Tom continued. "We're really going to miss you. If anyone's interested in relocating, let me know."

The locals cheered loudly.

"I'm serious; this is the best group we've ever worked with." Tom glanced around, then whispered loudly, "Don't tell the others."

We laughed, and after Tom singled out a few of the more awesome crew members by name, including Angie, he changed topics. "You've probably all heard about the appraiser that was arrested yesterday."

Minka. I prayed he would tell us that they threw the book at her.

"She's been released from jail."

No! I wanted to shout it out. *Noooooo! You're making a big mistake!* But I held my tongue. It wasn't easy.

"None of the book owners were willing to press charges," Tom said with a shrug. "And it's too much trouble for the show to get involved, since we'll be moving on to another location soon. But she's been fined and given a strong warning by the local police that they'll be keeping an eye on her."

Damn! I just hoped that would be enough to keep her from working with books—and me—again.

"One more thing and I'll let you all go back to work. I heard from Edward Strathmore an hour ago. He had an unfortunate incident occur at his house last night but wanted everyone to know that the party is still on."

There were more cheers, and I realized that this was the perfect moment to bring out the cupcakes. I ran back to get the big box, and a minute later I cleared a space on the coffee table and opened the box. Then I turned to the crowd. "There are cupcakes for everyone over here!"

You might have thought I'd let loose the hounds. The cupcakes were gone in less than a minute.

They all agreed they were great, although most of the guys

wolfed them down so quickly, I'm not sure they tasted them at all. I was really glad I'd set some aside for later.

*I*n my dressing room, I had finished my last round of research and was feeling nostalgic. I was about to appraise my last book. It was a moment to savor.

I glanced over at Derek, who was still working on his computer. "I've got to be onstage in a minute," I said, "so I'm having my cupcake now. Do you want one?"

"Not yet," Derek said, not looking up. "I'm afraid the clients have bollixed this budget again. I'm going to have to run some more numbers before I can call it a night."

There was a knock on the door. "Ten minutes, Brooklyn!"

"Wait for me, Angie," I shouted.

Derek started to close up his computer.

"It's okay," I said, waving him back. "You're still working. I'll walk out with Angie. I'll be fine."

He seemed to weigh the options, then nodded. "Stay with Angie."

"I will." I grabbed my cupcake, then gave him a quick kiss.

"I'll be out there in five minutes," Derek said, glancing at his watch.

"Okay."

I joined Angie in the hall. "How's Randy feeling?"

"He looks like crap," she said. "I don't know. He was fine earlier, but now he's got it bad, whatever it is."

"Should he go back to the hospital?"

"He refuses." Clearly worried, she stuck her lower lip out in a pout.

"I'm sorry, hon. Any news on the moving front?" I asked.

"He's been too sick to talk about it."

"I think we need some cheering up. Good thing I have an

extra cupcake." I held it up in front of her face. "And I'm willing to share."

"Oh, my God, is that chocolate coconut?"

"Yup." I took a big bite and handed the rest to her.

"Are you sure? Really?"

"Yes," I said. "And look, there's a chunk of creamy chocolate in the middle."

"Oh, my God. Oh, my God. I'm not worthy."

"Then give it back."

"No way!" She took a bite and moaned. "It's so good. I want to meet your cupcake friend and kiss her."

I laughed again. "You've got coconut frosting on your nose."

She pointed at me. "You've got it streaked across your cheek. How did that happen?"

"I don't know. Guess I got carried away." I tried to wipe it off.

"You're making it worse." She snorted.

"You're not helping," I said, laughing. "I'd better go to Makeup."

She made a face. "I've got to get back onstage."

"No, wait for me." As we reached Randy's dressing room, I noticed the door was open so I peeked in to make sure it was safe. Randy was gone. "Where is he?"

"He's already out onstage. And I'm in deep doo-doo if I don't get out there now."

"Okay, you go ahead. I'll just be a second. I'm going to use Randy's mirror. He's got his own deluxe makeup kit in here."

"I'll see you out there," she called from the hallway. "Oh, hi, Garth."

I popped my head out and waved to the friendly old janitor sweeping the floor near the door that led to the stage.

I stared at the vast selection of makeup in the tiered case on Randy's dressing table. *It's nice to be the star of the show,* I thought. The makeup man came to him instead of the other way around.

I grabbed a tissue from the box and wiped the frosting off my cheek. Then I picked up a pot of pale cream makeup that matched the color of my skin and found a clean sponge. Dabbing it into the makeup, I leaned in close to the mirror and brought the sponge up to my face.

"No!"

Somebody slapped my hand and the sponge flew across the room.

"Wha—?"

Garth stared at me, his eyes wide with panic.

"Why'd you do that?" I demanded.

"It—it's . . . nothing!"

"What's nothing? What are you talking about?"

"The makeup," he shouted, and moved closer. "It's been poisoned."

I tried to step backward but my hip hit the makeup table. "You saw someone put poison in Randy's makeup?"

He swallowed convulsively. "I . . . I . . . yeah. I saw someone do it."

"Who was it?"

His eyes were shifting wildly. That's when I noticed that we were the same height.

But that was impossible. Garth was several inches shorter than me. I remembered from when he'd helped me with the stage flats.

"Garth, are you all right?"

"Gotta go." His voice was deeper than usual.

He turned to leave, and I noticed his shoulders weren't as hunched over as they usually were.

I recognized that deep voice.

"Gerald?"

"Nope, that ain't me," he said, his voice sounding crackly and old like Garth's.

"Gerald, I know it's you."

He spun around. "Shut up! Shut up! Why can't you leave it alone?"

"You've been here all along! You were Garth, the janitor. You've got a fake beard and shaggy eyebrows. No wonder nobody noticed you."

"Nobody ever notices the janitor." He rubbed his hand over his mouth and pulled something out from between his teeth. His cheeks were no longer sunken in. The appliance he'd been wearing had been giving him that gaunt look, and now it was gone. Garth was gone.

"When you came in yesterday as Gerald, I knew I recognized you from somewhere."

He reached for the door and slammed it shut. He had dropped the pretense of being a shorter, weaker man. Now he was tall and strong. And angry. At me.

I held up both hands. "Just let me walk out of here, and nobody will ever have to know."

He shook his head like a temperamental bull. "It's too late for that, isn't it, Brooklyn? And it's your own fault."

"My fault?" I said. *What nerve!* "Was it Randy's fault that he was hired and you were fired?"

"Yes!" His mouth screwed up as if the words spilling from it tasted as nasty as they sounded. "He was the only one standing in my way."

"That doesn't make it his fault. It doesn't give you the right to torment him." I took a slow, steady breath and tried to calm down. I had to try cool logic. I didn't have much else. *Why* hadn't I stayed with Angie? "He just happened to be filling in while you were sick, and the audience liked him."

"It was my show!" he shouted. "Mine!" He charged over and jabbed his finger inches from my face. "I came up with the concept. I made it what it is today. They had no right to take it away from me."

"No, they didn't," I said, trying not to show my nerves. He was starting to lose it, and that scared the hell out of me. "They behaved very badly. You have every right to be angry."

"That's right."

"But you shouldn't have poisoned Randy."

He was scowling at something only he could see. "They took my show away. They gave it to *him*."

He wasn't addressing my questions, just sticking to his own twisted reasoning. He was talking to himself now, devolving. That was never a good thing. I had to get out of here.

Without warning, I screamed as loud as I could.

"Shut up!" Gerald slapped his hand over my mouth. "I like you! I don't want to hurt you. I-I saved you! You would've been poisoned, too. You have to stop screaming."

"No," I mumbled behind his hand. I tried to scream again, but the sound was completely muffled.

"I saved your life!" he shouted. "You can't betray me now!"

This was probably not a good time to point out that my life wouldn't have had to be saved if he hadn't put poison in Randolph's makeup. "You tipped over those stage flats on top of me. And you put that snake in Randy's dressing room."

My stomach lurched again at the memory.

"I didn't do it to you," he muttered angrily. He began to babble, insisting that he didn't want to kill Randolph, exactly. He just wanted him off the show so Tom and Walter would give him another chance. It was *his* show, not theirs.

"Now I've got my chance," he said, his voice growing more manic. "Randy's still sick. They'll make him go back to the hospital and I'll take over."

"You know tonight's the last show," I said cautiously.

"Be quiet!" he shouted. "I can't think." He shook his head and rolled his shoulders as though he were working out the kinks in his neck muscles. Was he loosening up and getting ready to attack me?

I tried to flatter him. "You really fooled us all with your Garth disguise. How did you learn to do that?"

He smiled vaguely, as though he were remembering the past. "I was an actor."

"I'll bet you were really good."

He preened a little, which was better than his rage-induced craziness. "In Cleveland theater circles, I was known as the master of disguise."

"I can see why."

"I don't want to hurt you," he said, his tone reasonable. "I have to figure out what to do."

"Nobody will even bat an eye if you walk out of here and leave the studio. I won't tell a soul."

He looked at me, paced a few feet back and forth, then stopped and looked at me again. "No. I can't trust you. You'll tell your boyfriend. Women always tell. You ruined everything."

He stepped closer, then closer still, until his face was right up next to mine. "You. Ruined. Everything."

All of a sudden he grabbed me by the throat. I couldn't breathe. I slapped at his arms but he wouldn't let me go.

His lips were thin with rage and his hands tightened around my throat. "I didn't want to hurt you but you wouldn't shut up. Why don't women ever shut up?"

So it was my fault, I thought, as I tried to get my legs to work. I kicked at his shins, but he didn't react. He was in some other world. But here in this world, I was about to pass out.

I had a sudden vivid image of my self-defense class, of Alex coming at me, reaching for my throat, trying to teach me how to fight back. Over and over again. What had I done? How had I reacted to her? She'd come at me again and again until I got it right.

But that was fake. This was real. *Real* was harder. Oh, hell. It took every ounce of will I had left in my head to relax my shoulders and go completely limp.

I must have shaken him, because he gasped and pulled his hands away. But just as quickly, he slapped my face. "Wake up!"

First he's trying to kill me and then he's slapping me to bring me around? He was insane, for sure. *Had I angered him by pretending to lose consciousness?* Fine. That worked for me.

I slid a little lower. He started to slap me again. But this time I lifted my hand and slammed it, backhanded, into his, deflecting the blow just as Alex had showed me.

It shocked Gerald and I took advantage of that. It felt like slow motion as my body followed the movement of my hand, spinning around until I had my back to him. Then I elbowed him in the stomach and kept turning until I was facing him again. I kicked him in the shins and this time it made an impact. While he was reacting, I slammed my foot down on his instep.

He yowled in pain.

"I liked you better as Garth!" I shouted.

The door flew open and Derek rushed in, roaring at the top of his lungs. He yanked me out of the way and slammed his fist into Gerald's face. I cringed at the sound of bones crunching, followed by an unearthly scream of pain. I saw blood spurt across the mirror and spatter on the wall.

I heard myself moan, right before I passed out on the floor in a dead faint.

They canceled the last three segments of the show, which meant that we would all get to come back on Monday and finish it up.

"You should feel a lot better by then," Tom said to Randy, as we watched Gerald being carted off to jail.

"I feel better already," Randy declared, even though he still looked deathly pale.

I was glad one of us felt better. I was still a little woozy and more than annoyed that once again, I'd taken the brunt of his stalker's vicious anger. I decided I wouldn't hold it against him, though, since he had his arm wrapped securely around Angie's waist and they made the cutest couple.

Earlier, when I'd been locked up with Gerald in the dressing room, Derek had gone out onstage to find me. He'd run into Randy, who'd told him about the phone call he'd just received from the doctor at the hospital.

"He says I've been ingesting poison through my skin. That's so weird. I can't figure out how that could've happened."

Derek had taken one look at his pasty complexion. "It's in your makeup."

They'd hurried back to find Chuck, but as Derek passed Randy's dressing room, he'd heard Gerald's howl of pain. That's when he'd slammed through the door and rescued me.

Of course, by then I was doing pretty darn well on my own. I had made Gerald scream like a baby, and I was about to make my escape when Derek arrived. Everything would have been fine if he hadn't gone and broken Gerald's nose and cheekbone and caused all that pesky blood to go flying.

I never had reacted well to the sight of blood.

Still, faint notwithstanding, I was pretty proud of myself. I'd gotten out of trouble all on my own. I was lucky, though, to have a man rush to my rescue—even if I didn't need rescuing after all.

Chapter Twenty

I slept remarkably well that night, probably because of the two heaping glasses of wine I'd consumed when we got home. I'd given Alex a quick call and begged off trying on dresses. She'd completely understood and suggested I come by in the morning and I'd promised I would.

I couldn't wait to tell her how her cupcakes had played a role in unmasking a vicious stalker.

Saturday morning, after gulping down a hearty protein drink and a cup of coffee, I zipped over to Alex's place.

"Come in," she said, swinging the door open. She searched my face. "Are you feeling all right?"

"Sure, why do you ask?" She didn't quite make eye contact and it didn't take much to figure out why. "I see. Mr. Big Mouth told you what happened."

"It's not Derek's fault," she said. "After you called to cancel our dress fest, I was concerned so I texted him. He said you'd had a run-in with someone, but the guy is in jail." She gave me a hug. "I'm so glad you're safe."

In the kitchen she made a café latte and served it with mini cupcakes while I gave her the whole scoop.

"My run-in last night wasn't with the guy who attacked me. It was with the stalker."

"The one who was targeting the host of the show?"

"Yes. Turns out it was the ex-host."

"That makes sense."

I gave her the play-by-play, and when I was finished she laughed and clinked her latte cup with mine.

"Congratulations—you did it! You fought back. You rock."

"Let's not get carried away," I said, but I was beaming with pride. "Oh, what the heck? It was pretty exciting. Not the preliminary, psycho-chase-scene-where-I-was-scared-to-death part, but the part where my brain finally kicked in and I worked the moves you gave me. I was a fighting machine."

"You're awesome."

"Yeah. Until I fainted dead away."

She laughed until she realized I was serious. "You didn't."

"I did." I sipped my latte and tried not to shudder. "It was the blood. When Derek clocked Gerald, it flew everywhere. It was gruesome. I blame Derek."

"He left out that part."

"That's because he knows I would smack him if he told anyone I passed out."

"I don't blame you. It sounds gruesome." She put our cupcake plates in the sink. "Ready to try on some dresses?"

"I should tell you, Alex. I rarely wear dresses. I have a few long skirts, but otherwise . . ."

She waved away my comment. "It's never too late to start. Come on."

Her extra bedroom was a revelation. The entire room was a walk-in closet, just as she'd said. It was ruthlessly clean and orderly. There were two levels of hanging clothes and she explained that they were switched every six months, depending on the season.

Everything was hung in order of color, naturally. Dresses, pants, blouses, suits, and coats.

In the center was a chaise longue, because why wouldn't you take a quick nap in your walk-in closet?

The woman had at least a hundred pairs of shoes, too, all neatly arranged by color and style. There were hooks for belts and scarves, a long row of purses, and dozens of drawers filled with sweaters and lingerie. Three long, thin drawers pulled out to reveal dozens of cubbyholes for every type of jewelry known to man. Or woman.

"You are my idol," I whispered.

She laughed. "I've selected a few things that I thought you might like. They're over here. If you don't like something, I won't be offended."

"My tastes are pretty simple."

"I don't agree," she said, "but we can argue about it as we go along. Here's the first thing I thought would suit you."

She held up a simple black suit. *Not simple at all,* I amended as I stared more closely at the gorgeous material and the softness of the lining.

"It's pants and a jacket," I said.

"It's a tuxedo suit. Yves Saint Laurent. Black pants, black jacket. Silk. Simple, elegant, sexy."

"It's beautiful." The jacket was the thickest, softest silk and fitted through the waist. "The shoulders are perfect. Do you have a blouse that you wear with it?"

"No."

"Ah . . ."

"Try it on."

I tried it on and was truly surprised. I looked sexy. And high-powered, and taller than usual. Did I mention sexy? The pants were slim around the hips and flared at the heel. "I want."

"I have a fabulous black bustier you're welcome to wear with that. I've also got a few dresses I want to show you. And if you happen to see something still hanging that appeals to you, grab it and try it on."

"Have you worn everything in here?"

She scanned her clothes. "I have a few new goodies I haven't worn yet, but mostly yes. I like variety. And I like to keep people guessing, even if it's just them wondering what I'm going to wear that day. It sounds silly, but keeping them guessing about my wardrobe is just one more way to make an impression. And it amuses me."

"You do make an impression," I murmured. "You really do."

I tried on twelve dresses and six pantsuits, although it was difficult to call them pantsuits. That term conjured up a dowdy image that didn't appeal to me, while Alex's suits were sharply tailored and powerful and gorgeous. And they all looked fantastic on me. It was such a revelation. And fun. Who would've guessed?

After three hours, I had whittled my choices down to two.

"I absolutely love the black tuxedo, but I think I want to go for this dress." I held up the little black silk dress that fit me better than anything I'd ever worn.

"It's Halston," she said on a sigh.

"He was a genius." The dress wrapped around me like a sarong while hiding flaws and accenting my better parts. It was a simple design yet it made me feel glamorous and powerful. How did they do it?

"Derek will be in heaven."

"I was just thinking the same thing," I said, tingling a little. "But he would love the tuxedo, too. I wish I could find something like that somewhere."

"I'll call my shopper at Nordstrom and have her hunt one down."

"You have a shopper?"

"Yes, she calls me when something comes in that she thinks I'll like."

"We live different lives."

"Maybe a little." She stared at my shoes.

"I guess I'd better go shoe shopping," I said, my spirit sagging.

"Won't be necessary." She strolled over to her shoe rack, found what she wanted, and handed the pair to me.

"Oh, my goodness," I whispered, staring at the black satin pumps. "Those are sensational. But I can't—"

"Try them on." She smiled serenely. "Men like those shoes."

"You're the devil." But I tried them on and looked down at my feet. I didn't recognize them. I stood and wobbled over to the full-length mirror. "Oh, my."

"Very sexy," she said. "You'll practice walking. Take them with you. And this." She handed me a small black bag.

"It's so pretty. It's perfect. I can't."

"It'll make me happy if you will."

I laughed. "You make cupcakes and loan me clothes. I am bringing nothing to this friendship."

"That's where you're wrong. I've had more fun in these past three hours than I have in months. That's much more precious than cupcakes."

*B*efore I left, Alex took a small velvet box from a drawer and pulled out a slim diamond necklace and matching earrings.

"Absolutely not," I said. "This is crazy. You've been too generous. I can't take anything else from you. Besides, I would worry all night, wearing those."

"First of all, they go with the dress," she insisted. "It's a package deal. All or nothing. Second of all, you'll be accompanied by two ex-operatives so I think you'll be safe. And third, I'm getting everything back tomorrow, right?"

I laughed. "Yes. But still, this is crazy. I don't know how to react to all this."

"Not to contradict a former first lady, but *just say yes.*"

"Oh, hell."

"Resistance is futile," she said in an alien voice.

"Okay, fine. Yes, I'm taking everything, but only because you insist and because I'm weak. And because you'll get everything back tomorrow. Except I'll dry clean the dress first."

"That's a deal." She folded everything in tissue and tucked it all, except for the hanging dress, into a big shopping bag.

At the door, I gave her a hug. "I'm pitifully grateful that you kept me out of the shopping mall."

"It was my pleasure. But I warn you: payback is a bitch."

I frowned. "What does that mean?"

"One of these days, you and I are going to hit Nordstrom together."

"If that's a threat, it's just plain mean."

"Don't worry," she said, patting my shoulder. "We'll have fun and reward ourselves with cocktails afterward."

"Ah. Okay." I nodded. "Sign me up for that."

*D*erek loved the dress. A lot. It was black and short and slinky and yet simple and elegant. He liked it so much that he made a very strong case for my taking it off and the two of us missing Edward's party altogether.

I was delighted and vowed to buy pretty dresses more often.

In the end, though, we soldiered up, grabbed Alex, and drove off to Belvedere. As the three of us approached the entryway to Edward's home, a tuxedoed server opened the door.

"Right this way," he murmured, and escorted us over to a small elevator I hadn't noticed before. We descended to the bottom floor, and when the elevator opened we all gazed out at the massive space before us.

"Who has a ballroom in their house?" I wondered.

"Good question," Derek murmured.

Even here in the spacious ballroom, Mae West reigned supreme. Her movie posters filled the walls and a screen behind the bar was showing one of her films, minus the sound.

There was a good-sized orchestra and a dance floor at the far end of the room. On the opposite end, six serving stations offered various types of cuisines. Two long tables were piled with bite-sized fruits and veggies and cheeses, plus dips. For those who preferred to eat dessert first, two large-sized chocolate fountains were surrounded by all sorts of goodies for dipping.

"I love a good chocolate fountain."

"Who doesn't?" Derek remarked.

There was an open bar on either side of the room along with waiters circulating with champagne flutes. Derek handed each of us a glass and took one for himself.

I recognized a number of friends from the television studio already out on the dance floor. Angie and Randolph were slow dancing to the upbeat tune and seemed to be oblivious to the rest of the world. Other guests stood on the sidelines, making conversation and nibbling on chocolate-drenched angel food cake chunks. A few of Edward's movers and shakers were probably negotiating and closing deals at this very moment.

Alex seemed to know all of their names and many of their little secrets, which she was more than happy to share with us as we stood on the sidelines with our champagne.

The room was filled to capacity, but not uncomfortably so. The balcony doors were open and guests wandered in and out. More waiters made the rounds, offering hors d'oeuvres and drinks. Raucous laughter and sly whispers blended with the big-band sound.

Even though many were dressed in black, because the cool people always dressed in black, it was a colorful scene with glowing tans and glittering jewels everywhere. The snatches of conversation were equally colorful.

Alex wore a silver sequined and beaded, formfitting creation with strategic cutouts that managed to be both revealing and demure. She was gorgeous, of course, and many of the men looked our way as soon as she walked into the room. I thought she would go off to mingle, but she seemed content to chat with me and Derek.

"If you want to go off and talk to other people," I whispered loudly in her ear, "don't worry about us. I saw all those men looking your way when we walked in."

"They were looking at you, Brooklyn," she said.

I laughed at her comment and flagged a passing waiter. His tray held little pancakes rolled up and stuffed with bits of grilled lobster and a light sauce. I hummed in pleasure as one slid down my throat.

From another waiter I took a prosciutto-wrapped melon to cleanse my palate, then wasn't sure what to do with the long plastic toothpick and napkin, so I shoved them into my purse. You'd think I didn't get out much.

Yet another server offered tiny quesadillas stuffed with champagne grapes and melted Brie. I grabbed a quesadilla and popped it into my mouth. "Oh, my goodness. I love this party."

I gazed around, watching all the different people and trying to guess what their stories were.

A waiter jostled one woman's arm as he passed her. She winked at him.

Three women nearby burst into laughter. The man standing with them scowled and slugged down half the contents of his highball glass.

Another man was dressed in a foppish white shirt that billowed out from beneath a tight black velvet vest. He was alone at the moment and I could see why. He resembled some sort of

Charles Dickens villain, complete with bad posture and little rodent teeth.

Alex explained that he was a local bigwig for one of the political parties. She wouldn't mention which one.

Everyone was having a great time enjoying Edward's eccentric furnishings, delicious food, and excellent band. But where was Edward? I hadn't seen him since we'd arrived, but he had to be here somewhere.

I was debating whether to embarrass myself out on the dance floor when part of the crowd shifted and Edward appeared a few yards away. Looking thin and elegant in a vintage tuxedo, he greeted guests with kisses on the cheek or hearty handshakes. When he reached me, he gave a slight bow. "Brooklyn, dear, how wonderful to see you again."

"Edward, thank you so much for inviting us."

I introduced him to Derek and Alex. He shook Derek's hand, then took both of Alex's hands in his. "Oh, I know this remarkable young lady. How are you, my dear?"

"Fine, Edward," she said. "Wonderful party."

"We have our fun," he said demurely.

A sudden buzz arose near the entryway and spread instantly throughout the room. Edward looked toward the door and gasped. I whirled around to try to see who had just walked in.

"Oh. My. God." I held my hand over my mouth in complete shock. It was horrifying. I wanted to look away, but I couldn't. It was like viewing a bad accident on the freeway. To ease my distress, I swigged the rest of my champagne in one long gulp.

"Do you think it's a joke?" Alex whispered. "Who is that?"

I couldn't form the words to answer her, but it was no joke. It was Minka, fully transformed into Mae West.

Minka's hair was platinum blond now, a large, curly ball of fluff with spit curls plastered all over her glistening forehead.

Her lips were painted siren red, not the best color for someone whose lipstick always seemed to migrate to her teeth and whose smile resembled a demented prairie dog's.

The white halter-top gown she wore was a blindingly shiny polyester blend that looked as if it had been glued—badly, with rubber cement—to her more than ample body. The clingy material showed off every one of her flaws—and they were countless—and threatened to rip apart at the seams any minute now. In fact, the dress was already beginning to shred along the back seam at her butt. I took a step backward because when that thing blew, it was not going to be pretty.

Not to change the subject, but it was a darn shame that she wasn't still in jail. Too bad the studio and the book owners had decided not to press charges.

The same couldn't be said for Garth, or, rather, Gerald, thank goodness. Having attempted to murder Randolph—and me!—on more than a few occasions, he would be staying in prison for quite a while. And I intended to make sure of it.

But meanwhile, I was watching Edward, who tittered with glee and lightly clapped his hands together with every bump and grind Minka tried to pull off. It was terrifying to watch her and Edward's slavering adulation just made it that much worse.

"Don't go anywhere, my dear!" Edward cried out over the music, and skittered across the dance floor to speak with the big-band leader. With one sweeping wave of his hand, the man stopped the music.

Edward rushed back to Minka, took her hand, and kissed it. For a long moment, he gazed into her eyes with something resembling adoration.

"Hello, sweet lady," he crooned.

"Hello, big boy," Minka said in an abysmal attempt to imitate Mae West. She placed her hand provocatively on her hip and wiggled around a bit. "Why doncha come up and see me sometime?"

I glanced up at Derek in time to see him grimace in pain. I knew how he felt. She had misquoted Mae West slightly, but that wasn't what pained him. No, it was Minka's nasally, high-pitched voice that hit us both like nails scratched on a blackboard.

I was reminded of Vinnie flirting with Suzie in her Mae West voice. She had been funny and charming, while Minka was just icky and awkward.

Edward turned and gave another grand signal to the orchestra leader, who instantly cued the band to begin their own special rendition of "Brick House."

No! No, no, no. This was so wrong. I could hear Derek trying to suppress his laughter.

Edward urged Minka gently toward the dance floor and they began to move to the music. It was awkward, because Minka could barely walk in that getup, let alone dance.

But now it all clicked into place. Edward Strathmore was grooming Minka LaBoeuf to be his very own real-life Mae West. The man was more than a little twisted, but that's what happened when you had so much money, you could buy—

"Oh!" I struggled for breath, understanding in that instant what I'd missed the last time I was here. I'd known something was wrong at the time. I just hadn't known what it was.

I glanced around. I would need to double-check one thing before I could do anything about it.

With every eye on Minka and Edward, including Derek's and Alex's, I was able to slip away to the elevator. I pressed the button for the top floor and made my way back down the wide hall to Edward's private library. When I reached the door, I glanced around to be sure I wasn't being followed. Then I tried the door handle but it was locked.

Darn! I felt along the top ledge of the doorjamb, but no key was hiding there. I lifted the edge of the beautiful oriental carpet runner to check, but again no key.

Derek had once shown me how to pick a lock, but I had nothing to use as a pick.

Yes, I did! My prosciutto-melon toothpick. I pulled out the plastic toothpick and wiped it with the wadded napkin a few times, just to be sure it was clean enough. Then I slid it into the lock.

I twisted and turned it and tried to spin it. The plastic bent back and forth and I knew this wasn't going to work. Someday I would insist on another breaking-and-entering lesson from Derek and perhaps a little pouch with my very own burglar's tools—which I'm sure he would love to give me. But for now I wondered if maybe I could find the actual key in Edward's bedroom or his office. I didn't want to leave here without confirming what I'd seen before.

I turned and almost collided into Edward.

"Is this what you're looking for?" he asked, dangling a key in front of my eyes.

"Oh, Edward, what perfect timing." It was an effort to hide how badly startled I was to find him there. "I was just coming down to get you. I wanted to take another look at your collection of Cosway bindings one more time, but I didn't want to disturb you while you were entertaining. But since the door was locked, I was on my way to find you and, well. Here you are."

I was babbling.

"Yes, here I am," he said smoothly. "I saw you leave the ballroom and I had a feeling where I might find you." He slipped the key into the lock and opened the door. "Let's go inside, shall we?"

Crap, I thought. *Another confrontation with a lunatic.* My head was still pounding from last night's adventures with Garth/Gerald.

"Oh!" I squealed with ultrafake enthusiasm as I sprinted over to the glass-in display of Cosway bindings. "I can't get enough of these lovely books."

"I should warn you," he said as he followed at a more sedate pace. "We had an unfortunate incident occur two nights ago. A man tried to break into the house and I had to shoot him."

I glanced at him, feigning horror. "That must've been terrible for you."

"Yes, and for him. He was going to steal from me and now he's dead."

I tried to react calmly, but how could I? He wasn't quite the eccentric charmer I'd met the other day. Did he think I was here to steal something?

"Ah!" I cried. "And here are the Frances Hodgson Burnett beauties." I stared at the trio of books one more time. "Stunning." They really were, but I could barely see them. My mind was racing through various scenarios of how I might get out of here gracefully.

"You didn't really come here to see these, did you, Brooklyn?"

"Why, Edward." *Stay calm,* I told myself. "Who wouldn't want to see these beautiful images again?"

He laughed. "You're a terrible liar."

He was right. I was an incredibly bad liar. But that didn't mean I was going to confess anything to him.

"The last time you were here," he said, "I neglected to show you the portrait I had commissioned. Let me give you a private viewing."

He pulled a cord and the velvet curtain parted, revealing the portrait of himself with Mae West.

"She was so lovely," he murmured. "So smart. So filled with life and vigor."

"That is remarkable," I said.

"But you've seen it before, of course."

"I'm not sure what you mean."

"Don't be coy, my dear. I'm talking about the security cameras I have in every room in the house." He pointed up at one corner of the room, where I could see a small hole in the wood grain. "When I left you alone in the library the other day, you peeked."

"Ah." *Hmm.* I had nothing.

"Even without the cameras, I saw the curtain swaying when I came back into the room."

I took a deep breath and decided to play along. As they say, when in Loony Town, do as the loonies do.

"Yes, I did peek," I confessed. "I saw the closed curtains and I was curious. I took one look at that portrait and was mesmerized by the look of love on both your faces."

He patted his heart. "Oh, my dear, I know what you mean. This painting reveals my inner truth. I have nothing to hide. I love Mae very much. It shows, I think."

"But . . . that isn't Mae West in the painting, is it?" I said.

"No." He gave me a sly look. "It's Vera Stoddard, as you well know. You met her on your show when she brought in the stolen book for you to appraise."

Stolen? I ignored that for now and stared at the painting. "She's very pretty."

He gazed at the portrait. "She was very young when this portrait was done. I had high hopes for her, but she aged badly. It was such a disappointment. She was supposed to be my Mae, my muse."

"She's still a lovely woman," I said. Or she *was*, before she was gutted with a stylish pair of English gardening shears. A weapon that seemed tailor-made for Edward Strathmore's small bones and delicate nature.

"You and I both know that's not true, Brooklyn." He sighed. "I finally had to confront Vera with the truth, that she was no longer good enough to be my Mae. She had grown old and fat. Her hair was thin and gray. I believe she did it to me on purpose. She was so jealous of Mae. Who could blame her?"

He continued to stare at the painting and seemed to have forgotten I was in the room.

So the no-good boyfriend Vera had been seeking revenge on was Edward. I was beginning to sense a sorry theme. Vera had grown old and Edward had banished her and sought a replacement in Minka. On the television show, Gerald had grown old and been fired and replaced by Randolph. In both cases, the older people had been dumped callously, without regard for their feelings or their futures. But in a twist, neither Vera nor Gerald had taken their rejection cheerfully; they weren't satisfied to drift away quietly on a metaphorical ice floe.

Revenge could be a real bitch.

"Somehow Vera got hold of that book," he said after a while, his eyes darkening with resentment. "She couldn't have stolen it because I would've seen her in the security cameras. They're all over the house. But someone stole it and then, I don't know how, but Vera had it." His voice was rising in anger. "And she took it on that television show and bragged about it! Called it a lucky garage-sale find. Liar!"

"If the book is rightly yours, the show will get it back for you."

He smiled sadly. "Oh, Brooklyn. Vera's not the only liar, is she?"

"What do you mean?" I asked innocently.

"I know you have the book. You were going to restore it for Vera. She was going to pay you."

"Yes, I have the book, but why do you think I was planning to restore it?"

He shrugged artlessly. "Vera told me herself."

Icicles of cold fear formed along my spine. I was almost afraid to ask, but I had to know. "When was that? When did you talk to her?"

"The morning she died."

Was this a confession? I glanced up at the corner of the room. Were those cameras rolling?

"You . . . killed her?"

He blinked, as though I'd broken the spell he was under. "No. Good heavens, of course I didn't kill her."

Now who was the liar? But I wasn't going to push it. Instead, I played along. "Edward, do you know who killed Vera?"

"Perhaps I do." He sighed again. "I'll probably have to turn them in to the police. I don't want any dark clouds of negativity hanging over me as I begin my new life with my new Mae."

I almost choked. "You mean Minka?"

He giggled and quickly covered his mouth with the tips of his fingers. It was weird. "Yes. Isn't it wonderful? She's agreed to be my muse."

"That's so nice," I said, trying to swallow the bile that was rapidly rushing up to my throat. "You two make quite the couple. But you said something about turning Vera's killer over to the police. Would you like me to call them now?" *I have them on speed dial,* I thought to myself.

He seemed to consider it. "No, I hate to disrupt the party. I'll call tomorrow."

My cell phone was inside my bag, itching to be grabbed and used. But I needed more information first. "Edward, do you think Vera knew that the book had been stolen?"

"Oh yes. She knew."

"But on the show she told me that she found it at a garage sale. The man who sold it to her didn't seem to know much about it. He demanded only three dollars from her."

"Because he's an idiot," Edward said calmly. "And that's why he's dead."

"And you killed him!" a woman screamed.

We both turned and saw Mrs. Sweet standing in the doorway. Edward's housekeeper looked enraged enough to murder, and it didn't help that she was holding a gun pointed directly at us.

"Mrs. Sweet," Edward said nervously. "We were just talking about you."

"Don't you think I know? I was watching the security cameras and heard you say you were calling the police. People are stealing the silver downstairs, by the way."

"That's to be expected," Edward said reasonably.

She shook her head in disgust. "People suck."

This was not the happy-clappy housekeeper I'd met the other day. No, this woman wore a black taffeta party dress that showed off a mighty amount of cleavage. She looked like a Mob queen, large and in charge, ready to mow down her enemies with that semiautomatic weapon in her hand.

I heard heavy footsteps out in the hall and dared to hope it was Derek.

It wasn't.

Grizzly stopped short of knocking over his mother. "Mom, I told you I'd handle this."

Mom?

Mrs. Sweet was the mother of those two criminals? But it made perfect sense in a horrible, twisted way.

"You?" She smacked Grizzly's arm and he cowered. "The last time you handled things, you got your brother killed."

He hung his head in shame. "Sorry, Mom."

"Worthless brat." She looked over at me and shrugged. "But what're ya gonna do? We love our kids, right?" She rubbed Grizzly's arm where she'd just punched him and his lower lip trembled.

Was he going to cry? Good grief, the man could crush her with one fist. But mothers held strange and mighty power over their kids.

"Mrs. Sweet," Edward said, his tone all saccharine and syrupy. "Why don't we go to the kitchen and talk about this over a nice cup of hot cocoa?"

She snorted. "Why don't you just stick a sock in it, Eddie? You and I have nothing to talk about, and there's no way you're calling the police."

"Really, Mrs. Sweet," he began.

"Enough with the Mrs. Sweet crap. We both know I'm not married and I'm not sweet." She glanced at me. "He likes to pretend I'm a servant and not his sister. It's always amused me enough that I played along. Until now."

They were brother and sister?

Edward gulped, but didn't speak. It looked like this household was even sicker and more twisted than I'd thought. And if she'd heard us talking about the police, then she really had been monitoring the security cameras.

Since she was pointing a gun at us, I didn't have a whole lot of choice here. But I wasn't going to go down without a fight, and I wanted to find out exactly what had happened.

"Were you friends with Vera?" I asked the housekeeper.

She nodded. "Oh yeah, she was a good girl. She brought flowers every day, and not just for the house. She brought them for me, too. I guess she wormed her way into my little heart and I ended up trusting too much. I confessed to her that Grizzly had taken the book and was going to sell it to add to our little nest egg." She cast a damning look at Edward. "I'm pretty sure this genius here will leave all his money to a cat hospital or something. And no way am I living on skid row in my golden years."

I glanced at Edward and figured his long-suffering housekeeper might be right. He did seem fond of his Siamese cat.

"My Prinny has been loyal to me," Edward insisted, then sniffed. "Unlike you, Mrs. Sweet."

"I told you to drop the act, brother dear."

I was still shocked that Edward made his sister work as his housekeeper. Was she working off some loan or something? No wonder she was so filled with anger!

Ignoring Edward, Mrs. Sweet—or whatever her name was—continued. "Vera always had a soft spot for my boys, and she wangled her way into Luggy's heart. He had a gentle one." She sniffled and patted her chest in fond recollection. "Not much of a brain, though. Anyway, Vera convinced Luggy to give *her* the book because she wanted to get back at Edward for dumping her. She promised Luggy she would finagle another book for us to sell, but, obviously, she never got around to it."

Luggy? I figured she was referring to her son Lug Nut, of blessed memory.

"When I found out the book was gone," Mrs. Sweet said, her voice growing colder, "I was angry. And when I get angry, things go downhill."

"Did Luggy, er, Larry kill Vera?" I asked.

"Oh no, miss. You don't know my boy, but let me assure you he could never harm a fly. He might *scare* a fly, but . . . no, it wasn't him."

Actually, I *did* know her boy, and he was a vicious slug. But I let that go for now.

"No," she continued, "I was the one who went to visit Vera that morning, right after Mr. Edward left. I tried to talk to her, tried to get the book back, but she was just not going to cooperate. It wasn't about me and the boys, you understand. She wanted to turn the screws on Mr. Edward. I couldn't blame her for that because he said some hurtful things to her."

"I told the truth," Edward insisted.

"You're a mean old coot who's going to die alone!"

"I won't! I have my Minka!"

"So, what happened then?" I asked, trying to get this lunatic train back on track.

Mrs. Sweet gave Edward—her brother—the evil eye before continuing. "I've got to admit, Vera really rattled my cage and I let her get the best of me. Before I could even think straight, I had those shears in my hand. Next thing I knew, she was on the ground, bleeding out. I hightailed it on home and told my boys to get that book back or there'd be hell to pay from their mama."

So Mrs. Sweet—was that even her real name?—had orchestrated the entire mess.

I glanced at Edward, who looked completely wigged out. His face was pale and he kept shaking his head in disgust and disbelief.

"So it was you, Mrs. Sweet?" he whispered. "You had your

son, my nephew, steal my book?" He shuddered a little at the word *nephew*. I couldn't blame him.

"Oh, right, you knucklehead. Forget that Vera's dead. Forget that my son is dead. It's all about your precious books. Yes, it was me! I figured you wouldn't miss the damn thing because you've got, what, six more freaking copies of it?"

"But there was only one signed by Mae," he wailed.

"But you told me you already had two copies signed by Mae," I said, confused.

"What did you expect me to do?" he said with contempt. "I wasn't going to steal it from you in broad daylight."

"No, you were probably going to send your goon here to steal it for you," I said scornfully. "Too bad he already tried and failed miserably."

"But it's my book," he moaned. "Signed by my Mae."

Mrs. Sweet rolled her eyes. "Jeez, Eddie. I'll agree that Mae West was a good actress. And I always admired her for not letting men boss her around. She was smart and funny, too. But don't pretend you ever met her."

"I met her! She kissed me!"

She shrugged off his outburst. "I doubt it, but even if she did, it's not like she would've put up with your crap for one hot minute. She'd have beaten you with a stick and left you for dead." She glanced at me and winked. "Just keeping it real."

"I need my Minka," Edward whimpered.

"And . . . there he goes," she said sarcastically. "He's off to Wonderland." She stared at us for another few seconds, shaking her head. Then she looked up at Grizzly and patted his arm. "You handle this one, son. Don't screw it up."

"Okay, Mom." He bared his teeth at me and started walking my way.

"Wait!" Edward cried. "I'll give you money."

"Too late, brother," she snarled. "I'll take it for myself."

"Don't do this, Mrs. Sweet," I cautioned.

"Sorry, hon, but it's the only way," she said. Then under her breath she added, "And there's no way in hell I'm going to jail."

Grizzly lumbered toward us and I adjusted my feet on the ground, arranged my weight and body angle just right, and prepared to kick his ass. Then I realized I was the one in my own little Wonderland. There was no way I could hurt him. But I could outrun him.

I waited until he reached the glass display of Cosway bindings, and at the last second I dashed around the other side and headed for the door. Mrs. Sweet had disappeared, apparently determined to get the hell out of Dodge and leave her dear boy Grizzly to take the fall for her. He seemed amenable to that plan, but, then, he was an idiot.

I had almost reached the door when Grizzly caught up and yanked me by my dress—*oh, God, Alex's dress!*—and pulled me back. He wrapped one hand around my neck but I managed to thrust my elbow back and hit him hard in the gut.

"Oof!"

While he was holding his stomach, I turned and tried to shove him. But it was useless. He barely budged.

I glanced over his shoulder and my eyes widened. "Edward, no!" I screamed.

Grizzly took the bait and turned to look at nothing.

In that moment, I barreled into the big creep with sufficient momentum to shove him about six inches, but it threw him off guard enough that he stumbled and fell backward into the carefully arranged display of Fabergé eggs, which flew off the shelf in every direction.

"You'll be sorry for that," he swore, and struggled to his feet, bumping into another cabinet on his way up.

I stared as a very large, heavy, priceless Sevres urn on top of the cabinet tottered and plummeted, landing on Grizzly's head and knocking him out.

"That was almost too easy," I said, my legs trembling a little.

"My urn," Edward cried as he cowered in the corner.

"Oh, please," I muttered, exhausted. I leaned back against the matching cabinet to catch my breath. "It just broke the handle. You can glue it back. And you're welcome, by the way. I just saved your sorry ass."

Edward screamed and pointed. "No, the other one!"

I looked up and saw another massive porcelain urn wobbling and quickly steadied the cabinet. The urn managed to stabilize and I breathed in relief.

"Brooklyn!" Derek dashed into the room and grabbed me. I glanced around and was pleased that no books had been ruined in the melee.

Alex's dress, on the other hand, was torn badly.

Epilogue

Two weeks later, Alex was still telling stories about my valiant effort to catch another killer, just as Vinnie had promised her I would.

The night of the party, when Derek ran into the library and saved me from Grizzly and the falling urns, Alex had been right behind him. She was shocked to see all the destruction, but also secretly tickled that she'd been an eyewitness to the wrap-up of another successful murder investigation by the amazing Brooklyn. Or so her story went.

She was laying it on a little thick, but I wasn't about to ruin all her fun. I owed her too much. For one thing, she had helped stop Mrs. Sweet in her tracks. The murderous housekeeper had been sneaking down the stairs to make her escape when Derek and Alex came running upstairs, looking for me. Alex had chased after the woman and forced her to stay put while Derek ran ahead and saved me from the monstrous Grizzly.

And, for another thing, Alex hadn't cared about the damage to her dress, which she insisted could be fixed. She was more concerned about me. And not just because I had been confronted by that monstrous woman and her two criminal sons.

No, Alex's main concern for me had stemmed from her having experienced a mind-numbing conversation with the dreadful Minka. It was during the party, after I had already run off to the library.

Alex had stood at the bar with Minka and, in an effort to make small talk, she'd mentioned that she was my friend. The vitriol began, with Minka spewing all sorts of vile and semi-intelligible insults about me.

I was used to Minka's despicable wrath, but Alex had never heard anything like it. I brushed it off, but she claimed to fear for my sanity if I ever had to work with Minka again.

Meanwhile, Vera Stoddard had a lovely niece who came forward to claim her meager estate. Unfortunately, since *The Secret Garden* had been stolen from Edward, she wasn't entitled to the book. But she was happy to take over running Vera's beloved flower shop.

I was shocked—pleasantly so—to hear that Edward Strathmore had decided to donate *The Secret Garden* to the Covington Library's children's collection. Ian explained that Edward felt so guilty about Vera being killed by his housekeeper—his own sister!—as well as me being attacked by his horrible nephews, all over a "silly" book, that he no longer wanted to have it in his house.

He must've been carrying around a whole boatload of guilt if he'd been so willing to give up that exquisite book with the added bonus of Mae West's signature on it.

I found out from Inspector Lee that more than ten years ago, Edward had bailed Lug Nut and Grizzly out of jail and paid some big bucks for their legal defense. In return, Mrs. Sweet had agreed—or been coerced, more likely—to become his housekeeper. Essentially, she'd signed on as an indentured servant in exchange for her sons' freedom. It was Edward's way of keeping her and her violent boys under his thumb. So much for brotherly love.

The inspector also revealed that Mrs. Sweet's second husband was Mr. Sweet, so her name had come to her honestly. Still, it was quite possibly the most ill-suited name I'd ever heard.

The dust had settled on the case, and it seemed like a good time to pay Alex back for everything she'd done for me. She had taught me those defensive moves that had probably saved my life and she'd loaned me that beautiful dress which, it turned out, was indeed easily repaired by her tailor.

So one Saturday night, Derek and I invited Alex over for dinner. Derek was pouring champagne for the three of us when the phone rang.

"Should we answer it?" I asked.

"It might be important," he said apologetically.

I saw Ian's name on the screen and grabbed it. "Hi."

"Hey, I've got news," Ian said.

"What is it?"

"Did you hear about Minka?"

"Oh no. What has she done now?"

"She's moved."

I frowned at the phone and pressed the speaker button so Derek and Alex could hear, as well. "So where did Minka move? County jail?" I cringed in fear that Ian might tell me she was moving into our apartment building.

"No, you probably heard that the charges against her were dropped," he said. "But after what she did on the show, she couldn't find a job. And then, all of a sudden, she got a phone call and was hired within days."

I almost hated to ask. "So where's she going?"

"To the National Library of Kosovo."

"Kosovo," I mumbled. "As in Eastern Europe? The Balkans? *That* Kosovo?"

"Yes, that one," he said, chuckling. "It's much safer than it was a few years ago. They've built a fabulous new library in the capital, and Minka starts working there next week as the head archivist. I gave her a glowing recommendation."

I stared dumbfounded at the phone, then looked at Derek. He shook his head, equally mystified. I happened to glance at Alex, who was gazing innocently at the ceiling as she sipped her champagne. The kitten pounced on her foot and Alex smiled, set down her wine, and reached for the tiny bundle. It reminded me that Derek and I still hadn't come up with a name for the little fuzz ball.

"Thanks for the great news, Ian," I said distractedly. "Talk to you soon."

I hung up, still confused. It took me a moment to fathom the truth, but finally I said, "Alex? Weren't you assigned to Kosovo once upon a time?"

"Who, me?"

"Is there something you want to tell us?" Derek asked.

"You did this," I murmured.

She glanced from the kitten to me and fluttered her eyelashes. "Whatever are you talking about?"

I looked at Derek and whispered, "Her powers are awesome."

He nodded. "Truly awesome."

"Not really." Alex sighed and set the kitten down on the floor. "After the party, I couldn't sleep for several nights and it had nothing to do with catching a killer. It was all because of that horrible Minka and those nasty things she said about you." Alex shivered slightly and rubbed her arms. Her eyes narrowed down to pinpoints and her lips flattened in fury. "Nobody talks about my friend that way. She had to go. I knew I couldn't have her killed, so I did the next best thing. I hope you don't mind."

Derek and I stared at each other and began to laugh.

"Are you laughing with me or at me?" she asked, cautiously glancing from one of us to the other.

We both reached for her and enveloped her in a group hug.

"With you," I said. "Even though you terrify me."

"Me, too," Derek admitted, and grabbed the champagne bottle to fill our glasses.

I picked up the kitten. "To celebrate, let's name this little girl tonight."

Alex smiled. "You could always name her Cupcake."

"I love cupcakes." I nuzzled the kitten's soft neck.

"I still like Charlemagne," Derek said. "Charlie for short."

"I do like Charlie," I admitted, "but what's the attraction to Charlemagne?"

He hesitated, twirled his wineglass, refusing to meet my questioning gaze. "It's silly, I suppose, but I had a dog when I was young. Ugly little thing. Runt of the litter. He wasn't expected to live, frankly, so we got him for free. I was studying the Western emperors at school, and I thought if the pup were given the name of one of the greatest rulers in history, he might find within himself the will to live. So I called him Charlemagne. He grew up to live a good, long life." He glanced at me and smiled. "But that's a ridiculous reason. Forget it."

"No, it's sweet," I said, melting a little.

Derek took the furry creature from me and held her in his big hands. There was something overwhelmingly attractive about a strong man cuddling a tiny kitten.

I smiled up at him. "Let's call her Charlie. Charlie Cupcake."

Author's Note

This story is a work of fiction except for a few historical details. Both the actress Mae West and the author Frances Hodgson Burnett were real people. Both lived in or near New York City from 1911 to 1912. Mae West first began performing on Broadway in 1911. Frances Hodgson Burnett published *The Secret Garden* in 1911, and her *Little Lord Fauntleroy* had long been a popular Broadway play, as well as a novel. Many of the details about Mae and Frances are based on research, but my suggestion that the two women met and exchanged books and/or memorabilia is purely a product of my imagination.